A
DEADLY
INFLUENCE

OTHER TITLES BY MIKE OMER

ZOE BENTLEY MYSTERIES

A Killer's Mind

In the Darkness

Thicker than Blood

GLENMORE PARK MYSTERIES

Spider's Web

Deadly Web

Web of Fear

A
DEADLY
INFLUENCE

MIKE OMER

THOMAS & MERCER

Text copyright © 2021 by Michael Omer
All rights reserved.

Published by Thomas & Mercer, Seattle

www.apub.com

Amazon, the Amazon logo, and Thomas & Mercer are trademarks of Amazon.com, Inc., or its affiliates.

ISBN-13: 9781542022873
ISBN-10: 1542022878

Cover design by Faceout Studio, Spencer Fuller

Printed in the United States of America

A
DEADLY
INFLUENCE

CHAPTER 1

The bedraggled man sat huddled on a rickety scaffold, staring at the thousands of lights glittering in the dark night. He wore baggy jeans and a faded corduroy jacket that seemed too thin for the chilly wind. Abby peered at him through the bare, unfinished window, trying to judge if he was about to jump.

"He's been out there for the past fifty minutes," the patrolman said behind her. "Doesn't answer when we call out to him. Won't even look in our direction."

Abby nodded distractedly, never taking her eyes off the man. He shifted uncomfortably and kept glancing down. He was building up his determination; she was certain of it. She didn't have a lot of time.

She took a step back and looked around her, assessing the situation. The space they stood in was still under construction, the beams bare, the windows paneless, rubble and building materials everywhere. The floor was scattered with food wrappers, and a couple of stubs and an empty cigarette box were tossed by her feet. Her colleague Will Vereen was talking on his shoulder mic, and farther away, two Emergency Service Unit guys stood waiting in case she decided they had to make a grab for the jumper outside.

It was windy up there on the fifty-second floor of the unfinished skyscraper. To talk to the man from the window, she'd have to shout.

Her voice tended to be shrill when she shouted, hardly the reassuring tone of a calm negotiator.

She glanced at Will, wondering if he should be the primary negotiator this time. He had a deeper voice and could shout louder. But she had a hunch that the man outside might think of Will as threatening. She was better in this instance.

"Do you need the bullhorn, Lieutenant?" The officer held up a blue bullhorn.

She shook her head. "If I shout at him through that, he'll jump just to make it stop. I'm stepping out."

One of the ESU guys helped her latch the rope to her rappelling harness. Then, swallowing hard, she stepped out of the window and into the void.

Once she was outside, the wind was much worse, buffeting her body relentlessly. She grabbed the scaffolding pole, her heart beating wildly, and tried to ignore the creaking and groaning of the metal frame. The rappelling harness felt almost like a joke now, a flimsy strap that would never hold her weight if she lost her balance. A wave of dizziness shot through her, bile in her mouth.

She forced the fear away, focusing on the man who sat at the far end of the scaffolding, dangling his legs over the abyss. She took a step closer. He glanced at her, unblinking, his lips trembling. His cheek was scratched twice, two angry red lines, jagged and raw. Another step. She was three yards away from him.

"Don't come any closer! I'll jump!" His voice was hoarse, desperate.

She raised one hand slowly, palm facing outward. "Okay. I'm staying here."

"I swear I'll do it!" He leaned forward.

Abby carefully sat down on the ledge of the scaffold. "See? I'm right here. I just want to talk."

He turned away, facing the New York skyline, his thin hair fluttering in the wind. Coughing, he patted his pockets, then hawked and spat.

"I'm Abby Mullen," she said, keeping her voice calm and carefree. As if they were two strangers who had randomly bumped into each other while taking a stroll on the scaffolding, hundreds of feet above the street.

He ignored her, lost somewhere in his own mind.

"What's your name?" she asked after a few seconds.

No response.

She waited, letting the time stretch. She was comfortable with waiting. Her arrival had interrupted the man's focus, and he now seemed to be frozen in indecision. Whatever determination he'd mustered before had dissipated.

It was cold. Abby had her long coat on, a sweater underneath, and a woolen hat. But she'd left her scarf and gloves back in her car. She had one hand shoved in her pocket, but she gripped the freezing scaffolding with the other, and wasn't about to let go. Her nose and ears already felt like icicles.

The words *I'm cold* hovered on her lips. It was basic human interaction. If you were cold, you mentioned it, because it was something to say and it was a way to create a connection, to start a conversation. But even such a simple comment hid a trap within. Because *I'm cold* was about *her*. And the worst thing she could do right now was make it seem like she wanted to talk about herself.

"It's cold," she said instead. "You're probably freezing."

His eyes stayed fixed on the horizon.

"It seems like you're in a lot of pain," she said. "What happened?"

His jaw clenched as if the question prodded his thoughts. But he also shifted slightly away from the edge, turning so that he could see her from the corner of his eye. Abby waited, hoping he'd talk again. She needed something, anything, to get him inside. She knew Will was

3

frantically trying to find out this guy's name and the reason that had driven him to go up fifty-two floors and step out a window.

Finally she said, "Do you want to get inside and tell me what happened?"

She didn't expect him to agree. She wanted him to say no. It would be a start. And it would give him a sense that he controlled the situation. If he said no, they'd be in a much better place. But instead, he ignored her, his eyes vacant. He patted his pockets again, his motions erratic, clumsy. The movement of a drunk.

"Do you want a warm drink? I can get you a thermos with hot coffee or tea." Those sounded amazing to her right now. Surely they sounded just as good to him. But he tightened even more. As if the suggestion made him suspect trickery.

Was it getting colder? She let go of the icy metal pole and shoved her other hand in her pocket as well. Even though she sat safely on the scaffold, letting go felt like a mistake. She accidentally glanced down, and the darkness below yawned endlessly. Another wave of dizziness hit her, even worse than the first one, and the blood drained from her face. She dug her fingernails into her palm as hard as she could, the pain clearing her mind.

She quickly raised her eyes and focused on the skyscrapers. It was an amazing view from up here; she had to give the guy that. He'd chosen the location well. There were few things Abby found more awe inspiring than New York's skyline. Brightly lit spires and countless rooftops. The Empire State Building, awash in white, and beyond it the colossal Freedom Tower, its blue light almost spectral. Surrounding them stood numerous buildings and towers, each dotted with dozens of windows offering small glimpses into the lives beyond. Even now, at four in the morning, there were still scores of lit windows as well as many cars traversing the streets below, their red and yellow lights glimmering in the night.

"How did you get those scratches?" she asked.

On and on she tried, asking questions, labeling his feelings, prodding for a way in. She did so tirelessly, making sure her mounting frustration and concern didn't creep into her tone. The man seemed to tense up, fidgeting more, shutting his eyes, taking fast, shallow breaths. She was about to lose him. It was time to call the ESU guys.

Would they get to him in time? She doubted it. But she was out of options, and they had to try.

And then she thought of the stubs and the empty cigarette box on the floor by the window. The way he'd patted his pockets as if searching for his cigarettes. She could imagine him standing by that window earlier, having his last smoke before climbing over the windowsill and stepping out.

She didn't want to offer him a cigarette, remembering his reaction to her previous offer. Instead, she turned to the window and said, "Hey, I'm dying for a smoke. Does anyone have a cigarette?"

One of the ESU guys handed her a cigarette and a lighter through the window. She carefully reached over and grabbed them both. Then she placed the cigarette between her lips and lit it. She hadn't smoked since college, and the taste of it in her mouth nauseated her. But she sucked on the cigarette as if it were the best thing in the world, then expelled the smoke slowly.

The man turned to watch her. She took another drag from the cigarette.

"Mind if I have one of those?" he finally said.

"Absolutely," she said and turned to the window. "Can I have another one for the guy over here?"

The ESU guy held out the entire box.

"Toss it over," the man said.

She'd hoped he would reach for the box. It would have forced him to let her come closer.

Still, at least he was talking. She carefully tossed the box over to him. A gust of wind nearly knocked it off the scaffolding, but it ended up on the edge. The man pried one cigarette out and lit it with his own lighter. It took him four tries, his fingers trembling, the wind puffing out the lighter's flame. Finally he managed it and took a long drag.

"Thanks," he said.

"Can I get you anything else?"

"No." He gave her a small sad smile. "I'm Phil."

She returned a smile. "Nice to meet you, Phil. What made you come here?"

He took another drag. "Life."

She was used to vague answers, knew how to pry the truth out. "Life," she echoed.

"Yeah. Life. Things didn't go the way I wanted, I guess."

Once she got them talking, her main role was to keep them talking, and to *listen*. Good negotiators didn't talk much at all. They mainly listened, prodding their subject to keep on going. Buying time. Gathering information. Looking for the things that would help influence the subject.

"The way you wanted?" she repeated his words. It was the number one tool in any negotiator's arsenal—mirroring. Repeat the subject's words, demonstrate that you were listening, and make them elaborate more.

A few seconds of silence followed, and then he said, "My sister died two days ago."

"I'm sorry. It must have been very painful to lose her. How did she die?"

"Cancer." He glanced at the cigarette between his fingers. "Lung cancer. She didn't even smoke."

"I see."

"I went to her funeral, and I could see every person there thinking the same thing." He exhaled a cloud of smoke. "That it should have been me."

Abby waited. The words were pouring out now. All she needed to do was listen.

Phil took another drag from the cigarette. "I've been drinking my life away for the past twenty years. Spent two of those years in prison. My parents gave up on me. But not my sister. She kept trying to get me to go to AA or to talk to her priest."

"She sounds like a good sister."

"She was. And a good daughter. Gave my parents three lovely grand-daughters. She was an amazing mother." He stubbed out the cigarette on the scaffolding. "You know what I thought as they lowered the coffin?"

"What?"

"That now I have no one left to disappoint. What a terrible thing to think, right?"

"Why is it a terrible thing to think?"

"Don't you get it?" He raised his voice. "I was already looking for a way to drink. My sister died, and I used it as an excuse to drink."

"It sounds like you were in a lot of pain."

He shrugged impatiently. "So I drank. And then in the morning, I bought another bottle and drank some more." He seemed to lose his train of thought, staring vacantly at the city skyline.

She tried to find a way to paraphrase his words, to make him see it in a better light. "You were grieving. So you slipped."

"I guess." He didn't sound convinced. "My neighbor keeps playing loud music at night."

"Loud music?"

He paused and took out another cigarette, then lit it. "Really loud music. So I get up around midnight, right? And I'm angry. My head is pounding, and I feel like shit."

He took several puffs from the cigarette, his fingers trembling. The smoke curled and dissipated in the wind.

"I have a gun at home."

Oh shit. If he'd shot and killed his neighbor, it would make this much more difficult. It would be hard to convince him to come back inside if he knew prison waited for him on the other side of the window.

After a few seconds, when he didn't expand, she said, "A gun?"

"I need to pee," Phil suddenly said. "Been needing to pee for some time."

"We can get inside, you can go pee, and then we can finish this conversation."

Phil grinned at her. "I don't think so."

He stood up, cigarette still in his mouth, and Abby's heart missed a beat as he seemed about to jump. "Wait—"

He unzipped his fly, and a few seconds later an arc of piss trickled into the night. "Hope no one's down there," he muttered. After finishing, he zipped himself. Then he took out the cigarette and expelled a jet of smoke, grabbing the metal pole for balance. "So I grab my gun, and I walk over to my neighbor. I pound on the door, and he opens it."

"Okay," Abby said, taking a slow breath, calming her beating heart.

"I step inside. He has a few friends in there; they're all listening to this music, kinda stoned, right? And I empty my entire gun on his damn stereo."

Thank god. "Then what happened?"

"One of his crazy friends goes apeshit, starts kicking and scratching me." Phil shook his head. "So I push her and run outside. I hear them say they're calling the police."

"I see."

"So that's it. I would have shot myself except I emptied all my ammo in that stereo. I came here instead."

Abby nodded sympathetically and adjusted her tone of voice. Gone was the carefree, conversational stranger. Now her voice became deeper, slower, reassuring. She inflected it downward, every sentence becoming a statement. "It sounds like your sister was the one person who was there for you when you were down," she said. "She really wanted you to pick your life up."

She paused, letting the silence sink in, doing her job for her.

He blinked, seemingly startled. "Yeah, that's right."

"How about your nieces? You said they were lovely. Do you see them often?"

"Yeah. I mean, I did when my sister was alive. They're really great girls. The oldest one . . ." He grinned. "She has this crazy sense of humor. She could really crack me up."

Abby let the seconds go by. Let him come to his own conclusions. His nieces were still there. He could still laugh with his oldest niece. A glimmer of hope in his future. If he only would come inside with her.

"How would your sister feel about you taking your own life?" she finally asked.

"It doesn't matter; she's dead."

"What do you think she would have said if she was still alive?"

"I guess she wouldn't have been happy."

"What do you think your nieces, your father and your mother, will feel when you're gone, immediately after your sister?" Abby asked.

He cleared his throat. Then, apparently trying to buy some time, he placed another cigarette between his lips and took out his lighter. It slipped from his fingers.

He fumbled at it and, with that sharp movement, lost his balance. He waved his arms, panicking, tilting into the void. A scream rose in Abby's throat.

Then his hand clutched at the scaffolding, and he managed to gain his balance. His face was white, his mouth wide open. Abby's heart thudded in her rib cage. She remained silent, not trusting her voice at the moment, but locked eyes with him. The wind howled in the background.

"Phil," she finally said. "Do you want to go back inside?"

"Yeah." His voice trembled. "I'm not sure I can. I'm scared I might fall."

"That's okay; don't move. I have a couple of people here that'll help you."

9

CHAPTER 2

Abby's relief at feeling the solid floor beneath her feet was palpable. Walls and ceilings were an underestimated commodity. She felt an urge to lie prostrate on the floor just to get the full floor experience. But before she started the floor fan club, there was work to do.

"He's ready to come in," she told the ESU guys. "But he needs you to help him."

They walked out the window like it was a common occurrence. As if they traipsed hundreds of feet between heaven and earth every Tuesday. Show-offs.

She shook her head and turned to Will. "Is the mental health consultant on the way?"

"Already waiting downstairs with the ambulance." He grinned at her. "Nice work with the cigarettes."

She returned his smile, letting his reassuring, serene demeanor calm her down.

Ask a cop about their partner, and you'd get a myriad of responses. "He will always have my back." Or "I can trust him with my life." Or maybe "We're a family."

To Abby all this was true. But her first and foremost thought about Will was that around him, she could let go. She didn't need to stay on guard, to think about how she acted or what she said. He was one person with whom she could just relax for a bit. He was one of the few people she could trust.

Trust didn't come easy, not to her.

Will was tall. Tall enough that half the time when he met people, they invariably said, "Oh wow, how tall are you?" which was why Abby, who'd never actually asked him how tall he was, knew that he was six foot five. Inevitably, when hearing his name, people would say, "I never knew wolverines were so tall," sometimes adding, "Get it? Wol-vereen?" Will usually chuckled as if it were the first time he'd heard it.

His skin was a rich umber, and his bushy eyebrows and wide nose gave him the appearance of a father who'd found out you'd gone joyriding with his car. But he was actually a softhearted kitten trapped in the body of a nineties-movie action hero.

"I'm exhausted." She leaned against the wall, shutting her eyes.

"Well, saving lives is hard work."

She glanced out the window, watching the two ESU guys carefully helping Phil stand up. "I wish we could take the day off."

"We have two simulations scheduled for today."

"I *know* that. I just wish we didn't. What about Kimberly? Did you two have a nice evening?" Will had celebrated his five-year anniversary with his wife the day before. Abby had helped him pick a restaurant.

"It was *very* nice. But we went to bed late—"

"Spare me the details."

"I wasn't about to offer any. Still, went to sleep at one a.m.; then the call came after three. The phone rang for ages before I managed to pick up. Kimberly kept snoring. I swear, that woman could sleep through anything. What about you? Who's with the kids?"

"My mom, as usual. You can imagine how happy she was when I woke her up." Still, even though her mother had sounded exhausted, she'd showed up on Abby's doorstep ten minutes after the phone call.

"Well, you're lucky your parents live nearby, or you'd have to call Steve."

"Ugh. I don't want to imagine what that would be like."

"I'm going back to bed for a few hours." Will rubbed his eyes. "Then I'll go to work. Otherwise I'll be a zombie all day."

She checked her watch. Four forty-five. The kids needed to wake up at six fifteen. "I think I'll grab a cup of coffee once we're done here, then go back home to relieve my mom and get the kids prepared for school."

They both stopped talking as Phil came through the window, now secured with a rappelling harness of his own. The ESU guys followed. Phil gazed around him bewildered, his eyes wide open. Abby had seen this look before with other men and women brought back from the brink of death. A wonder at still being alive. Often, it was enough to keep them from trying to kill themselves again.

"How are you feeling?" she asked him softly. "Do you need water?"

"I'm good, thanks," he said sheepishly.

"Phil, I'm Will Vereen," Will said. "I'll walk you downstairs. There's an ambulance waiting for you."

"I don't need an ambulance. I'm not hurt."

"They just want to make sure." Will was already by the man's side, walking him toward the stairs.

"Thanks." Abby smiled at the two ESU guys.

"Sure." One of them smiled back. "It was nice working with you again, Mullen."

She recognized his face now. He had been on the ESU team from the bank siege eight months before.

"You too!" she said brightly, hoping it wasn't glaringly obvious that she didn't remember his name. "See you around."

She turned and followed Will down the stairs. She had a long day ahead of her.

CHAPTER 3

He woke up with a burning need, inflamed by a half-remembered dream. Gabrielle was there, smiling, kissing him, the touch of her lips as soft as a cloud. When he opened his eyes, the harsh reality was too empty and cold, and he tried to fall back to sleep, to clutch at the loose threads of his dream. But it was gone, and all he had left was a gnawing hunger he had to satisfy.

He had to see her.

But first, there were things he needed to do. Obviously, he had to brush his teeth. And Gabrielle liked it when he shaved before seeing her.

He took his time, made sure his cheeks were smooth. "I like a man's face as smooth as silk," she'd once told him. And he'd shaved off his mustache that very day.

He returned to the bedroom, where he removed his shirt and his pants, then folded them and placed them on the nightstand. He took off his underwear next. When he met Gabrielle in the morning, he preferred to be naked, just like she often was.

That done, he lay on the bed and grabbed his phone. Then he tapped the Instagram app. She'd posted a new story like he'd known she would. He touched her profile photo gently, his finger brushing her lips, a ritual that never got old.

She'd taken a selfie in bed, only her bare shoulders visible. He didn't need to see more. He knew she was lying nude, those satin bedsheets she'd bought two months before twisted between her legs.

Good morning, the caption read. She was smiling that sleepy half smile that never failed to stir him.

"Good morning," he whispered back.

Need shone in her eyes, a lust that mirrored his, and he lowered the phone, her mouth caressing his torso, his stomach, pausing between his legs. He squeezed the phone hard, his body spasming as he reached his relief.

Later he lay in bed and they talked. He scrolled through her posts, reading the captions or her comments. And then he answered her. Pillow talk.

I wish I could stay in bed all day, one post said, with her peeking under the blankets, grinning mischievously.

"Me too." He smiled at her.

Another post had her standing on the beach, the wind toying with her hair, and the caption was, *Do something your future self will thank you for.*

"I plan to," he said. "Today's the day. And future *you* will thank me too."

He scanned other comments on her posts, reading the inane blather her fans wrote, rife with grammar and spelling mistakes. *Your so beatiful,* one of them wrote, adding an emoji of a heart and another one with a rose. Her fans didn't realize an emoji meant nothing. If you wanted to send a rose, you sent an actual rose.

Of course, her fans didn't know she wasn't posting for them at all. Sure, they put bread on her table. But for more than a year, all her posts had been aimed only at him.

He scrolled a bit more, another glimpse before he started the day, and then suddenly paused, frowning at one of the images. A recent picture of her eight-year-old brother in his bedroom.

Something in the background caught his eye. A new drawing.

"Damn it," he muttered, getting up. He put on his clothes, feeling irritable. It was a good thing he'd spotted it before it was too late.

He stomped to the adjacent room. A boy's bed stood in the corner, with *Star Wars* bedsheets. A small desk and a dark-blue chair. A Harry Potter poster by the window. A nightstand with some plastic toys and a bed lamp. And a corkboard with a few crayon drawings pinned to it.

He tapped the screen of his phone and compared the image there to the room he stood in. There was the bed. Same bedsheets. Same poster. The nightstand was identical as well; it had taken him weeks to find all those toys.

The corkboard was almost the same. The one on the screen had seven drawings pinned to it. This one had six.

He zoomed in on the missing drawing, frustrated by the low resolution of the image. It was a drawing of a family. A mother, a big girl, and a smaller boy. The girl was obviously Gabrielle. He had to smile at the child's bad attempt at drawing his sister. Her body a rectangular block, her hair a few straight brown lines.

Sitting down at the desk, he took out a box of crayons and a sheet of paper from one of the drawers. Carefully and painstakingly, he copied the drawing. He had to start afresh twice, once when he got the mother's shirt color wrong and once when one of the boy's feet was too long. On the third attempt, he managed to get it reasonably similar. If he'd had time, he'd have made several additional sketches, trying to get it just right. But time was short. He had to get things ready. He copied the signature he already knew so well—*Nathan*.

He checked the image on-screen again. The picture was attached with a blue pin above the drawing of the spaceship. He found a blue pin in the drawer and stuck it in the exact same location.

Taking a few steps back, he compared the image on the screen to the room.

Perfect.

While he had been working, she'd posted a new image on her feed. It was her, dressed up for her photo shoot. She wrote, *How do I look?*

He commented, writing, *Gorgeous as always.*

She liked his comment almost immediately and replied, *thanks!* coupled with a blushing emoji.

He kissed the screen tenderly. "You're welcome," he breathed.

CHAPTER 4

Standing in the bathroom of the NYPD's police academy, Abby stared at herself in the stained mirror as she washed her hands. It was only noon, but she was completely drained. She'd hardly gotten four hours of sleep before the call about the jumper had woken her up. And the night before had been just as difficult because Ben had woken her up, and it had taken her ages to fall back asleep.

He'd had a terrible nightmare about spiders. Which in itself wasn't unusual—a lot of kids had nightmares about spiders. Abby herself had had a few when she was young. However, Ben's nightmare was that Jeepers, his pet tarantula, had died.

Sometimes your children's nightmares were your own shameful fantasies.

Ben's eighth birthday was coming. Abby ticked the tasks in her mental checklist. The invitations had been sent, and his best friends had already RSVP'd. She still had to figure out the refreshments and cake. There was a kid with a nut allergy in Ben's class, so her usual go-to recipe for Ben's birthday, german chocolate, would have to be adjusted. As for the rest . . .

Lowering her gaze, she frowned at the running water. She'd been scrubbing her hands raw. How long had she been washing them? Two minutes? Three? And she'd been scraping her skin with her fingernails.

She snatched her hands away and turned off the water. Damn it. Third time this week. It got more and more frequent. To think that only a few months ago, she'd thought she'd gotten over this habit.

Maybe there was no getting over it. Maybe, like the small red patch on her neck, it was a scar that would never entirely heal.

Wiping her hands, she checked the mirror. Presentable. She patted her wavy blonde hair, making sure it covered her ears, and straightened her glasses. Her sandy complexion was a bit paler than usual, and her eyes were slightly puffy from lack of sleep. But there was nothing she could do about that right now.

She stepped out of the bathroom, checking the time. She still had an hour before the next simulation started. She walked back to her desk and sat down, then jostled the computer mouse to wake up her laptop. Lately, it had been going into sleep mode every five minutes if she didn't move the cursor, as if the computer were the one who was sleep deprived. Maybe the computer had it right. She could try to sleep whenever no one talked to her for five minutes and only wake up if someone moved her cursor.

It almost sounded like weird sexual innuendo. *How was the date last night? Did he move your cursor? Nudge, nudge.*

Not that she'd gone on a date last night. She had no interest in anyone moving her cursor at the moment. She just wanted a good night's sleep.

She yawned and focused on the screen. The transcript she was reading was dated August 2019, two months before. It was a conversation between Sergeant Gutierrez, one of the NYPD's hostage negotiators, and a man who had barricaded himself in his ex-wife's apartment, threatening to shoot himself. The man, thanks to Gutierrez's efforts, hadn't killed himself or anyone else.

A big part of Abby's job was to dissect the transcript, figure out what Gutierrez did right and what he did wrong. Then she would incorporate it into the protocols and training material. She was in charge of the department's crisis intervention course as well as the training of the force's hostage negotiators. She had, in fact, trained Gutierrez.

She skimmed over the pages, noting approvingly how Gutierrez had managed to keep the man talking for over two hours. It had taken an hour and a half for Gutierrez to start nudging the subject softly, letting the man convince *himself* to unlock the door and hand his gun to the cops.

After a while, she found herself reading the same line over and over again, her brain not even registering the words. She sighed, minimizing the transcript window. Leaning back, she rotated her neck gently, letting her hands drop to the sides of her body. If only they had a masseuse in the office. Just a nice woman who'd walk by every hour or so and give your shoulders a relaxing massage. She glanced at the framed photo on her desk, Ben and Sam smiling at her. Well, Ben was smiling, and Sam was doing that thing she did when told to smile for the camera. A sort of grimace, not unlike the face she'd make if electrocuted.

Abby straightened the photo. Went over some paperwork on her desk, reshuffling it. Tried the four pens in her pen holder, verifying they all worked. Watered her succulent plant with her water bottle. Her very own procrastination ritual. Then, almost compulsively, she double-clicked an icon on the laptop's desktop, opening another transcript. This document was older, a scanned handwritten report. It was shorter than the Gutierrez transcript. Much shorter. And she knew it by heart. She skimmed it, reading fragments of sentences as if this time they might be different.

. . . *a gun pointed at my head. He says if you come closer, he will shoot. He says you should stay back.*

. . . *put him on the phone?*

. . . *together in the dining hall. All sixty-two* . . .

Hearing footsteps behind her, she guiltily closed the document and turned around. One of the instructors walked by, smiling at her distractedly. Abby smiled back, her cheeks flushed as if she'd been caught doing something she shouldn't.

And perhaps she really shouldn't have.

She tried to get back to work, but couldn't focus. The skin on the back of her hands stung from the recent abuse. She should really buy some cream for that. Though that would only cement the problem. It would be better to just stop doing it.

Her phone blipped, and she glanced at the message. It was her friend Isaac. How was last night? Better?

She sighed and tapped back, Ben didn't wake me up tonight, but I had to answer a call. I'm exhausted.

I'm sorry :(anything serious?

Yes, but it ended well

Oh, good. Did you see the new forum post?

Her interest was piqued. Checking it now

She opened the browser, then logged into the support forum. She and Isaac had both been members for years. She checked it daily, rarely participating herself. She wasn't there for the support. She was there for information.

A new user had joined the forum. Like many others, she wasn't sure she was in the right place. After all, the forum was for cult survivors. And she wasn't really in a cult. At least, she didn't think so. It was a dedicated group, the woman explained, and the guy who managed it had become difficult. Abby read the post about the so-called-group, whose goal was to follow and spread some sort of revolutionary diet. The woman detailed the increasing demands for their loyalty. The punishments for perceived disloyalty or other infractions, which became more and more severe. The pressure to donate money to the group. The woman had been encouraged to cut connections to family and friends, who were a "distraction." And then came the pressure to give more and more of her time. Until she lost her job.

Finally, after two years, the woman had gathered the courage to quit the group.

It wasn't a cult, she explained again, as if trying to convince herself. After all, they didn't commit any crimes, and they weren't even some sort of fanatic religion. It was a diet group.

"Then why are you here?" Abby muttered. Because obviously, the woman knew the truth. It had been a cult. A cult didn't necessarily follow a religion. And often, it wasn't illegal. All a cult needed was a very devout following centered on one thing. Sometimes it was a religious belief. Sometimes it was a person. And yes, sometimes it could even be a diet.

Some cults caused no damage. But often, they became destructive. And usually, all it took was that the leader would become, as the woman in the forum put it, difficult.

Abby skimmed the posts that followed, noting the name of the group. The addresses of its two hubs in New York. The name of the founder. The number of members. Every bit of information the woman offered. She stored it all in her ever-growing document detailing dozens of cults in the area.

She added the locations to her online map. Two red pins, among many others, all over New York State and adjacent states as well. It looked like any other Google map, and to a random viewer, the locations seemed like any other point of interest. A restaurant, or a shop, or a favorite park. But for Abby, each pin represented a small cancerous growth.

One day she might be called to one of these places. And she'd be prepared. History would not repeat itself, not if she could help it.

CHAPTER 5

The school bus dropped the kids by the East Elmhurst Playground in Queens. There, he knew, the group of children split. Only a couple of them turned north, up 101st Street. The two, Nathan Fletcher and Daniela Hernandez, weren't friends, but they had that strange connection children at school bus stops had. They walked home side by side in companionable silence. And after one block, Daniela reached her home, and Nathan continued alone another block.

He knew all that because he'd watched it transpire several times.

It took Nathan, with his short eight-year-old legs and his dreamy pace, two minutes to walk the remainder of the way.

That was the only window of opportunity.

Originally, he'd figured he would park nearby and wait. But he quickly saw the problem. In this suburban neighborhood, an unknown car parked at the curb would be noticed. People might take a minute to glance inside, maybe get a look at the driver. He couldn't let that happen.

So instead, he decided to drive around the block and wait for the school bus to show up.

Round and round and round he went. The school bus was late. Or maybe, for some reason, it had been very early, and he'd missed it. He'd driven around the block three times already, getting familiar with its little peculiarities. *Hello, tree that looks like a woman. Nice to see you again, misspelled graffiti. Fancy meeting you for the third time, faded plastic Halloween pumpkin.*

Someone could notice the car circling the block. Was that too paranoid? Gabrielle had once written, *Just because you're paranoid doesn't mean they aren't after you*, and he loved it so much that he'd printed it and hung it above his bed. Sure, he knew it was a quote from *Catch-22*, but for him it would always be a quote from Gabrielle's Instagram post in the summer of 2018.

He thought of Nathan riding the school bus. His emotions about the kid were complicated. In some ways, Nathan was part of his own family. One day he would be. But of course, Gabrielle had mentioned more than once that Nathan was by far her favorite man in the universe. And that was . . . well.

It was complicated, that's what it was.

There! That yellow color of the school bus. Four kids this time, not five as usual, and his heart skipped a beat as he scanned them. But there was Nathan's blond hair and Avengers backpack. He exhaled, trying to figure out the best way to handle it. He couldn't just drive slowly after them. The kids would surely notice him, and he didn't want that brat Daniela seeing his face. On the other hand, if he went on another drive around the block, he'd miss his window of opportunity.

He decided to stop by the curb and check his phone. Just a guy texting a message to his wife.

Except instead, he opened the Instagram app and saw that Gabrielle had posted a new story. His finger hovered above her icon, almost tapped it, an instant reflex. No. No time.

He closed the app and started scrolling through his contacts, up and down, while glancing at the kids walking farther and farther away. A few teenagers were playing basketball on the court a dozen yards from his car. The ball went bounce-bounce-bounce, and his finger slid the screen along with the rhythm of the ball. Strange, the things the body would do when you didn't notice. Were any of the teens paying attention to the cars around them? To one guy sitting in a vehicle, mindlessly fiddling with his phone?

No, they were too intent on their game.

Using the time to review his plan one last time, he glanced at the McDonald's bag on the passenger seat. A Happy Meal with a burger with no vegetables. Gabrielle's March 17, 2019, Instagram story— *The hell with eating healthy today, I'm getting a quarter pounder with extra cheese, and Nathan is having his usual, a burger with absolutely no vegetables.*

He practiced his greeting. "Hey, Nathan," he said to himself. Getting the words just right, with a tone of familiarity. A greeting to someone you've seen a few times in the past.

He had to convince the boy that he was a friend of the family. Not a stranger to be wary of. And really, in this day and age of social media, was anyone a stranger? Everyone was a friend of a friend, or a follower, or someone who liked your TikTok clip.

In the distance, Daniela turned to her home. He pulled away from the curb, making sure to drive casually even though his hammering heart told him to *floor it* and get to the kid before he reached his home.

Nathan walked unusually fast. Usually the boy would walk at a snail's pace, stopping to appreciate a bug scuttling on the sidewalk or to pick up a leaf that drew his attention. But now he practically ran home.

Did the kid know?

CHAPTER 6

Nathan hurried home as fast as he could, his mind intent on reaching the bathroom. He'd needed to pee for over an hour, but he hated asking to go during class, especially when Mrs. Covington was teaching. She always frowned when pupils asked to go to the bathroom, like it made her angry that they couldn't hold it in. And then he'd had to hurry to the school bus. The ride home had been an increasing nightmare with every bump making him squirm uncomfortably.

But now, finally, he was almost home.

"Hey, Nathan."

The voice startled him. He turned to face the street. A man had pulled up in a white car, the passenger window open. He smiled, his expression friendly. Nathan squinted at him, trying to figure out who he was. One of their neighbors, maybe?

"Hello," he said politely.

The man laughed. "You don't recognize me, do you?" he asked. "I'm Gabi's friend."

Now that he said it, maybe Nathan *had* seen this guy with Gabi one time. Gabi had lots of friends, and she worked with a lot of people, especially in the past year. This was probably one of them. Yeah, he was definitely one of them. "Oh right, I remember you now."

"Gabi sent me. We're preparing a surprise party for your mom for tomorrow. You're in charge of the decorations. Gabi said you have a crazy talent for drawing."

Nathan smiled, embarrassed. He loved drawing, and he really thought he drew well, but he was always shy about showing his pictures to people. "Yeah, I'm not bad."

"Great! So get in. We need to pick up some candles on the way. I can't wait to see her trying to fit forty-five candles on the cake, right?"

Nathan had a pang of unease. Get in? Sure, this guy was Gabi's friend, but Nathan didn't know him so well. It was probably best to go home and ask Gabi about it. "I need to ask Gabi first."

"Gabi is already there. She asked me to pick you up. We're eating McDonald's." He raised a McDonald's takeout bag to the window. "Your favorite, right? Gabi said to get you a Happy Meal with a burger and absolutely no vegetables."

Nathan relaxed. His favorite meal. And right now, thinking of the burger inside, he felt his mouth watering. "Thanks! I just want to go home for a minute, I have to use the bathroom."

"If your mom sees you, it'll ruin the surprise," the man said, opening the passenger door. "Get in, we'll stop at a gas station, use their restroom."

"Okay." Nathan stepped over to the car and then paused. "Wait."

The smile on the man's face faded. He glanced at the rearview mirror. "What is it?"

"Gabi said we'd get those candles shaped like numbers this time," Nathan said. "So we don't need to fit all the candles on the cake."

"Oh yeah!" The man smiled again. "But in case you and I don't find any, we'll get regular candles, right?"

"Right." Nathan slid inside the car. He hoped the man would drive slowly, because the bumps really made him want to pee.

"Buckle up!" The man grinned at him.

And they drove away.

CHAPTER 7

The sounds of Samantha's violin greeted Abby even before she climbed the front steps of her home. She sighed wearily as she twisted the key in the lock. Her head pounded, and she'd hoped for a quiet and soothing evening nursing a cup of warm tea. But *quiet* did not characterize Sam's music, and frankly, neither did *soothing*.

When she pushed open the door, she could also hear the background music to Sam's violin—a fast-paced drumbeat and high-pitched electronic vocals. Abby tossed her bag on the dresser by the door and shouted, "Kids, I'm home!"

Ben appeared almost instantly, running at her full speed, his dark eyes sparkling with joy. Abby crouched, opening her arms to enfold her son in a hug. Her smile wavered as she noticed the creature held in Ben's palm—Jeepers, his pet tarantula. But it was too late to do anything about it; son and spider both sank deep into her arms. She lowered her face into Ben's smooth honey-blond hair.

"Hey, Mommy," Ben chirped.

"Hi, hon," she said, glancing at his palm to make sure Jeepers's furry limbs weren't touching her. "How was your day?"

"It was okay. Sam said she's gonna squash Jeepers." He sounded deeply offended. "You need to tell her not to."

"Did you take Jeepers to her room again?"

"No! I just let him walk on the table for a bit."

"The kitchen table?" Abby asked faintly, standing up. "I don't want it walking on the kitchen table, Ben."

Jeepers started climbing up Ben's arm. Abby suppressed an involuntary shudder. She'd been sharing her house with this creature from hell for over six months, and she still wasn't used to it.

"She can't squash him, Mommy, you need to tell her."

"I'll talk to her, but I want you to keep Jeepers off—"

"Oh, and Dad said you should call him because he wants to take me on my birthday to the Museum of Natural History. He said I could bring three friends."

"He what?" She clenched her fist. "Ben, we're having a birthday party for you and Tommy together, remember?"

"Yeah, but maybe we'll do that next year? Because Dad said—"

She took out her phone. "I'll talk to your dad right now. Hon, take Jeepers to your room, okay?" Abby could face only one vile creature at a time.

Ben and his eight-legged horror retreated to their lair, and Abby dialed Steve.

"Abby," he answered almost instantly. The way her ex-husband said her name when she called him was unique. He started with a very quick "A," and as if to compensate, the "bby" stretched forever. So it was actually "Abbyyyyyyy." His intonation always sounded like the godfather welcoming a beloved son who had just made an unfortunate mistake. Adoring, patronizing, and sorrowful. It never failed to enrage her to the point of homicidal urges.

"Steve," she said, trying to summon her calm, soft voice. "I talked to Ben, and he said you want to take him to the—"

"The Museum of Natural History with some friends. I thought it's a great way to celebrate his birthday. You know, because he likes insects so much."

The way he belittled their son's hobby spiked her rage even further—if that was possible. "The thing is, we already agreed that on his birthday we're celebrating with Tommy. They're inviting the entire class and—"

"I never agreed to that."

"I mean, I agreed with Ben and Tommy's parents." She recognized her misstep a second too late.

"Tommy's parents agreed, did they?" Steve's voice wasn't even fake warm anymore. "It's nice that Tommy's parents were consulted. When were you going to tell *me* about my son's birthday? At some point down the line from Tommy's parents, I suppose?"

"I was about to tell you today," she lied airily. "In any case the museum visit—"

"I think it would be nicer if Ben will be the focus of the party, don't you?" Steve interrupted her. "He shouldn't need to share it with another kid."

"He doesn't need to . . . he wanted the joint party . . . we discussed this . . ."

This conversation was a recurring moment of irony in her life. As a negotiator, Abby could face deranged criminals armed to the teeth, holding numerous hostages, while her voice remained measured, each word de-escalating the situation. But when she talked to the guy she was married to for twelve years, her voice automatically adopted the style of nails dragged on a blackboard, and she couldn't think of a single word to utter aside from expletives.

"You can come along; this isn't about pushing you away," Steve said helpfully.

With her right ear exposed to her ex's infuriating voice and her left ear being subjected to the torturous sound of Samantha's violin practice, Abby went through an internal meltdown. She had to end this conversation before she said something she'd regret. "Tell you what," she said, summoning her calm, slow voice from years of training. "I'll think it over, and we'll talk about it tomorrow, okay?"

When in doubt, always buy time.

"Sure," Steve said. "Tell the kids I said good—"

She hung up, her fingers tightening on the phone. Before Ben had taken an all-consuming interest in invertebrates and Squamata, he'd been obsessed with superheroes. He'd had superhero toys, posters, clothes, and bedsheets. To Abby they all seemed boring and interchangeable, except for She-Hulk. Now *that* was a superhero she could identify with. These phone calls always left her with the urge to morph into a seven-foot green giant and growl, "Abby Smash."

Instead she put the phone down and followed the sound of music to the closed door. She knocked on it, and the violin stopped, leaving just the electronic background music.

"Yeah?" Samantha said, her voice muffled.

Abby opened the door and stepped into her fourteen-year-old daughter's room. Samantha sat on a chair with her violin still in the crook of her neck. Her smooth copper-brown hair was tied in a haphazard, typical ponytail.

"Hey, Mom," she said, the words barely audible above the music. "I didn't hear you come in."

Abby let her stare slide over the room's disarray—clothes on the floor, stacks of music sheets everywhere, Samantha's schoolbooks scattered on the desk. Keebles, Samantha's dog, sat on the bed, eyeing Abby with disapproval. She was a white Pomeranian spitz that Samantha had gotten for her tenth birthday from her grandmother. Recently, Samantha had colored Keebles's tail pink and purple, which made her look like a tiny dog-unicorn breed. The white furry creature, who adored Samantha unconditionally, viewed the rest of the world as a disturbance. Sometimes, it was like Abby had two teenagers in the house.

"Hi, Sam." Abby smiled at her. "Can you turn off the music for a sec?"

Samantha paused the playback. Keebles tilted her head and almost seemed to roll her eyes. Abby imagined her thinking, *Ugh, human parents are the worst.*

"How was your day?" Abby asked.

"Fine."

"What are you practicing?"

"A song for the band."

Some days, Samantha could go into a two-hour-long monologue about her music. Other days all Abby got were a few monosyllabic grunts. It seemed today was a grunt day. Keebles shifted on the bed and yawned.

"Was Grandma here?"

"Yeah, she left an hour ago. She said she'll call you. Something about an urgent question about Ben's birthday present."

Ben, right. "Ben said you told him you'd squash Jeepers."

"Mom, he put that *thing* on the table while I was *eating*."

"I told him not to put it on the table, but you can't say things like that. Imagine him saying that he'll kill Keebles. How would that make you feel?"

Samantha and Keebles exchanged looks. Now they both seemed to roll their eyes.

"I'm sorry, but how do you expect me to act if he puts that creature near my plate?" Samantha asked calmly.

"Tell him to take it away."

"Take it away?"

"Yeah, tell him you're uncomfortable with it and that he should take it back to his room."

"Take it back to his room."

"Listen, tell you what, I'll talk to him again, make it clear in no uncertain terms to keep it away from the kitchen table."

"It seems like you think that would help."

It took Abby a few seconds to catch on. Samantha's voice was slow and measured; she'd mirrored Abby's words, labeling the situation and asking open-ended questions. She was *handling* her mother like Abby would handle an out-of-control subject.

It wasn't the first time. Samantha had been seven when Abby became a hostage negotiator. She'd grown up with it in the house, and as kids did with useful information, she'd soaked it up like a sponge.

And of course, it had already worked like a charm. Abby had promised to talk to Ben again. She'd calmed down, trying to find a solution to the problem instead of demanding things from her daughter.

She was both infuriated and proud. Grinning at Samantha, she said, "I'll start making dinner in a bit."

Samantha nodded. "Today is a no-meat day for me." She turned the music back on.

Abby shut the door behind her, shaking her head. They should insist all prospective negotiators have kids. Nothing prepared you better for crisis management.

CHAPTER 8

Eden Fletcher called out to her kids as soon as she walked through the door but got no response. She took off her coat, hung it on the coatrack, and made her way to the kitchen. She wanted a cup of tea. She'd spent the last half hour of her shift rescheduling an appointment for one of Dr. Gregory's oldest clients. The woman was hard of hearing, and Eden had to half shout through the phone while constantly giving the irate people in the waiting room apologetic looks. By the time she'd ended the call, her throat was raw and her nerves shot to hell.

She made her tea with a spoonful of honey, which she normally didn't like, but this time it hit the spot. As she took the second sip, she noticed with some surprise that there was no plate in the sink. Nathan usually made himself a sandwich when he got home, and he always placed the plate in the sink afterward. It was possible he'd washed the plate and dried it, then put it back in the cupboard, but it was also possible that she was a long-lost princess.

As she took her tea back to the living room, a second discrepancy caught her eye—Nathan's schoolbag wasn't discarded by the door.

She went to his room and scrutinized it. It was a mess, as usual, but the schoolbag wasn't there either. And neither was Nathan.

The door to Gabrielle's room was shut. Eden knocked on it tentatively. "Gabi?"

"What?" Gabi asked from beyond the door.

Eden opened the door. Gabi was sprawled on her bed, eyes glued to her phone, one finger on the screen.

"Where's Nathan?" Eden asked.

"I don't know. Probably in his room." Gabi's words were sticky, the syllables mushing into each other. She really communicated better typing than talking.

"He's not. Did you see him when he got home from school?"

"No." Gabi was still fully intent on her phone. "He probably went to a friend's house. Maybe that kid down the block, uh . . . Mikey?"

"I'll check," Eden said with unease. Nathan had never gone to a friend's home straight from school. But he was growing up, and it wasn't like she didn't allow it. It was possible.

She checked her own bedroom to make sure Nathan wasn't there for some reason and then went back downstairs. Dialing Mikey's mother's phone number, she paced the living room impatiently. The woman answered after a few rings. A steady noise hummed in the background, like a vacuum cleaner.

"Hello, Rita?" Eden said. "It's Eden, Nathan's mom."

"Oh hi," Rita said, her voice laced with feigned politeness. "How are you?"

"Good. Is Nathan there?"

"No, he isn't." Rita's voice shifted. Now it sounded like fake concern. Maybe it wasn't really fake. Maybe Rita was just one of those people who sounded fake no matter what. "He isn't home?"

"No . . . can you ask Mikey if he knows where he is?"

"Sure, hang on."

Eden listened as Rita asked her son about Nathan. The words were garbled, swallowed by the sound of the vacuum cleaner. Finally, the woman said on the phone, "Mikey said he saw him get off the school bus but that he went home."

"Oh okay. He's probably at another friend's house," Eden muttered, wondering why she'd said it. As if she was trying to reassure the other woman that nothing was going on.

She hung up and tried Nathan's other friends. She had a total of four phone numbers. As she ticked them off, her breathing became shorter, erratic. Her lungs wouldn't compress all the way anymore because fear had settled inside them. After hanging up the last call, she held the phone, staring at it wide eyed, her fingers trembling. She had no idea what to do. She'd run out of life's protocols, out of the plausible stories she could tell herself to feel better. New stories came to mind, stories laced with darkness.

She went upstairs to the bathroom and turned on the water. Grabbing the soap and the scouring pad, she began scrubbing her hands furiously. She scrubbed for three minutes, her skin becoming raw and painful, but the anxiety didn't abate. In fact, it got worse.

Should she call the police? It seemed like a crazy thing to do. Nathan would show up in a minute, and it would turn out he'd been playing outside the entire time.

Then again, what if he wasn't outside? What if something had happened? And she had wasted precious time scrubbing her hands, as if that were going to help.

She got out of the bathroom and looked for her phone. Where had she left it? Kitchen. She hurtled down the stairs and grabbed it, her heart pounding like crazy as she switched on the screen.

It came to life in her hands, ringing as if it had waited for her to pick it up. The caller ID was unknown.

"Hello?" Her voice was cracked, consumed by fear and worry.

"Eden Fletcher?"

"Yes, who—"

"We have your son."

She was in one of those dreams in which she fell into an elevator shaft or a chasm. That sensation of dropping helplessly, a scream lodged in her throat. Except those always ended abruptly when she woke up.

There was no waking up from this phone call. "Is he okay?" Trembling, feeling faint. "Let me talk to him."

"He's fine. Sleeping." The voice was wrong, warped, metallic. This was what evil sounded like. The voice of a man corrupted beyond hope.

"What do you want?"

"Five million dollars. Or your son dies."

"You can't be serious. I don't have that kind of—"

"Better start finding it if you ever want to see your son again. We're watching you. Five million dollars. We'll talk soon." The line went dead.

The phone tumbled from her petrified fingers and clattered on the kitchen tiles. She let out a guttural moan as she sank to the floor, leaning against the wall. Nathan. Her sweet, angelic boy, so full of life, always laughing, always curious. And these men had him. Where? Was he locked in some dark basement? Nathan was afraid of the dark; they couldn't do that to him. She could already imagine his terrified cries begging them to let him out, to—

"Mom? Mom!" Gabrielle shook her. "What is it? What's wrong?"

"Nathan," she breathed. "They took Nathan."

"What? Who took him? What are you talking about?" Gabrielle's voice was angry, hysterical, shards of glass against Eden's ears.

Eden curled into a fetal position and hid her face between her knees, hoping Gabrielle would leave her alone. There was nothing she could do right now. She couldn't call the police. Couldn't call anyone else—she had no one in her life who could help. And she couldn't get $5 million. She should have never allowed Nathan to walk on his own from the bus stop. She'd demanded for years that the school bus add a stop closer to their house, but they'd never listened to her, thought she was hysterical. And now . . .

"Mom!" Gabrielle shook her violently. "Don't do this now. Who took Nathan?"

"A man called me," Eden said. "He wants five million dollars. Or they . . . or we never see Nathan again."

"We need to call the police," Gabrielle said.

"No! He said they were watching us. Five million dollars? I don't have five million dollars." She picked up the phone and tried to dial the number the man had called from. She had to talk to him, to explain they'd targeted the wrong family. There was no way in hell she could get even $1 million, not to mention $5 million.

The number was unavailable. She tried it again. Unavailable. She tried it a third time. Unavailable. Gabrielle said something, but she couldn't understand what because there was roaring in her ears, and she couldn't hear the words above the din.

She stumbled to her feet and made her way back to the bathroom. Turned on the water, washed her hands, scraping all the germs away. People didn't understand; those germs were everywhere, and if you didn't wash them away often, it caused all sorts of problems. Diseases, and suffering, and your son being kidnapped, and—

Someone pulled her away from the sink, and a sudden sting of pain shot through her face.

She blinked, focusing. Gabrielle stood in front of her, panting hard. She'd slapped her.

"Mom, I'm calling the police." Gabrielle already had her phone in her hand.

"No!" Eden shrieked and yanked the phone away from her daughter. "He said they were watching."

"We need to do *something*."

Her daughter was right. Nathan needed her to do something. She couldn't lose herself to her usual routines. And it occurred to her that she did have one person to call.

"I know someone. Someone who might help."

"Who?"

"She's a cop." Eden walked back to the kitchen and picked up her phone from the floor. "She'll know what to do."

"How do you know her?"

We've gone through hell together.

"She's someone I used to know." Eden found Abby Mullen in her contact list and made the call.

"Hello?" a woman answered.

"Is this . . . Abby Mullen?" It wasn't. It didn't sound anything like her.

"Yes, who is this?"

"My name is . . ." She paused for a fraction of a second. She couldn't tell the woman her real name, not yet. Abby might hang up. "Edie Fletcher. I live in East Elmhurst. I need your help. My son has been kidnapped."

There was a long pause. "Edie, did you try calling 911?" Abby finally asked.

"No. They're watching me; I can't call the police. But I saw you on the news a few months ago. You can help me, right?"

"Edie, there are people better suited to handle a kidnapping case. I can connect you to—"

"Please," Eden sobbed. "I need you to help me."

Another long pause. Nathan's life hung in the balance, teetering on the edge of a chasm, as Abby Mullen decided what to do.

"I don't live far; I'll come over," Abby said. "What's your exact address?"

CHAPTER 9

The rain spattered on the windshield, the wipers working frantically, fighting a hopeless battle against the downpour. Abby peered through her drop-spotted window at the house. Whatever attempts had been made to differentiate this house from the row of identical structures on the block had met with failure. Like the houses to the left and right, it had a tiny front yard, an uninviting front door, and a shaded window facing the street. Two more windows on the second floor, and a third shuttered window hinting at a tiny attic. The rain and the darkness served to make the house even smaller.

She should have been more insistent with that woman on the phone. But there was something in Edie's voice, a sort of desperation Abby couldn't ignore. And the drive from her own house at College Point to East Elmhurst wasn't long. She'd left as soon as her mother showed up to pick up the kids, brushing off a question regarding Ben's birthday. They could talk about that later.

Sighing, she switched off the engine, the wipers freezing midswipe.

She exited the driver's door and struggled to get her umbrella open. By the time she managed it, her glasses were completely spattered, turning the world into a blur. She hurried to the front door and rang the doorbell.

The door was yanked open, and a large woman stood before her, her face cast in shadow.

"Edie Fletcher?" Abby asked.

"Come in," the woman said, tears in her voice.

Abby stepped inside, taking off her eyeglasses, wiping them on her shirt. While she did that, she glimpsed the fuzzy shape of another younger person—the woman's daughter?

"Thank you for coming," Edie Fletcher said.

Abby turned to face her, still wiping the lenses of her glasses, then put them back on, and the woman shifted into focus. She was instantly struck by a sense of familiarity. She knew this woman, but from where? Edie had a fair, pink complexion; deep blue eyes; and wavy brown hair. She wore a loose purple shirt, and Abby could glimpse parts of tattoos above the collar—a flower on one side and letters on the other. Her face was blotchy with tears, her lips trembling.

"Sure," Abby said, taking off her coat. The woman's daughter took it from her. She was a few years older than Samantha, maybe eighteen or nineteen, with blue eyes like her mother's and cascading blonde hair. Her face was pale, crumpled with worry.

"Can you tell me what happened?" Abby asked.

"Nathan didn't come home from school today," Edie said in a trembling voice. "And I got a phone call—"

"I'm sorry, how old is Nathan?" Abby interrupted.

"Eight. I called all of his friends. They saw him get off the school bus, but he never came home. And then I got a phone call from a man who said they have Nathan. And they want five million dollars."

Abby nodded, a sinking feeling in her gut. Most child abductions were by someone in the family. A ransom demand was unlikely in that case. And the ridiculously high sum was worrying. "Okay, when was this?"

Edie blinked, confused. The daughter said, "My mom got the phone call an hour ago."

"Okay." Abby glanced around her at the tiny kitchen, the dark living room. "Is Nathan's father here?"

"N . . . no," Edie said. "We're divorced."

"Do you have sole custody?" Abby asked.

"Yes."

"Did you tell Nathan's father about any of this?"

"No, I have no way to reach David. He hasn't been in touch for years."

They would have to investigate this further. Ransom demand notwithstanding, the father was a likely suspect. For now she let the matter drop. "Do you have a picture of Nathan?"

"Sure." The woman fiddled with her phone, then handed it to Abby. Cute kid with a faraway smile, staring dreamily at the camera almost as if he didn't notice his mom taking the picture.

Abby sent herself the picture from the phone. "Can I look around the house?"

"Why? Nathan isn't here. I mean, I checked."

"Sometimes, in abduction cases, there are important details that can really assist us." Also, often, the kid *was* in the house, hiding or even simply asleep. And in some cases there were details that shed light on the family's life. Because there was another suspect in this case: Edie Fletcher herself, who was the only one who'd talked to the supposed kidnappers. Missing children often turned up dead, murdered by their own parents. Abby would search for anything that stuck out. She would know what she was looking for when she saw it.

"Sure," Edie said. "Anything that would help bring Nathan back."

Abby had already glimpsed most of the ground floor, which included a cramped kitchen with a small metal dining table, and the family's living room—one couch facing a TV. There were other framed pictures on a dresser. Abby checked any possible hiding spot—kitchen cupboards, behind the fridge. She also opened the dresser drawers, as Edie hovered behind her, but saw nothing that drew her attention. She would make sure the place was searched more carefully later. A small bathroom was empty, a trail of water on the floor and a wet rag hinting at plumbing problems that could be temporarily ignored.

"Nathan's bedroom is on the second floor," Edie said.

Abby climbed the stairs. Two bedrooms on the second floor.

"Nathan's room is over there," Edie said behind her.

Abby opened the door. The room was cute, cheerful. A bed with *Star Wars* bedsheets and a small plushy. A desk scattered with crayons, a few drawings tacked to a corkboard. A distinct, unsettling emptiness loomed in the room, a vacuum shaped like a child. Abby imagined the boy she'd seen in the picture on the bed or sitting at the desk, drawing. She walked over to the desk and inspected the drawings more closely, looking for signs of abuse that a child would perhaps let show. But these were all innocent, childish. A spaceship, a dragon, a family. The family only had a mother and two children. No hidden father figure there. Like Edie had said, the father seemed out of the picture, literally and figuratively.

The door clicked shut behind her, and she turned around, surprised. Edie leaned on the door, looking wary.

"What is it?" Abby asked. Something about the woman's demeanor unsettled her. She was tense, as if about to pounce or flee, her eyes wide.

Edie's lips moved, not making a sound.

"Ms. Fletcher," Abby said. "I'm not sure—"

"Abihail? Don't you recognize me?"

The name, emerging from the ancient past, shocked Abby to the core. She leaned on the desk as if to steady herself.

A memory flashed in her mind. A girl standing in a beautiful flower field, her arms folded, her cold blue eyes fixed on Abby. "This is my garden, and *you're* not welcome."

And then, months later. Huddling with the girl and another boy in the back of a police car, the dark night lit by tall shimmering flames, a man's hushed voice saying, "So many of them. This is terrible."

Abby shivered. The past had a tangible chill to it. "Eden?" she whispered.

The woman let out a sob.

Modern culture provided ways to handle meeting people from your past. Little ceremonies and phrases aimed to bridge the gaps of decades. A wide smile, the meaningless phrase *how have you been*, perhaps the mention of a mutual acquaintance.

All those were practically useless in this case. Abby felt lost. It was difficult enough to just stand there, holding back the tide of memories that threatened to drown her.

"Is your name now really Edie?" she finally asked.

"No. It was for a while. I changed it back to Eden. And you—"

"I'm Abby," she said sharply, severing any misunderstanding. "*No one* knows me as Abihail. Okay?"

"Okay, I won't call you that." Eden seemed afraid of her reaction.

She was obviously frightened Abby would walk away. Eden seemed to really think Abby was her son's best hope.

It wasn't surprising. Eden probably still had a built-in suspicion of law authorities. In her mind, the police were your enemy, not your friend. And when you needed something, you turned to your family.

"How did you find me?" Abby asked, suddenly realizing she had no idea.

"You were on the news a few months ago," Edie said, her voice faint. "I saw you. You haven't changed."

The bank siege, her fifteen minutes of fame. Seven hostages, two desperate men—and her team had managed to get them to surrender without anyone getting hurt. She had been the primary negotiator, and even better, a woman. The media had loved her, at least until the next shiny thing came their way. But she still had people telling her they'd seen her on TV.

So Eden had seen her back then and recognized her. Amazing, after all this time. She would never have identified Eden. Time had not been kind to the girl . . . no, the woman in front of her. Only the blue eyes, which had seemed so familiar when Abby first saw her, remained the same.

"So how did you get my number?" Abby asked.

"I don't remember. I probably found it online."

She hadn't. The number wasn't listed anywhere. Abby had a feeling she knew how she had gotten it. She waited, letting the silence between them stretch.

Eden glanced sideways uncomfortably. After a few seconds passed, she blurted, "You know something? I saw someone. A man I didn't recognize hanging around the block. Saw him three times in the past few weeks. He was just . . . standing there. Do you think he could be involved?"

"Can you describe him?" Abby asked, more out of instinct.

"I think so. He had black hair. And he had a beard—"

"Not to me." Abby shook her head. "We should get you to the station. Take a look at some pictures. Maybe get you with a sketch artist."

"But . . . the man said they were watching me. I can't go to the police."

"I'll drive," Abby said. "I'll make sure nobody is following. This is the best thing for Nathan."

Eden's shoulders relaxed as Abby told her what was to be done. Up until now, Eden had been lost, helpless. Now Abby had taken charge.

Abby checked the rest of the house quickly, making sure she hadn't missed anything glaringly obvious. Eden's bedroom was in the attic, cramped and dark, a single tiny window facing the street.

The rain was even worse when they left. Eden insisted that Gabrielle join them, terrified to leave her daughter alone in the house. Eden's umbrella flipped on the way to the car, and she was drenched as she bundled into the passenger seat. Abby looked at the woman, strands of wet hair sticking to her cheeks, her face wet with rain, or tears, or a mix of both. And those eyes, peering from more than thirty years before.

Abby started the car, praying Eden wasn't bringing their shared past hurtling into the present.

CHAPTER 10

When Nathan's eyes blinked open, he had that feeling he got when he slept at a friend's home. That unfamiliarity of the bed, the sheets, even the way the *air* was not the same. He got up, fragments of his recent memories resurfacing as he rubbed his face with his hands.

He was in his room after all. These were his bedsheets, that was his desk on the far side of the room, his drawings on the wall. He yawned, shaking the cobwebs of sleep away. But he couldn't. His head was foggy, heavy, the world blurry at the edges.

He couldn't remember what day it was. Saturday? If it was Saturday, it was already Mom's birthday. He and Gabi had agreed they'd bring Mom breakfast in bed on her birthday.

Thinking of his mother's birthday brought back the car ride with Gabi's friend. They were going to get supplies for Mom's surprise party, right? What had happened? He remembered eating the burger and fries and drinking the Coke that Gabi's friend had bought him. And then he became sleepy. It was a long ride.

He must have dozed off. And maybe Gabi and her friend had decided to take him home after all. He pulled off the blanket and saw he still wore the clothes from the car ride. Maybe it wasn't Saturday after all. It didn't feel like he'd slept all night.

"Mom?" he called out.

He waited and then called again, "Mom!"

No one answered. The door to his room was shut, which was strange. It was never shut. He liked sleeping with the door open.

He got off the bed and stood up. A wave of dizziness hit him, and he wavered unsteadily. It was as if he had cotton balls in his head; it was hard to concentrate. The room felt . . . weird. Like the walls were closing in on him, everything seemingly more cramped. The desk was too close to the bed, the door too close to the desk. He didn't like it.

He shuffled to the door, his hand went to the doorknob, and he froze. The doorknob was different. This one was shiny, its shape rounder. Had Mom switched the doorknob of his room? Last year, she'd said she wanted to make some changes in the house. She'd even brought a guy who said the walls needed painting and that they could fix the bathroom window. But later she said it was too expensive and that they'd have to wait.

He grabbed the strange doorknob, twisted it, and pushed the door. It was stuck.

He twisted harder, pulled and pushed. "Mom, the door is stuck!" he shouted. "Mom!"

There was no answer, and he started panicking. He didn't like being in his room alone, didn't like the door closed, and he didn't like this new doorknob that didn't work properly. He shook the door, then kicked it and hurt his foot. He whimpered in pain and sat on the floor, holding his bruised toe.

"Mom! Gabi!" he cried. "I'm hurt."

They didn't come. They never left him home alone. Well, sometimes Mom would leave him alone for only ten minutes to get something from the store across the street, but she always told him she was leaving. And while she was gone he *always* watched TV because otherwise he noticed all the empty rooms in the house, and he would start to imagine they were filled with creepy monsters.

His heart beat faster as he breathed from his nose, gritting his teeth. They'd left him alone without telling him, and they hadn't even noticed the door was stuck because of the new doorknob. He would yell at them when they came back. And tomorrow he *wouldn't* bring his mom her birthday breakfast in bed, because of what she had done.

He cried on the floor, his toe throbbing with pain. After a while he crawled back to the bed and lay on it, hugging his Yoda plush doll. It took him a few minutes to notice that it, too, was different.

Several months before, Yoda's ear had been ripped, and his mom had sewn it back on, but she'd sewn it wrong, and the ear had a lopsided angle. But now it wasn't lopsided anymore. And the bright-green thread his mom had used to sew it was gone. So was the chocolate stain on Yoda's foot. And it didn't smell the same.

Neither did the bedsheets. They smelled different. Like new bedsheets.

He got out of bed, feeling as if ants were crawling on his neck. What was going on? Now that he was searching, he saw small differences everywhere. The torn corner of his Harry Potter poster was fixed. The wardrobe was not exactly the same color. And . . . and . . .

There was no window.

How had he not noticed it before? The small window above his desk was just . . . gone.

His drawings were still all there, the only thing that could not be replaced.

Except they weren't his. In this drawing, Mom's eyes were too small. The stars were wrong in the spaceship sketch, and it was flying the wrong way. And there was the drawing of his imaginary dog. He hadn't drawn this. *His* drawing of the dog was cute. *This* dog leered at him, his teeth too sharp, his tongue too long, a bad dog. A dog that ate children.

He had to get out of this room. Something was very wrong with it. He rushed to the door and rattled it. "Gabi!" he screeched. "Mom!"

They still didn't come, and he was beyond finding an explanation for it. Beyond understanding what the hell was going on. He had trouble breathing; a constant thudding in his ears disoriented him further. He needed to pee—or to throw up—but to do that he needed to go to the bathroom, and the door wouldn't move; it was stuck—*he* was stuck.

He recalled a movie he'd seen with his mom. In the movie, these two guys needed to open a locked door, and they used a crowbar. He remembered how impressed he had been by the sound of the wood cracking as the door was flung open. He didn't have a crowbar, but he had a metal ruler in his desk drawer. He could wedge it in the door's crack and lean on it. It had to work.

He went over to the desk drawer and yanked it open.

There was no metal ruler in it.

Instead, there were more drawings. A stack of drawings. The top one almost looked like the one he'd drawn of their family, except his own feet were freakishly long.

He took out a stack of drawings and spread them on the table.

They were all his drawings, but they weren't. Some were slightly different, a wrong color used, a person that seemed misshapen. A few were hideous, badly drawn people and then an angry scrawl, as if he had scratched out the drawing in frustration. In one of his drawings of Gabi and him, Gabi's image had been circled over and over with a red crayon. His name was on almost every page, but on some it wasn't his handwriting, and on others it was similar but not quite right. And on one page, his name was written over and over and over.

Nothing in this made sense, and of all the things he'd experienced in the past twenty minutes, this for some reason frightened him the worst. His bladder released, a stream of urine running down his pant leg and trickling on the floor.

A sudden click made him whirl, facing the door as it opened. A man stood in the doorway, the same man who'd said he was Gabi's friend. He held a bucket in one hand and a bottle of water in the other.

"Oh," the man said, glancing at the puddle of pee on the floor. "I guess I'll go get a mop."

Nathan didn't answer. His eyes were fixed on the man—and the space beyond him.

This was not his house at all.

CHAPTER 11

"It's crucial that we contact your ex-husband as soon as possible, Ms. Fletcher," Detective Jonathan Carver said.

His gaze was fixed on Eden, and he seldom broke eye contact except to scribble quickly in his notebook.

Abby knew cops who were diligent and caring, but when talking to civilians, they seemed aloof. Typing their report into the computer while talking or pausing the interview to answer a phone or check something. Carver listened, and *conveyed* that he was listening. He had been the same when they were in the academy together. When he talked to you, you felt like he was really fascinated by what you had to say.

"I really don't know how to reach him," Eden said. "We separated less than a year after Nathan was born."

"Do you have any shared friends? Maybe on social media?"

"I'm not on social media."

Abby had been surprised when Carver showed up at the front desk of the 115th Precinct station. She hadn't seen him since the academy. Now she had yet another opportunity to see how time changed people. In this case, unlike Eden, it was less shocking, and time had been kinder. Still the same thick brown hair, a small scar on his tawny chin. The age difference hid at the corners of his almond-shaped green eyes, where a hint of crow's-feet showed.

"Ms. Fletcher, the reason I'm asking is that maybe the kidnappers approached your husband as well, or maybe it's someone your husband knows. In more than ninety percent of abduction cases—"

"I have no idea how to contact him," Eden said. "Don't you think I'd love to get the child support payments?"

They sat in a small office away from the hubbub of the detective squad room. Carver had brought them chairs and sat to the side of the desk so that it wouldn't stand between them. Abby took the chair in the corner between Carver and Eden.

"Gabrielle," Abby said. "When was the last time *you* talked to your dad?"

"Seven years ago," Gabrielle said guardedly.

"Did he ever try to contact you?"

"No. My dad has nothing to do with this; he doesn't give a shit about us."

Carver nodded, letting it go. He then walked her through Nathan's motions when he usually came back from school. Eden answered with short sentences, speaking fast, as if she wanted to hurry the process along.

"When did you get concerned that he wasn't returning home?" Carver asked.

"I came back from work—"

"Where do you work?"

"I'm an office assistant at a dentist's. Dr. Gregory. When I got home around six, I saw he was missing, and I began to make calls."

Carver walked Eden through the calls to Nathan's friends and then the subsequent phone call from the kidnapper. Next he asked for her phone. "I'll see if our guys need it for anything," he said. "Lieutenant Mullen said you saw a stranger hanging around the block?"

"A few times in the past month."

"We'll show you some mug shots later. See if you can pinpoint the guy. We'll also see if a sketch artist is available to come over, okay?"

"Okay."

"Earlier you mentioned you called Nathan's friends," Abby said. "And that someone saw him get off the school bus?"

"Yes. A boy named Mikey."

"And where does the bus usually drop them?" Carver asked.

"Two blocks down. It's a quick walk home. I don't like him walking alone, but I'm working, and the school wouldn't add another stop by our house. I asked a few times, but maybe I didn't try hard enough . . ."

Abby had seen this before, parents finding the little things they could have done. Small decisions morphing into lifelong regrets.

"What time does the bus drop them?" Abby asked.

"Around three fifty. It depends on the traffic."

Carver scribbled in his notebook and glanced at Abby. "I'm going to talk to some people, get the search started. Then we can continue this talk. Do you all need anything?"

Both Eden and Gabrielle shook their heads, the plastic water cups still full on the desk. Carver walked out of the room.

Abby wished she had a recording of the phone call between Eden and the kidnappers. Her job hung on a thousand tiny details. The tone of voice used, a word spoken out of place, a long pause. All these things gave her information, let her build an idea of the person she was handling. "I want to go over the phone conversation you had with the kidnapper again," she said.

"It was a short conversation," Eden said. "All he said was that they had my son, and they demanded five million dollars or they'd kill him."

"Did he say they'll kill him?" Abby asked.

Eden gritted her teeth in frustration. "I just said—"

"I need to know the exact words, Eden," Abby said softly. "Did he say they would kill him? Did he say how? Or when? For example, did he say, 'We're going to shoot your son if you don't get the money in three days'?"

Eden flinched. "No . . . he never said they'll shoot him. He said . . . he said . . ."

"Take your time," Abby said. "Close your eyes. Breathe deeply. Imagine the moment you answered the phone. Can you do that?"

"I . . . yes," Eden said, shutting her eyes. She took a long breath. Abby matched her breathing rhythm to Eden's and softened her voice. "Where were you when you answered the call?"

"In the kitchen. By the counter."

"Okay, that's good." Abby's words matched the pace of her breathing. "Were you standing up or sitting down?"

"I . . . I was standing. I just came from upstairs."

Carver stepped inside and shut the door behind him. Abby shot him a quick look, and he remained silent.

"What was the first thing he said when you answered the phone?" Abby asked.

"He said my name." Eden placed her palms on the table, seemingly to stop them from trembling.

Abby glanced at Eden's hands, saw the multiple scratches, and identified them for what they were. She didn't mention it. Instead, she said, "Did he say your name? Or did he ask if it was you?"

"He didn't ask if I was Eden Fletcher, but he made it sound like it was a question."

"So he intoned it," Abby suggested. "Like this. Eden Fletcher?"

"Exactly. And then he said they kidnapped my son."

"Did he say *kidnapped*?" Abby frowned. She doubted those were the words the man had used. Eden's memory was fragmented by fear. They would have to take her words with a grain of salt.

"Y . . . yes. He might have said *taken*; I don't remember. He definitely said they took my son."

"And then what?"

"He said they want five million—"

"Hang on. He said they took your son. What did you say in response?"

"I . . . I wanted to . . ." Eden let out a hiccuping sob. "I wanted to speak to him. He was probably so scared."

"Did the man let you speak to him?"

"He said Nathan was sleeping."

So far they had no proof that Nathan was even alive. But saying he was *sleeping* was an unusual phrase. Usually, if the kidnappers couldn't let the hostage talk, for whatever reason, they'd say something ambiguous like "He's not here right now" or a similar phrase. It was possible the man had lied, but Abby believed he'd have chosen a simpler lie. It was more likely he was telling the truth, and Nathan was really sleeping—or was unconscious. Perhaps he'd been drugged.

"Did he say Nathan was sleeping?" she asked. "Did he use his name?"

"I . . . I don't remember."

"Okay," Abby said. "Then what?"

"He asked for five million dollars and said they'll kill Nathan if I don't get it."

"Did he say it like that?"

"I don't remember."

Abby gritted her teeth and then, in spite of herself, said, "Eden, I want you to focus. Focus on your *core*." She repeated the words she'd heard endless times as a child. "I want you to imagine your core as a glowing light that spreads through you. It cleanses you. Breathe deeply as your core cleanses you."

Abby felt Carver's surprised stare boring into her, but she ignored him. Eden's breathing became deeper, calmer.

"All your negative emotions are cleansed away. Cleansed with . . ." Abby took a breath. "Cleansed along with the germs. Your thoughts are clear."

Eden's body was getting lax; the trembling stopped. Sadness coursed through Abby's body. Even after all these years, the words still held such control over this woman.

But it didn't matter, not right now. "You asked to talk to Nathan, and he said he was sleeping. Then what did he say? What were his exact words?"

There was a long pause, and then Eden said, "He said they wanted five million dollars, or Nathan dies."

"What did you tell him?"

"I tried to tell him I can't get that kind of money, and he answered that I better start working on getting it. And then he hung up. I tried calling him back, but the phone was offline."

"Your *son*, are you sure he didn't say *your son* before hanging up, instead of *Nathan*?" Abby asked.

"I don't know." Eden's eyes snapped open. "What does it matter?"

Perhaps it didn't, but Abby wished she knew. If the kidnapper had said *your son* or *the boy*, it was a form of abstraction. It was a way to build an emotional detachment from his hostage, to view him less as a human and more as leverage. And it might possibly mean that the likelihood of Nathan returning unharmed was slimmer.

"It doesn't," she said. "But the more information we have, the better our chance to return Nathan home safely."

"Will you?" Gabrielle asked abruptly. "Get him back home?"

It was impossible for Abby not to compare Eden's children with her own, not to imagine herself in the same spot as Eden. Human beings always searched for connections even when there were none. She and Eden had come from the same place. Now, decades later, each had a teenage daughter and a younger son. Each of them apparently a single mother. And when Gabrielle asked her if she'd bring Nathan back home, she could almost see another reality in which Samantha asked the same question about Ben. It sent chills up her spine.

And she had only one possible answer to it. "We'll do everything we can," she said, catching the girl's eyes. "I promise you that."

The girl's sharp stare made it clear that the vague promise did nothing to make her feel better. If anything, it made her angry—and afraid. She'd wanted to hear a confident yes.

CHAPTER 12

The rain had dwindled to a light drizzle by the time they left the station. They'd been there for hours as Eden had first looked through mug shots with no result, then described the man she'd seen to the sketch artist.

Eden appeared as if the adrenaline had worn off, her body slumped in the seat. She stared out the passenger window morosely. Gabrielle sat in the back, hands in her lap.

"How will I be able to get the money they're asking for?" Eden asked weakly.

Abby sighed, turning on the engine. "Eden, what I'm about to say might be difficult to hear, but it's important you understand." She paused, giving the mother and daughter a few precious seconds to steady themselves. "Even if you had five million dollars in the bank, and you could transfer it all tomorrow, there's no guarantee that Nathan would return home safely."

She maneuvered the car to the road, letting her words sink in. When convincing anyone to change their point of view, silence was the most important tool. It gave them time to think about what was said, about the implications, hopes, and fears. The fast-talking salesman might get someone to buy a vacuum cleaner, but he'd never manage to coax a jumper off a building or convince a trapped robber to surrender. Abby needed to make Eden understand that this was much more complicated than a business transaction, $5 million for boy.

Gabrielle was the first to break the silence. "Why not? If they got what they want, why wouldn't they let him go?"

"Because maybe the money isn't what they want at all," Abby said. "Maybe they took him for a different reason, and they are using the ransom demand to buy time." Unless they twisted her arm, this was as close as she was willing to get to saying, *Maybe your brother has already been raped and murdered.*

"But he asked for the money," Eden babbled. "He kept talking about the money."

"Which I find strange," Abby said. "He took Nathan in a very limited time window, which makes me think he'd been planning this, probably watching, scouting ahead of time. He knew who you were. And you don't look like you have that kind of money. I think there's something he's interested in beyond the ransom."

The streets were much emptier now. They would get back to Eden's house in no time.

"It's also possible Nathan can identify them," Abby added. "He was taken in broad daylight from a city street. I'm willing to bet they didn't wear ski masks when they grabbed him. Why would they let him go if he saw their faces?"

"Why are you telling us this?" Gabrielle raised her voice. "Just to scare us?"

"I'm telling you this because, like I said, we will do what we can to get Nathan back," Abby answered. "But that's not the same as saying we will do whatever the *kidnappers* say to get Nathan back. Because doing what the kidnappers say doesn't guarantee us anything. Instead, we can use the conversations with the kidnappers to buy time, to learn more about what they want, about who they are and where they are. And meanwhile, we also talk them down. Lower the ransom. See if they're willing to let us talk to Nathan. It probably won't be a quick process. But I'll help you through it. And I'm very good at what I do."

Eden's eyes welled up, and Abby drove on in silence, giving the woman some time to adjust. She glanced in the rearview mirror, checking on Gabrielle. Only the top half of the girl's face was visible in the mirror's frame, and her eyes seemed vacant. Abby couldn't figure out what was going through the girl's head. She focused on the road, running the next steps forward in her mind. The kidnappers would call again, probably tomorrow, and it would be best if she or one of the other negotiators took the call. She would know exactly what to say and when to stay quiet, how to prod the subject and keep him talking while giving him a growing sense of control.

The problem was that the kidnappers probably didn't even know the police had been contacted. And it should stay that way for now.

"We need to talk about the next call," she said. "How you should talk. What you can and can't say."

"When will he call?" Eden asked.

"I don't know. It's best to be prepared as soon as possible." Abby's fingers drummed on the steering wheel. "First of all, I want your voice to remain steady when you talk to him. When this kidnapper calls, he's stressed and wary. If you fall apart, start screaming at him, or if your voice is tense, it'll only make matters worse. He might react badly."

"Badly how?"

"It might cause him to hang up," Abby said—and didn't add that Nathan might suffer from that loss of control. "We want him to stay on the line, right? So we can try and trace his phone, send police to where he's calling from. And so that he keeps talking to us, giving us information."

Eden nodded, her lips trembling.

"When the phone rings, I don't want you to answer immediately. I want you to take a few breaths. You can let it ring a few times, maybe eight rings."

"What if he hangs up?"

"He won't; he wants to talk to you. Remember, both of you want something, not just you. He'll want to make it seem as if it's all about getting your boy back, but he's got a huge stake in this. He'll wait for you to answer. Let it ring, breathe, prepare your calm voice, okay?"

"What if he asks me why it took me so long to answer?"

"Tell him you're sorry, but you were in the bathroom. Be apologetic but not hysterical. We want him to feel in control, okay?"

"Okay."

"I want you to take a breath before every sentence you say. Use this breath to think about your next sentence and to maintain your voice."

"He might get mad if I don't answer fast enough."

"He won't. People don't get mad at someone taking their time. Trust me. The most important part is for him to feel like you're listening to him. So you need to sound like you're attentive. It's good to say things like 'I understand,' or 'Okay,' or 'I see.' You can repeat the last few words he said. So for example, if he says, 'We want five million dollars,' you can say, 'Five million dollars.'"

"It'll make her sound dim witted," Gabrielle said from behind.

"That's not a bad thing," Abby said firmly. "He'll feel more in control and talk more to make sure you understand. And to make him talk even more, we need you to ask him questions that start with *how* or *what*. These questions are open ended and will make him talk his way out of it. They are also very nonaggressive questions, so they'll make him calmer. So you can ask him, 'How can I pay you the ransom if I don't know my son is okay?' Or 'How do you want me to pay you?' Or 'What if I can't get the money in time?'"

"Questions." Eden seemed dazed. "I won't remember all of that."

Abby put a reassuring hand on Eden's wrist. Eden started in surprise at the touch but didn't move her arm.

"I'll go over it again when we get to your home," Abby said. "We'll go over it several times, okay? We'll even do a practice call, see how you do. And there'll be someone with you all the time, at least in the next few days, to help you when they call."

"All the time?"

"Yeah," Abby said resolutely. "We'll do shifts. You'll need someone with you."

"But who'll stay tonight?"

Abby wanted to say she'd call it in, see who was available. The words were practically on her lips when she glanced at Eden, saw the pleading look in her eyes.

Damn it.

"I'll stay at your home tonight—until tomorrow morning," she said tiredly. "And then we'll see, okay?" She'd have to call her parents, let them know. The kids were staying there for the night anyway.

Eden shifted her hand and squeezed Abby's palm. "Thank you so much for helping us," she said, her voice barely a whisper.

CHAPTER 13

The girl's hair was tousled from sleep, and she was obviously confused and scared to have been woken up. Detective Jonathan Carver had to kneel to question Daniela Hernandez, and she answered the questions while clutching her mom's hand. He always found that particular gesture sweet. As if holding their parent's hand would protect them from danger. And maybe they were right. After all, if Nathan Fletcher had had his mother's hand to clasp when he had been taken, he probably *would* have stayed safe.

"Daniela," Carver said. "You walk back home with Nathan Fletcher after school, right?"

"No."

Carver blinked. "Do you get off at the same station?"

"Yes."

"And you walk in the same direction, right?"

She wiped her nose on her mom's shirt. "Yes."

An important distinction. They didn't walk together; they just happened to be walking side by side in the same direction. "Did you see him today after school?"

Daniela raised her eyes to her mom. "I want to go to bed."

"In a minute," her mom said. "Answer the nice man's questions."

She didn't say *nice* as if she meant *nice*. Mrs. Hernandez apparently didn't like cops. Daniela glared at him, saying nothing.

Carver suppressed a sigh. "Did you see Nathan when you got off the school bus today?"

"Yes."

"And you saw him walking home?"

"Yes."

"Did he talk to anyone?"

She frowned. "No."

"Did you see him approach anyone? Or a car maybe?"

"No. He walked home."

"Did you see any grown-ups in the area?"

She scrunched her forehead, then shook her head.

"And when you got home, he kept walking on his own?"

"Yes."

"Did you see anyone then? Or a car driving by?"

"I saw Mommy. She was in the kitchen. She made pea soup." Her expression clearly signified that the pea soup was, in fact, a suspicious development. As far as Daniela was concerned, the police should probably investigate the pea soup incident further.

Carver stood up. "What time did Daniela show up today?"

"I think it was the usual time. Around four," her mom said.

"You don't know the exact time?"

"I didn't check. But it's always around four."

"Okay. Thanks, Mrs. Hernandez. Sorry to have bothered you so late in the evening." Carver smiled at Daniela. "Thanks, Daniela. You've been very helpful."

Daniela tightened her hold on her mother's hand. Carver nodded at them both and got out of the house. Shoving his hands down in his pockets, he stepped past the Halloween skeleton that hung by the front door and crossed the tiny yard back to the sidewalk. Instead of going on to the next house down the block, he stared at the tree in front of him, his breath misting in the chilly air.

Monika used to say he sometimes "got stuck." He would be putting on his shirt, and then, one sleeve in, he would gaze at the wall, motionless. Or he would be doing the dishes and suddenly stop, the water running. She'd found it exasperating. She'd found a lot of things about him exasperating. Maybe that was why she'd finally left.

The occasional fake pumpkins and spiders that decorated the front yards and fences in the street struck Carver as oddly inappropriate. The local residents didn't need to furbish their neighborhood with fake spookiness. Not when true fear had seeped into their lives. Just hours ago, Nathan had paced this very sidewalk like he'd done dozens, if not hundreds, of times before. Following life's motions. And then something had swept in and taken him. The illusion of safety shattered.

Trick-or-treating would be tense on the block this year, with the parent chaperones sticking very close to their children.

"Carver." A uniformed officer approached him. "We found something. This guy across the street saw Nathan get into an unfamiliar car."

Yes. They'd already gone door to door through half the block with no result. Daniela Hernandez was the best eyewitness so far. Now, finally, they had something better. Carver followed the officer to a small house close to the street corner. No light illuminated the front yard, and Carver could barely see the shadowy forms of a discarded hose and a rake on the ground. The officer knocked on the door, and it instantly opened, as if the man had been waiting on the other side, his hand on the doorknob.

"Mr. Doyle, this is Detective Carver," the officer said.

Doyle—pale, tall, and sinewy—said, "Well, like I told the officer, I saw Nathan—"

"Sir, is it possible to talk inside?" Carver asked politely.

Doyle hesitated for a second, then said, "Sure, come in."

Carver and the officer stepped inside the house. Doyle closed the door behind them. The house seemed bare and neglected. Carver glimpsed an ashtray brimming with cigarette stubs on a small wooden table in the living room. A single beige armchair faced a television set, and that was pretty much the extent of the living room furniture. The entire place was stuffy, every window draped, every door shut.

"Like I told the officer," Doyle said again, "I saw that little boy get inside a car."

"Good," Carver said, ceremoniously pulling out his notebook. He didn't need it; he was recording the conversation. But the notebook made people pay attention. "What's your name again?"

"Frank. Frank Doyle."

"Okay, Frank. When was this?"

"At two minutes to four. I was in the kitchen making a fresh pot of coffee, and I looked out the window. And I noticed the car, which instantly drew my attention."

"Why did it draw your attention?"

"I know the cars of the people on the block, and it wasn't anyone's car. It was sort of muddy. And it stopped in the middle of the street."

"Muddy?"

"Yeah. Like the bottom part of the car was spattered with mud."

"What sort of car was it?"

"It was white."

"Did you notice the make?"

"I don't really know a lot about cars."

"And the license plate?"

"I didn't get a good look; it was far away. But it was covered in mud."

"And then what happened?"

"The driver talked to the boy."

"Which boy?"

"Nathan Fletcher."

"Are you sure it was him?"

"I've been living on this block for three years," Frank said. "I know the Fletcher family. It was Nathan Fletcher."

65

"So the driver stopped at the side of the road and talked to Nathan. And then what happened?"

"They talked for a minute or two. And then Nathan got inside the car."

"Are you sure Nathan got inside? The driver didn't grab him?"

"I'm sure. The driver opened the passenger door, and Nathan got in."

"Can you describe the driver?"

"I didn't see him too well. I'm pretty sure he was a white guy."

"Could you tell his age? Anything about him?"

"No. It was pretty far away. I could barely see anything from the kitchen window. And Nathan smiled when he talked to this guy; it seemed like he maybe knew him."

Carver jotted the details, using the time to think it through. He would show the man a few car model images later, see if he could get an actual make. If Nathan knew the man, it tightened the circle of suspects significantly. A relative? A teacher? A parent of a friend?

"Can I see the kitchen window?"

"Sure." Doyle led them to the kitchen. A faint smell of stale food and burned oil hovered in the air. The man gestured at the window, a dirty rectangular pane of glass facing the street.

"Where was the car exactly when you saw it?"

Doyle pointed. "See the tree over there? By the trash can? There."

A few steps from home. Carver peered out the window. To see the mentioned tree he had to lean to the left. Doyle hadn't just glanced out the window like he'd claimed. He'd had to have leaned uncomfortably against the kitchen counter to see the exchange between Nathan and the driver. Something must have felt wrong to him. If he'd only called Eden Fletcher that moment . . .

People, Carver often found, didn't want to make a scene. They didn't want to seem as if they were sticking their nose where it didn't belong. Frank Doyle had probably rationalized the events at the time, told himself it was Nathan's uncle picking him up. How dumb would he sound if he called Eden Fletcher hysterically saying that Nathan had just driven off with a stranger?

And then he'd carried on with his day. While Nathan Fletcher had disappeared.

CHAPTER 14

Eden wasn't even sure why she was lying in bed. Was she just going through the motions? Or setting an example for Gabrielle? Sleep was completely unthinkable. No matter how late it was, she couldn't stop her churning mind. She couldn't even slow it down.

Nathan had to be terrified, trapped in a strange place with these awful men. Her sweet Nathan, who'd had nightmares for three days in a row after seeing Disney's *The Lion King*, was in a basement, or a dark room, or a cage somewhere, crying for his mom.

Had she doomed her son by calling the police? Maybe he wasn't in a basement at all. Maybe his body was already in a ditch somewhere. And what if she'd known that he was missing sooner? He had already been gone for two hours by the time she'd gotten back from work. Why did she have to work every day until five thirty? If only she'd looked harder for a job that allowed her to be home earlier . . . maybe if she had been there to notice he was missing, if she'd called the police in time, Nathan would be home by now.

It would be beyond wonderful to have him back. She pictured him coming home right now. *Mom, I managed to sneak out the window, and a nice woman gave me a ride home.* She let out a whimper, knowing there was no way that would happen.

She tried to think of something else, perhaps what she'd say to the kidnappers when they called again or of the different ways she could get the ransom. But her mind always returned to Nathan.

At some point during the night, she went to Nathan's room and lay in his bed, hugging his Yoda plushy. The bed smelled like him, and shutting her eyes, she could imagine him lying in bed with her. He always slept curled with the blanket up to his eyes.

Had they given him a blanket? Or had they let him lie shivering in the cold? A flash of rage followed by a wave of helplessness.

It was her birthday, she realized. For as long as she remembered, birthdays had been a time for disappointments. Reality never matched her expectations. But no birthday had come close to this. In all likelihood she would never celebrate her birthday again. The date was now permanently stained with the worst thing that could ever happen.

At three in the morning, she padded to the kitchen to get a glass of water. Were they giving Nathan enough to drink? Enough to eat? Or was he hungry as well as scared?

To her surprise, Abby was awake, sitting in the darkness by the kitchen table. The woman's laptop was in front of her, the screen illuminating her face in a ghostly pale light. Her hair was slightly disheveled, one of her ears protruding. Abby had always had large ears, and they stuck out, drawing attention to them. Even as a small child, she'd carefully hidden her ears under her hair. And the other kids had loved taunting her about it, calling her Dumbo.

Abby turned to face her, and blood rushed to Eden's cheeks as if Abby could hear her thoughts.

"I'm sorry," she said clumsily. "I wanted a glass of water."

"You don't need to apologize," Abby said gently. "It's your own home."

She kept talking in this placid, soft voice. Had she been like that as a child? Eden remembered Abihail differently, shouting a lot and prattling endlessly.

She poured herself a glass of water and turned back to her bedroom. But up there, all that waited were more endless hours of staying awake and torturing herself with useless thoughts and regrets. Here, in Abby's company, her mind seemed to calm down, even just for a bit. Abby seemed to be in control of the situation. She knew what to do. She had seen it all before.

Eden sat opposite the woman and took a tentative sip from her glass. "I couldn't sleep."

Abby nodded. "I'd be surprised if you could. You should probably get something to help you sleep tomorrow. The next few days will be very difficult, and you'll need to get some rest."

The next few days. "How long do these kidnappings usually take?" Eden asked.

"It varies. Some end really quickly; others can drag on." Abby sighed and shut her laptop. "They'll probably call tomorrow. Do you feel ready for that call?"

Eden would never feel ready. She wished someone else could do this. Maybe Abby could take the call and pretend to be her. But they would know. And then they'd kill Nathan. "Yeah," she said. "I'm ready. Ask questions. Keep my tone calm. Take a long breath before saying anything."

"That's right."

Eden took another sip from her water. "Oh, I didn't offer you any—"

"It's okay." Abby motioned at two mugs on the kitchen counter. "I made myself some tea earlier."

"Abihail—"

"Don't call me that." Abby's affable tone evaporated. "It's not my name."

"Sorry. I like Abby."

"Me too. That's why I chose it."

"Do you have kids?" Eden asked heavily.

"Two, like you." Abby smiled at her. "A boy and a girl."

Then Abby surely knew what Eden was going through. "Are you married?"

"No, divorced. What about you? Who was your kids' father?"

"A guy I met a while ago. It didn't work." Eden was desperate to change the subject. "What happened after . . . after we left the Wilcox Family?"

Abby froze for a moment. Had Eden gone too far? The woman clearly didn't want to reopen that part of her life. Her jaw clenched tightly, eyes glazing as if the question brought back dark memories.

"They put me in a foster home," Abby finally said. "They ended up adopting me."

"Oh." Eden felt a pang of jealousy. "Were they nice?"

Abby smiled. "Very nice. My mom is actually with my kids right now, watching them. What about you?"

"I wasn't adopted. But the fifth foster home they put me in was really good, and I stayed there until I finished school." It was a ridiculous summary of a life with as much turbulence as hers. But it served the purpose of "catching up." As if now, after they'd both given a succinct outline of the years since they'd last seen each other, they could continue like nothing had happened.

"How did you end up in New York?" Abby asked. "I thought you'd go live somewhere more rural."

Eden frowned. "Why?"

"You spent your entire time in the wildflower fields behind the farm."

The sudden memory almost made her smile, which in turn consumed her with guilt. Here she was, having a casual conversation while her son was being held by malicious strangers. "I totally forgot about the fields," she said, her voice cracking slightly. "When Father noticed that I spent all my time there, he started calling them the Garden of Eden, remember?"

Abby nodded. "They were beautiful."

"Were they?" Eden couldn't recall how it had looked. All she could summon was the feeling of the rugged soil between her fingers and the smell of the wet earth after it rained.

"Yeah, they were." Abby smiled sadly.

"I really should have gone somewhere rural. I did for a time, but I ended up here. And if I lived somewhere else, Nathan wouldn't have been—"

"Don't blame yourself."

But now that she'd started going down that road, she couldn't stop. "Do you think that if I'd called the police when I first saw that guy in the street, Nathan would be home now?"

"I don't know."

She should have done it. She should have insisted more about the bus stop's location. She should have found a job that let her be home in time to meet her son after school. A tapestry of terrible mistakes and moments of weakness culminating in her son's abduction.

"Eden," Abby said. "I have to ask. Did you get my number from Isaac?"

Eden hesitated before answering. "Yes. When I saw you on the news, I wanted to reach out. He didn't want to give it to me at first. He said you left the past behind you and that he didn't think you'd be happy to hear from me."

Abby didn't seem about to contradict her. Eden exhaled and added, "I finally convinced him to give it to me but promised I'd sleep on it a few days before I called you. And I guess I never really managed to go through with it. Reach out, I mean."

Abby nodded, her jaw clenched.

"I chat with him every week," Eden said. "And before, we stayed in touch with actual letters. He was like my pen pal."

"Same here," Abby said. "I didn't want to stay in touch at first. Just wanted to leave it all behind me. But he sent me letter after letter, and eventually I succumbed."

"He was right to insist," Eden said. "Family's the most important thing."

"It wasn't a family," Abby said. "You know that."

"It was a family for me," Eden answered defensively.

"You just think it was. It was *never* a family." Abby's tone became sharp again. "And Moses Wilcox was never *Father*. It was a cult. And Moses Wilcox was the bastard who created it. And in the end, he was the one who took everyone with him to hell."

CHAPTER 15

After Eden went back to bed, Abby opened her computer and sat motionless in her chair, gazing at her laptop's screen. Long-lost memories were floating to the surface of her consciousness. She could feel them emerging, lone fragments—a bowl of soup in the mess hall, the laughter of her biological parents when she said something funny, her Sunday dress stretched on her bed, so white and clean. But behind those glimpses, she knew that other memories lurked. Not the ones she'd forgotten but the ones she'd repressed, pushing them into a dark corner in her mind. Now that the dam was cracking, they'd gush out as well.

It was talking about the Garden of Eden that had done it. Just mentioning it brought back the scents. The sweet smells of the flowers Eden tended to. What were they? Abby recalled purple flowers . . . lavender? And underneath that scent, something else. A stench that didn't belong.

Chicken feed.

The sudden realization knocked her breath away. The Wilcox community had been nearby a poultry feed mill, and on some days, depending on the wind, everything smelled like fermented grain.

What was it her mom used to say?

It smells like—

"—*the armpit of a skunk here," Mommy said. "We're knee-deep in flowers, and all I can smell is that awful chemical stench.*"

She was carrying two large buckets as they paced through the field. A pair of scissors was wedged in her belt. Every few steps she'd halt, snip a few flowers, put them in one of the buckets, and move on.

Abihail followed behind her, a handful of flowers clutched in her fist. She loved picking flowers with Mommy. Later, she knew, Mommy would make beautiful bouquets from the flowers she picked, and her daddy would go sell them in the flower shop that the Wilcox Family owned in the nearby town. Father Wilcox sometimes said that Mommy was a genius of beauty and color. And whenever he said that, Abihail's chest would fill with pride.

She picked another flower, a small yellow one, adding it to her own bouquet. Bees hummed around them. A bee had stung her several weeks before, and Abihail had refused to enter the fields afterward—until Father Wilcox told her she had to. He explained that like them, bees did God's work, spreading beauty in the world. And if a bee had stung her, it was only doing God's work, and it was probably a small punishment for Abihail's impure thoughts.

Abby clenched her fists as the images tumbled through her mind. She hadn't remembered that the Family had owned a flower shop. But it made sense, of course. The perfect facade for what really went on at that farm. And Abby's own biological parents had been the ones who'd maintained that facade. In the Wilcox Family, everyone pitched in, and each had their job. Even the children—

—were playing hide-and-seek. Eden was counting loudly, her face against a large tree. Abihail stood frozen, unsure where to hide. Eden always found her easily, no matter what.

A hand clutched her own.

"Come on!" Isaac pulled her, grinning his wide bucktoothed grin.

She ran after him through the flowers, colors rushing past her: purple, yellow, red, and pink. She stumbled a few times as she tried to stick close to him. He always ran so fast; it was like trying to keep up with the wind.

He led her to a patch of tall flowers that towered above her. She hesitated, but he just dove in, the flowers hiding them completely. Green walls closed around them on all sides. After a few steps they stopped, and Isaac lay on his back. Abihail lay beside him, staring at the blue sky and the pink flowers that rustled in the wind overhead.

"Do you think she'll find us?" she whispered.

"Eden can look all day and never find us here." Isaac grinned at her, then frowned. "What's this?" He reached out and plucked an object from the ground by her head.

Abihail peered at it. It was a small metallic cylinder. Part of it was sort of brown, but the other part was golden, shimmering in the sun.

"Maybe it's a holy ancient relic," she said. "Like Father's staff."

"It's not a holy relic, stupid," Isaac said, rolling it between his finger and thumb.

"Why not?"

"Because it's not ancient. It's a bullet, Dumbo."

Abihail was already sniffling. Being called stupid *was bad enough, but being called Dumbo, and by Isaac, of all people . . .*

"Aw, don't start, Eden will hear us." Isaac handed her the bullet. "Here. You keep it. Put it with your treasures."

Abihail let out a shuddering breath, wiping her eyes. "Really?" She stared at the small smooth object. "Is it gold?"

"No, the casing is brass."

"Won't it explode?" She couldn't take her eyes off it.

"Nah, you don't have to worry, it's—"

"Found you!" Eden's voice, victorious, shrieked beside them . . .

Abby shook her head, blinking. To her surprise, she realized her eyes were tearing up as if that memory of the decades-old hurt had squeezed them out.

What had happened to that bullet? And to her box of treasures? She now recalled the box, hidden under her bed, full of stuff she'd found—a funny-looking rock, a feather, a metal spring. Real childhood treasures.

She took out her phone, opened the chat with Isaac, then realized it was four in the morning. She wondered if he remembered playing hide-and-seek. After all, he'd been much older back then. Abby had been barely seven and—

—a half. But still, the big kids had agreed to include her in the game. And it was her turn to count. Covering her eyes with her hands, she counted aloud.

"One . . . two . . . three . . ."

She heard the kids' scuffling steps as they ran, searching for places to hide. A spurt of giggles, and then just the wind.

". . . seven . . . eight . . ."

She peered through her fingers but saw no one. She quickly shut her eyes again, kept counting, aware of the weight of the bullet in her pocket.

". . . nineteen . . . twenty!"

She opened her eyes, her smile evaporating.

Father Wilcox loomed in front of her, his long black-gray hair fluttering in the wind, his flinty eyes narrow and severe. Had she been counting too loud? Or maybe he knew about the bullet?

"Abihail," he said, and she could hear that she really was in trouble. "What are you doing?"

"Playing hide-and-seek?" she said meekly. Suddenly she wasn't sure if it was allowed. Was playing hide-and-seek a sin?

"Look at your hands."

She did. They were brown with dirt. Oh no.

"And you put those hands on your face," Father said.

"I'm sorry."

"Spreading all those germs on your mouth and eyes and nose. Letting Satan crawl inside your body."

She could feel them crawling all over her face. She started crying.

"Your body is not yours to desecrate!" Father roared. "You are to be the mother of the Messiah's children. Do you want your children to be corrupt with germs and filth?"

"I'll wash them," Abihail blubbered. "I'll wash them right now."

"You do that." Father knelt in front of her, his piercing gaze unwavering. "And you apologize while you do it. Apologize to God. Apologize to me. Apologize to your future children. Apologize to every—"

Abby exhaled sharply, her fingernails digging into her palms. She was not ready for those memories to return. Not now. Perhaps not ever.

CHAPTER 16

Abby stifled a yawn, the third one that morning. It had been a terrible night. Even when she'd finally fallen asleep, around five, her slumber had been rife with nightmares.

She checked her watch. Where was her replacement? She wanted to go home and get a quick shower before returning to work, but she didn't want to leave Eden alone. She glanced at the woman who sat on the couch, her eyes glazed. Eden kept staring at her phone as if to make sure it was on, that it had enough reception.

When it rang, they both started. Eden's eyes widened with fear. Abby quickly checked her laptop's screen, the number calling Eden flashing on the monitor. It wasn't the same number as the day before, but it didn't match any of Eden's contacts either.

She quickly sat down on the couch by Eden's side, laptop on her knees. "Remember, ask questions. Mind your tone. If I squeeze your hand, it means you need to pause and take a deep breath to regroup, okay?"

Eden nodded, lips trembling. Gabrielle hurried into the living room and stood by the couch, watching her mother. Abby put on her earphones and took Eden's clammy hand. She gave it a small squeeze. Eden took a deep breath and answered the phone after the sixth ring.

"Hello?" Her voice trembled.

"It took you long enough to answer," a metallic voice said. Eden had described it as pure evil, but as Abby had guessed, it was merely the result of a voice modulator. She watched the graph of the sound wave on-screen, knew that in the situation room, someone was listening in, trying to undo the voice modulation, tracking the location of the caller. The longer this call was, the better.

"I'm sorry, I . . . I was in the bathroom," Eden blurted.

Abby squeezed her hand again. Eden turned to look at her, a desperate glint in her eyes. Abby did her best to give her a reassuring stare.

"Do you have the money?" the man asked.

For a second Eden seemed lost. Abby mouthed *how*.

"How can I get five million dollars?" Eden asked. Her voice was strangled, but she managed to get the words out in a steady pace.

"I don't care how; that's your problem. Sell your car, take out a loan, rob a bank. Just get that money."

Eden was about to answer when Abby squeezed her hand again. The first mistake people always made when negotiating was thinking they had to answer fast. As if the other person would hang up with impatience if she took a moment.

Eden took another deep breath. When she spoke, her voice seemed slightly calmer. "How can I get the ransom if I don't know Nathan is okay?"

"He's okay. Don't worry about him."

"How can I be sure of that?"

"Eden, don't mess with us. Do you want us to hurt your son? Do you want us to cut his finger off?"

Eden's hand went to her throat, eyes widening. Before Abby had the time to squeeze her other hand, she blurted, "Don't hurt him, don't hurt my boy. I'll get you your money, just please, please, don't hurt him."

Her voice cracked, then shattered, the last words punctured by deep, wet sobs. She tried to say something else, but the phone tumbled from her hand, dropping to the floor.

"Then you'll get that money for us, right?" the voice in Abby's earphones asked.

Abby picked up the phone and held it out to Eden while squeezing the woman's hand hard.

"Hello? You don't worry about your son; he's fine. Get us the money, you got that?"

Abby pushed the phone into Eden's hand. Eden put it to her ear, her lips moving, but all she could do was weep.

In one swift move, Gabrielle snatched the phone from her mother.

"Hello?" she said. "This is Gabrielle; I'm Nathan's sister. I want to talk to Nathan."

Abby waved at Gabrielle and whispered, "Questions."

A few seconds of silence followed, and then the man said, "Nathan can't talk at the moment."

"Then how do you expect us to believe that he's okay?" Gabrielle asked.

Abby's heart sank. The way Gabrielle phrased her question, it didn't sound like a request, an attempt to work together to solve a problem. Instead, it came out as finger-pointing, assigning blame. The anger in her tense voice didn't help the situation either. Instead of disarming the situation, she was escalating it.

"If you give us trouble, my associates won't be happy," the man said, his voice sharp. "They might hurt your brother. I don't want that to happen."

"We're not giving you any trouble; we just want to know that he's okay. Why won't you let us talk to him? Put him on the phone."

"He can't come to the phone right now—"

"Why not?" Gabrielle raised her voice. Tears were running down her face. "Did you hurt him? Is my brother even alive? I want to hear him say that he's okay—"

The line went dead.

Gabrielle let out a shuddering breath and slumped on the couch. Abby watched the mother and daughter crying, feeling sick to her stomach. This call had made things worse.

CHAPTER 17

He sat in his car, heart pounding wildly, bile in his mouth. A loud honk made him start in panic. The traffic light was green. He tried to control his breathing as he drove slowly down the street. Hundreds of vehicles on the road, and only one of them driving away from the cops, who had surely tracked his phone . . .

His phone. He'd forgotten to turn it off. He fumbled, grabbing the phone from the passenger seat, one eye on the road. He hit the power button, pressing so hard his finger whitened with the effort. The phone turned off. He struggled with the battery, attempting to remove it with one hand, but it was impossible. He took his other hand off the steering wheel and grappled with the battery. Damn it, the thing wouldn't come loose. Enraged, he smashed the phone on the dashboard, and the battery finally popped out. Then, raising his eyes to the road, he hit the brakes, his car pausing inches away from the bumper of the car ahead of him.

He was breathing fast, as if he'd gone on a five-mile run. How could he have forgotten to turn off the phone? The police could easily track a cell phone. And if Eden Fletcher had called the police . . .

Maybe she hadn't. He hoped she hadn't. But he couldn't take that risk.

He glanced furtively around him but saw no cops rushing into the street. No sounds of multiple sirens. He was in the clear.

Did you hurt him? Is my brother even alive?

What did she want from him? He'd said repeatedly the boy was fine. Her voice, so angry and hysterical—she sounded like an electric drill, whirring furiously.

Bitch! He'd done it for her; didn't she get that? Didn't she already realize this was the best thing that could have happened to her?

He drove down a side street and found a parking spot. Taking out his other phone, he tapped the Instagram app and watched as her feed appeared on-screen. No new stories or posts. No surprises there. Still, she could have posted *something*. Even just saying she would be offline for the next couple of days.

He scrolled down to her post about her new shirt and tapped the comment button. There were already 364 comments on that post with emojis and numerous exclamation points. All of them things like *beautiful!!!* And *you're so gorgeous!!*

Oh, he could add his own exclamation-marked comment to the pile. Tapping furiously, he wrote, *Ungrateful bitch!!!!!!!!!!!!!!!!!!!*

He needed the right emoji. He scrolled through them, searching for the right one. Thousands of tiny useless drawings, none of them really encapsulating what he felt. The betrayal, the hurt.

Finally he added three furious emojis, his finger hovering above the "Post" button.

What the hell was he doing?

He deleted the entire thing, put the phone aside, and shut his eyes, taking a deep breath.

Of course she was angry. He had kidnapped her brother. It wasn't like he'd given her a detailed bullet point plan explaining how, in the long run, she'd realize it had been the best day of her life. She didn't know the specifics. It was important that she didn't know.

She would thank him later.

And her mother had a point, as much as it vexed him. They needed to see the kid was alive. He'd take care of that.

He picked up the phone again and scrolled down to one of his favorite posts. The one where she'd sent a kiss to the screen. The caption read, *Thank you.*

"You're welcome," he whispered back.

It was time to return to the house. It was a long drive back, and the kid was probably already hungry.

CHAPTER 18

Abby knocked on the door of the meeting room and then opened it without waiting for an answer. Five men sitting around a large oval table all turned to face her as she entered, followed by Will.

"Sorry we're late," she said.

"That's fine," Griffin, the 115th Precinct commander, said. Abby had met the man twice before. He had an uncommonly large bald head, and his scalp seemed to shine so brightly it almost looked as if it were coated with oil. Abby found it distracting.

"I understand the kidnappers called again," Griffin said.

"Yes, we came soon after the call ended," Abby said. Two empty seats were located at the far end of the table, and she took one, sitting down by Carver. Will took the seat to her left.

Griffin cleared his throat. "This morning, Chief Harris and I agreed to form a task force to investigate the Nathan Fletcher kidnapping case. I will be leading the task force." He gestured at Carver. "Detective Carver is the detective from the 115th Precinct who originally got the case and did the preliminary investigation. Detectives Marshall and Barnes are from the Major Case Squad. Agent Kelly will be our FBI liaison. And Lieutenant Mullen and Sergeant Vereen are our hostage negotiators."

Abby quickly memorized the names. Marshall looked like a father from Sam's school whose name was Marshall. Barnes was similar to

Barney from *The Flintstones*. She had nothing for Kelly, but his name was easy. Griffin was . . . well, his head looked like a huge egg. Perfect.

"Carver was about to summarize what we have so far," Griffin said.

Carver cleared his throat. "Yesterday at three fifty-five p.m., eight-year-old Nathan Fletcher got off the school bus at the corner of 25th Avenue and 100th Street. He walked straight home with another pupil, Daniela Hernandez. She verified Nathan was fine when she got home. From there it was a quick walk to his own house. But a neighbor, Frank Doyle, saw him talking to someone driving a white car, and step inside it. The car drove away."

"White car." Griffin grunted. "Is that the best the neighbor could do?"

"He couldn't name a car model, but I showed him some pictures, and he thought maybe it was a Nissan Sentra," Carver answered. "He didn't notice the license plate number. He thinks the driver was a Caucasian male."

"Traffic cameras?" Griffin asked.

"We're getting the footage now. There are no traffic cameras on 100th Street, but we have several in the immediate perimeter." Carver flipped a page in his notes. "A man called Eden Fletcher's cell phone at quarter past seven. He used a voice modulator and said they have Nathan, demanding a five-million-dollar ransom. The call had come from a phone that was turned on a few seconds before. Another call was made this morning with a different phone, also switched on just for the call. Neither number has any previous use. It's safe to assume they're using burners."

Abby's phone buzzed in her pocket. She took it out and glanced at it. A cryptic message from Samantha—A snack? Srsly? Abby wrote back, held up at work. Just order some pizza. She should have told her mother to have lunch with the kids. Abby always took them out on Saturday. She'd have to make it up to them at dinner.

She tuned back in to what Carver was saying. Both calls had been made from busy locations. The assumption was that the kidnappers had called from these locations on purpose to make tracking them difficult.

"He told Fletcher she's being watched," Abby said. "But didn't tell her not to call the police. It sounds like he assumed she would and didn't want it to be a deal breaker."

Griffin glanced at her with displeasure, clearly not happy with her talking out of turn. She was fine with that. Her main goal in this meeting was to stick out. She didn't want to blend in with the rest—that would make it easier to replace her with someone else. She met his stare wearing her soft, innocent face, aimed to disarm. He really did look like a modern version of Humpty Dumpty.

Carver moved on. "The voice modulator the caller used is a common app, but it does its job. We can't reverse the modulation. Eden Fletcher says she'd seen a stranger in the vicinity of her home, and gave us a sketch." He took out a sheet of paper with the printed sketch and passed it around the table.

Abby gave it to Will after glancing at it briefly. She'd seen it the day before when Eden had described the man to the sketch artist. The face of a man with a high brow and a full beard.

"We also went through some mug shots," Carver said. "But so far, she couldn't ID the person she'd seen. We'll show her additional mug shots today." He tapped his stack of papers on the table. "That's what we have so far."

"Okay." Griffin leaned back, intertwining his fingers. "So we're checking traffic cams, right? We can look at cams from the areas where the call was made from, search for cars matching that model. What else?"

Abby's phone buzzed yet again. Annoyed, she checked, thinking it would be another message from Sam, but it was Isaac this time. Just heard from Eden. This is horrible.

It was weird seeing Isaac refer to Eden. In all the years they'd stayed in touch, Abby and Isaac had done their best to avoid discussing anything from their shared past. Aside from their involvement in the cult survivor forum, they tried to focus on their everyday lives. Now, in a way, the three of them had been brought together again. The Moses Wilcox survivor group.

She hesitated, finger hovering over her phone screen as she listened to Griffin outline their search efforts. She was still angry that he'd given Eden her number all those months ago. He knew better than to do that. Still, this was not the time to discuss it. She tapped, It really is. She'll need a lot of support

Absolutely. Any progress?

We have a few leads

Do you have suspects?

I can't discuss that. I need to go. She shoved the phone in her pocket and turned her full attention back to the discussion.

"I need a few officers from the precinct to interrogate local sexual predators," Carver said.

"Is it really necessary?" Griffin asked. "This sounds like a kidnapping for ransom."

"I'm not sure that's the case," Abby said.

Again, all eyes were on her. She leaned forward, intertwining her fingers like Griffin did, mirroring his body language.

"The caller asked for a very high sum," she said. "In both phone calls he didn't give any indication he was willing to compromise. Since he kidnapped Nathan in broad daylight during a very narrow window of opportunity, it means one of two things. Either that he was a predator on the prowl, looking for a kid walking alone, *or* that this kidnapping attempt was well planned, and Nathan and his family were watched for a while. If it's really the second case, the kidnappers should know five million dollars is practically an impossible sum for Eden Fletcher, a single mother who works as an office assistant."

"Then why ask for the ransom?" Carver asked.

"To buy time," Abby answered. "Maybe Nathan is dead, and the kidnappers get a kick from calling the family. Or maybe he's alive, and the kidnappers are calling to feel a measure of control. We don't know enough to make any solid assumptions, but I don't think we should rule out a sexual predator."

"We shouldn't rule out a family member either," Carver said. "Nathan entered the car willingly. Maybe the caller used a voice modulator so that Eden wouldn't be able to recognize him. We're trying to find Nathan's father, David Huff. They broke up seven years ago, and the family hasn't heard from him since."

Griffin nodded. "I want another door-to-door canvassing. Perhaps someone else noticed the stranger that Eden Fletcher saw. If it wasn't a random prowler, the kid *was* watched, and that could be our ticket in."

"There's another option," Will said.

Abby glanced at him. She'd asked him last night to do some research on the Fletcher family, but they hadn't had time to talk before the meeting and discuss his findings.

"I did some digging on the family," Will said. "Gabrielle Fletcher is a successful social media influencer. I mean, semisuccessful—she's no Paris Hilton, but she has quite a few followers."

"How many is 'quite a few'?" Abby asked.

"About seventy thousand across all platforms, mostly on Instagram. And lately she's posting about her family life. There are a lot of posts about Nathan. And there's a lot of information there."

Abby felt queasy. "How personal does it get?"

"Enough so that the kidnappers would have a very good idea about Nathan's hobbies, the things he likes, and so on. Just from scanning her

Instagram posts, I can tell you Nathan likes swimming and drawing, that his birthday is in June, that he loves *Star Wars*." Will shrugged. "That kind of thing."

"Was there enough in Gabrielle's posts to give the kidnappers an idea what time Nathan comes home from school?" Carver asked.

"I don't know," Will answered. "I didn't have time to go over all of them; there are a lot. And that doesn't include Instagram stories, which are removed from the feed after twenty-four hours, or any post Gabrielle herself removed. I'll be able to see those if Gabrielle gives me her password."

"Regarding the kidnappers, we should tell Ms. Fletcher to ask for proof of life," Marshall said. "We need to know Nathan Fletcher isn't dead."

"You're right," Abby agreed. "We're already working on—"

"Eden Fletcher should have demanded proof of life from the kidnappers." Marshall raised his voice. "We've done it before. We can get some details from her regarding Nathan. Then we formulate a few questions she can ask the kidnappers. What's Nathan's favorite color. What does he want to be when he grows up. Things like that."

"The kidnappers can find these things from Gabrielle Fletcher's Instagram page," Agent Kelly pointed out.

"We can scan that Instagram account, verify that we use information that wasn't exposed on social media," Barnes said.

Abby and Will exchanged frustrated looks.

"That's a good idea," Griffin said. "So—"

"I agree that we need to get proof of life," Abby said. "But that's not the same as *asking* the kidnappers for proof of life."

"The kidnappers won't give us anything we didn't ask for," Marshall said. "They're not exactly the giving type. That's why we ask proof-of-life questions. It's the easiest way to get what we want."

"The problem is that proof-of-life questions do more harm than good," Abby said. "Suppose Nathan is alive. The kidnappers ask him those questions, give us the answers. Now they feel like we owe them something. Tit for tat, right?"

"It's in their best interest to prove he's alive," Marshall said. "They want the ransom."

"Like I said before, we don't know what they want. And even if it's in their best interest, they'll still feel like they gave us something. Not to mention they'll probably realize that those proof-of-life questions were not Ms. Fletcher's idea. It's a telltale sign of police intervention. Now the kidnappers are edgy because they know the police are involved. *And* they feel like we owe them something. And to make things worse, Nathan could say his favorite color is green, but his mother might think it was blue, so we don't even know if he's alive."

"Then what do *you* propose?" Marshall asked sharply. "That we continue blindly, not even knowing if it's a kidnapping case or a murder?"

"I think you made a good point, and we need proof of life," Abby said, not mentioning she'd already discussed it with Eden the night before. "But we'll tell Eden to use open-ended questions like, 'How can I pay the ransom if I don't know if Nathan is alive?'"

"How does that help us?"

"It makes the kidnappers do our work for us. Maybe they'll offer to let Nathan talk with his mother on the phone, or they send us a video. It'll force them to spend time thinking about this problem, which is great because we're trying to buy time. And they'll think about it from Ms. Fletcher's point of view, which is also useful, because we want them to see her as a person. And when they finally do give us proof of life, they won't feel like they did us a favor, because we never actually asked for proof of life; it was their idea."

"Okay," Griffin said. "Let's do that."

Abby leaned back in her chair. *Yes,* she thought. *Let's.*

CHAPTER 19

For some reason, long meetings always put Abby in a carnivorous mood. It was a primal reaction to sitting in a room with a group of people—usually men. Perhaps her reptilian brain thought of the meeting room as a cave, and the men were therefore her tribe. And they were about to hunt mammoths.

Or maybe after listening to a bunch of administrators talk, she just wanted to bite into something and draw blood.

Whatever the reason, after the meeting finally ended, she and Will went to Pauline's Burgers. Just the mention of *burgers* made her mouth water.

The smell was the first thing that welcomed her as she stepped through the door. It hugged her like a loving friend, whispering about the wondrous food she was about to consume. They sat at one of their usual tables—the tables that let them sit across from each other while neither sat with their back to the door. Cop mannerisms.

"I'm starving," Abby said. Her stomach growled, and she raised her voice as if to drown out the rumble. "Good catch with Gabrielle's social media. Are you going to keep digging?"

"Yeah. How's the mother?"

"Tired. Scared."

"She didn't do so well with the phone call this morning."

"She'll get better." Abby wasn't sure Eden *would* get better, but she would do whatever she could to try and prepare her. "Listen, I have an important phone call with Steve today about Ben's birthday."

"That does sound important."

"Scoff all you want. When *your* precious daughter will be old enough to celebrate birthdays with the rest of her class, that's when shit gets real."

Will raised his eyebrows. "Point taken. Important conversation."

"I want to simulate it with you."

Will slumped in his chair. "Oh no."

"It's an important—"

"I get it, I get it. An important conversation. Okay, when do you want us to do it?"

"Right now would be great," Abby said.

"No way," Will said. "Not before you eat."

She frowned, annoyed. "We don't have a lot of time, and I really need to be prepared—"

"Abby, you know I'd do anything for you." Will spread his hands. "But remember in June, when we did the simulation about the summer camp?"

"That was a one-time thing—"

"You skipped lunch, and within ten minutes you were ready to kill me. I don't even want to mention the conversation about Ben's homework from last year. No, never again. That's my one rule. No ex-husband simulations when you're hungry."

Abby was about to retort, but Pauline approached them, smiling widely.

"Abby," she said warmly. "How ya beenerble warble garble deerbleing?"

Abby glanced up at Pauline, her mind parsing the woman's words.

She knew some people who stayed away from Pauline's, simply because they couldn't understand anything the restaurant's owners said.

Pauline spoke really quickly and enthusiastically, her mind churning words much faster than her tongue could utter. As a result, the words mashed together into an almost-incoherent ramble. Pauline's husband, who did the cooking, had a thick Scottish accent that some people found even more difficult than Pauline's unique way of talking. As a result, the customers had to learn to talk Pauline dialect if they wanted to get something to eat.

Pauline's burgers were worth learning a new language for.

"I'm good." Abby grinned at Pauline. "What about you?"

"Ah, not bad. Son's poodle gorble feedleburg on the floor with two balls, it was a messuple warbelung, had to get a guy. Ya hungry?"

"Starving. Can I have a King Lear, medium rare, with extra onions and fries on the side?"

"And I'll have a Mercutio," Will said. "Medium, also with fries."

Pauline jotted that down. "Okay, anywan garink?"

"Two Cokes," Abby said.

Pauline nodded and turned away.

"Anyway," Abby said. "About Steve—"

Will raised one finger. "When we get our food. Not before that."

Abby sighed. "Fine. There's something else we need to talk about."

"What is it?"

"Eden Fletcher." Abby took a long breath and began fiddling with her napkin. "I knew her long ago. As a child."

Will frowned. "From school?"

Abby cleared her throat. "No, it was . . . before that."

Will's eyes widened, but he said nothing.

Abby had shredded her napkin to bits. She sighed, gazed at the street beyond the door. The truth would come out sooner or later. She'd known that as soon as she'd involved herself with this case. It was better to talk about it first with Will, her closest friend. Soon she'd need to talk to Carver and Griffin about it. And Will was the only one who knew about Abby's history in the Wilcox cult aside from her parents. Even her kids didn't know.

Abby took a long breath. "When we were kids, it felt like a family, you know? It's not like we were walking around thinking we were in some sort of religious cult. Kids had a lot of free time there, and we didn't know anyone outside the cult. Eden was older than I was, but we still played together."

Abby could read body language and facial expressions like open books. Know someone long enough, and that book became one of your favorites. The kind of book in which the pages were worn, and the spine was falling apart because you read it so many times. Will's demeanor—the parting of the lips, the narrow eyes, the tenseness in his shoulders—was so achingly familiar and touching she had to glance aside and blink a tear away.

"No one knows yet, but they'll figure it out," she said.

"They might," Will agreed.

"Carver already noticed something yesterday. I needed Eden to calm down, so I used one of Wilcox's meditation speeches. And Carver looked at me like I was a loony tune."

"It must have brought back memories, seeing her like that," Will said.

For an instant she was seven again. *The cold, hard muzzle of a gun pressing against her temple. The phone in her hand. Moses Wilcox's soft voice saying, "Tell them."*

And then, huddled in the back of the patrol car with Eden and Isaac. Flames flickering in the dark. A man's voice. "So many of them. This is terrible."

Pauline strode over with a tray. She let out a string of nonsensical syllables as she placed their dishes in front of them and marched away. Abby carefully picked up her burger with both hands and took a large bite. The juicy hamburger tasted like heaven. She chewed twice, swallowed, and took another bite, hardly stopping to breathe.

After finishing about a third of her burger, she said, "I'm not starving anymore. Can we please do the simulation now?"

"Abby, hang on—"

"I don't want to talk about me and Eden. Not right now. I need some time, okay?"

Will mulled it over. "Okay."

"Thanks." Abby smiled at him. "Onward to the simulation."

Will sighed and picked up a fry, then dipped it in ketchup. "Sure. What's the conversation about?"

"I told you. Ben's birthday. I have a party all organized, and now Steve wants to take Ben and his friends to the science museum on the same date."

"Uh-huh. And I assume you want me to be Steve, and you'll be Abby?"

Abby blinked. "That would be the logical way to do it."

"You might get more by being Steve," Will suggested. "Get into his brain."

"I don't want to be Steve. You be Steve, and I'll be Abby."

"And the negotiation goal?"

"To beat him into submission."

Will rolled his eyes. "Which in this case means convincing him to cancel the museum or change the date."

Abby shrugged and picked up her burger to take another bite.

"I'll start," Will said, putting his hand to his ear as if mimicking a phone call. "A-bbyyyyyy."

Abby slammed her burger down on the plate, sprinkling a handful of fries all over the table. "Do you have to do the voice?"

"Last time you *told* me to do the voice. You said it's important. Are you sure you're not hungry? Maybe you should finish that burger first."

"Ugh, no, I'm fine. I wasn't prepared. Okay, let's start again." She plucked a french fry from her plate.

"A-bbyyyyyyy."

"Hi, Steve," Abby said, holding the fry to her ear. "I wanted to talk about Ben's—"

"You want to talk about the science museum thing, right?" Will asked.

After years of training, Will could do Steve almost better than Steve himself. Interrupting her, using that infuriating patronizing tone, mansplaining things that needed no explanation. Abby was impressed by Will's ability to channel her ex, but she also suspected he enjoyed this much more than he should.

"The museum thing, that's right." She mirrored his words, injecting a pleasant, upbeat tone into her voice.

"I know you wanted to have that little party for him," Will said. "But you and I both know Ben really would prefer a day at the museum with his friends. And I already cleared my schedule for that day."

"You cleared your schedule." She tried to maintain the same cheerful tone, but it was diminishing, replaced by that scraping, cold, furious tone she retained for her ex. She grabbed the burger and took a quick bite for moral support.

"That's right," Will said brightly. "And I'm sure you can postpone your neat little party to a different date; your job is much more flexible, and besides—"

"My job isn't more flexible, you pompous asshole," she snapped at him. "And I *can't* postpone the party because it's scheduled with another boy. Not to mention I've been planning it for weeks, and I was *about* to tell you about it, so don't get all offended. Also, both you and I know you don't give a shit about what Ben would prefer; you're doing this to make it seem as if you're the better parent. And you're not fooling *anyone*. So you can take your schedule with all the appointments with students you're sleeping with, and shove it up your ass!" She squeezed her burger with rage, and a large dollop of ketchup dripped on her collar.

"Feeling better?" Will asked.

"Well, I have ketchup on my shirt, so not really," she muttered, wiping the stain with a napkin.

Will turned to look at the aghast patrons staring at them. "Don't worry, everyone. She's just *pretending* to hate my guts."

He had suggested the Steve simulations four years before, after Abby repeatedly showed up in the morning fuming as a result of an argument with her ex. Will had pointed out that they simulated events with jonesing drug addicts, suicidal drunks, armed men with multiple hostages. They spent hours every week honing their craft so that when the real crisis occurred, they were ready. Surely they could do the same with Abby's ex, which was, in a way, an ongoing, never-ending crisis.

At first Abby liked the idea because she thought it would help to prepare her better. But it turned out it was also useful as a venting venue so that later, when she talked to Steve, she wouldn't lose her cool.

"I'd say maybe a bit more tactical empathy and active listening," Will suggested. "And maybe a little less calling him names and listing items he can shove up his ass."

"That's a valid point."

"Also, it wouldn't hurt if you remember that Steve is a good dad. He was just a shitty husband."

"How is he a good dad?" Abby asked. "By sabotaging the party that might get kids in Ben's class to like him more instead of calling him a freak?"

"He's a good dad because he wants to make his son happy," Will said. "And if he can also seem the better parent, that's icing on the cake for him. So let him feel like the better parent. Give him the illusion of control in the conversation. That's what you'd tell me if this was an actual crisis."

"If this was an actual crisis," Abby said, jabbing a fry in some ketchup, "I'd try to get him to end his misery once and for all."

CHAPTER 20

Nathan had never gone a whole day without seeing his mom.

The longest he'd gone was when Dennis had had a sleepover party at his home over the summer. Nathan had gone to his house on Friday afternoon, and his mom picked him up after lunch on Saturday. But he was distracted the whole time; they watched *The Last Jedi* and played the PlayStation. And even then, when Dennis fell asleep, Nathan wanted his mom to show up and kiss him on the forehead like she did every evening.

Now, after not seeing his mom for what felt like almost two days, all he could do was lie in bed crying.

He needed her hug. He needed to feel the tickle of her hair as she leaned over to kiss him. Even just to hear her telling him that he had to take a bath, had to change his clothes.

His throat was hoarse from crying, the pillow wet with tears and snot. And no matter how hard he prayed for it, even when he really concentrated, his mom didn't open the door.

He needed to pee, but he didn't want to pee in the bucket. He held out for as long as he could, curling in bed, crossing his legs, but finally he couldn't hold it any longer. He bolted out of bed and went to the corner of the room. When he peed in the bucket, it made a weird sound that almost made him start crying again. But it was a relief not to need to pee anymore. He gaped at the pee in the bottom of the bucket. What would happen when the bucket overflowed? Would the man get angry?

What would happen when he needed to poop?

He had nowhere to wash his hands. His mom repeatedly told him that he *had* to wash his hands after peeing, that there were tiny germs in pee, germs he couldn't even see, and those germs could crawl all over him if he didn't wash his hands. But there was no sink there. His palms itched. Were those the germs? He imagined them as tiny worms. Were they crawling all over his fingers? His wrists? His arms?

He took the bottle of water the man had given him and poured some on his hands above the bucket. Some of the water splashed on the floor, but at least the itching was gone.

His stomach rumbled. Usually he ate cereal when he woke up, but when he had gotten up from bed earlier, there had been no food waiting for him. He sat down by the desk and opened the drawer, then took out a few empty sheets of paper and the box of crayons. He drew his mom and Gabrielle. Then, unable to help himself, he drew the man from the car, taller than both of them. He colored the man's eyes red.

The sudden click behind him sent his heart racing. He whirled around just as the man opened the door. He held a pizza box in his hand.

"How are you doing today? Feeling at home, I see."

The smile on the man's face made Nathan's skin crawl. He acted as if they were friends, but he kept him locked here in this strange room that was both his and not his.

The man stepped into the room, looking around him in satisfaction. "That doll wasn't easy to buy, you know. It was out of stock when I searched. They had a new version, but it was all wrong. You wouldn't have liked it. Finally found this one on eBay. Still in the box. Cost double, but I wanted to get it just right." The man winked at him. "Gotta get your man cave the way you like it, right?"

Nathan had no idea what the man was talking about. He shrugged.

"I brought you some food; are you hungry?"

Nathan nodded.

The man sighed. "Well, if you are, you're going to have to talk. You're shy—I get that; I was the same at your age. But I made all this effort. And I bought you food. It's polite to say thank you."

Nathan stared at him. Did the man really expect him to say thank you? He opened his mouth, then shut it, not sure if he should thank the man or yell at him.

The man took two fast steps forward and slammed the pizza box on the desk. "Say thank you!" he roared, his eyes bulging from his flushed face.

"Th . . . thank you," Nathan whimpered.

The man's breathing was fast, furious. Nathan cringed, afraid the man would hit him. But after a few seconds, the man seemed to relax.

"Good," he said. "You can talk after all. I need you to say a few words to your sister and your mother."

Nathan's heart leaped. Were Mommy and Gabi here? He glanced behind the man, but the strange hallway beyond the door was empty. The man knelt by Nathan and handed him a newspaper.

"Can you read that?" He pointed at a headline.

Nathan glanced at the paper, then nodded. "Y . . . yes," he said aloud before the man got angry again.

"Okay," the man said, tapping on his phone. "I want you to say hi to Mom and Gabi. Tell them you're okay. And then read this."

"Can they hear me?" Nathan asked, his voice trembling.

"Not right now. But I'll send them a recording of what you say so they know you're fine."

Nathan gaped at the phone, the words frozen on his lips. He wanted to tell his mom the man had locked him in here and that he'd made him pee in a bucket. But if he said the wrong thing, the man probably wouldn't send her the recording.

He swallowed. "Hi, Mommy. Hi, Gabi. I'm fine. But I want to go home." His voice broke.

The man gestured at the paper. Oh right, he wanted him to read this.

Nathan frowned. "I need to read this to you." Then he read slowly, "'Jessica Meir and Christina Koch made the first all-female space walk . . .'"

The man patted him on the shoulder. "That's enough, good job, Nathan, you read really well." He flipped open the lid of the pizza box. "Green olives, right?"

"Yes." He glared at the pizza, again wondering how the man knew. Perhaps he could read minds. If he could, then he knew how much Nathan hated him. The very thought made him want to flee.

The door was open. The man had never shut it behind him.

For some reason, Nathan couldn't move.

"Your sister will be really glad to get your message," the man said. "Here, hold this." He handed Nathan the newspaper.

Nathan took the newspaper, not understanding what he was supposed to do with it.

"Hold it next to your head so I can take a picture," the man said impatiently.

Nathan complied, holding the newspaper up. The man aimed his phone at Nathan and took a few pictures. Then he left the room and shut the door. A second later Nathan heard that click again. The door was locked.

He took a pizza slice and wolfed it down. It was cold but tasted amazing. He ate another one, then drank some water. Then he shut the pizza box lid and lay on the bed.

The man had become so angry before. He'd looked like he was about to hit him.

If he had superpowers, he could kill the man when he opened the door. He could shoot lasers from his eyes, or punch him really hard.

And then he could escape. He imagined how it would feel, striking the man down and then running away.

Or if he only had his baseball bat, he could hide and, when the man walked in, hit him with it. If he hit the man's legs hard enough, they would break. And he could run away, and the man wouldn't be able to chase him.

But the bat wasn't here. At home, he kept it in the closet, but here, all the closet had were some clothes.

A sudden thought occurred to him. Back home, he'd discovered he could detach the bed's headpost by rotating it. He'd used it as an imaginary light saber and almost hit the TV. His mom was furious and told him he wasn't allowed to do it again. The metal bar was dangerous; he could break something—or accidentally *hurt* someone.

But now, he wanted to hurt someone. And if this was the same kind of bed . . .

He went to the bed and tried to rotate the headpost. It was stuck. He put both hands on it and gritted his teeth, pushing as hard as he could.

With a sudden jolt, it moved. He kept rotating it and, after a few seconds, managed to pry it free. He gazed with awe at the metal rod in his hand. He swiped it in the air, heard the satisfying whoosh.

What if he hit the man's legs with that?

They would break for sure.

CHAPTER 21

On her way home, Abby had a very specific fantasy as to the progress of the next few hours. She would get home, take off her sauce-stained blouse and slept-in clothes. She would take a scalding-hot shower followed by a two-hour nap, which she felt she'd earned. Once she woke up, she'd call Steve and get him to postpone his birthday museum trip. Then she'd take the kids to dinner. It sounded like a good plan. A great plan, since the hot shower and the nap came first, and plans that started with hot showers and naps were great plans. In fact, you could call them master plans.

When she opened the door and saw Steve sitting in the living room, it threw a big wrench in her master plan. Steve was supposed to come *after* the shower and the nap; that was the plan. The plan was now upside down. It was a nalp.

"How did you get in?" she blurted, which perhaps wasn't the best way to start the conversation.

He raised an eyebrow. "Your mom let me in. She just left; I told her I'd wait for you. I'm here to pick Sam up."

Abby blinked. "Picking her up? This is my weekend with the kids, not yours."

Steve's eyes focused on the sauce stain on her shirt. It shouldn't have bothered her. If there was one man on the entire *planet* she didn't need to impress, it was Steve. But it nevertheless irritated her, as did the fact that her clothes were rumpled, her eyes bloodshot, and her hair frazzled. She desperately searched for something neglected in his appearance, but he was immaculate as always.

"I thought Sam told you," Steve said. "She said she wants to stay at my place this weekend because of that creature."

Abby rolled her eyes. "She's overreacting. I told Ben to keep his pets in his room."

Steve frowned. "Overreacting? Abby, your mother went too far. That thing's almost a foot long."

This was the moment when reality shifted for Abby. Because neither Ben's tarantula nor his chameleon were a foot long. And there were her mother's constant attempts to question her about Ben's birthday present. And . . . oh no, Sam's weird text message about a snack, which could have easily been an autocorrect mishap . . .

She turned away from Steve and stormed to her son's room. *Please god, anything but this, please please please . . .*

"Hi, Mom," Ben said softly from his bed. Abby barely glanced at him.

There was a new vivarium in the room, and in it, coiled in what could only be described as a nefarious manner, was a yellow-brown snake. Abby glared at it. The snake seemed to glare back with its beady eyes. She was having a staring contest with a reptile. She probably wouldn't win, but she could damn well try.

The snake would have to go. She was furious at her parents for putting her in this position, making her break Ben's heart, but there was no way in hell that this *thing* was staying in her house.

She turned to face her son, bracing herself for the difficult talk. He gazed at her with his typical Ben expression, somehow mixing hope and sorrow together. This always stirred that guilt she carried with her. Because if she'd been able to stomach Steve's infidelities and stay married to him, Ben would have had both parents at home instead of just his often-absent mother. He would have had a normal childhood and . . . and . . .

Damn it.

Her resolve was like an ice cube floating in a cup of hot tea. A cup of hot Ben's-sad-stare tea.

"Hi, sweetie," she said, her voice strangled. "Grandma gave you an early birthday present?"

He nodded. "It's a corn snake. They're harmless!" He seemed to be searching for another positive aspect of the snake. "He's not fussy, he can eat frozen rodents, he doesn't even need live ones."

What a wonderful personality trait. She sighed. "Ben . . . I know that you wanted a snake."

"He's very curious. And I can hold him. *You* can hold him if you want. He's named Pretzel. Because he can make a pretzel shape with his body."

She exhaled, trying to get the words out of her mouth. The snake was one step too far. It would have to go. Maybe they could get Ben another spider instead.

"The pet store owner said the last family abused Pretzel and finally gave him away."

Great. The snake came with a sob story. Now, if she made Ben return it, he would always remember poor Pretzel, who never found a home that loved him.

When Ben had become obsessed with superheroes at the age of four, Dr. Rosen, the kids' therapist, had explained the obvious. Ben was trying to replace his father figure with Iron Man, and Thor, and Captain America. Then Ben switched his superhero obsession to a fascination with invertebrates and Squamata. Dr. Rosen explained that Ben was trying to get closer to his dad, the academic. But Abby preferred to indulge in her own theory: that, realizing his father would never come close to being Captain America, Ben had decided that he could be replaced with something more similar, like a spider or a lizard.

So now Ben had tried to replace Steve with a snake. Abby could relate to that.

"Can I keep him?" Ben asked.

Abby sighed again and sat on the bed next to Ben. "We'll see, sweetie. I need to think about it."

Her heart clenched as she watched her son. Eden's missing child was so close to Ben's age. She wondered how many times Eden had told Nathan that he couldn't have something—just like Abby had been meaning to do. And she probably regretted each and every one of those occasions.

Abby wrapped her arms around Ben, hugging him forcefully as if she were trying to squeeze out his precious and sweet Ben juice.

"Mom, you're hurting me."

She pulled back. "Sorry. I'm going to talk with your dad now, okay?"

She got off his bed and returned to the living room. She tensed, knowing that if Steve said something snarky or critical right now, she would have to kill him. It was a pity because the NYPD frowned upon cops who killed their ex-spouses. But some things were unavoidable.

Luckily, he just met her eyes, saying nothing. Impressive restraint.

"So where's Sam?" she asked.

"Just getting her bag ready," Steve said.

"I'll pick her up tomorrow night?"

"Sure."

"Can we talk about Ben's birthday now?" she asked.

He smiled at her, but a spark of a challenge kindled in his eyes. "Absolutely."

She sat down next to him so that he wouldn't need to look up at her. That would only make him defensive. He waited for her to speak. But he was an amateur when it came to waiting. Abby gave him a demure smile.

"I thought *this* year I could take a more active role in Ben's birthday," he finally said. "Usually you plan everything. And I thought we could do something different."

"Something different," Abby said encouragingly.

"Ben loves insects and reptiles. Why not do something he really likes for once?"

Abby could think of a dozen reasons. And the words *for once* were clearly said critically to make it sound like *she* never did anything Ben really liked for his birthday. No, according to Steve, Abby just made Ben *suffer* on his birthday, perhaps by making him do more homework that day or purposefully feeding him broccoli.

The words rose, about to bubble out. That angry tone of hers, reserved only for Steve, settled in her throat.

Taking a deep breath, she recalled Will saying, "Maybe a little less calling him names and listing items he can shove up his ass."

The thing was, it was hard for her to put her life with Steve aside. The good parts and the terrible parts, they all niggled at her whenever they talked.

She decided to imagine this was a crisis. She'd been called in the middle of the night to a 7-Eleven. A man, high on MDMA, had barricaded himself with a gun aimed at the store owner. And he was threatening to kill both of them if Abby didn't agree that he would take Ben to the museum for his birthday. Now *this* drug-crazed man, unlike her ex-husband, she could talk to.

"It seems like you feel that maybe I've been dominating Ben's birthdays," she said, her tone becoming pleasant, calm.

Steve blinked. "I guess so. I mean, last year you invited me the day before. And when he was six, you took him to Florida, so I wasn't even there. So I thought I'd organize Ben's birthday for once."

She nodded agreeably. "Which of Ben's friends did you want to invite?"

"Well, Dennis, obviously. And Kyle."

"Dennis . . . and Kyle?" she repeated, her voice becoming quizzical. Kyle was a nightmare of a kid, but he was also Ben's best friend. The idea of taking him to the science museum probably made Steve nauseous.

"Maybe not Kyle," Steve said after a second. "We could ask Ben who he wants to invite."

She waited a few seconds, letting Steve stew with that conundrum. Then she said, "I wish I hadn't already agreed to that joint party with Tommy. How can I call it off now?"

"Tell Tommy's mother that something came up."

"How can I do that without it impacting Ben's relationship with Tommy?"

"You . . . um . . ." Steve frowned, searching for an answer.

Which was what she wanted. To make him try to solve her problem. Try to see it from her point of view.

"I don't see why it should impact anything," he finally said.

"It shouldn't impact anything?" she repeated.

He sighed. "I wish you hadn't agreed to this joint party without talking to me first, Abby. This is exactly what I'm talking about."

This was not Steve talking, she reminded herself; it was a drug addict barricaded in the store. "I'm sorry," she said. "You should be consulted about these things."

"Yeah, that's exactly right!" he said, encouraged.

She'd gotten him where she wanted him to be—feeling as if he was in control. But also ambivalent. He didn't want to postpone the museum trip, but he didn't want her to cancel the party she'd organized either. Now she had to prod him in the right direction.

"You remember Sam's third birthday?" she asked, smiling. It was the only birthday they'd planned together.

He snorted. "I'll never forget it even if I tried. That cake was *everywhere*."

"I laughed so hard. And that mother with the health food agenda—"

"Oh god, she wouldn't shut up." Steve shook his head, bemused, and then said in a high-pitched squawk, "Why don't you serve carrots? Carrots are healthy."

Abby burst out laughing—actual, spontaneous, true laughter. Steve could always imitate people's voices well. He grinned at her.

Sighing, she adopted a calculated sad expression. "We should do Ben's birthday together next year."

"Okay. And I'll postpone the museum visit so that you don't get into hot water with Tommy's mom."

She touched his arm briefly. "Thanks."

Samantha strode into the living room, her face full of indignation. "I'm ready, Dad."

Abby got up from the couch. Sam had her bag slung on one shoulder and her violin case held in her hand. Keebles pattered after her and gave Abby a scathing stare. *Bye, Human Mom. We're going to Human Dad's house. Where it's way better.*

"So you're going to your dad's for the weekend?"

"I'm going to Dad's until that snake returns to the pet store."

"We'll talk about it later," Abby said, choosing her battles. "Enjoy your weekend."

She gave her daughter a hug. Keebles seemed torn between her wish to be petted and her desire to scorn Abby. Finally she approached Abby, losing her angry-teenager scowl for a second. Abby bent and scratched the dog behind her ear.

As soon as they left, she called her mother.

"Hi, honey." Abby's mother sounded completely at ease. Almost as if she didn't know what a mess she'd created in Abby's life.

Abby walked to her bedroom and shut the door so that Ben wouldn't hear her side of the conversation. "You bought him a snake?" she hissed, wrestling her laptop out of her bag. She wanted to see if there were any updates on the case.

"He's been asking for one for six months."

"Yes! And we all told him when he goes to college he can have one." She sat down on the bed, opening the laptop on her knees.

"It's his eighth birthday." Her mother said *eighth* as if the number had significance. As if it weren't simply the number that came after seven.

"Mom, you knew I wouldn't agree to this. And you knew Samantha would be furious, and you—"

"Samantha will get over it like she did with the chameleon and the tarantula. It's a corn snake, Abby; it's harmless."

"This is the last time you do something like that." Abby's voice trembled with rage.

"You're angry, honey. Let's talk about this when you've calmed down, okay?"

She was about to tell her mother that no, they would talk about it now, when she saw a new email from Will with the subject *Nathan's Father*. She clicked it and skimmed the text briefly. Will had found a picture of Nathan and Gabrielle's father in Gabrielle's Instagram feed.

She glanced at the photo. Her mouth went dry.

"Hello? Abby?"

A man was smiling at the camera, crouching and hugging a girl that had to be Gabrielle as a child. Another man stood beside him.

She knew that man.

Eden had lied to her.

CHAPTER 22

Abby knocked on Eden's front door and then almost immediately rang the bell. She was breathing hard, as if she had run all the way to Eden's house. Gabrielle opened the door.

"Hi," Abby said. "Is your mom home?"

Gabrielle moved aside, motioning for Abby to come in. "She's in the bathroom."

"Okay." Abby shut the door behind her. The faint sound of running water could be heard in the small apartment. "I'll wait."

The negotiator on shift, Hernandez, sat in the kitchen fiddling with his phone. A young man sat on the living room couch.

"Hello," he said hesitantly.

"Hi," Abby said. "I'm Lieutenant Mullen."

"I'm Eric."

Abby kept her eyes on him, saying nothing, letting the silence stretch. He wore a baggy sweater and a worn pair of jeans. His hairline was receding, and as if to compensate, he had a stubbly beard.

"Eric Layton," he blurted, fidgeting. "I'm Gabrielle's . . . I work with Gabrielle."

"Work with Gabrielle?" Abby asked.

"Just helping her out with image filters, and uh . . . social media maintenance."

Abby nodded. "Eric, can you please let me talk to the family in private?"

"Sure." He jumped to his feet. "I was leaving anyway."

"Is something wrong?" Gabrielle asked. "Is there news about Nathan?"

Abby waited as Eric brushed past her, leaving the house. Then she shook her head. "No. I just need to talk to Eden about something." She took out her phone and opened the image Will had sent her. She showed it to Gabrielle. "You posted this on your feed a while ago. This is your father, right?" She pointed at the man hugging the little girl.

"Yeah," Gabrielle said. "And that's me."

"And who's the other man?"

"He's this guy we all used to live with. On his farm."

Jesus. "His name is Otis, right? Otis Tillman."

Gabrielle's eyes widened. "You know him?"

Abby knew *of* him, but this wasn't a discussion she wanted to have with Gabrielle. "Did you live there for long? At Otis's farm?"

"Yeah. Most of my childhood. Is this related to Nathan's kidnapping in any way?"

"It's too early to tell." Abby frowned. She could still hear water running. *Damn it.* She marched up to the second floor and knocked on the bathroom door. "Eden?"

"Just a moment," Eden called from inside, her voice sounding panicky.

Abby twisted the doorknob and opened the door. Eden stood by the sink, washing her hands violently with a metal scrubber. The water pooling in the sink was pink with blood. She jumped, startled, as Abby stepped in.

"I was just—"

Abby yanked the scrubber from Eden's grip. "That won't help Nathan." She turned off the water and then, more gently, took one of

Eden's hands and examined it carefully. The back of the hand was raw, beads of blood emerging on the pink skin.

"It's just . . . when I'm anxious," Eden said, her voice cracking.

"I know." Exhaustion flooded Abby. "Let's bandage you up. Do you have any gauze or something?" She opened the medicine cabinet and stared.

The bottom shelf was filled with what seemed like prescription pills, but that wasn't what caught Abby's attention. The shelf above it held a framed picture of Moses Wilcox, the "father" of the Wilcox cult.

"Mom?" Gabrielle stood in the doorway.

Without knowing why, Abby slammed the medicine cabinet shut, as if to hide the contents from Eden's daughter. Eden's face was flushed, her lips trembling.

"Is everything okay?" Gabrielle glanced at her mother's hands. Abby saw no surprise in the girl's eyes, only distaste. She'd seen Eden do this before; Abby was sure of it.

"I'm fine," Eden blurted. "I'll be out in a moment."

Gabrielle strode out of the room. Abby gently closed the bathroom door, shutting both of them in the tiny space. Then she opened the medicine cabinet again. It was a picture she'd never seen before, Moses sitting in a chair in a hotel room, his signature benign smile plastered on his face.

"When you get anxious," Abby said, trying to keep her voice steady, "you go here, open the cabinet, and scrape the skin off your hands as Moses looks at you."

"Sometimes," Eden whispered. She took a roll of gauze and wrapped it around her hands in practiced motions. Crimson dots materialized on the white sterile cloth. "Don't you?"

"I stopped doing it when I was eight. My mom helped me."

"Your mom?"

"My adoptive mother," Abby clarified. "It's a terrible habit. Implanted in our heads by a man who controlled us with fear. It doesn't help with anything."

"The germs—"

"The germs are not the issue here. You know that." Abby watched as Eden finished bandaging her hands. How many times had the woman done this in the past years? "Where did you get that picture? I never saw it before."

"Isaac sent it to me. Years ago. He managed to keep it when everyone . . . when we left."

"He never told me that."

"Maybe he realized you didn't need it."

"You don't need it either. And neither does Isaac." Abby sighed. This was not the time to fix years of damage. There was a more pressing case. She took the phone out of her pocket and showed the screen to Eden. "This is Otis Tillman."

Eden leaned on the sink to steady herself. "Where did you find this?"

"Your daughter posted it on her Instagram feed. She told me you lived there."

"Yes. But we—"

"He recruited you?"

"How did you know who—"

"How do I know who Otis is?" Abby asked. "He has a police file. He's a local cult leader. *Of course* I know him." She didn't mention her own obsession with cults. The database she maintained on a daily basis. Otis Tillman had been on it for years.

He had a small following, never more than seventy people. As far as the police knew, there were just a few guns on the premises. Aside from a statutory rape accusation that had been investigated and dropped, the community on the Tillman farm stayed off police radar. But there was no telling what went on beyond those fences.

"It's not a cult," Eden said defensively. "It's a community. I was searching for someplace to call home. A place where I could be loved again. Like I had been loved as a child."

"And Otis found you. Recruited you to his *community*."

"It was actually David, my ex-husband, who met me and introduced me to Otis. And they seemed so happy. So full of purpose. They didn't *recruit* me. They invited me for a weekend there—to meet the rest of the community. And when I got there, people were so nice. And they liked me. They *really* liked me. I felt like I belonged."

It was called a love bomb—a strategy cults used in recruitment. Abby didn't bother pointing that out. Eden probably knew that on some level. After she'd joined, she must have done it to others. Showered them with endless affection when they came, made them feel like they'd finally found their place.

"Is David still there?" Abby asked.

"As far as I know, yes, he is."

"You told me you don't know how to contact him. You said he's irrelevant. If he's at the Tillman farm, he's *very* relevant. He lives nearby, and he's part of the Tillman cult. As you were, and Gabrielle, and Nathan."

Eden lowered her eyes. "We left."

"What if Otis Tillman decided he wants you back in his so-called community? What if he wants the kids?"

"He wouldn't—"

Abby lost her patience. "Eden, you can't know what he would or wouldn't do. And if Tillman told Nathan's father or anyone else from that group to take your child, to 'bring the lost child home' or whatever, would they hesitate?"

Eden said nothing.

"This is the first thing we needed to investigate. Before anything—"

"Mom!" Gabrielle sounded distraught.

"Just a second, Gabi, we'll be out in a moment."

"Your phone is ringing!"

Eden froze, a deer staring at the incoming headlights. Abby grabbed her by the arms firmly.

"Breathe. Talk to him. Remember, ask him open-ended questions; buy us time. Don't mention the Tillman farm. Do your best to keep your voice steady."

"Mom!" Gabrielle pushed the door open, holding the ringing phone as if it were a bomb about to go off.

Eden stepped out of the bathroom and took the phone in her bandaged hand. She put it to her ear.

"Hello?" she said.

It took Abby a second to gather her wits and activate the wiretapping application on her own phone. She caught the end of the sentence: " . . . to your daughter."

Eden blinked, paused, and then said, "I'm sorry, why do you want to talk to her?"

"I'm not talking to you anymore," the metallic voice answered. "Give the damn phone to your daughter right now, or I'll hang up."

Eden glanced at Abby, eyes wide. Abby gave a tiny shake with her head.

Eden took another breath and said, "How can I—"

"Put Gabrielle on now! If I hear you say another word, I'll hang up, and Nathan will be hurt!"

Eden practically shoved the phone at Gabrielle. "He wants to talk to you," she whispered.

Gabrielle took the phone. "Hello?"

"Hi, Gabrielle," the metallic voice said. Despite the sound modulation, it was clear that its tone had softened. "I'm glad to talk to you again."

Gabrielle glanced at Abby fearfully. Abby mimed breathing deeply. Gabrielle blinked, then took a deep breath. "Um . . . is Nathan okay?"

Yes-or-no questions were useless, and Abby winced. She should have been ready for this, should have prepared Gabrielle like she'd prepared Eden.

"Nathan's fine," the man said. "How are you? I noticed you haven't posted anything on your account."

"You're following my account?" Gabrielle whispered, her face twisting with horror.

"I've been following you from the start. Why aren't you posting?"

Abby leaned over and whispered in Gabrielle's ear, "Open-ended questions."

Gabrielle let out a shuddering breath and then said, "How can I post anything on Instagram when my brother is gone? When I don't even know if he's okay?"

Abby nodded at her and gave her a thumbs-up. That had been a perfect response.

"Good point," the man said. "I have a message from Nathan. Let me play it for you."

"Can I talk to him?" Gabrielle blurted.

For a few seconds, there was no answer. Then, a child's voice, frightened, trembling: "Hi, Mommy. Hi, Gabi."

"Nathan," Gabrielle sobbed. "Are you—"

"I'm fine. But I want to go home," Nathan said. "I need to read this to you. 'Jessica Meir and Christina Koch made the first all-female space walk.'" He spoke slowly, as if struggling with the words, fumbling at the astronauts' names.

"What?" Gabrielle asked. "What was—"

"Like I said, he's fine," the metallic voice said. "I'll send you a picture in a moment. Are you working on the ransom?"

"I don't understand," Gabrielle said. "Why did he say that? Can I talk to him?"

"It was a recording," the metallic voice said. "He's not here now. But like you heard, he wants to go home. And we are getting impatient. How are you doing with the ransom?"

Abby waved at the girl, trying to catch her attention. There were so many ways to respond to this question. Mirror his words; pose an open-ended question, a difficulty; try to make the man see things from her point of view. She should talk slower, buy some time, wait a few seconds between each sentence, watch her tone . . .

"We can't get that amount of money!" Gabrielle shouted. "We're trying to get it, but we can't get so much. I need to talk to my brother. Please let me talk to him, I—"

"I don't know how much longer I can hold my associates off," the metallic voice said coldly. "I'm sure you don't want your brother harmed. Do what you need to do to get that ransom. Talk to whomever you need. I'm sure you can find people who would be glad to help you. I will call soon." The line went dead.

For a few seconds, none of them said anything; then Gabrielle whimpered, slumping against the wall, then sitting on the floor.

"I want this to be over!" she cried. "I want him back."

The phone blipped, an incoming message. Gabrielle tapped it. It was a photo of Nathan holding a newspaper. The image of the astronauts outside the space station was on the top of the page.

"What the hell is this?" Gabrielle said. "Why would he send us this?"

"It's proof that Nathan is alive," Abby said. "See? He's holding the *New York Times* from today."

"But . . . that can't be," Eden said. She scrutinized the phone closely. "It has to be an old photo."

"This paper is from today." Abby pointed. "I saw this story on the news."

"But this is Nathan's room," Eden said. "The photo is from Nathan's room."

Abby stared at her, then at the photo. She was right. Nathan's bed stood in the background, and the same Harry Potter poster hung on the wall. Even a corner of the corkboard with the drawings. For a second, all three of them raised their eyes to the doorway. Nathan's bedroom was just across the hall.

But of course, it was empty and dark.

CHAPTER 23

He didn't want to be in this position. Causing Gabrielle grief, risking his own life. He was doing it all for her. In a way, she'd *asked* him to do it. And now she was acting like he was the bad guy.

He was the only one on her side. The only one who really gave a damn. It was easy to be a mindless sheep, one of her many followers. Liking her posts, adding the occasional bleat of a comment—*Beautiful* or *You're so pretty* or a wordless string of emoticons.

He was more than that. He wasn't a follower. He was part of her team.

He remembered to turn off the phone this time and remove the battery. He drove aimlessly for a while, listening to the radio, his fingers tapping on the steering wheel as he hummed along with the music.

Finally, deciding he was far enough from where he'd made the call, he parked in a parking lot and took out his other phone. The one he used only to watch her. He opened the Instagram app—still no updates. Were some followers noticing the gap? Wondering if she was okay? Gabrielle normally posted throughout the day. In the past year, she'd only skipped two days—one when she'd had that nasty flu, and the other when she'd broken up with her boyfriend. Two dark days, a void.

Of all her followers, only he knew what was going on, and it connected them both by an intangible thread.

But even knowing why she wasn't posting anything, even though he had talked to her twice, seeing that the last post was a day old made his heart squeeze, his hands becoming clammy. A million invisible ants crawling on his skin. He imagined that was what heroin addicts felt like when they needed their next fix. No wonder they would do anything, *anything* to make it stop. If he could give blow jobs to strangers just to see Gabrielle post again, he would. It would be a small price to pay.

He scrolled down her history, a trip down memory lane, and paused on her best posts. His own virtual methadone.

That one morning when her smile seemed to be aimed only at him. That day at the swimming pool, her hair fluttering in the wind. New Year's 2019, when she'd blown a kiss to the lens, to *him*, thanking all of her followers.

A quick swipe with the finger, dozens of Gabrielles flashing across his screen. Smiling, pouting, dancing, kissing. The feed stopped on the post of her hugging her brother. Both of them in Nathan's room, the caption reading, *In my brother's man cave. When I get my dream house, it'll have a room for him just like this one.*

And her fans had reacted with heart emojis and gushing platitudes. None of them had realized it was a request.

No one but him. And for him, every wish she made was his command.

He closed the Instagram account and opened the photo gallery to scroll through his private collection of her photos, finally finding his favorite series from the photo shoot during the 2017 road trip. Standing in the forest, the mist around her like a veil. In two of the images she was out of focus, and in one, she was about to blink, and one eyelid was half shut. But the rest were a tapestry of perfection. He swiped through them one at a time, the tension seeping away from his body.

Finally, the pain diminished; the restlessness lessened. He put down the phone, turned on the engine, drove back to the cabin.

Maybe tonight he would eat with the boy. After all, in the future they would become a family. There was no reason for Nathan to eat alone in the room. He'd gotten them some Chinese food. He wasn't sure if Nathan liked Chinese, but the kid couldn't sustain himself on pizza and burgers.

He left the city behind him, the traffic becoming sparser. Finally turning down the long gravel road leading to the cabin. He shivered as he stepped out of the car; it was a chilly night. Entering the warm cabin was an instant relief.

He walked over to the locked room, turned the key, and opened the door. To his surprise, the boy wasn't in bed or sitting by the desk. The door hid the left side of the room, and he stepped inside, glancing around.

Movement, spotted from the corner of his eye. Time slowed down as he turned, trying to react. The boy stepped forward, swinging something that whistled as it tore through the air.

And then a blinding pain in his knee.

CHAPTER 24

Nathan hesitated for a fraction of a second.

The hours he'd spent imagining this moment and practicing his swing had helped. But in his imagination, the man's face was twisted with malice. He was a monster in human flesh. Instead, the man walking through the door smiled, holding a bag of takeout. His nose was red from the cold.

So when Nathan took the swing, he didn't do it as hard and fast as he could. The steel bar connected with the man's leg, the shock vibrating through Nathan's palms, nearly making him drop it.

The man's face changed. He was no longer smiling. Nathan saw the burning rage and pain in the man's eyes, heard his snarl.

The scream that left Nathan's lungs was pure terror as he swung the bar a second time, hitting harder this time—and lower. The man toppled to the floor, roaring in agony.

Nathan took another swing, aiming at the man's chest. The man's hand moved so fast it was a blur. The rod hit it, the man screaming as his fingers gripped the metal. And with one swift pull, he yanked the rod away from Nathan.

Nathan bolted through the open door, leaving the man hollering behind him. He stumbled down the hallway, breathing fast, panicky breaths, finding the front door. He tried to yank it open, and it rattled, staying shut. He grabbed the dead bolt, twisted it, could hardly make it move. Whimpering, he tried harder, heard the lock click, tried to open the door again. Nothing.

A second dead bolt high above his head. He stretched, stood on his tiptoes, could touch it with the tip of his finger.

The man wasn't screaming anymore. Instead, he moaned in pain. Nathan glanced back down the hallway. No one was chasing him.

He needed a chair to stand on so he could reach the second dead bolt. He looked around him, noticed a small kitchen, a table, a white metal chair.

"Nathan!" the man roared. "Get back here, you little shit! I swear to god, if I need to chase you, you'll regret it!"

Sobbing, Nathan lurched to the kitchen, grabbed the metal chair. Then his eyes went up to the wall, and he froze.

Gabi was smiling down at him.

It was an enormous picture of her; it took up almost the entire wall. Nathan couldn't tear his eyes away from it. His sister appeared so happy in the picture, so calm. But there was something wrong in the image. A strangeness in the colors. Almost as if the picture was made of tiny square patches.

He took a step toward it, details swimming into focus. The picture was, in fact, a collage of dozens of smaller pictures. No, not dozens. *Hundreds.* And each one of those tiny pictures was also an image of Gabi. She was sitting in a restaurant, or in her bed, or outside in the street. In many of those pictures, there were friends. Nathan's gut lurched. In some of the images, Gabrielle was naked.

"Nathan!"

The voice was closer. Nathan glanced at the hallway. The man was crawling, his face a mask of pure hatred, teeth clenched in pain. He dragged himself along the floor, grunting, muttering.

Nathan grabbed the chair, pulling it to the door. He climbed up, clutching the top dead bolt, twisting it. He heard the man behind him moving faster, didn't look, turned the dead bolt as hard as he could.

It moved, clicking.

He got off the chair and yanked the door open, and a gust of cold air filled the room.

A grip on his ankle. The man's fingers tightening. Nathan screamed in panic. Stomped the fingers with his other foot as if stomping a cockroach. The man let go with a visceral scream of pain.

Nathan fled into the darkness, leaving the screams behind him.

CHAPTER 25

Carver had called Abby and told her to get to the incident room in the 115th Precinct. When she arrived at the station, she didn't even need to ask for instructions. She followed her ears.

The incident room was a large room with two large tables, crisscrossed with cables and phones. It was full of people bustling around, talking on their cell phones, or writing on the four whiteboards that lined the walls. Carver stood by one of the whiteboards, next to which a large map of New York was taped to the wall. At the far end of the room, the top of Griffin's head, bald and even shinier than usual, was visible. Will sat by the table, face glued to his laptop's screen. He rubbed his eyes tiredly, but there was something else there. The hint of a satisfied smile.

"You found something?" Abby asked hopefully, walking over.

"This is Gabrielle's Instagram profile." Will gestured at his screen. "She opened it two and a half years ago. As far as I can tell from the engagements on the early posts, she had a few hundred followers, no more. Then she and her friends decided to go on a road trip. Gabrielle posted images of herself in various locations with the hashtag *whereAmI*. And people had to guess. She would send a prize to whoever got it right. Like a signed postcard or something."

"Uh-huh," Abby said, trying to curb her impatience. Information was negotiator oxygen. There was no knowing what was relevant and what wasn't. And Will, who'd been a detective in the Computer Crimes Squad for six years, had a talent for extracting endless information from online data.

"So she got maybe a few more hundred followers from that stunt, but then she posted *this* picture." Will switched windows, displaying an image in full screen. Abby exhaled slowly.

It was some sort of forest or marsh; it was hard to figure out the details. Thick mist curled between the tree branches and the foliage, a blanket of white. And in the center, Gabrielle standing, arms arched above her head, apparently nude. Except the mist hid her body just enough that you couldn't be 100 percent sure she *was* nude. Maybe she was wearing a body suit or a skimpy bathing suit. It was unclear, and obviously, that was the point of the image. And the caption simply read, *#whereAmI*. Abby had to hand it to her—the image was gorgeous.

"This image went viral," Will said. "Within a day, Gabrielle's Instagram account exploded. A reporter from the *New Yorker Chronicle* was working on a story about influencers, and he tagged along for the road trip. His article made her profile even more popular. By the end of that road trip, she had over fifty thousand followers. She did two more road trips with the same friends and got to seventy thousand followers. A lot of female followers who love her—but a lot of men too."

"I'd imagine," Abby muttered.

"I've been going over Gabrielle's followers. First of all, she blocked seventy-three of them in the last eighteen months. Fifty-seven men, sixteen women. I've made a list of those—"

"Why did she block them?"

"Rude comments, dick pics, trolls, who knows? We'll have to ask her. Then I ran a Python script—"

"A what?"

"Python? It's a programming language. So I ran a script to make a list of all the followers who comment or like Gabrielle's posts. I have two lists. One is the superfans, right? Those who comment and like almost everything. And the others who never actually respond to her posts, which is maybe also weird? Like stalker-ish? I don't know. Let me show you." He turned to the laptop and began typing.

Abby waited. After a few seconds she said, "You know, a python can eat an entire antelope."

"Really?" Will asked.

"It unhinges its jaw so it can swallow the antelope whole."

"That's amazing." Will's tone did not, in fact, reflect any shred of amazement. He hit the "Enter" key, and an Excel spreadsheet opened on-screen. "See? These are the five hundred most-engaged fans that Gabrielle has. Now check out number one hundred twelve." He scrolled down to someone called Karlad345 and tapped the link next to the name. An Instagram page opened. The profile picture was of a man about twenty-eight with a full black beard and a high brow, leaning against a tree.

"He looks like the guy in the sketch that Eden described," Abby said.

"Check out his followers and following."

Abby glanced at the stats. Karlad followed seven people. He had no followers.

"So he's not very active on Instagram," Abby said.

"Like I said, he's the one-hundred-twelfth-most-active fan Gabrielle has. He's on Instagram *every* day. Commenting all the time. But his Instagram profile is almost solely about Gabrielle."

Abby stared at the screen. "Can you print this picture for me? And I want a list of all his comments on Gabrielle's posts."

"On it. There's a printer over there." Will pointed at the far end of the room. "I'll send the printout of the profile image to it."

Abby went over to the printer and took the page as it slid out. She scrutinized the picture of the man again. On paper, he somehow seemed creepier, his beard wild, his clothing hanging loose on his body. She imagined him lurking around the block. Not surprising that Eden had noticed this guy.

She walked over to Carver, who was now speaking to Griffin by the map.

" . . . anything from the last call to Ms. Fletcher?" Griffin was asking.

"The call was made from a new number," Carver answered. "And again, the caller turned off the phone as soon as he ended the call. Same voice modulator, which we can't reverse, but we *can* be certain it's the same guy in both cases. It was made in the vicinity of the corner of 66th and Park Avenue in Manhattan. We can estimate that he called within two hundred yards of that location. We *think* he called from his car, but it's possible he called from one of the buildings in the vicinity."

Carver took a blue thumbtack and plugged it into the map at the location he'd mentioned. There were two other blue thumbtacks in Manhattan—the locations of the previous calls. They weren't particularly close to each other. Another red thumbtack marked the presumed location of the abduction.

"We sent a patrol over to the location with our sketch." Carver gestured at the whiteboard where the sketch was taped. "Nothing so far."

"Agent Kelly sent the photo of Nathan for analysis," Griffin said. "It's most likely photoshopped, but they're making sure. Our current assumption is that the kidnapper found an image of Nathan in his room holding up something, probably a picture he drew. And the kidnappers inserted today's newspaper on it. It's likely that he found the image on Gabrielle's feed."

"If it's an altered image, it could mean that Nathan's dead," Carver said heavily. "The kidnappers modifying an image of him would indicate they can't take a picture of the actual boy."

"That was what I thought," Griffin said. "Except we have a recording of him reading the text, right?"

He was right. It made no sense. Why would they go through the effort of modifying an existing image if Nathan was fine?

"We have a probable ID of our suspect," Abby said, interrupting their conversation. She taped the photo to the whiteboard. "This guy is a rabid fan of Gabrielle's Instagram profile. Will is looking into it. And I also have some other people we should check." She opened her bag and took out a folder she'd prepared earlier.

Inside was a photo, which she handed to Carver. "This is Otis Tillman. He was convicted of three charges in his twenties: illegal arms trafficking and two counts of sexual assault. He spent four years in prison. These days, he has a large farm in Suffolk County. There are over sixty people living on that farm. The ATF raided the place six years ago, but as far as I know they came up empty."

Abby thumbed through the folder, looking through her printouts and notes. "Two years ago, the police investigated a case of statutory rape, but the charges were dropped. I talked to the detective who investigated the case, and she was convinced this so-called community was a cult with Tillman as its leader."

"What's Otis Tillman's relation to this case?" Griffin asked.

Abby took out another picture and showed it to them. "This is a picture of David Huff, Eden's ex-husband, alongside Otis Tillman. That's Gabrielle Fletcher as a child with them. David was the one who recruited Eden to Tillman's cult. She lived there for over thirteen years."

Carver and Griffin gaped at her. Then Carver taped the picture of Tillman to the board.

"So Eden Fletcher was part of a cult?" Griffin said. "That might change our approach to the entire case."

"She'd been in a destructive religious cult as a child," Abby said. "It made it easier to recruit her."

"How could it make it easier?" Carver asked. "I'd have thought that if a person had been in a cult once, they'd want to stay as far away as possible."

131

Abby shook her head. "It's complex. When people are in a cult, they have a tight community. And you have a purpose. When they leave, all that is gone, and that feeling is hard to replace."

"So she wanted to find that feeling again?" Carver asked.

"Yes. There's a phenomenon called cult hopping. It sounds frivolous, but it's anything but that. People who leave cults are often badly hurt. They have a void they need to fill. Or they've been abused and emotionally scarred. And people like Otis Tillman, or Keith Raniere, or Jim Jones swoop in and take advantage of that. They tell you that they can help you get better. That you were in a bad group, but *this* is the right group. And if those predators catch you at the right moment, when you're alone and isolated and lost, there's *nothing* you can do."

Carver looked at her strangely. "Did you have dealings with the Tillman cult before?"

"No, but negotiation with extreme groups and cults is one of the cornerstones in crisis management," Abby said. "I've done my research."

"Does David Huff still live at Tillman's farm?" Griffin asked.

"As far as Eden knows. She hasn't been in contact with him since she divorced him and left the cult."

"Why did she leave the cult?"

"We haven't had the time to talk about it yet."

"Cult or not, I need to talk to David Huff tonight," Carver said.

"You should avoid rushing in there," Abby said quickly. "These guys don't like cops, and there's a good chance they're heavily armed. Showing up in the middle of the night, lights flashing, will get you a lot of itchy trigger fingers."

"I'll talk to the police commissioner in Suffolk County; I know her," Griffin said. "We should coordinate this with them. You'll go tomorrow morning."

"Can you brief me on how to approach these people?" Carver asked Abby.

"Why don't I join you?" Abby suggested. "I can brief you on the way."

He raised one eyebrow. "Sure."

"Hey, Abby," Will called from his seat. "You guys should see this."

Abby walked over, Carver and Griffin following behind her.

"What is it?" Abby asked. There was a paused video on Will's screen.

"Gabrielle just posted this Instagram story," Will said. He clicked play.

Gabrielle sat on her bed in her room, her face tear stricken. She wasn't wearing the same clothes she had before. She had changed to a white dress, her feet bare.

"Hi, all," she said, her voice trembling, cracking. "Yesterday afternoon, as my brother returned home from school, a man took him."

Abby's gut sank as she watched Gabrielle wiping the tears with the back of her hand.

"We got a phone call," Gabrielle continued. "The kidnappers told us they want five million dollars to give him back. We don't have that much." At this point she broke down, hiding her face in her hands as she sobbed.

"What the hell does she think she's doing?" Carver asked angrily.

"Quiet," Abby said, tense.

Finally Gabrielle got a hold of herself and with a shudder said, "We will raise whatever we can to get Nathan back, of course. But for now, I wanted you all to know that this is what I'm going through, and this is why I haven't been around." Then she blinked and straightened. "And if the kidnappers are watching this, please don't hurt Nathan. He's a little boy. He likes drawing and swimming, and he still loves to cuddle. Keep him safe, and we'll get you your money, okay?"

She let a few seconds go by as she sniffled and then, with a barely audible whisper, said, "Thank you."

The video ended.

"Well, the shit just hit the fan," Griffin said. "How many people watched that?"

"Gabrielle has over sixty-five thousand followers on Instagram," Will said. "About seven thousand on YouTube and Facebook, though some are duplicates. And obviously not everyone saw it just this minute, but the video is live, and she pinned it."

"Pinned it?" Griffin asked.

"It means it isn't removed after twenty-four hours. Also she posted about it, see?" Will pointed at a new image of Gabrielle's tearstained face. The caption read, *terrible news, just posted story about it. Your prayers are needed.*

"So a shitload of people are about to see it, is what you're telling me," Griffin said. "We need to tell her to pull it down."

"I'm not sure she would, and I'm not sure we should either," Abby said. "It's what the kidnappers wanted. He told her to use whatever resources she has to get the money. He knew she would do that. She's going to raise the money from her followers."

"But she didn't ask in the video for money," Carver said.

"Because she's smart," Will said. "Someone else will start a fundraiser for her. And it'll seem much more heartfelt."

"They knew from the start," Abby said. "This is why they demanded to talk with her. This is why they never told Eden not to contact the police—they wanted this to be public. That man had told her he was sure she would find people who would be glad to help her."

"Due respect to her followers, she won't raise five million dollars from seventy thousand randos online," Carver said skeptically.

"Seventy thousand right now," Will said. "I'm betting news will be out pretty fast. This number will shoot up, no doubt."

Abby stared at Will's screen, at Gabrielle's tortured expression. "They targeted her all along. It was never about kidnapping Eden's son. It was about kidnapping Gabrielle's brother."

CHAPTER 26

Nathan tore through the darkness, gravel rattling under his feet. He glanced behind him, spotted the silhouette of the man in the doorway of the cabin on his knees, like a predatory beast. The man screamed after him incoherently, a string of furious syllables that froze Nathan's heart in fear. Whimpering, he dove left, farther into the darkness, away from the gravel road, away from the light that came from the cabin. Deeper into the night.

Soon, he couldn't see the ground, couldn't see anything around him. He let his feet fly, thinking of how he always did so well in gym class, was always one of the fastest kids. He needed that speed now. Needed to get away from—

His right foot sank into a deep puddle, and Nathan stumbled, fell to the ground, his leg and palms instantly blazing in pain. He whimpered, clenching his jaw, knowing that he couldn't scream. The man would hear him, would come for him. And although earlier that hadn't scared him so much, *now* he was terrified. The rage in that man's face when he'd hit him with the metal bar . . . Nathan had never seen a grown man so angry. He wasn't even a man anymore; he was a monster.

He got to his feet and started limping, his right foot now squelching with every step, completely soaked. His palms burned; he was sure there was *blood* on them. He was scared of blood, and his mom always applied a Band-Aid when he scratched himself. His leg ached, no matter how lightly he tried to walk on it.

After his puddle accident, he was terrified to blunder into another hole—or a tree—so he moved much slower, waving his arms ahead of him, peering at the ground, avoiding darker spots that could be holes or rocks.

It was cold, so cold. It had never occurred to him to wear his coat before attacking that man. He'd left it discarded carelessly on that duplicate bed. If only he had it with him. When he got out of the house, he'd assumed he'd run into a street. He would find someone to help him, or knock on doors and scream for help. Someone would call his mom; he knew her phone number because she'd had him memorize it. Or they'd take him home; he knew his address as well.

But instead, he'd run out into this . . . emptiness. Where *was* he? Where had the man taken him? It must be much farther than he'd thought. He was probably out of New York City.

The idea terrified him so much he nearly turned back. He would apologize to the man. Mom always said if you apologized, and you were truly sorry, people would forgive you. And he *was* sorry. He should never have done that. The man hadn't hurt him. It had seemed like he was taking care of him.

But now . . .

Now the man would hurt him if he ever caught him. Nathan had no doubt.

He kept on going, and when he glanced back, the cabin was small; he could hardly see it. The door was shut now, and the only way he could even make it out was because of the lights in the windows. Maybe the man had given up on catching him? After all, Nathan had hurt his legs; he couldn't catch him crawling and—

A bouncing light. A flashlight. It pointed down at the ground, the beam swiveling like an evil eye, and then it pointed up again. Bouncing closer.

The man was following his footprints in the mud.

Nathan sobbed and tried to move faster, but his leg actually hurt more, and it was freezing, and he was in pain. He wanted to lie down and stop. The man wouldn't kill him if he just lay there, right?

Collapsing to the ground, he shut his eyes and thought of home. Of Mom. Of Gabi. Of being warm again.

The man's footsteps were getting closer, squelching in the muddy ground.

"Nathan!" he hollered. "Get back here! You'll get lost."

He was already lost. He opened his mouth, about to call out. The room back in the cabin was warm. He got fed. And the man seemed to like Gabi. Surely he would send him back eventually. "I'm—"

"Get back here right now! I'll carve you to pieces, you little shit."

The words died in Nathan's throat. He looked around frantically, saw a dark shape, maybe a bush, a few feet away. Very carefully, he crawled over to it.

The footsteps got closer. The man was limping because of what Nathan had done, and it made the sound of his steps uneven—squelch, thump, squelch, thump—like a monster in the swamp, the flashlight beam flickering as it swept over the muddy ground. Nathan managed to reach the bush, huddled behind it as the beam slid nearby.

"Nathan." Hardly a word, more like a growl.

Squelch. Thump.

Nathan crouched, holding his breath.

Squelch. Thump.

The footsteps receded. His lungs were about to burst, but he didn't dare breathe.

I'll carve you to pieces.

Squelch, thump, squelch, thump.

Perhaps the man was far enough away. Perhaps he wasn't. It didn't matter; Nathan couldn't hold his breath any longer, and he exhaled, trying to let it out as softly as possible. Carefully, he got to his feet and moved away from the searching flashlight.

He nearly blundered into the wire fence. His fingertips brushed it as he took that extra step. He froze, breathing hard. Touched the top wire and ran his finger along it. It hit something spiky, a pang of pain flashing. He pulled his finger back and fumbled around, found two more wires. Three wires, running from left to right. And each had those nasty spiky things.

He could crawl above the bottom wire and below the middle wire. They were spaced really far from each other.

He crouched, trying to push the middle wire upward, but it was taut. Very carefully, he moved his right hand over the wire, and it touched grass on the other side. His left hand landed in something wet and sticky—mud. Gently, he maneuvered himself under the wire. His eyes glimpsed the flashlight. Moving toward him again. Too close. In a panicked moment he lunged to the other side, and agony tore through his back. *Now* he screamed.

Behind him, the man called, "Nathan! Don't move, you little shit!"

He couldn't get away; the fence held him back. With another lunge, he managed to pull free, hearing his sweatshirt rip. And he was on the other side. He could glimpse the silhouettes of tall, looming trees above him.

Running into the forest, he left the man and the fence behind him.

CHAPTER 27

His leg hurt like hell. As he limped back to the cabin, he cursed the boy over and over. He should never have bothered to befriend the kid. Perhaps he should have throttled Nathan as soon as he slid into the car. Instead, he'd gone to all that effort, re-creating Nathan's room, buying him his favorite food. And for what?

The kid had attacked him like an animal as soon as he'd had the chance.

And now . . . well, now everything was ruined. His entire plan had unraveled. If the kid managed to get to safety, he could identify him, and the police would show up. And if the kid got lost in the woods and died . . .

That wouldn't be *so* bad. He could work with that.

He barged through the door and slammed it behind him. Went to the medicine cabinet and took two ibuprofens, swallowing them dry. He limped to the kitchen, sat on one of the chairs, and rolled up his pant leg. A large purple bruise had materialized on his shin.

Shit.

Maybe he should get that x-rayed. No, of course not. What would he say? That he'd accidentally kicked a metal rod with his bare leg? No, it'd be fine. Pain relievers would be his friends for a couple of days, and he'd get better.

What he *should* do was get ready. Because if the kid got to safety, he had to disappear—and quickly. He should prepare a bag with some necessities, withdraw some cash.

His eyes went to the large picture on the wall, and hundreds of Gabrielles stared back at him. It had taken him over thirty hours to make this picture. He'd gone through thousands of images he had of Gabrielle—mostly from her Instagram, some manipulated to match his needs. Creating her nude images had become much easier since the DeepNude application had been released.

Could he take the picture with him? It would fill the entire back seat of his car. He imagined the border guard looking at it, asking him questions. No, he would have to leave it behind. He would have to leave everything behind.

He let out a sob. He'd done it all for her. And this was what had happened.

He grabbed a beer from the fridge and chugged half of it, trying to ignore the throbbing pain in his leg. Then he fished his phone from his pocket and tapped the Instagram app.

A new story *and* a new post, saying she had urgent news. Had Nathan already managed to return home? But no, that was crazy; it couldn't be. The kid had been gone less than fifteen minutes.

His trembling finger tapped the story. He watched Gabrielle on-screen, talking about her brother's abduction.

Finally. He had started thinking she'd never figure it out.

She'd dressed in her white dress; he remembered her buying it. At the time she'd planned to wear it to a spring dance of some kind. But she never had, or at least, she'd never posted about it. She had called it *pure* when she'd bought it. But for him, it had inspired a different word. *Bride.*

"We don't have that much," she said and sobbed into her hands.

His heart squeezed. He couldn't bear it when she cried. He took another long sip of his beer, drinking her tears away.

"If the kidnappers are watching this, please don't hurt Nathan. He's a little boy. He likes drawing and swimming, and he still loves to cuddle. Keep him safe, and we'll get you your money, okay?"

He exhaled. She was right. Nathan was a little boy. He'd been thinking of him like a *thing* that could be discarded, left to die in the woods. But he couldn't do that. He needed to *keep him safe*. Gabrielle had spoken to him directly, not even hiding behind her usual facade of pretending to talk to all her fans.

She was talking to *him*. Telling him to keep her brother safe.

And then, that whispered *thank you*. She'd never thanked him directly before. He'd always done what was needed for her, but she'd never expressed any gratitude. And in a way, he'd never minded; he didn't expect anything else. But those two words tasted so sweet.

He played the video again.

Keep him safe.

Thank you.

Exhaling, he got up from his chair, his leg hardly hurting anymore. Perhaps it was the ibuprofen and the beer, but perhaps it was just Gabrielle, instilling him with renewed energy.

He grabbed his flashlight and phone, then stepped back into the night, determined to keep Gabrielle's brother safe.

CHAPTER 28

After stumbling in the freezing dark for what felt like hours, Nathan felt drowsy.

His right foot, wet and muddy, almost didn't hurt anymore. It was numb, and moving it was like lugging a large rock forward with every step. His back still hurt, the fabric of his torn shirt now sticking to his skin. When Nathan had tried to peel it away, the stinging pain had been so unbearable that he'd been unable to go through with it.

His teeth chattered occasionally—but not so much anymore. Really, it was getting better. Maybe the cold was getting better too. He needed to get some sleep.

In the distance, an animal screeched. He listened to it, detached, no longer scared.

Just exhausted.

He finally lay down by a tree, trembling. He curled into himself, hands hidden deep in his sleeves, face tucked into his sweatshirt's collar. He would just rest for a few hours, maybe until morning. And then he'd keep walking.

New York City couldn't be far.

The reassuring nothingness of sleep enveloped him, taking away the agony, the fear, the cold. His trembling diminished. Just a short rest.

A noise startled him. He wasn't sure if he'd even managed to fall asleep, but something had prodded him awake, bringing back the chill, the stinging pain in his back. What was it? What was that noise?

He heard it again. A faraway rumble.

A car engine.

A road was nearby.

Roads sometimes had streetlights. They had cars—and people. A road would mean help.

When he got up he found himself teetering, almost falling. His right foot hardly worked anymore; spots danced in front of his eyes. He leaned on the tree, letting out a soft breath. Or a whimper.

Then he took a step, and another, following the memory of that sound. Searching for the road.

There.

Almost invisible in the myriad of shadows, a black patch of ground, clearly man made. It curved, disappearing into the trees. Nathan narrowed his eyes, not sure if he was really seeing it. But he was.

His feet took him to the road, and as they touched its hard surface, relief flooded his body. The road was flat and smooth—no thorns were scratching his legs; no hidden tree trunks or holes threatened to trip him. All he had to do was put one foot in front of the other until this road took him somewhere.

One foot in front of the other. Over and over again.

His eyes were half shut as he did so, trudging down the road. His body was getting heavier, dragging him down. One foot in front of the other. The right shoe always making a wet sound as it hit the asphalt. He could hardly see the road. Could hardly see anything.

Could hardly see the pair of white lights as they hurtled toward him.

At the last second he gasped and tumbled out of the way. The car seemed to veer slightly, a rush of wind against his face as it passed inches away from him. He stumbled to his feet, jumped up and down, waving his arms, screaming as it got away, the red taillights turning into dots in the night.

He burst into tears. He couldn't take it anymore. He wanted his mom.

And then, amazingly, the car stopped. Turned around, drove back. It slowed down as it got closer, and he had the presence of mind to move to the side of the road.

A sudden fear hit Nathan. What if the driver was *him*? He stood frozen on the road as the headlights came closer and closer.

CHAPTER 29

Abby read the article on her laptop's screen, almost oblivious to the scenery outside the passenger window. Carver drove, one hand on the steering wheel, the other casually resting on the driver's side windowsill.

"I don't know how you can read in a car," he said. "If I tried to do that, I'd throw up my breakfast after two minutes."

"I don't get motion sickness," Abby said distractedly, scrolling down the article. It was the third one she'd read since they'd passed a four-car accident on the Grand Central Parkway and continued east on the Long Island Expressway, heading toward the Tillman farm. All three articles covered the Instagram story that Gabrielle had posted the night before. This one was on the *New York Post* website. And from there it would presumably get to CNN, Fox News, and the rest of them. Nathan's kidnapping had become national news.

Or more to the point, Gabrielle's Instagram story had become national news.

"So what does *that* one say?" Carver asked.

Abby sighed. "Pretty much the same as the rest. 'Instagram influencer Gabrielle Fletcher shocked her followers last night when she announced her brother had been kidnapped.' Then comes a brief recap of the story with a link. A picture of Nathan. A two-line commentary from the NYPD. And of course, the inevitable mention of the fundraiser."

The emergency crowdsourced fundraising of the ransom had begun faster than Abby had predicted. Only two hours after Gabrielle had gone public, one of Gabrielle's followers, TanyaThePixie, had posted a dramatic Instagram post of herself holding a large sign that said **Save Nathan** in purple bubble letters. She'd added a link to the fundraiser she'd started. Gabrielle had almost instantly reposted it on her own account, adding a tearstained Instagram story of her own in which she thanked her fans for the incredible initiative. Now, less than twelve hours later, $112,000 had been collected, and every time Abby checked the number, it leaped up. It was still far from the $5 million goal, but after this morning's exposure, Abby had no doubt the rate of donations would increase tenfold.

She had three tabs on her browser. One was open on Gabrielle's Instagram page, where she monitored the comments and likes pouring onto Gabrielle's post, as well as the hashtag *bringNathanHome* that was becoming increasingly popular. The second showed the fundraiser sum, which had already risen by $7,000 since she'd sat down in Carver's car. And the third she used to read the articles. She didn't really care much about the articles themselves. But the kidnapper read them; of that she was almost certain. And she wanted to see his perspective on the events.

A message from Isaac popped up on-screen. She'd written him the night before, asking if he'd known that Eden had joined the Tillman cult. He'd only answered now.

She tapped the chat and read his message. I knew she found a community, and that she met her husband there, but she never gave me details. We lost touch for a few years back then, but I never knew she'd joined a cult!

He added a horrified emoji.

Okay, thanks, she wrote back.

Are you checking it out?

146

Yeah, we need to talk to her ex-husband. He might still be there. On our way there now

Be careful

Like her, Isaac had firsthand experience of how a police visit to a cult could go wrong. For a second an image blinked into her mind. *Holding the phone, a gun pressed against her temple. Isaac's frightened eyes meeting hers. Then running. Smoke.*

A shout: "Abihail, get away from there!"

Isaac's hand on her shoulder.

A searing pain in her neck.

She shook her head, tearing herself away from the memories. She sent him a thumbs-up emoji and put the phone away.

Glancing out the window, she said, "Oh. Trees."

"I always thought you were unusually perceptive when we were in the academy," Carver remarked. "And now I see I was right."

At some point they'd left the busy urban landscape of the city, and now trees lined the road on either side, and traffic was pleasantly sparse. When had she last driven out of the city? It had to be months. More than a year? Surely not.

Okay, possibly more than a year. That camping trip at Cranberry Lake. Why hadn't they done that again? It had been so much fun. Ben watching the fishermen, more interested in the worms they used as bait than the fish. Samantha reading a book while sunbathing. And then later, a night of a crackling fire, fingers sticky from endless s'mores.

She took out her phone and sent her daughter a message asking if she was awake.

Sam didn't respond. No way to know if she was asleep or simply ignoring her. Abby sent her another message asking her to let her know when she woke up. She also checked up on Ben, and her mother wrote back that Abby's father had taken him to the park.

"So when do you think the kidnappers will call again?" Carver asked.

"I don't think they'll call today," Abby said. "We can see from their behavior so far that they're careful. They know these calls are risky, which is why they use burners and call from different locations. They called frequently at first because they wanted Gabrielle to get the message and start raising the money. But now they can just wait. In fact, they can literally see the ransom being raised from the comfort of their own home. They have no reason to call as long as the ransom fund keeps rising."

"Do you think this hurt us?"

"I think it's not ideal," Abby said. "If she'd come to us beforehand, we could have told her to wait, let the kidnappers call a few more times. We would have crafted a better message for her to post, one that gives the kidnappers reasons to keep contacting us."

"Yeah," Carver muttered moodily.

"But she did a pretty good job of humanizing Nathan. If the kidnappers are trying to distance themselves from him, it'll make it harder for them. And she made them feel like things were going their way. They feel in control, which is a good thing."

"Because they *are* in control."

"For now." Abby shut her laptop and slid it into the bag. "Listen, can I put some music on?"

"Sure, feel free."

"What's your jam?" Abby hooked her phone to the auxiliary cable.

"My jam?"

"Yeah, what do you like to listen to?"

"I don't really listen to music."

Abby blinked. "What? At all?"

"Well, when I drive, I usually listen to podcasts. And I can't really concentrate with music, so I don't listen to anything while I work. And in the evenings I prefer watching TV or reading a book." Carver mulled it over. "I usually listen to music when I do my annual income tax paperwork."

"Once a year. You listen to music once a year."

"Yeah, I guess so."

"So how does it feel to be dead inside? Is it like . . . sad? Or just very relaxed?"

Carver glanced at her, grinning. "I get along fine. Okay, you know what? I do enjoy music. I like that new song they keep playing on the radio."

"Which song?"

"By that band. You know. Na-nana-naaaa-na-na."

"I never heard that. It doesn't really sound like anything."

"Oh, come on. It's super popular."

"That song you just hummed. Whose words you don't know, by a band whose name you don't remember."

"You know what? I changed my mind. You can't put music on."

"Too late. You're getting educated." Abby scrolled through her music library. "Okay, this might awaken even your husk of a soul." She hit play, and the fast notes of "Baba O'Riley," by The Who, began playing.

"Oh, I know that song," Carver said beaming at her. "It's 'Teenage—'"

"No."

"Yes! I know this song from high school. It's 'Teenage Wasteland.'"

"It's *not* 'Teenage Wasteland.' There's no song called 'Teenage Wasteland.' It's called 'Baba O'Riley.' But plebeians think it's called 'Teenage Wasteland' because it has those two words in the chorus."

"You know something, Lieutenant Mullen? You're a musical snob."

She laughed. "I get that from my daughter."

"That's not how genetics works."

"Sometimes it does."

"How many kids do you have?"

"Two. Ben, who's eight, and Samantha—she's fourteen."

"Fourteen, huh? You must have had her soon after we finished the academy." He frowned. "I remember you were dating that guy . . . Steve? Is he the father?"

She cleared her throat. "Yeah."

"Brilliant!" Carver beamed at her. "I really liked him. He was a math teacher at Columbia University, right? I had a long chat with him during our graduation barbecue; he seemed like a really fantastic guy."

"Not as fantastic as you might think. We're divorced."

"Oh. Sorry." Carver looked embarrassed.

"Eh, it's fine, I'm over it. Listen to the violin solo; that's the best part of the song."

Dave Arbus's incredible solo always made Abby think of Samantha playing it, biting her lower lip, trying to get it right. Guilt crept into her mind. Her daughter was still at Steve's place, fuming over Ben's new snake. Abby would have to make it up to her.

The song ended and "Bargain" started.

"Do you have kids?" Abby asked.

"Nope. I have a lot of nephews and nieces, though."

"How many is a lot?"

Carver didn't answer, frowning.

"Carver? How many nieces and—"

"Hang on, I'm counting."

"You're *counting*?"

"Nineteen."

"*Nineteen?* You're making it up."

"I'm not. See, one of my sisters wanted a big family."

"So she had nineteen kids?"

"What? No, of course not. She had seven. But Dewey—that's one of my brothers—he had a kid, and he was like, well, I want two. Except the second kid was actually a triplet. So that brings us up to eleven. Dana had three, and Holly had one. And Jake—"

"How many siblings do you have?"

"You made me lose count. I have four—"

"That's a lot."

"—sisters. And three brothers. Eight altogether. My mom also wanted a big family. That's where my sister got it."

"And what do they think about you not having kids? Are you like the black sheep of the family?"

"No, that would be Gerald. He's in prison."

"God, I'm sorry, I didn't mean—"

Carver laughed. "No worries. He's a con man. He had a scam selling rocks online. Which he claimed were moon rocks, complete with certificates signed by supposed astronauts."

"Seriously?"

"Yup. He managed to sell over three hundred rocks before he was arrested. Got two years. We take turns visiting him."

"Wow. Is the website still up?"

"No, of course not."

"I'd have bought one. Just to say that I have a pretend moon rock."

"No, you wouldn't."

"No," she conceded. "I wouldn't. So you have seven siblings. And nineteen nieces and nephews. What do you do on Christmas?"

"Dewey has a farm down in Texas. We usually celebrate Christmas there. It gets very loud."

"I can imagine."

"I don't think you can." He grinned at her. "I don't think anyone can. It gets *really* loud."

She laughed. "Okay, fair enough, I guess I can't imagine."

Eight siblings. How had it been, growing up like that? Hectic for sure. But her own childhood, even after her parents had adopted her, had been quiet and often lonely. A brother or sister would have made things easier.

"So . . . ," Carver said. "You were in the Moses Wilcox cult with Eden?"

Abby's heart sank like a stone. "How did you find out?" she asked, her voice barely a whisper. Had Will told him? It would crush her if he had. Will never—

"I didn't, really. I wasn't sure up until this moment."

She was such an idiot. She'd fallen for the oldest trick in the book. She stared out the window, saying nothing.

"That thing you told Eden about the germs was weird. I couldn't figure it out," Carver said. "But it felt like you two had a connection. Something that went far beyond a casual acquaintance. And yesterday, after you said she was in a cult as a child, I did some research. Moses Wilcox's obsession with germs is well documented. And when you talked about cults, it didn't sound like you just did your research. It sounded . . ."

"Personal," Abby said hollowly.

"Well, yeah. The identities of the Wilcox siege survivors were hidden. But the press mentioned three children. A seven-year-old girl, a thirteen-year-old girl, and a twelve-year-old boy. The ages matched."

"It doesn't impact the case."

Carver glanced at her. She gazed stonily forward, trying to contain her emotions. She was furious at him, as if he'd read her secret journal. But he hadn't. He'd only done his job.

"It might impact it," Carver said. "If it ever goes to trial. They'll find out the connection. But I don't care about the trial right now. I just want to get Nathan Fletcher back home."

"Me too."

"And your personal knowledge about cults might turn out to be helpful. Can you be objective when we get there? It's important, Mullen."

"Yes. You don't have to worry about me."

"Who else knows?"

Abby counted on her fingers. "My parents, Will Vereen, and anyone else you told." She spread her hand.

"I didn't talk to anyone about this. And if it doesn't hurt the case, I'll keep my mouth shut."

"Okay."

"They'll probably find out sooner or later."

"Yeah. But I won't fall for the cheap trick you pulled on me again."

As if on cue, the track ended, and the song "Won't Get Fooled Again" started playing. Abby had to smile at the perfect timing. She tweaked the volume. God, she loved this song. They drove in silence, listening to the music, the trees rushing past them.

CHAPTER 30

As they'd agreed beforehand, Detective Wong from the Suffolk County Police waited for them by the side of the road about half a mile before the Tillman farm. She leaned on the hood of her car, smoking a long cigarette. As Carver parked the car, Abby scrutinized the woman. Wong was tall with perfect tawny skin and smooth brown hair pulled back into an immaculate ponytail. She wore a black jacket and matching sailor pants that Abby knew from experience she could never in a million years pull off.

Abby opened the passenger door and stepped out of the car. "Detective Wong? I'm Lieutenant Mullen."

Wong nodded, exhaling a plume of smoke, and walked over to shake Abby's hand. "I remember you. We talked a couple of times on the phone a year ago."

"And this is Detective Carver from the NYPD." Abby gestured at Carver. "He's the lead detective on the Nathan Fletcher case."

"Your case is getting a lot of publicity this morning," Wong said, shaking Carver's hand. "Do you really think the Tillman farm is related?"

"Well, both of Nathan's parents lived there," Carver said. "And it's possible the father still does. We need to find the father in any case, regardless of the Tillman farm. What can you tell us about it?"

Wong shrugged. "Lieutenant Mullen already knows most of it. Two years ago a teacher in the local high school approached us saying a fifteen-year-old girl in her class, Ruth Lindholm, had told her that she had sexual relations with a grown man. Ruth lived on the Tillman farm. I came over to the school and interviewed her there with the school psychologist present. She told me there was a man on the farm who had sexual relations with her twice. She also said her parents knew about it."

She paused every few seconds to take a long drag from her cigarette, smoke punctuating her sentences. "We went to the farm and arrested the man. A day later Ruth showed up with both parents alongside Otis Tillman and said she'd made up the entire thing. We tried to investigate further, but after a few weeks, we had to drop the case. No one there would really talk to us except for Otis. And he's . . . well, I don't know if you can believe a word he says. Not even hello."

"Does the man who assaulted Ruth still live on the farm?" Carver asked.

"Oh yeah. They all do. One big happy community." Wong took one last drag and dropped the stub on the ground, then squashed it with her foot. "Come on, let's get there before lunch starts. During meals Otis usually does one of his sermons, and those can go on for hours."

They got back into the car and followed Wong as she drove down the road. Abby's phone blipped, a curt message from Sam letting her know she was awake. Abby quickly texted that she'd call her later.

They turned right at a rough gravel path and drove a few hundred yards until they reached a closed gate. A barbed wire fence stretched in both directions, presumably circumnavigating the entire farm. Abby watched Wong's silhouette in her own car as she called someone.

"So you talked to Wong a year ago?" Carver asked.

"Yeah."

"Why?"

Abby stared through the window. "One day I might be called to a police siege on Otis Tillman's farm. On that day, I want to be prepared."

"So . . . what? You research all the cults and weird religious movements in New York City and Long Island?"

155

She eyed him, deadpan. "And the rest of the state. And three in Pennsylvania."

He raised his eyebrows. "Okay."

"These things have gone terribly wrong before."

"I know they have. But—"

"The gate's opening." Abby pointed.

The electric gate opened slowly, and as soon as there was enough space, Wong drove through with barely an inch left on each side of the car. Carver waited patiently for a few seconds more, then followed her into the farm.

Otis Tillman waited for them by the large house.

Abby's body tensed up as she saw the man. He was thin and pale, his hair curly and frizzy. He wore a large pair of thick spectacles. As they stepped out of the car, he smiled, exposing a slight overbite. Everything about him seemed harmless, clumsy, perhaps even endearing.

Abby knew the truth. This wasn't a sheep. This wasn't even a wolf in sheep's clothing. This was a cancerous growth in sheep's clothing. It didn't just attack you. It killed you from within.

"Detective Wong," he said warmly, approaching her. "It's so nice to see you again."

He held out his hand, and Wong coldly offered hers. He grasped it with both hands, shaking it with gusto. Then he turned to Abby and Carver.

"And you must be the NYPD detectives I've been told to expect," he said, the smile staying on his face. He practically beamed at them. "Welcome to my farm. Can I get you anything to drink?"

"No, thank you." Abby's eyes went to one of the windows on the second floor of the house, where a couple of tiny faces gaped at them with curiosity.

"So what's this about?" Otis asked.

"You have a man living here," Carver said. "His name is David Huff. We would love to have a word with him."

Otis frowned. "David? What do you want to talk to him about?"

"Just a few routine questions regarding a case," Carver said.

"Well, lunch starts at one, so we have a bit of time. Let's see if he's around." Otis took a cell phone from his pocket and dialed. As they waited, Abby looked around, taking it all in. The fence seemed to circle the entire perimeter. Aside from the large house, she spotted a few cabins farther south, as well as something that seemed like a barn. Several men and women were toiling in a field.

And three men stood a dozen yards away by a pickup truck, looking at them. These guys, she was certain, were armed.

If things went south, how would it play out? Would Tillman's followers barricade themselves in the house? Shoot at the police from the windows? Were there automatic rifles stowed on the second floor, a few feet away from the kids who were staring at them?

"Tell them." Wilcox, handing her the phone. "Tell them what will happen if they come near us. Tell them about the gun."

The cold muzzle, pressing against her temple.

"He's not answering," Otis said.

"Imagine that," Detective Wong said dryly.

"Let's search for him," Otis suggested. "He's probably around back."

"Maybe he's in the house?" Abby suggested.

"Not likely," Otis answered, smiling at her disarmingly. "David sleeps in one of the shacks out back, and during the day he's either working the field or in the office."

"What's the office?" Abby asked, catching up to Otis as he strode toward the field.

"Just a small caravan we use to store all of our paperwork. David's our accountant."

"How long has David lived here?" Abby asked.

"David's one of the earliest members," Otis said with a fatherly smile. "He practically helped me build this place."

"So what *is* this place exactly?" Abby asked, feigning curiosity.

"We're a Christian community," Tillman answered. "We're trying to make this world better."

"Make the world better?"

"That's right. We search for lost souls, and gather them. Protect them. Heal them. And we try to contribute to worthy causes. Racial inequality being the chief one. Did you know that Suffolk County is the most segregated area in the United States? More than eighty percent of the county is white."

"I didn't know that." Abby looked around again to get a feel of the place. She had to hand it to Otis; he ran a tight ship. The ground was weeded; the gravel path was well surfaced; the walls of the shacks and the caravan, as well as the main house, were freshly painted. It was easier to maintain a farm well when each of the workers was completely and utterly devoted to you, willing to work eighteen or even twenty hours a day.

Otis kept talking. "In *our* community, twenty-two percent of our members are African American, twenty-one percent Latino, and fifteen percent Asian." He pointed at the men and women working in the field. "And we strive for gender equality as well. Women and men are treated equally here."

"Treated equally?" Abby suspected that if she repeated Tillman's words to him, he would keep talking forever. He warmed up to her, walking closer, his hands and shoulders relaxing.

"That's right. We have an equal number of men and women on the board. And the tasks are rotated equally. We have as many men doing the laundry and cooking as the women."

"Admirable." Aside from the hushed statutory rape story, of course. Abby could almost feel Tillman's speech crawling on her skin, a hungry parasite, searching for a way in.

"Otis!" one of the men called from the field. "We have a problem here."

"Just a second," Otis called back. He glanced around him, then brightened. "Ruth! Can you come here a minute?"

He waved his hand. A young woman approached them, her face blank. Detective Wong, standing by Abby's side, inhaled sharply. Abby glanced at her, saw the detective's expression twist in pain. And then it was gone, Wong's cool expression back in its place.

Tillman placed a fatherly hand on Ruth's shoulder. "Can you please show the detectives where the office is? They want to talk to David."

Ruth raised her eyes to the man. That stare. Damn it. That look of complete devotion, of reverence and love. Abby wanted to grab the girl. To drag her away from this place kicking and screaming and spend days, or weeks, or months talking with her. Do whatever it took to deprogram her.

"Sure," Ruth said, glancing at each of them, Otis's hand still on her shoulder. "Come on, it's this way."

Otis left them alone with the girl, and she led them down a gravel path.

"Ruth, do you remember me?" Wong said.

"Of course," Ruth said. "It's nice to meet you again, Detective Wong—"

"You can call me May."

"I'm glad you came. I never got the chance to apologize about that whole mess," Ruth said.

"There's *absolutely* no reason to apologize," Wong said emphatically.

Abby had no doubt Otis had left them alone with the girl intentionally. He knew Ruth would confess absolutely nothing. He wanted Wong to see that as well. And perhaps he was demonstrating his trust to Ruth, another test—and another measure of control gained over the girl.

"I was looking for attention," Ruth said. "I have a very vivid imagination. But I never dreamed it would get so blown out of proportion." She spoke casually, her voice genuine and full of sorrow.

Wong's face twisted in pain again. "Ruth, if there's anything you want to tell me, no one can hear you right now. Or you can come to the station *whenever* you want. If anyone touched you, or hurt you—"

Ruth seemed confused. "No. Like I said, I made it all up. I wanted to apologize." She gestured ahead at the caravan. "The office is over there. Oh, and there's David. He can take it from here." She turned and left them.

Abby had only seen David in the one photo from Gabrielle's feed, the one with Otis. Otis had hardly changed since that photo, and she'd expected the same from David—he had been wide shouldered, handsome, with a thick mane of hair. But the photo was ten years old. David Huff had spent them in the Tillman cult, away from his wife and children.

He was almost skeletal, his eyes hollow, his hair gone. His face was pale, almost white. At first, he didn't move, and for one crazy second, Abby thought he was already dead. But then he walked over to them, his steps slow and weary.

It seemed like the past decade in the Tillman cult had sucked David's life away. And all that was left was a dying husk.

CHAPTER 31

"David Huff?" Abby asked, thinking that it couldn't be, that surely this was his father or grandfather.

"That's right," the man answered.

Carver flipped his shield. "Sir, we're from the NYPD. I'm Detective Carver, and this is Lieutenant Mullen. Would you mind if we ask you a few questions?"

"Well, Sunday lunch is about to start. If you care to join us—"

"This will only take a few minutes," Abby said. "We gathered from Otis that lunch starts at one o'clock. We have some time until then."

"I usually help set up."

"We won't hold you for long," Abby answered. "Were you married to a woman named Eden Fletcher?"

David's eyes flickered behind them, over to the field where Otis was speaking to the workers. "Yeah." His tone became sharper. "Is this about Eden? I signed the papers and gave her what she asked for. Did she come for more?"

"It seems like you're still angry at her," Abby said, her tone slowing down, softening.

David took a deep breath. "I'm not angry. It is the burden of God and his emissaries to be wrathful."

"But you regret her decision to leave?" Carver asked.

"Yes. She didn't consult me. She just left with Gabrielle and Nathan. Came a few weeks later with divorce papers."

"And you signed them?"

David's eyes flickered toward Otis again. "Yes. 'No one, having put his hand to the plow—'"

"'—and looking back, is fit for the kingdom of God,'" Abby said, echoing Moses Wilcox's voice from long ago.

"That's right," David said with a surprised smile.

"I do some Bible reading from time to time," Abby clarified.

Some of the Bible, anyway. Cult leaders loved religious phrases about forgetting the past. It enabled them to change stances, to rewrite history, to confuse and obfuscate. Abby knew many of those phrases by heart.

Why had Otis Tillman told David to sign the divorce papers? She would have to ask Eden.

"Did you stay in touch with your children after Eden left?"

"No, I didn't know how to get in touch. I decided to let them go."

"You didn't even try searching for them?" Carver asked.

A long pause. Then David said, "Like I said, I decided to let them go. I'm blameless and upright." He smirked as if he'd made a joke that none of them got.

"Can you tell us where you were on Friday?" Carver asked.

David shrugged. "Sure, I was here on the farm."

"Anyone see you?"

"The entire congregation, probably. We work together all day, Detective. This is a very close community. And it's unusual not to see everyone both during morning and evening prayer."

And there they were. Abby could already tell from the way he'd said it, smoothly, practiced, almost bored. This was a well-rehearsed answer given to outsiders all the time. She was certain all the cult members would say pretty much the same thing. An unbreakable alibi for each and every one of them.

It was time to shake things up. "Mr. Huff, on that day, on his way back from school, your son, Nathan, was kidnapped. Do you know anything about it?"

Cult members were incredible liars because they *believed* everything they said. Even when they knew they were lying, they were certain they were doing it for a greater good, so the lie, in a way, became the truth.

But their world, and everything they believed in, was dictated by their leader. Typically, cult leaders discouraged curiosity and offered abstract answers for questions that might arise. That was how they handled any doubts about their leadership, any complaint, and especially criticism from outside.

So when you went completely off script, saying something the cult leader didn't anticipate, it was easy to tell. Because at that moment, the cult members had to think. They had to search for the right answer. For a fraction of a second, they regained their individuality. At that moment, the cult members weren't good liars. They were the *worst* liars.

Abby saw the surprise in David's eyes, the long stare toward Otis, as if searching for guidance, and at that moment she became certain that David Huff didn't know that Nathan had been kidnapped.

"But that's . . . ," David finally blurted. Then he regained his composure and paused. "How?" he finally asked, his voice cracking.

"We're still looking into it, sir," Carver said. "We would appreciate your cooperation."

"Of—of course. Whatever you need."

"You didn't know?" Abby asked. "It was reported on all the local news."

"We don't have televisions here, and most of us don't own cell phones. We try to avoid the media. It's a distraction."

"Who *does* have a cell phone here?"

"Well, Otis, of course, he needs it to run the place. And—" David paused, and his head rose as he gazed farther out on the horizon.

The sound of an engine made Abby turn around. A pickup truck drove down the road by the side of the house and stopped by the field, raising a cloud of dust. Two men stepped out and approached Otis. One of them glanced over.

Abby peered back at the man. Making sure that she wasn't wrong.

There was no doubt about it. The man who had arrived was the same one Eden had described. The one who'd hung around their block. And he was the one who maintained the Instagram profile Karlad345, which had been created to cyber stalk Gabrielle.

CHAPTER 32

"Carver," Abby said, her eyes still locked on the man in the field.

"I saw," Carver said. "We need to bring him in."

Abby's eyes went to the people around them. Four men and three women working in the field. One still in the pickup truck. The three men who had been watching them had followed from a distance.

Abby had spent countless hours studying cases of major hostage situations. She'd shown up to dozens of crises and untangled the knot, figuring out how they'd gotten to this dangerous point. She'd learned to recognize the causes that could spark a crisis.

These people's vision of the world was warped, a cultivated mentality of *us* against *them*, and she had no doubt that she, Wong, and Carver were *them*. She had good reason to believe there were guns on the premises, some just out of sight. Tensions were already high.

To make things worse, she had no idea what Tillman's agenda was here. Was his cult really involved in Nathan's kidnapping? If it was, Nathan could be on the premises right now, and Tillman and his men might do anything to keep the police from searching the grounds. Or from interrogating one of their own members.

Carver took two steps toward their suspect. She watched him as time slowed down around her. Saw the change in Otis Tillman's stance as he registered Carver's approach. One of the men tensed, his hand shifting to his back. Behind her, she could sense Wong reacting, preparing for whatever was about to happen.

She took a few hurried steps to Carver and lay a hand on his shoulder. "Wait," she said in a low voice. "Stay back. Let me handle this."

She felt the knotted muscles underneath her palms. Carver's jaw was clenched tight, and she could guess he was flooded with adrenaline. Like her, he knew instinctively this might go sideways. But unlike her, he didn't know how to avoid it. They couldn't walk away and risk this man disappearing. They *had* to take him in.

"Trust me," she muttered. "Please."

Carver stood in place, his brow furrowed. Finally he said, "Okay. Wong and I are just behind you."

Abby nodded and swept her hair behind her ears, plastering the most casual, nonthreatening smile on her face. She had practice, knew it seemed authentic. Some people had fake smiles that never reached their eyes. Abby's fake smiles spread to her eyes, her brow, her body language. In fact, Abby's fake smiles seemed more authentic and infectious than her real ones. The fact that she was a small woman with silly-looking ears also helped to alleviate the tension. Her own casual smile was reflected in the stance of the men she approached. They still glanced at Carver and Wong suspiciously but deemed her as safe.

"Mr. Tillman, can I have a word with one of your men?" she called out.

She made sure to keep her pace steady as she met Tillman's eyes. At the moment, he was the only one she cared about. The rest of the cult members, she knew, were single minded and hostile. In the cults' everyday business, compromise was normally unheard of. People were indoctrinated by the leader to believe they were working for a higher purpose, that the law was the enemy, that the world was against them. In such a tense and extreme atmosphere, the moment she tried to make an arrest, there would be pushback—and violence.

Ironically, the only man who probably wasn't a fanatic, and who might agree to compromise, was Otis Tillman, the cult leader who'd radicalized everyone else. It was in his best interest to maintain the status quo, to avoid bloodshed.

Unless he'd bought into his own bullshit. If that was the case, this would get very ugly very fast.

"Lieutenant Mullen," Otis said. "Mr. Adkins here updated me with some upsetting news."

Mr. Adkins. Karlad345 was Karl Adkins.

"You can call me Abby." She halted a few feet from Otis and Adkins.

"David's child has been kidnapped." Otis looked shaken up, but it was impossible to say if it was an act or not. Adkins's face was completely impassive, but Abby noticed the reactions of the people around her. Eyes widening. Shocked whispers. As she'd surmised, the majority of the cult didn't know about Nathan. But Adkins did.

Did he know because he'd seen Gabrielle's Instagram story? Or because he'd kidnapped Nathan himself?

"That's right," Abby said. "Detective Carver and I are investigating Nathan's kidnapping. And we were wondering if Karl would mind coming with us to answer a few questions." She intentionally called Adkins by his first name, which Otis hadn't used, to verify that she'd gotten it right.

"He can talk to you here." Otis folded his arms. "There's no need to go anywhere."

"That's not a bad idea," Abby said. "In fact, we would appreciate talking to everyone here. Someone might have information that could help us."

"Absolutely. After the Sunday meal—"

"I'm sorry, I'm afraid we can't wait that long. When a child is missing, every minute counts."

Otis's body tensed. "Eden and her children haven't lived here for seven years. I don't want you to waste your time."

"It won't be a waste of time," Abby reassured him, smiling placidly. "Eden and her children lived in this community for over a decade. I'm sure people here know her well. Perhaps some have stayed in contact."

"They haven't," Otis blurted.

Abby frowned, acting surprised. "They haven't?"

Of course they hadn't. The deadliest thing to a cult was its ex-members. People who left realized that almost everything they'd been told was a lie. The world didn't end if you left the cult. Not everyone was out to get them. Life outside still had meaning. In fact, life outside could be *better*.

So the first thing almost every cult did when its members left was to sever all connections and demonize the people who'd left. Painting them as selfish traitors, as collaborators with the enemy. That way the cult leader made sure no one would be influenced by them, and it also made it harder for additional members to leave.

"As far as I know, Eden disappeared completely," Otis amended his statement. "Perhaps David told you—we tried to search for her but had no luck."

Abby stared at him quizzically. "But Eden said . . ." She froze and then shook her head. "No. Of course, you're right. You know your community best."

Abby was certain Otis Tillman was a world-class actor. There was no inkling of distress in his body language or face. But she knew she'd struck home. She'd threatened to talk to his entire community before he had time to control the narrative. And she'd just hinted that someone in the community was talking to an ex-member. Which could only mean his control was slipping. Otis would feel the need to propose an alternative, which would make it seem as if he were in complete control.

"You can talk to Karl in our cabin in the presence of our attorney," Otis said. "I'll start the Sunday meal, and as soon as you finish talking to him, you can interview the rest of our members."

"I'm sorry," Abby said apologetically. "I have witnesses that identified a man who matched Karl's description at the crime scene. How can I rule him out as a suspect if I talk to him here?"

"When did they see him?"

"A few times in the past month."

"He was here the entire time."

Abby glanced at the pickup truck Karl had ridden in. "The entire time?"

"I'm sure we can get to the bottom of this—"

"This seems like a very tight-knit community. I'm sure you want to do everything you can to rule Karl out as a suspect. *And* to help us get David's child back to his mother, of course."

She waited for the cogs in Otis's mind to turn, and glanced at Karl apologetically, as if she were sorry she was dragging him into this mess. He ignored her, looking only at Otis. Abby had almost no doubt this man would kidnap a child or, in fact, kill a child if Otis told him to.

Otis glanced at Karl, and Abby could imagine him deciding to cut him loose. He would find a way to contextualize it, make it easier for his people to swallow. He wouldn't let them arrest Karl in front of all these people.

"So you want to take him for your lineup?" Otis asked. "To verify he isn't your guy?"

Just a quick lineup and he'd be back for dinner. No questioning, no interrogation by the enemy. Abby's eyes flickered over the faces around her to see how they were taking it. A few angry frowns but no threatening gestures.

"Absolutely," she said. "Just a lineup to rule him out. We don't want to waste any time."

"Karl, is that okay with you?" Otis asked.

The rest was playacting. Karl said, "Sure, whatever I can do to help." And the tension in the crowd dissipated. Abby exhaled, relieved.

"He'll follow you in his pickup truck with our attorney, Richard," Otis said.

Abby didn't let her hesitation show. Unless they were willing to arrest Karl right now, it was the best they could do. "Absolutely."

Otis motioned for Karl and another man, presumably the attorney, and the three of them strode aside to have a quick word. Abby examined their faces—the attorney was clearly worried; Otis appeared calm. Karl's face was impassive. The rest of the community walked toward a large barnlike structure, which was presumably where they had their meals.

"I'll stay behind," Wong told her. "Look around."

"You're not alone," Abby answered in a low voice, glancing significantly at a large man who remained outside the house, studying them.

"If the boy is here—"

"If he's here, they won't let you get near him. You'll need a search warrant and a lot of backup," Abby said. "Just be careful."

"I didn't think you'd manage it," Wong said. "Force them to let you take Karl like that."

"I gave them something in return," Abby said darkly. "I gave Otis time to talk to his flock about the kidnapping. And after he's done, we won't get anything useful from them. I just hope we can get something out of Karl."

CHAPTER 33

Abby let Carver start the interrogation of Karl Adkins without her. She wanted to talk to Eden first and get as much information as she could about the Tillman cult beforehand. As soon as they got to the station, she took her own car and drove to Eden's house.

Eden looked worse every time Abby saw her. The intense fear and pressure she was going through would crush anyone's spirit, and in some ways, Eden was more fragile than most. She was wilting, her eyes watery and empty, her posture stooped.

Abby smiled at her, touching her shoulder briefly as she stepped into the house. She paused just a few steps beyond the threshold. Gabrielle sat in the living room alongside a man in a cheap suit. Gabrielle talked, tears in her eyes, as the man listened sympathetically. Gabrielle's phone was in her hand, and she showed it to the man.

"And after the call and the recording . . . they sent us this image." She let out another sob. "See? It's Nathan with the newspaper. It's proof he's alive."

The man shook his head in dismay.

"Can you send me the photo?" the man said.

"Sure." Gabrielle sniffed and tapped on her phone.

Abby took three quick steps inside. "Are you a reporter?" she asked sharply.

The man got up and smiled at her. He held out his hand. "Tom McCormick. I write for the *New Yorker Chronicle*."

"You can't publish that photo," Abby said. "There are details in it that we want to keep from the public."

He blinked, and then his face brightened. "Aren't you Lieutenant Abby Mullen? You were the hostage negotiator who saved those people during that bank robbery. Are you part of this case?"

She sighed. "Mr. McCormick, publishing details about the investigation might hurt our chances of getting Nathan back safely. I would really appreciate it if you waited before publishing anything—"

"I asked Tom to do this interview," Gabrielle said, her voice raw. "He's interviewed me before. And we need the media on this. We need the public's awareness."

Abby hesitated. Gabrielle wasn't wrong. More exposure meant more donations. And if the kidnappers saw that their payout was on its way, they would have good reason to keep Nathan alive. Besides, they could use the article to send a message to the kidnappers. "Don't publish the photo," she said. "And I would appreciate it if you run your article by me. When do you intend to publish it?"

"I promised Gabrielle that we'll post it on our website this evening," McCormick said. "And it'll be published in our paper tomorrow."

"Let me go over it before you publish it, and I'll give you a quote," Abby said.

McCormick nodded. "I'll send it to you in a few hours."

Abby gave him her phone number and email and then glanced at Eden. They went up to the third floor, leaving Gabrielle and the reporter to proceed with their interview. They entered Eden's bedroom and shut the door behind them.

"I went to the Tillman farm this morning," Abby said in a low voice.

"Oh." Eden sat on the bed heavily. "Is . . . is David still there?"

"Yes." Abby examined her carefully. "Eden, the man you described, the one you saw a few times in the past month, is part of the Tillman cult."

The blood drained from Eden's face. "It . . . it can't be."

"You didn't recognize him?"

"He must have joined after I left. I've never seen him there."

"His name is Karl Adkins. Does that ring a bell?"

"No, I've never heard that name before."

That made sense. If Otis Tillman wanted to send someone to stalk Eden and her family, he'd send a member Eden wouldn't recognize.

"Any idea why a man from Tillman's farm would stalk your house?"

"No." Eden seemed stunned. "I told you, we'd left that part of our life behind us. I was sure we'd never see any of them again."

"We took him in for questioning," Abby said. "And we want you to point him out in a lineup, to make sure he's the guy you saw."

"Now?"

"No. We'll need time to organize it, and we want to interrogate him first." Abby leaned against the wall. "I need to know more about the Tillman cult. Anything I can use when questioning Karl."

"I don't know how much I can help you. I haven't been in touch with them for seven years."

"Back then, how was it? Tell me anything you remember."

Eden stared at her hands. "When I joined, it was a very small group. Maybe a dozen people. David was like Otis's right-hand man. Otis was very religious, and he had interesting ideas. He believed confessions should be more than a report of your sins. It was more like therapy. Each of us had three confession sessions every week. And he would help us through our difficulties. He was very intuitive—and sensitive. I always left those confessions feeling so . . . free and light. I just waited for the next one."

"What did you tell him during those confessions?" Abby asked, keeping her tone natural.

"Everything, Abby. There were no secrets during confessions. No judgment. And it wasn't just the confessions. He preached a lot. He could preach for four or five hours, quoting long passages from the Bible word for word."

Long sermons were used by some cult leaders to induce a trancelike state in their members. During such a state it was much easier to plant ideas in their heads. Reverend Jim Jones, whose cult had ended in the Jonestown mass suicide, had been known to talk for hours, intermingling his Bible preaching with his social agenda while constantly hammering in the importance of single-minded loyalty.

"We felt important," Eden continued. "He kept telling us we were changing Christianity, modernizing it. Armageddon was coming, and it was our job to make Christianity more accessible to the younger generation, to save their souls."

"Was there a date for Armageddon?"

"It changed a few times. Otis received signs God was postponing it because he saw the good work we were doing." Eden's voice was monotone. "I know how it sounds—"

"Never mind how it sounds," Abby said softly. She'd heard much crazier cult dogmas before. For cult members, no matter how strange the preachings of the leader were, they became the absolute truth. "Just tell me."

"The community grew. I was really happy at first. I had a purpose. I loved the people around me. I fell in love with David, and we had this wonderful child." Eden's voice cracked.

"But then . . . ?"

"Otis began saying the FBI was after us. Satan was using the FBI as his army. We got guns, and we all learned to use them. We were constantly afraid the FBI would attack. And we knew that if anyone left the cult, he was at risk of being killed by FBI assassins. As long as we stayed at the farm, Otis could protect us."

"Where were the guns stored?"

"They kept stashing them in different places and moving them around. At some point I couldn't keep track anymore. I couldn't shoot straight anyway, so it didn't matter. My job, if the FBI attacked, was to pray for God to smite them."

"How did you leave?" Abby asked. "You must have been terrified."

"I was, but . . . I had Gabi and Nathan. And the confessionals . . . Otis said if we really want to be pure, we should do the private confession sessions with nothing materialistic to weigh us down."

"Like what? Money?"

"Like clothing."

Abby's heart sank with every word.

"So I left," Eden said. "It was hard. Much harder than I thought. I was terrified. And empty. Otis was furious, and warned me we would all die without him. I still did it against his will. It wasn't like when we were kids, when Moses chose us to leave unharmed."

"Moses didn't *choose* us," Abby said, startled. "We were lucky."

Eden blinked. "He chose us. That's why we weren't in the hall when . . . when it all ended."

"Eden, we *were* in that hall," Abby said. "Don't you remember? Moses held a damn gun to my head and told me to tell the police to stay back. He said if they tried to break inside, he would shoot me."

Eden shook her head. "No, we were in a different room. He told us we were chosen to be saved."

"I read the transcripts of that phone call," Abby told her softly, sitting on the bed by Eden's side. "I told them everything. He held a gun to my head. We were all together in the same hall. We were never *chosen*. Moses wanted us *all* to die."

"That's impossible," Eden blurted. "Then why do I remember—"

"We went through a terrible trauma," Abby said, taking Eden's hand in her own. "Our minds had to come to terms with what had happened. Moses told all of us over the years that we were chosen. And then, when we survived, your mind manufactured a false memory in which Moses chose us to survive. But, Eden, he didn't. We were there with everyone else. We were all supposed to die."

CHAPTER 34

Abby sat in her car, the traffic sludging forward at a snail's pace. She thought about Eden, envying the woman for her fuzzy memory of those last days in the Wilcox cult. If anything, Abby's memories were just getting sharper by the day.

She now remembered the other children. She recalled a chubby boy, and a girl with glasses, and other faces, and even a name or two. The recollection of one of their last days sprang to mind. All of them—

—*washing their hands, standing side by side above the large metal sink outside. Abihail was scrubbing her hands violently. She'd obtained a fresh metal scrubber from her mom, and it was doing a wonderful job. Her hands throbbed with that cleansing pain that she'd learned to love. Some of the other children just washed their hands with soap, but Eden had taught Abihail how to really get the job done, scrubbing away every bit of dirt. And Abihail had found out that when her palms were raw with pain, when they were scratched and bleeding, the grown-ups in their community treated her differently. They smiled at her more. Commended her on her devotion. The pain she felt was a sign of her purity.*

Maybe soon, they'd let her work in the flower fields. All the bigger kids were working there now. Abihail had no one to play with throughout the day.

She finished, stepping away, spreading her fingers, tiny pinpricks throughout her hands. She joined everyone else waiting for Father Wilcox's sermon.

Everyone seemed worried. The grown-ups were talking in hushed whispers, the children silent, looking confused and scared. Abihail didn't know what was going on. She caught snippets of words that meant nothing to her.

" . . . Chopper went by twice today . . ."

" . . . think I saw someone watching . . ."

" . . . Someone told the cops . . ."

Cops.

A jolt of fear shot through her. The cops wanted to tear down their Family. She knew that. They were guided by corruption and hatred.

Where was Father Wilcox? He should have been there, preaching, calming everyone down. When Father talked, everyone always relaxed.

Abihail stepped out of the crowd, went to Father's study to see if he was there. But the structure was empty, the windows dark. Then she noticed a lone figure standing in the flower field, his white robe flapping in the wind, the setting sun casting its last rays on his face. Father.

She walked over to him hesitantly. "Father Wilcox? Everyone's waiting."

He didn't budge, didn't acknowledge her, staring straight ahead, his eyes distant. Abihail had never seen him like this. She'd seen him angry, of course. And often she'd seen him excited. But right now he looked sad. And tired.

After a few seconds, he said, "Consider the lilies, Abihail."

She knew the rest, had heard it dozens of times in Father's sermons. "'How they grow,'" she said. "'They toil not, they spin not . . .'" She paused, trying to remember the rest.

Father Wilcox smiled. "'And yet I say unto you, that Solomon in all his glory was not arrayed like one of these.'"

"I like lilies," Abihail said.

"I like lilies too. The lily is the state's wildflower; did you know that?"

"Yes, of course." She didn't.

"We're just trying to spread beauty here, Abihail. Using God's blessings to enrich the world. But the police are after us."

"Flowers can't be bad."

To her surprise, Father laughed. "Out of the mouth of babes." He knelt beside her. "You take after your parents, Abihail. You're a very clever girl."

She felt the blood rushing to her face as she smiled shyly. "Thank you."

"What are your favorite flowers in the Garden of Eden?"

"The ones over there." She pointed. "The tall ones."

He looked at her thoughtfully. "Like I said, very clever. Why are they your favorite?"

There was a right answer to that; she was sure of it. But she'd just liked them since Isaac had taught her to hide there. "Because they're beautiful?" They weren't that beautiful, not really. They didn't really work in a bouquet. Her mom never used them in the flower shop; they were too tall.

But still, that was where all the children worked every day now with small knives, cutting the pods.

"They're our most precious possession," Father said. "You know what they're called?"

"Yeah," Abihail said. "Poppies."

A sudden honk made Abby start, lost in the past. She exhaled, letting her car drift slowly down the road, recalling the poppy field in the Garden of Eden.

CHAPTER 35

Carver waited for Abby in the monitor room, staring moodily through the one-way mirror. Abby shut the door behind her and stepped to his side. Karl Adkins and his attorney, Richard Styles, sat in the interrogation room together. Their eyes were shut, their lips moving softly.

"Praying?" she asked.

"Yeah," Carver said. "Karl likes praying. He does it every time I ask a straightforward question about the case. If I say, 'Karl, what do you think about the weather today?' I get a long, exhausting answer. If I ask why he's stalking Gabrielle online, I get . . . this." He gestured at the one-way mirror.

"Eden didn't give me a lot to work with," Abby said. "The Tillman cult have some automatic firearms on the premises, but she doesn't know where. When she left, Otis was using his position for sexual gratification with the women in the cult."

"So much for female empowerment."

"He taught his cult members to be wary of the law, particularly the FBI." Abby clenched her jaw. "I doubt we'll be able to get much by questioning Karl, but it's worth a shot."

"I talked to Wong on the phone," Carver said. "Otis showed her around and let her look inside each of the cabins and the rooms in the house. She didn't see Nathan, but they didn't exactly let her search the premises thoroughly."

"We need a search warrant."

"She's trying to get one, but she's getting pushback from the judge. Sounds like Otis made a lot of friends in Suffolk County. Since all we have so far is one cult member who followed Gabrielle online, the judge said it's not enough for a search warrant. Can't argue with that; she has seventy thousand followers."

"More like ninety thousand," Abby said. "She's getting new followers by the bucketload. But Eden saw Karl by her house—"

"She didn't ID him yet; all we have is a sketch, and apparently, sixty members of the Tillman community say Karl hasn't left the farm for more than ten minutes in the past month."

"We need to organize that lineup."

"I have a guy on it. It'll be ready in a few hours."

Abby checked the time. "Damn it," she muttered.

"Late for something?"

"I forgot to call Sam," she answered. "I need to pick her up, but she won't come home with me."

Carver frowned. "Why not?"

"There's a snake there."

"In your house?"

"It's my son's new pet. Never mind, I'll go pick her up from her dad as soon as this is over." Abby was fairly certain Sam would go home with her without a fuss—if she sweetened the deal enough. If she couldn't negotiate *this*, she didn't deserve her job title.

She quickly sent a text to Samantha. I'm sorry, things are hectic at work. I'll call you in an hour. She'd call Sam, negotiate a truce, and pick her up.

"Let's have a chat with Adkins," she said.

"Okay. I didn't have any luck so far, but maybe together we might be able to squeeze him."

181

That sentiment made Abby pause. She and Carver had interrogated together before, more than fifteen years ago when they were at the academy.

It hadn't been great. To use their instructor's own poetic description, "A debacle of epic proportions such as I've never seen in all my many years of service." Which had been an exaggeration. Probably.

They'd kept interrupting each other. At one point, Abby had made a point, and Carver had contradicted her. They'd *argued* in front of the bemused suspect, or rather, the recruit who simulated the suspect.

"Can you let me lead the questioning?" she asked lightly.

Carver shrugged. "Sure."

Abby strode into the interrogation room, her eyes adjusting to the harsh neon light. She smiled at Karl and his lawyer, taking the chair across the table. Carver sat by her side, folding his arms.

"I'm sorry for the wait," Abby said apologetically. "We're organizing a lineup, but it's taking longer than we anticipated. Can we get you anything? Water? Coffee?"

"No, I'm good," Karl said, just as the lawyer said he'd love a cup of water please.

"We'll get you that in a minute." Abby smiled at Karl. "The lineup is a formality, really. We need to cross out even the most unlikely suspects. Obviously, you have a solid alibi. We've already talked to a few people who said they saw you on the day in question in the . . . how do you call it? Community?"

"The Progressive Christian Community," Karl said.

"Right," Abby said brightly. "Otis told me about it. Do you like living there?"

Karl's muscles seemed to relax a fraction. "Yes," he said. "It really changed my life."

"When did you join the community?"

"Seven years ago."

Abby's face remained blank, hiding her surprise. Eden had told her she'd never seen Karl before. She'd left when Nathan was less than a year old. Assuming she was telling the truth, it sounded like Karl had joined the community immediately after Eden had left. Had Otis recruited Karl to the cult because of Eden's sudden departure? "Do you remember the exact date?"

"How is that relevant to your case?" Styles asked.

"Just connecting the dots. You know how it is." Abby had found out long ago that if she said *you know how it is* to an aggressive man, he often wanted to seem as if he knew how it was, which made everything easier. The lawyer nodded, satisfied. He knew how it was.

"I joined the community at the beginning of February. And the year would have been . . . 2012."

Less than two weeks after Eden had left. It couldn't be a coincidence. Could Otis have planned this seven years ago? "What were you doing back then?"

"Well, when I joined the community, I mostly worked in the apple orchard."

"I meant, what did you do *before* you joined the community?"

"Oh." Karl seemed startled. He paused for a moment as if trying to remember. "I was a writer."

The shift in Karl's expression was subtle, almost impossible to notice if you didn't look for it. But Abby had been waiting for it. Cult members were often indoctrinated to leave their past lives behind. But you couldn't really erase the past. It just got suppressed. Ask a cult member about their life before they joined the cult, and the memories came flooding back. For a short time, before the cult dominance in their mind reasserted itself, you could glimpse the person as they used to be.

"Really?" Abby asked. "What did you write?"

"Short stories. Sci-fi and fantasy mostly. I got a story published in *Extraordinary Dimensions*."

"Extraordinary Dimensions?"

"It was a very popular online magazine. They paid me three hundred dollars for it."

"Fantastic. So did you publish additional stories for them?"

He frowned. "No. They didn't want the next one I sent. And after that I didn't have time to write. Because I had a lot to do in the community."

She waited for a moment, letting the long silence punctuate his sentence, give it significance. Finally she asked, "How did you join the community?"

"Well, my uncle suggested it."

"Your uncle?"

"Yeah. Otis."

Karl Adkins was Otis Tillman's nephew. How had they missed that up until now? Now that he said it, there were tiny similarities between the two men's chins and noses. She nodded agreeably. "Right! Otis approached you?"

"Yeah. I was between jobs, and he suggested I come work on his farm."

"I'm impressed." Abby grinned at him. "You were, what, back then? Eighteen? And you were happy to drop everything and go work at the apple orchard?"

Karl let out a short laugh. "I didn't want to at first. But . . ." He paused. She could see him trying to recall that moment. How *had* his uncle eventually convinced him? And then his eyes seemed to glaze, and she knew she'd lost Karl the writer. Karl the cult member was back. "He suggested I come over for a few days. To talk to some people. They were doing this amazing work. I wanted to be a part of it."

"Wasn't it difficult? Giving up all the things you were used to doing? There was your writing, of course. And TV, right? I mean, I can't go a week without bingeing a TV series. David Huff told us you aren't allowed to have TVs there. Or cell phones, for that matter."

The atmosphere in the room seemed to tense up.

"We do important work," Karl said. "It's not that we aren't *allowed* TVs or phones. We just don't need them."

"Of course," Abby said. "I forgot. You still have a phone, right? You even have an Instagram account."

Karl said nothing.

"You opened the account, uh . . ." Abby pretended to check her folder. "Three years ago. Four years after you joined. So you got along fine without social media for four years. And then what happened?"

Karl's eyes shut, and his lips moved as he prayed silently.

"Whose idea was it to open that Instagram account?" Abby asked. "*You* didn't need it, like you said. So why open one? An account that essentially follows only one person—Gabrielle Fletcher."

"My client is not answering any more questions," Styles interjected.

"Did you ever meet David Huff's wife, Karl? Her daughter? Or her son?"

Karl kept praying. Carver's phone rang, and he stepped out of the room. Abby asked a few more questions about Nathan, about Gabrielle, about his presence nearby Gabrielle's house. But like Carver had said, all she got were prayers and the lawyer's adamant statements that they were done answering questions.

Finally she said, "I'll go get you both that cup of water," and stepped out of the room.

Carver stood outside, talking on the phone, his expression grim. He motioned for her to wait.

"We're on our way," he said on the phone and hung up.

"What was that all about?" Abby asked.

"A civilian noticed a smear of blood on the door of a Toyota Corolla parked in a parking lot in Staten Island," Carver said. "He called the police. The patrol officer on scene popped the trunk and found an unidentified dead body stuffed inside."

"So why did they call you?" Abby asked. "That's not even in your precinct."

"Forensic team found a muddy shoe under the front passenger seat," Carver said. "It matches the description of the shoes Nathan Fletcher wore when he was kidnapped."

CHAPTER 36

Abby rode with Carver, and the only one speaking in the car was the navigation app. She stared out the window, exhaustion and worry clouding her mind. Details about the crime scene had been sparse. They'd said the body was male. But was it an *adult* male? Dispatch wasn't sure. They were checking. Time went by with no response.

It was also possible that the kid's shoe they'd found wasn't really Nathan's. After all, it wasn't like Eden had bought Nathan's shoes in a boutique. She'd probably bought them at Walmart or Target. There were thousands of kids walking around New York with the same shoes.

But had those kids left just one muddy shoe behind? In a car with a body in the trunk?

"There," Carver said, turning off the navigation app. The red-and-blue lights of the two patrol cars were now their beacon. As they got closer, they saw the ME van, the forensics van, and the unavoidable media vehicles that homed in on crime scenes with unerring instinct.

Carver drove over to the cordoned area, where a young patrolman in uniform handed them the ripped page from a crime scene logbook. Both of them signed their names and were let inside. Abby was the first one out of the car, crouching under the tape, hurrying toward the trunk of the vehicle illuminated by a bright spotlight.

As she got close enough to see the large body inside, she exhaled, realizing that she'd been holding her breath. She'd been expecting to see the body of a small boy in the trunk.

She put a hand up to block the harsh glare of the spotlight as a silhouette of a tall woman took a step toward her. "Lieutenant Mullen. You got here just in time. We were about to remove the body." The woman wore a face mask, but Abby recognized her voice easily. Dr. Valeria Gomez had been the ME in many of her homicide investigations over the years.

"What do we have, Gomez?" Abby asked.

"Male victim in his early fifties. Rigor mortis has fully set while the body was in the trunk, so it is in a rigid fetal position."

Abby peered at the pale body, smelling the unmistakable metallic scent of blood. The victim had been stuffed roughly in the trunk, lying on top of the spare tire. A tripod and a few metal cases were stacked around him as if they had been shoved aside to make room for the body. Whoever had put him in the trunk hadn't bothered emptying it first.

The victim's neck was covered in blood and marred by several dark stab wounds. The man's beige shirt was soaked in blood as well. His eyes were wide open, mouth ajar, a trickle of blood staining his chin.

"On initial inspection livor mortis seems to have appeared only on the lateral right side of the body," Gomez said. "So in all likelihood the body was placed in the trunk very soon after his death."

"Or before?" Carver suggested.

Gomez shrugged. "Medically speaking I can't discount it yet, but all the blood on the driver's seat tells a different story according to our forensics expert. In addition to the stab wounds on the throat and chest, there's a shallow stab wound on the left palm as well as a minor incision across it."

"Defensive wounds?"

"Probably. The blood on the body's lips and mouth indicates trauma to the respiratory system, and the likely culprit is either of these." She pointed at two of the numerous wounds on the throat.

"Time of death?" Abby asked.

"For now, the best I can say is sometime last night, maybe early morning," Gomez answered. "I'll do the autopsy first thing tomorrow, and maybe I'll manage to narrow it down."

Abby took a step back, and took a deep breath. The air in the parking lot smelled like exhaust, trash, and urine, but it was a significant improvement from the odors that rose from the car's trunk. She scrutinized the people working the scene. She didn't recognize the detective and the uniformed cop who were busy sketching it. Carver approached them, shaking the detective's hand. As for the rest—she'd worked with the police photographer before, a dour man with a pretentious demeanor. She was glad to recognize Ahmed Nader from CSU kneeling by the driver's seat.

"Hey, Ahmed," she said, sticking her hands in her pockets.

"Abby Mullen," he said, straightening. "What? You decided that you miss homicide? Or were you just longing for my company?"

"Definitely longing for your company," she said. "But I'm also part of the Nathan Fletcher kidnapping task force. What are you looking at?"

"A muddy footprint on the floor mat of the driver's seat. It's a good print, and it doesn't match the victim's shoes. It seems like a twelve, maybe even thirteen."

Could they be Karl's shoes? He had a pair of worn-out tennis shoes, but they weren't particularly large. "If I send you a shoe sole photograph, would you be able to see if it matches?"

He straightened. "Maybe. Talking about shoes, I suppose this is the one you're really interested in."

He produced a plastic bag from a nearby container and held it up to the spotlight. A small shoe. "We found it on the floor of the front passenger seat underneath a man's coat. The coat is definitely too large for a child; it could be the victim's."

Abby peered at it through the translucent plastic. The shoe was covered in brown stains. "Is that blood?"

"No. Mud. The shoe is still soggy and is stained with mud both inside and out. Whoever wore it stepped in mud up to his ankle."

"Either that or he was buried in mud," Abby said. "It could explain the muddy footprint on the driver's side."

Ahmed raised an eyebrow. "Always finding the worst possible scenario for everything."

"You of all people should know a muddy article of clothing isn't good news."

Ahmed motioned her over to the other side of the car. "Come on, I need to show you something."

Abby followed him, and crouched by the open passenger door. The interior of the car smelled like a slaughterhouse. There was smeared blood on the steering wheel, the seats, and the dashboard. Multiple blood spatters on the top part of the driver's window as well as the inside of the door. The body had stab wounds on the left side. If the victim had been the passenger, the attacker had probably been the driver. But if he had been the driver . . . she glanced at the door. The attacker would have stood outside the car.

"What can you tell me about the blood trajectory?" she asked.

"We didn't measure it yet," Ahmed said. "But you see how the blood on the window is mostly on the top part of the window? Just one smear on the bottom. If I had to guess, our victim sat in the driver's seat, and the window was lowered. The attacker stabbed him through the window. Victim raised his left hand to protect his throat, got those two defensive wounds on the left palm. But that's not what I wanted to show you. Look here." He pointed at the vehicle mat on the passenger's side.

Abby leaned closer and saw what he was pointing at. Another partial muddy footprint.

"It matches the shoe we found under the seat. It seems like the kid who wore it stepped here before taking it off."

Abby wasn't convinced. "Or someone tossed the shoe here, and it later rolled under the seat."

Ahmed shook his head. "See those? Don't touch." He pointed at the back of the passenger seat.

"What am I looking at?"

"Two hairs."

She saw them. Two light-blond hairs, significantly below the headrest. As if a fair-haired child had sat in the seat. And left his footprint on the floor mat.

"You said the shoe was still soggy," she said, becoming excited. "Was the mud fresh? Can you estimate—"

"I can't estimate *anything* yet." Ahmed smiled. "But it's not likely they had a dead kid's body sitting in the front passenger seat, right?"

"It would be unusual."

"There's the understatement of the year. Now that I got you all excited, I have to be the bearer of bad news. See those stains of blood?" He gestured underneath the two blond hairs. Abby squinted and saw them. Two dark blots. Blood.

"They *could* be from our unlucky guy back there." Ahmed pointed toward the trunk. "He's definitely spread a generous amount of blood everywhere."

"But the trajectory doesn't work."

"Not really."

The blots were round, not oval, which indicated the blood hadn't come in a spurt from the side but rather that someone who was bleeding had leaned back on the seat.

"We'll do some blood comparisons," Ahmed said. "I'll tell you as soon as I have more information. The blood doesn't necessarily belong to whoever left those hairs there."

Abby nodded, straightening. She knew forensics could sometimes mislead. Initial conclusions were often scrapped when new details emerged. But for now, it appeared that Nathan Fletcher had been in this car, sitting in the front passenger seat. And he'd been alive and bleeding.

CHAPTER 37

Eden was alone in a room in the police station. They'd told her to wait a few more minutes as they prepared the lineup. Her heart pounded in her chest as she waited, wondering if she would recognize the man Abby had called Karl Adkins. A man from Otis Tillman's community.

Who'd been stalking them.

She shivered and hugged herself. Waiting. Alone.

Even at home, she was alone. Well, not really. Gabrielle was home. And there was always an officer downstairs in the kitchen in case the kidnapper called.

But the initial connection that had formed between her and Gabrielle when the kidnapper had first called had dissipated. Her daughter had become that distant girl she'd been lately, spending her entire time shut in her room or downstairs being consoled by her friends or that guy Eric. And now Gabrielle was busy managing the donations site, sending thank-you notes to the donors, getting more interviews. Eden was relieved her daughter had taken control of this crisis, that she was doing all she could to get Nathan home. But she couldn't shake the feeling that Gabrielle despised her for not doing it herself.

And those officers in the kitchen, an interchangeable group of men. All of them armed. Eden hadn't been this close to guns since her time in the Tillman community. Guns always made her uncomfortable. Cops always made her uncomfortable. The only one she trusted was Abihail. But now, whenever she talked to Abihail, her past came floating back.

And of course, there was a Nathan-shaped vacuum in her life. Every hug she didn't get, every bedtime kiss she didn't give, every moment she couldn't ask him how his day was or what he wanted for dinner, they all cut into her. Drained her.

For the first time in years, Eden missed David. Just because he was another person she could talk to who would share the difficult moments with her. Another person she could hug.

She took out her phone and opened her chat with Isaac. He'd been a real lifesaver these past two days, encouraging her, giving her strength to keep on going. He'd told her he'd also joined the fundraising for the ransom, donating some of his savings, and had gotten his friends to donate as well.

It's Nathan's bedtime, she wrote.

The three dots indicator appeared almost instantly. Isaac took special care to be attentive to his chat since the kidnapping. I'm sorry. I can't even imagine what you're going through.

His bedtime is the most difficult part of the day, she wrote. And it was. Because although Nathan was becoming more and more independent, at bedtime he needed her. He would go to sleep with his door open, verifying that she was downstairs and that she could hear him. Otherwise, he would get scared. It was the only time in the day he wanted her to kiss him. Any other time it was "Ew, Mom, cut it out." But the bedtime kiss was important.

But then, earlier she'd thought that the most difficult part of the day was making dinner, because she made dinner just for herself and Gabrielle. And before that, the most difficult part was the afternoon, when Nathan would usually run up and down the stairs. And before that, the most difficult part was in the mornings, when she woke up and he was still not there. And the night was the most difficult part because she couldn't sleep, and when she did, she had nightmares.

Every minute of the day was the most difficult part of the day. How's Gabrielle doing? Isaac wrote.

She's keeping herself busy. And she's doing wonders with the ransom fund

It's been rising really fast. You'll have the ransom in a few days. And then you'll get your boy back

She wiped a tear from her cheek. The tears came throughout the day, like a sneeze or an itch. Abihail said that even when we have the ransom, we might not get him back

Abihail is wrong, I'm sure of it.

She wished she had his optimism. I hope so. I'm at the police station now. For the lineup I told you about

Oh good. Do you feel like you can identify him?

Eden exhaled. Was she? I'm not sure

Don't let them rush you. Take your time and get it right.

Okay

After a few seconds he wrote, Any news about their investigation?

Not yet. They won't really tell me anything

You need to insist that they do

He was right. She would. I talked to Abihail today about the day we left the Family. She says I remembered it wrong. I remember we weren't in the hall with everyone. But she said we were. Do you remember that day?

She waited, watching the typing indicator as it blinked on and off a few times. Approaching footsteps made her put the phone away.

A pudgy officer entered the room. "Ms. Fletcher? We're ready."

She followed him, hardly breathing, down a neon-lit hallway into a dark room. One side of the room was just a large pane of glass looking out onto a gray chamber, six men standing against the wall. Eden paused in the doorway, petrified.

"They can't see you," the officer told her. "It's one-way glass."

She stepped into the room and peered through the one-way mirror. Six men, two of them bearded, the rest clean shaven. One was fatter than the others. All had black hair. And one . . .

And one was *him*. Number four. She could imagine him in the street, his eyes scanning around him, a predator in search of prey.

"Take your time," the officer said. "There's no rush."

"It's number four," she blurted.

"Are you sure?"

Something in his tone made her fearful. What if she got it wrong? They would have to let this Karl Adkins go. And if he had taken Nathan, if he knew anything . . .

She stared at each of them, their faces blending into a mix of noses and eyes and twisted lips.

"I'm sure," she finally said, half expecting him to sigh or shake his head, disappointed with her. But he didn't. He just nodded and marked something on his clipboard.

"Did I get it right?"

"I can't tell you that. You would need to talk to the detective."

"Where's the detective?" She'd expected Abihail . . . Abby, or that Detective Carver, to take her to the lineup. Not this unfamiliar man.

The officer hesitated. "He's been called to check something out," he finally said.

"Something about Nathan?"

"Ma'am, it would really be best if you talk to him about it."

Isaac had told her she needed to insist. But now her resolve melted; her shoulders slumped. "Was there anything else?"

"No, that's all. I'll walk you out."

As they stepped out into the hallway, someone said, "Eden?"

She frowned at the man, but it took her a few seconds to recognize him here, so out of place. It was her neighbor Frank.

"Oh hey," she said weakly.

"They brought me here for a lineup," he explained. "To see if I can recognize the man."

"Recognize him? You saw him around the neighborhood?"

"They didn't tell you?" Frank frowned. "I saw . . . well, I thought I saw Nathan get into his car."

"You saw it?" she whispered, shocked. "But why didn't you—"

"I wasn't sure," Frank quickly added. "Just when the police came over to ask me about it. I feel terrible, of course. If there's anything I can do to help . . ."

Anything he could do. Eden wanted to claw his eyes out. He'd *seen* her son being taken, and said nothing. Didn't call her. Or the police. Went on with his day like nothing had happened.

"How's Gabrielle doing?" Frank asked softly.

"She's doing fine," Eden said automatically.

"Tell her I said that if there is anything I could do, you can call me. I'd be glad to help. That's why I'm here. I want to help. I want—"

She couldn't listen to him anymore. She strode away, her head pounding, fists clenched tight. The officer led her outside, and she walked in a daze back to her car, slumped into the driver's seat, lips trembling.

Sobbing, she took out her phone, desperate to tell Isaac about her encounter. She saw he'd sent her a message while she was looking at the lineup. It took her a moment to recall what they'd been talking about.

I don't really remember that day. But I'm pretty sure Abihail's right. We were in the hall with everyone

She shut her eyes. If she couldn't trust her memory of that day, could she really be sure she remembered the man from the street? What if she'd gotten it wrong? Would they let him go?

She dialed both Carver and Abihail, but neither answered. That familiar crushing loneliness closed in again.

CHAPTER 38

"They were about to close," Will said, walking into the task force room with seven Chick-fil-A bags in his hands.

Abby raised her eyes from the crime scene photos. "Did you tell them to put—"

"Bacon and ranch dressing on your sandwich, yes." Will sighed, unloading the bags on the large table. "As I've told you before, I find your orders from fast food restaurants deeply ironic."

"Why are they ironic?" Carver rummaged in the bags and retrieved a chicken wrap.

"Will thinks I'm committing slow suicide by eating a lot of butter and bacon," Abby said. "While half my job is convincing people not to kill themselves."

"He's got a point." Marshall opened his salad container and poured in some dressing.

"Well, people need a reason to live." Abby located her chicken sandwich. "Butter and bacon are two very good reasons."

"Where are we with the search warrant for the Tillman farm?" Will asked.

Abby took a bite of her sandwich. Pure bliss. How did some people manage without bacon? "Wong still hasn't called me back." The man Eden had picked out of the lineup had indeed been Karl Adkins. With that, they felt they should easily have enough to get a search warrant, and Detective Wong said she'd take care of it.

"Just got a message from Detective Turner," Carver said. He was munching his wrap while reading something on his phone. Turner was the detective assigned to the murder case. "We have a probable ID on our murder victim. Liam Washington. The vehicle is registered to him, and his driver's license photo matches the body. We have an address in Albany."

"Could he be the one who kidnapped Nathan?" Will asked.

"The car doesn't match the witness account," Carver said. "But we can't discount it. The witness didn't get a good look at the kidnapper's face. He didn't point out anyone in the lineup."

"Albany?" Abby frowned. It wasn't anywhere near Tillman's farm on Long Island. But maybe the address was out of date.

"Suppose we have two accomplices, Liam and someone else," Carver said. "And two vehicles. One of them kidnaps Nathan, and they take him somewhere. Then, at some point, Liam decides to move Nathan."

"Maybe he saw they might actually pull this off and get the ransom," Marshall said. "It's one thing to plan this, and it's a different thing entirely to see the money being collected. He fantasized about it and figured he doesn't want to split the ransom. He put Nathan in the car and was about to drive off when the other guy shows up."

"The other guy knocks on the window," Carver said. "Liam figures he'll just sell him a bullshit story about taking the kid for a ride. Lowers the window, gets a knife in his throat."

"Or he saw Gabrielle's post and felt guilty," Will suggested. "Figured he'd drop Nathan at the bus station and drive off. Except his friend had other ideas."

"That works," Abby agreed. "Either way, the accomplice kills Liam, shoves him in the trunk, drives to the parking lot to drop the car, far enough to throw us off. And either someone picks him up, or he calls an Uber."

"Where are we with the shoe print?" Carver asked. "Did anyone check if it matches the sole of Karl Adkins's shoe?"

"Adkins's lawyer raised seven hells about it," Barnes said. "Said we can't take a picture of his client's shoe without a warrant, and his client isn't under arrest, and so on and so forth. We'll take care of that later."

"If the murderer knows what he's doing, he got rid of those shoes after he dumped the car." Marshall grunted. "And I'm not sold on the connection to the Tillman cult."

"Still, it's worth checking out," Abby said.

"I said we'll do it later," Barnes said, raising an eyebrow.

Abby decided to drop it. Arguing with the two men would only make them hostile. The last thing she needed right now was a face-off with a couple of Major Case detectives.

Carver got up and shoved his phone in his pocket. "Turner is driving to Albany. I'll join him, see what we find."

Abby considered joining them as well and glanced at her phone to check the time. "Oh shit!"

"What is it?" Will asked.

"I forgot to pick up Sam from her dad's." She shut her eyes as the waves of guilt washed over her. What was Sam thinking right now? She'd left home dramatically on Saturday, and Abby, instead of trying to talk to her, had ignored her completely for the entire weekend. Epic mom fail. To make things worse, Monday and Tuesday this week were Steve's days with the kids anyway, so Sam would just stay there.

"Be right back," she blurted and stepped out of the room. It was half past ten. She always gave Sam a hard time if she caught her using her phone after ten, which just increased the failure of what was about to transpire. She called Sam.

Sam let it ring for a good five seconds before picking up. "Yeah." Her voice was cold, impersonal. No better than Abby deserved.

"Honey, I wanted to come by and talk."

"Now?" Sam sounded incredulous. "Dad's going to bed soon."

Abby sighed. "There's an emergency at work."

"Uh-huh."

"I figured I could pick you up so you can sleep at home with us tonight."

"Well, I do need to pick up some clothes," Samantha said.

Abby brightened. "Of course. I'll pick you up in a bit."

"Just one question. Is the snake still at *your* home?"

"I guess it is."

"Then I'm not going near that place."

Abby sighed. "Sam . . ."

"Why do you care where I sleep? You aren't even there. I talked to Ben; he said he was with Grandpa and Grandma the entire weekend."

When Sam needed something from her, she handled her like a pro. But when she was angry, it was like talking to the embodiment of Abby's own guilt. Every sentence was a barb that hit home.

"How are you getting to school tomorrow?"

"Dad's taking me on his way to work."

"Okay," Abby said. "I'll come tomorrow afternoon to drop Ben, and we'll talk it over."

"Sure."

"Good night, hon, I love you."

"Night, Mom." Sam managed to inject enough venom into her tone to make it sound as if she'd been coerced to say even that.

Abby hung up and decided that for her guilt to feel complete, she should check up on her other child. Ben was asleep by now, she hoped, so she called her mother.

"Hi, dear," her mother said. "He's already asleep."

"I thought so. Did you have a nice day?"

"Yes. We bought some frozen mice for his snake. He was very happy."

"The snake or the birthday boy?"

"Both, really. Where are you, still at work? Didn't you say that in your new position there won't be any long weekends?"

"Something special came up."

"Still, Abby, when you divorced, you said—"

"I know what I said, Mom." Abby used the tone Sam had used on her only minutes before. "It really is something I couldn't have predicted. Do you . . . do you remember the two other kids from the Wilcox cult?"

"Eden and Isaac?" Her mother didn't even hesitate; the names came in a blink. "Of course."

"Isaac and I stayed in touch, but Eden disappeared." Abby swallowed. "It turns out she's been living in New York. It looks like she had a bit of a rough time growing up. And now her son has been kidnapped."

"Oh, Abby." Her mother's voice became a cracked whisper. "That poor woman."

"There's a good detective on the case. Jonathan Carver. But I can't just drop it." She struggled, trying to formulate the need to stay on this. To do whatever she could.

There was a long silence, and then her mother said, "My biggest regret is that you never had a brother or a sister. You know, me and Hank tried, but—"

"Eden isn't my sister, Mom. It's not that."

"You two grew up together, right? You've gone through terrible things." Her mother's voice was raspy. Was she crying? "When Hank and I decided to become foster parents, we wanted to take you and another child in. But the social worker said that the psychologist decided it was best for the three of you to be apart. They were worried that if you stayed together, it might hinder your development. You all had strange habits. The handwashing thing. You remember? You used to wash your hands until they were bleeding."

"I remember." She didn't tell her mother about her latest relapse.

"When I realized I was too old to have a baby, I regretted not insisting on it," her mother said. "Maybe if I'd insisted—"

"You can't know what would have happened."

"Still, I'm glad you're there to help her now. You're right to feel protective."

"Yeah." Abby leaned on the wall. "It's going to be a late night. Don't wait up for me. And I'll probably need you to get Ben ready for school."

"Of course, dear."

Abby hung up and was about to reenter the task force room, then thought better of it. Instead she called Ahmed.

"Hey, Mullen."

"Ahmed, that footprint? On the floor mat of the driver's seat?"

"Yeah. You said you'd send me a photo of the sole of your suspect."

"We're having some difficulties getting it. Listen, the feds have a footwear database, right?"

"Yeah. I can send it over to them, but it might take some time to get an answer."

"The task force has a liaison from the bureau. Maybe he can get us a speedy response."

"How speedy?"

"The suspect is currently detained, but we can't hold him for much longer. If his shoes don't match the manufacturer, we'll save a lot of time."

"Send me the agent's details. I'll let you know when I have an answer."

"Thanks. Oh, and Ahmed, don't mention my name when you talk to him. This was all your idea. There's a sort of pissing contest here, and I don't want—"

"No worries, Mullen, this call never happened." He hung up.

She sent him Kelly's contact, then went back to the room. Will frowned at his laptop's screen, a perplexed expression on his face.

"What is it?" she asked. "Something wrong?"

"We got an email from Agent Kelly. The feds are saying the picture of Nathan holding the newspaper in his room wasn't edited in any way."

She clenched her jaw. She'd had a feeling there was something wrong with the altered-image theory. It made no sense. But then again, how could that photo have been taken in Nathan's room? Unless Eden had really faked the kidnapping. But that made no sense either because then she wouldn't have made it so abundantly clear that the kidnapping was fake.

"There's no way that makes sense," she finally blurted.

"Yeah," Will agreed. "There's something we're getting wrong."

Abby looked closer at the image on Will's screen, trying to figure out what they were missing. But all she could see was Nathan's frightened gaze.

CHAPTER 39

Pitch dark, as if he'd gone blind. Nathan lay on the cold, hard floor, shivering, his teeth chattering uncontrollably. It had all gone so wrong. For a brief, wonderful minute, he'd thought he was safe. That he was going home.

But there was no home. Only this darkness, and cold, and thirst.

And the memory of that terrible, violent moment. The blade, flashing in the dark, a spray of warm blood hitting his cheek. The wrenching sound of a frantic, wet gurgle. Thrashing. More blood.

A terrible silence that followed.

He had only one shoe, couldn't remember where the other was. He tried to remove the remaining shoe, but the laces were soaked, the knot impossible to untie for his trembling, weak fingers. Finally he gave up, leaving the shoe in place as he curled in the blanket the man had carelessly tossed over him before shutting the door, locking it.

Leaving him in the dark.

There was skittering around him. At some point, something brushed against his fingers, and he pulled his hand back, screaming. Tossing the blanket over his head to protect himself from whatever lived in this small pitch-black space. It was hard to breathe within the blanket, but it was better than exposing himself to whatever was out there.

His back throbbed.

At some point he'd tried to remove his sweatshirt, but the sudden jolt of agony forced him to stop. The cloth was cemented to the deep scratch that ran down his back, the dried blood trapping the loose fibers. He couldn't take it off without tearing the wound open.

He couldn't lie on his back. He couldn't sit down, leaning with his back against the wall. He could only lie on his stomach, one cheek against the floor. Cocooned in the blanket. Trying to ignore the skittering. Trying to ignore the memory.

That wet, wheezing breath. The thrashing. The blood. The silence.

CHAPTER 40

Abby's phone blipped with a new email as she was about to leave and drive home. Rubbing her eyes, she tapped at her screen.

"We got an email from forensics about the shoe print," she said, scanning through the message quickly. Ahmed outlined the footprint's characteristics, detailing an increased wear pattern on the right side of the print as well as a distinguishable scuff mark on the heel. He pointed out that because of the tread-wear pattern, he would likely be able to match it accurately with the corresponding shoe as long as they found it soon. If they took too long to find the shoe, its wear pattern would change, making a match impossible.

Using the assistance of the bureau's footwear database, he'd managed to find the manufacturer and the particular model—a Hawkwell men's steel-toe boot.

"Was Karl Adkins wearing boots when you took him in?" Marshall asked, skimming the email.

"No," Abby muttered. "He wore tennis shoes."

"I guess forensics saved us some legwork." Marshall grinned. "Actually, they saved us some footwork, right?"

Hilarious people they had at Major Case. Abby clicked the link Ahmed had provided, which took her to Hawkwell's website, displaying a pair of brown boots. Definitely not what Karl had on.

She got up and stepped out of the room, dialing Wong for the third time that evening. To her surprise, the detective answered the phone.

"Hey, Mullen." Wong sounded exhausted.

"Wong, I thought you forgot about me."

"How could I forget the person who screwed my evening so thoroughly?" Wong said. "I left the Tillman compound five minutes ago."

"You searched it?" Abby smiled at Marshall and Barnes as they strode out of the room, their coats on, probably on their way home. They nodded at her.

"No. I didn't get the search warrant for the entire premises. The judge approved a search warrant only for Karl Adkins's cabin."

"What? But—"

"He said there was nothing linking the entire community to the crime. He pointed out that you don't try to get a search warrant for an entire neighborhood if one resident is suspected in a crime."

"But it's not a neighborhood. It's a cult."

"I guess definitions differ. As far as that judge was concerned, it's a religious community. He said that, and I quote, 'there's no legal definition for a cult,' and therefore he can't sign a search warrant based on such a definition. I told you. Otis Tillman has some friends in high places."

"So you searched Karl Adkins's cabin?"

Wong took a long breath. "I almost didn't. A bunch of those guys blocked the way. Armed with shotguns. Things got very tense. I had a really bad feeling there, Mullen. I think we were close to things getting out of hand."

Abby shut her eyes. She'd told Wong to be careful, but she should have gone there herself. "But they let you search it?"

"Yeah. Otis showed up and stopped it before things got ugly. Then he led us to Adkins's cabin."

"And?"

"No Nathan, no secret gun cache, no hidden compartments. Four men reside there, and for a bedroom of four men it's unusually tidy. Almost no personal belongings, a few Bibles, and that's it. No laptop or cell phone either."

Abby sighed. "Thanks."

"Sure. I'm going to get a drink, and then I'm off to bed. Good night, Mullen." Wong hung up.

Abby had a new email from Tom McCormick, the journalist who'd interviewed Gabrielle. He'd sent Abby the article like they'd agreed. She skimmed it, making sure he hadn't said anything about the photo or the voice message. The article was as clickbait-y as it could possibly get, with a lot of pathos and little content, mostly focusing on Gabrielle's rise to fame before the tragedy of her brother's kidnapping.

Abby had promised the man a quote. She had to assume Nathan was still alive. It was more than likely that whoever held him now was involved in the murder of Liam Washington. They were violent and probably very agitated at the moment. She didn't want them agitated. Agitated people made impulsive decisions. She wanted them to feel in complete control.

She replied to the email, writing that *The NYPD's first and foremost goal is to return Nathan back home, alive and safe.*

It was an empty sentence, which was obvious to most. But the kidnappers, in their state of heightened fear, might think the NYPD was mainly after them. She wanted to reassure them this wasn't the case. A ransom was being collected. It could be exchanged for the boy. As long as Nathan was alive, this was still a possibility.

She slipped the phone into her pocket and was about to return to the room when she had a thought. She dialed Wong again.

"What is it this time?" Wong answered.

"Did you see any extra boots in Karl's room?"

There was a short pause. "Yeah. Three pairs of identical boots."

"*Three* pairs?"

"I told you, the cabin housed four people. The boots were by the beds."

"Were they Hawkwell boots, by any chance?"

"Do you think I have a boot fetish? How would I know if they're Hawkwell boots? They were boots."

"I'm sending you a link. Let me know if those are the boots you saw." Abby hung up, and sent Wong the link from Ahmed.

A minute later, she got the response. Definitely the same boots.

Abby strode back into the task force room and sat down by Will. "Wong searched Karl Adkins's cabin. Three of the men had the boots matching the footprint at the crime scene."

"Three of them?"

"Tillman probably buys those boots wholesale for his people. Cheaper that way."

"Okay." Will listed on his fingers. "We have Eden's ex, David, in the cult. Karl Adkins from the cult, who stalked Gabrielle online and in real life. And now multiple pairs of boots, same as the ones used in the crime scene."

"Also, Karl Adkins joined the cult only two weeks after Eden left. With all the rest, it can't be a coincidence."

"What now? Get a search warrant for all the boots in the compound?"

"It might be difficult. The judge already made Wong's life difficult with the *first* search warrant. And Hawkwell is a common boot brand; it's not like this is a slam dunk. I think I'll go there tomorrow, do more digging."

Will leaned back in his chair. "How are you planning to do that?"

"Cults are mostly impenetrable to outsiders," Abby said, looking at Otis's photo taped on the whiteboard. "We need someone from the inside. Eden left too long ago. I need someone who left, or was kicked out, more recently."

"What if you don't find anyone?"

Abby thought it over. "Then I'll have to create my inside man myself," she finally said. "I'll get someone to leave."

CHAPTER 41

Carver counted to five before knocking on the door, Detective Turner standing behind him.

It was a strange quirk of humanity that dictated that if you got any news at nighttime, it was inevitably bad news. The lottery didn't contact you at midnight to tell you that you'd won. A mother didn't shake her child awake while the moon was still up to give him a puppy.

He knocked again and checked the time, though he knew it was half past one in the morning.

The woman who finally opened the door wore a faded green bathrobe, the eyes behind her spectacles swollen and red.

"Oh no," she blurted. "Liam. What happened?"

"Emilia Washington?" Carver said softly, showing her his badge. "I'm Detective Carver from the NYPD. Can we come in?"

She stood aside, let them in, her lips already trembling. He stepped inside carefully, as if the sound of his footsteps would be inappropriate right now. Turner followed, saying nothing. They'd agreed beforehand that Carver would handle the death notification. Carver had suggested it; Turner hadn't argued, hadn't insisted that it was his case.

"Please," Emilia said, shutting the door. "Just tell me."

"I'm sorry, Mrs. Washington," Carver said. "The police found Liam's car in a parking lot on Staten Island this evening. We found the body of a man matching your husband's description inside."

Carver had been a detective for six years, and he'd been a patrol cop before that. He'd done dozens of death notifications. Early on, he'd counted them. But he'd lost count at some point—or more accurately had made the conscious decision to stop counting. These moments stayed with him. A mother finding out that her son had overdosed, showing him a trophy the boy had won when he was eleven. A husband who wept uncontrollably at the loss of his wife, each sob sounding like the gurgle of a drowning man. People had cried, or stared at him in shock, or yelled at him, or fainted, or asked questions, or made accusations. A litany of hurt.

"In a parking lot?" Emilia whispered. "How did he die?"

"It seems like he might have been attacked," Carver said, his tone gentle. He kept his eyes on the woman, gauging her reaction.

"Attacked?" She blinked. "Who . . . ?"

"We don't know yet," Carver said.

"And are you sure . . . he wasn't even supposed to be on Staten Island . . . are you sure it's him?"

"The face matches the photo on his driver's license, and we have a positive ID on his car." Carver didn't add that the man they'd found in the trunk was identical to the one in the photo hanging on the wall behind her. The man who was hugging Emilia, a wide smile on his face, the Statue of Liberty in the background. "We'll probably have a positive ID in the morning, but it's definitely him. I'm very sorry for your loss."

He wasn't about to badger her for her husband's dental records or toothbrush for identification purposes right now. *That*, at least, could wait until morning.

She seemed to waver, as if about to fall. Carver delicately placed a hand on her arm and guided her to the couch. She sat down, her face pale.

"I thought he had an accident," she mumbled. "He always drives so fast at late hours. On those crappy side roads just to avoid the tolls."

Carver and Turner had talked to a cop from the Albany Police Department, finding out that Emilia Washington had called early the previous morning to report that her husband hadn't come home and that his phone was offline. She must have been waiting for her husband the whole day, minutes trickling by, constantly trying to get him on the phone, stuck in the limbo of not knowing.

"Detective Turner, would you mind getting Mrs. Washington a glass of water?" Carver asked.

"Sure," Turner said, already hurrying out of the room.

Carver glanced at an armchair in front of the couch, almost sat in it. But a sudden instinct told him that this was Liam's armchair. Instead, he sat down on the couch beside Emilia.

"Mrs. Washington, when was the last time you saw your husband?"

"Yesterday, around noon. He had a wedding he had to go to."

"A wedding?"

"Liam is a wedding photographer. He had a wedding in Manhattan on Saturday night."

"Isn't that a long way to drive for an evening gig?"

Emilia nodded, wiping her eyes. "I thought so. But his business was struggling. He accepted jobs all over. Manhattan, Long Island, Albany . . . he even drove to Boston a few weeks ago. He spent most days on the road."

Carver let her talk, his mind casually translating the details into motive, opportunity. A struggling business meant an urgent need for money. Going out more could mean that he was busy doing something his wife shouldn't know about. When he investigated a murder, every tiny detail got a dark, twisted tint.

She let out a long shuddering breath. "I only realized he was missing yesterday morning. He'd said he would be getting home late, so I didn't wait up for him. I should have waited up. But I was tired. I get tired in the evenings."

"Do you have his schedule?" Carver asked. "Maybe a list of clients?"

"I can look. I think he has a weekly planner somewhere on his desk."

"Did your husband seem troubled lately?"

"Like I said, his business wasn't doing well. He was worried about—how was he killed?"

"I'm sorry?"

"You said he was attacked. Was he shot?"

"The autopsy will be performed tomorrow, and we'll have the details by—"

"How do I get the body? Do I need to fill out a form or something? I need to plan the funeral. I need to call his brother. Is there a way to see him? Is he on Staten Island? You need to tell them to send him here. Will they send him here?" Emilia fired off the words without giving him an opportunity to answer, her eyes wide, desperate.

Turner reappeared with a glass of water and handed it to Emilia. She took it, gulped, her eyes shut.

"Mrs. Washington, would you mind if we look around?" Carver asked. "Maybe we could find something that would help us with our investigation."

She put down the glass. "Okay," she whispered.

He was about to step into the hallway with Turner when he glimpsed something outside in the darkness.

A shed in the backyard.

He exchanged glances with Turner. The other detective gave him a slight nod and said, "Mrs. Washington, you mentioned a planner? Can you show me where it is?"

"We have a spare room where he does his paperwork," Emilia said, her eyes distant. "I do my ironing there. Sometimes I put laundry on his desk. He hates that."

"Can you show me?" Turner asked.

The woman got up and shuffled down the hall, Turner behind her.

Carver unlocked the back door and stepped out into the yard. The ground was covered in grass, but it grew wild in some parts and was spotted with muddy patches. The shed lay ten yards from the house.

If Nathan had been held there, there was no chance that Emilia didn't know.

He switched on his pocket flashlight and walked over to the door, registered the large sliding bolt that held it shut. No lock. But if anyone was kept inside . . .

He slid the bolt and pulled the door open. A musty smell welcomed him as he let the beam of his flashlight run over the shed's contents. A few gardening tools, an old bicycle, a moldy mattress, three shelves with cans of paint, rusty metal boxes, something that looked like a dog leash.

There was enough room to keep someone here, especially a child. Liam could have kidnapped Nathan and kept him here. Then, at some point, maybe getting worried, he'd decided to move the kid. And his accomplice, displeased, had stabbed him.

It felt wrong. Liam and Emilia's backyard faced the neighbor's house. Someone would have noticed. Nathan would have made noise even if he was tied up. And it was just plain dumb. Not to mention that Carver doubted Emilia would have called the police so quickly if she'd recently had a kidnapped kid in the backyard shed.

He stepped out of the shed and slid the bolt shut. Looked down. A muddy puddle by the shed door.

Nathan's shoe had been soaked in mud.

He glanced at the house, then knelt by the puddle and took out a plastic bag from his pocket. He carefully scraped some mud into the bag. Forensics should be able to compare this to the mud on Nathan's shoe.

A movement in the house drew his gaze. Emilia's silhouette passing by the window, hunched under the weight of her grief. He was almost ashamed of his suspicions.

But Liam had been murdered, and Nathan's shoe had been found at the crime scene. The two were definitely connected. And Carver had to find out how.

CHAPTER 42

The morning sun was almost painful to Abby's sleep-deprived eyes. She adjusted the driver's visor, then fumbled for the cup of coffee and sipped from it, the overly sweet liquid already lukewarm. She'd gone to bed way too late and woken up ridiculously early to get ahead of traffic, and now she felt like death. Her life choices, she had to admit, were questionable. Two and a half hours of sleep were not enough for . . . well, for anything, really. It was a miracle she had managed to drive all the way across Long Island without smashing her car into a tree.

Carver had called her during the drive, filling her in on his meeting with Liam Washington's wife. He'd sounded just as exhausted as she was.

She'd agreed to meet Wong by the turn to the farm, but when she got there, Wong was nowhere to be seen. She checked her phone and saw that Wong had sent her a message. She had been delayed. Abby used the time to open the browser on her phone and search for Tom McCormick's article in the *New Yorker Chronicle*. She skimmed it quickly, making sure it matched the article he'd sent her the day before to review. He'd added her quote, naming her and calling her the "hero of the 2018 bank siege." He'd linked a different article in the online newspaper—the article that had been published on the day of the bank siege. The article had several photos of her—wearing a police vest, talking on the phone, and of course, the final photo that had been published everywhere of the hostages being released with Abby and a guy from ESU ushering them to safety.

She seemed like a hero in the article. But she remembered how she'd felt. The sudden terror that had gripped her when they'd heard a shot fired, and she'd thought the robbers had killed a hostage. That moment when she'd first gotten one of the robbers on the phone and couldn't hear his words because her heart was beating in her ears.

"Hero, my ass," she muttered.

Another link in the recent article caught her eye. A follow-up. She clicked the link. It was a Q and A with Eric Layton, the guy she'd met the day before. He'd told her he worked with Gabrielle. In the article he'd presented himself as Gabrielle's closest friend.

Most of it was fluff, Eric's story about an afternoon he'd spent with Gabrielle and her brother, how Gabrielle was the best sister anyone could hope for. That he would do anything to help her family get through this horrible ordeal.

The final lines drew her attention.

> Q: After two years of phenomenal success, this catastrophe must have hit Gabrielle extra hard, right?

> Eric: I think it would have hit anyone hard, regardless of what they went through. But Gabrielle's life wasn't easy even before. Their dad left them when she was a little girl, and they were kicked out of a community they lived in. She told me a few stories about those people you wouldn't believe. And her family nearly ended up in the street. She went through a lot, and she's much tougher than people think.

> Q: Do you think Nathan will come home?

Eric: Well, now that I see we have proof that he's alive, it makes me very hopeful.

Now that I see we have proof that he's alive. The reporter must have shown Eric the photo. Abby gritted her teeth in annoyance. At least the reporter hadn't followed up on the community Eric had mentioned. Dragging Otis's cult publicly into this could have been disastrous.

The sound of a car's wheels on gravel drew her attention. Wong had arrived and was parking her car behind Abby's. The woman stepped out of the vehicle, lit a cigarette, and exhaled a plume of smoke.

Abby got out of her car and walked over to her. "Thanks for meeting me."

"You *should* be thanking me, Mullen," Wong said, her face impassive. "Do you have any idea what a shitstorm you started?"

Abby blinked in confusion. "Over the search warrant?"

"The search warrant, taking Karl Adkins into custody, driving into the Tillman farm in the first place." Wong took another long drag of her cigarette. "Otis has been busy making calls."

"Calls to who?"

"Pretty much everyone, I'd say. Did you know the county executive has a grandson whose life was saved when he joined the Tillman community? Or so he says. He was suicidal when someone from the Tillman cult met him."

Abby's heart sank. "No, I didn't know that."

"Local newspaper loves them too. Apparently the Tillman community donates regularly to keep this vibrant form of free speech alive. They wrote a pretty nasty article about the NYPD's witch hunt in our county."

Abby leaned on Wong's car. "They must have done it just to handle situations like this one—"

"They did a great job at it. I was yelled at for ten minutes straight for collaborating with your witch hunt."

"Sorry. But it's not a witch hunt."

"Preaching to the choir, Mullen." Wong shook her head and dropped the cigarette to grind it with her heel. "I didn't drink the Tillman Kool-Aid yet. But you won't get any more help from us. I was told to meet you and tell you to turn back."

"What if I go on without you?"

"No way."

Abby bit her lip. "I have an ex-member who told me Otis Tillman is using his position to sexually assault his female community members."

"Can you prove it?"

"Maybe. I need to talk to a few of the cult members."

"They'll just give you the Otis Tillman spiel of the day."

"That's fine. I can work with that."

Wong paused for a second. "Maybe you just need to hear them verify Karl's alibi?"

Abby brightened. "Sure. A formality so we can release him from custody."

"But Otis might not let you talk to them alone. In fact, he might decide not to let you talk to them at all."

Abby smiled at the detective. "Leave that to me."

CHAPTER 43

The gate to the compound was closed, as it had been the day before. Abby waited, her fingers drumming on the steering wheel, staring at Wong's car. After a while, Wong switched off her engine, stepped out, and slammed the driver's door behind her.

"What's wrong?" Abby asked, getting out of her own car.

"They won't open the gate," Wong said. "Tillman is coming to meet us out here. I told you, he won't let you speak to anyone."

Abby took out her bag and locked the car. "We'll see what he has to say. Let me do the talking."

"I know these guys," Wong said. "I can try and convince them."

"For now let me do the talking," Abby said, brushing her hair behind her ears. "If I don't get anywhere after ten minutes, we'll switch."

Wong folded her arms. "Okay."

Abby checked her compact mirror. Her ears protruded sideways, even redder than usual due to the morning chill. Good. "I'll need you to be my tactical team replacement. Just loom behind me, looking, uh . . ." She turned to Wong, who leaned on her car, face impassive, arms folded, gun visible at her hip, her entire body rigid.

"In fact, just be you; it's perfect." Abby grinned.

"You know," Wong said after a moment, "even if Otis does let us talk to someone, he'll insist on remaining present."

"I know." Abby slid a plastic bag from her pocket. She knelt behind her car and scooped a sample of mud into it.

"Do you really think they'll give you *anything* while Otis is watching them?"

Abby straightened, snorting. "Not a chance."

"Then what are you doing here?" Wong asked, sounding frustrated.

"I'm hoping to get names of members who left the compound recently," Abby said. "Someone who could give me information."

"I doubt they'll give you that either."

Abby shrugged. "If not, I'll look for someone who's still capable of individual thoughts. I need someone on the inside."

"How can you spot someone like that?"

"There are a lot of small behavioral patterns to look for. How many times do they look at Otis for reassurance? Do they recite cult jargon automatically? How do they respond to questions about their former lives? The more that . . ." She paused as she spotted the men approaching.

Otis marched up to them with four other men, an entourage of goons. Two of them had shotguns in their hands. The other two were more worrisome since they held no visible weapon. Abby guessed that they had automatic weapons on their bodies within easy reach.

"You again?" Otis said, his warm demeanor from the day before gone. "Better turn your car around and leave, Officer. This isn't your jurisdiction."

Abby blinked, acting confused. "I'm sorry. I thought you *wanted* me to come."

Otis squinted at her. "Why? So you can arrest and hold more of my people? Harass us, and invade our privacy?"

Abby frowned. "But this morning I got a call from the NYPD chief. He said we had to release Karl Adkins as soon as possible. Apparently *he* got a phone call from some very angry people in Suffolk County. That's the only reason I'm here."

She saw the hostility and confusion fade from Otis's face. His lips quirked in a tiny smile. He was enjoying the narrative Abby was feeding him. The day before he'd made some phone calls, and lo and behold, the NYPD chief had hastened to free his nephew.

Power-hungry people always desired constant evidence of their own power. Cult leaders even more than most.

"I don't see Karl here," he pointed out. "And I didn't get any confirmation that he was released."

"I'm sorry; he's still in custody," Abby said apologetically. "Our witness identified him in the lineup. We asked him for his alibi, but he won't answer any of our questions. Detective Carver won't release him until the alibi is verified. So I need the people who saw him last Friday to come with me to the station and give me a statement."

"No one is going *anywhere* with you," Otis said, the smile gone.

"It'll just be for a few hours."

"That's what you said yesterday about Karl."

"Karl wouldn't answer our questions," Abby said.

"He doesn't need to answer your questions. He has the right to remain silent."

"But . . . he was identified in the lineup. My witness is almost certain." Her witness, Eden, was 100 percent certain, but she wanted to give Otis an opening.

"Well, your witness is wrong. It's their word against our word."

"You're right," Abby admitted. "If we had Karl's alibi, it would be my witness's word against his. But Karl won't talk to us, and neither will anyone here. How can I release him if I don't have their statements?"

Otis paused, and she could see him thinking it through. "I can let you talk to people here. But I won't have you taking them anywhere."

Abby feigned distress. "For the statement to hold up, I need them to give it at the station, where we can record it."

"That's not gonna happen."

Abby paused, opening her mouth as if to say something, then shutting it again and gritting her teeth. The choreography of frustration. She debated with herself if she should throw her hands in the air but decided it was too much and simply exhaled loudly instead. She waited a few more seconds, then said, "Can we at least have a quiet room where Detective Wong and I can talk to people privately?"

Otis shrugged. "Sure. You can talk in my study. But I won't let you violate my people's rights. I'll be present during their statements."

He was so pleased with himself for forcing her hand that he didn't notice Abby had managed to bring Wong in with her. She'd just convinced him to let both of them in.

She sighed, and turned to Wong. "Detective Wong, I'm sorry to take more of your time. Would this be acceptable?"

Wong's face was impassive as before, but a glimmer of appreciation flickered in the woman's eyes. "Fine," she said brusquely. "As long as this ends today."

CHAPTER 44

The newlywed couple weren't happy to talk to Carver at all.

"We really don't have time right now," the groom, Rory, explained. "We have to get on a flight in five hours. We're going on our honeymoon."

"It won't take long," Carver said, glancing around. There were dozens of flower bouquets in the apartment. The place smelled like a flower shop. His allergies were flaring up. He would *have* to finish this up fast, before the sneeze-athon started.

"We still need to pack," the bride said. Her name was Dori. Rory and Dori. What were they even thinking, getting married? "If this is about the cocaine at the wedding after-party, we didn't know it would be there. It was all Rory's uncle's idea. We didn't even do any."

"It's not about the cocaine at the party." Carver suppressed the urge to roll his eyes. "It's about Liam Washington."

"Who?" Dori asked, frowning.

"The photographer at your wedding."

"What about him?" Rory asked, glancing at his watch.

"Do you remember at what time he got to your wedding?" Carver's nose was about to implode. So. Many. Flowers.

"I don't know," Rory said. "Probably when it started. Around two."

"No, he took photos of me before the ceremony, remember?" Dori asked. "After the makeup. So that would have been around—"

Carver sneezed. And sneezed again.

"It would have been—"

Carver sneezed again.

"—around one," Dori said sharply, looking irritated.

"Okay." Carver blinked, his eyes tearing up. "And ad whad tibe did he leab?"

"I'm sorry?"

Carver sneezed again. This was why he hated flowers. Flowers were his kryptonite. He sneezed five times and finally pinched his nose shut.

"At what time did he leave?" he asked, doing his best to regain his composure.

"I don't know . . . eight, I guess?" Dori said. "We wanted him for the beginning of the after-party. That's why we paid for half a day. What's this about?"

"We really have to start packing," Rory said.

"Did he seem agitated in any way? Did anything strike you as odd?"

"He wasn't high, if that's what you mean," Dori said. "Only Rory's uncle was high."

Carver took his fingers off his nose. "Liam Washington is dead."

They both stared at him in utter shock.

"So I would appreciate it if you—" He sneezed again. He wished Turner were there. Then they could do a "good cop, sneezing cop" thing. But Turner had gone to the morgue, leaving Carver to this flowery nightmare. He pinched his nose shut again. "I would really appreciate it if you think it through, and tell me exactly when you saw Liam Washington last."

"I remember him saying he was leaving around eight," Rory said numbly.

"Oh god," Dori moaned.

"And during the wedding, did he seem stressed?"

Dori started crying. Rory hugged her, whispering soothing words in her ear.

"Now every time we look through our wedding photos, we'll think of death!" Dori wailed.

Carver waited impatiently for the girl to chill, his fingers still pinching his nose.

"You know," Rory hissed at him, "you could have been more sensitive. We're leaving on our honeymoon today."

"A man is dead." Carver tried to sound severe, but it was impossible in his current nose-clutching stance.

"But it's not our fault," Dori sobbed. "Did you really have to ruin our memory of the most special day of our lives?"

Should he arrest them both? The prospect was alluring. For obstruction of justice and for assault of an officer with pollen. Now *that* would really ruin their memory. Also they would miss their honeymoon flight.

His phone rang, interrupting his fantasy. It was Turner. He answered the call.

"Carver," Turner said. "I just got out of the morgue. The ME ruled it a homicide."

"Color me surprised," Carver said.

"Now for some bad news. I got the search warrant for the cell phone location for the past four days. I haven't gone through all of it, but it stops on Saturday at two fifty-three in the afternoon."

"He turned his phone off?"

"I don't think so. I talked to his wife, and apparently, Liam has been complaining about his phone's battery life lately. She thinks he repeatedly forgot to charge it. In any case, it's possible the battery just ran out."

"Where was he when it ran out?"

"Manhattan. I'll send you the location."

"Okay." He already knew what it would show. Liam Washington had been photographing the wedding on Saturday at that time.

"We might still catch a break," Turner continued. "The stomach contents contain partial remnants of a burger and some fries. The ME estimates he died an hour or two after the meal. If we find out when he ate, we'll have a tight time-of-death window."

"Hang on for a second." Carver turned to the angry couple. "Did you serve hamburgers and fries at your wedding?"

Dori flinched as if he'd slapped her. "Of course not!"

"Our catering was vegetarian," Rory said. "We weren't about to be responsible for the death of dozens of innocent chickens and cows just to celebrate our wedding."

"You don't seem too bothered about the death of your wedding photographer," Carver said. He wasn't proud of himself. But he was tired, and these two were a bit much.

"It wasn't our fault!" Dori shouted and sobbed again.

"Carver? What's going on there?" Turner asked.

"Nothing, I just—" Carver sneezed. And sneezed again. And again.

His record was seventeen consecutive sneezes. If he stayed in this flower apocalypse, he would beat it. "Danks bor your cooberation," he blurted at the couple and stumbled out of the apartment. "Oh god."

"Carver?" Turner sounded as if he was about to get on the radio and report that an officer was in trouble.

"I'b fide. Hang od." Carver rubbed his nose violently and sneezed a few more times. "I'm okay. Listen, let's check Liam's credit card charges. Maybe we'll get lucky and find where he ate those burger and fries. The happy couple said he was with them between one and eight."

"Okay. Oh, and I checked the victim's camera's memory. There are a lot of photos of weddings in there. No pictures of kidnapped boys, though."

"Yeah." Carver had already begun to seriously doubt their initial theory that Liam had anything to do with Nathan's kidnapping. Then what was the connection between the two?

Maybe there was no connection. Maybe Liam was just in the wrong place at the wrong time.

CHAPTER 45

Nathan phased in and out of sleep. When he was awake, everything hurt. He shivered weakly, his throat parched.

But when he slept, it was worse.

Because he returned to that car, the blood spurting everywhere, splattering on his cheek. That terrible wet, gurgling sound, the driver spasming.

"Look what you made me do."

When he'd walked down the road on the brink of exhaustion, the car had stopped for him at the side of the road. The passenger door opened, light shining on the driver's face. Relief coursed through Nathan's body. It wasn't *him*.

"Jesus," the driver said. "Are you okay?"

Nathan could hardly speak. He just cried.

"Are you lost?"

Nathan nodded, then blurted, "Can you call my mom?"

"Of course! You look freezing. Get inside. The heater's on."

Nathan did it without thinking, relieved to be out of the cold night air. The heater felt wonderful pointed at his face. He spread his fingers in front of it, feeling them thaw.

"How did you end up here?" the man asked, incredulous.

"I don't know." Nathan's teeth chattered. "A man t . . . t . . . took me."

"Okay, okay. Here, take this." The driver took off his coat and arranged it over Nathan like a blanket.

"Let's call your mom," the driver said, rummaging in his pocket. "Are you getting warm?"

"Y . . . yes." Nathan clumsily struggled with his shoelaces, taking the wet shoe off. He removed the wet sock as well, feeling the man's eyes on him. Wiggling his toes, he felt his foot for the first time in hours. He whimpered in pain.

"Do you know your mom's phone number?" the man asked.

For a terrifying second, Nathan's mind was blank. He couldn't remember the number or his address. Without them he would never get back home. But then the digits tumbled into his mind, and with a sudden relief he blurted them.

"Hang on, slow down." The man finally fished out his phone. "Oh. It's juiced out. This thing's battery is total junk. No worries, there's a gas station a few miles down the road. We'll call from there."

"O . . . okay."

A knocking sound drew Nathan's attention. He raised his eyes, saw someone was rapping on the driver's window. The driver rolled it down.

"Hey, is something wrong?"

The voice coated Nathan's heart with ice. It was *him*. He tried to say something, but he was completely paralyzed with fear.

"This kid was walking out here on the road in the middle of the night," the driver told the man outside. "I think someone kidnapped him."

"Seriously? That's terrible." The man peered at Nathan through the driver's window.

"That's him!" Nathan let out a gurgling scream. "That's the man who took me!"

The driver turned to stare at him in surprise. And at the same moment, something flashed in the man's hand. A blade. He jabbed it at the driver's throat viciously, over and over and over, the driver thrashing, his fingers clawing, trying to push the knife away.

Something wet spurted on Nathan's cheek as he gaped at the two men struggling. The blade kept jabbing. Five times, ten times. Jab. Jab. Jab. Long after the driver stopped gurgling, stopped moving. Jab. Jab.

The man breathed hard as he opened the driver's door. He crouched, gazing past the motionless, blood-soaked driver straight at Nathan, his face a mask of fury.

"Look what you made me do," he snarled.

All that blood.

Nathan barely understood what was going on as the man pulled the dead driver out of the car and thrust the body into the trunk. He drove the car, Nathan trembling in his seat, shutting his eyes as if it would make it all a dream. And then the man dragged him, stumbling, back into the cabin. This time, he didn't lock him in that strange room that mimicked his own. Instead he pushed him into a small dark alcove that held a bucket and a few rags. Tossed a blanket over him.

Left him in the dark.

Nathan shivered, his body numb, feeling far away. More than anything, he wished he were warm. He faded into sleep again.

Sometimes, in his dreams, the knife cut *his* neck as he thrashed, panicking. And sometimes, *he* was the one plunging the blade into the nice driver's throat, over and over and over, as the man tried to stop him.

"Look what you made me do."

CHAPTER 46

Otis's office had a large wooden table and two chairs. A shelf on the back wall was stacked to the limit by what appeared to be religious books. Abby skimmed the names, noting that despite Otis's words about race, equality, and feminism, his literary taste showed no correlation with those topics.

The room was meticulously clean, a strong scent of lilac in the air. But underneath that smell, there was something pungent, as if the fresh lilac was intended to overcome a different odor.

Otis sat down behind the desk. Abby and Wong waited while one of Otis's men dragged two more chairs into the office and set them near the empty chair so that they all had to sit in front of Otis. Abby sat down on the middle chair, her face giving away nothing. She didn't care about Otis Tillman's power plays. In fact, the more he felt in control of the situation, the better it was for her. Wong sat to her left.

"How many statements do you need?" Otis asked, as if he were a cashier taking an order in a statement drive-through.

"It's a long way from the city," Abby said. "Better take as many as I can so I don't make the trip twice."

"Let's start with Charlie O'Neal," Otis suggested. "He's Karl's roommate. He spends more time with him than anyone else."

He made a phone call to summon Charlie, and they waited. Otis asked them if they wanted any drinks, and they both refused. Abby already needed to pee after the long drive, and she didn't need additional stress on her bladder.

Charlie showed up pretty quickly, wiping his hands on his shirt. Abby pegged him to be in his midthirties.

"Nice to meet you, Charlie," Abby said. "I'm Abby, and this is Detective Wong."

He sat down next to them, facing Otis. Abby turned her own chair to face Charlie, her back to Wong.

"Charlie, how long have you been Karl's roommate?" she asked.

"About three and a half years," Charlie said, looking sideways at her while his body still faced Otis.

"And before that?"

Charlie glanced at Otis, then back at her. "Before that I lived in Hempstead."

Abby nodded. Wong dragged her chair so she could also see Charlie. She had a notebook in her lap and jotted in it as he spoke. Good.

"Did you live with Karl in Hempstead?"

Charlie blinked in confusion. "No, I lived with my wife."

"Oh," Abby said, acting surprised. "Is your wife here too?"

"No. She stayed behind in Hempstead. We got divorced."

"I'm sorry."

"It's okay. I'm blameless and upright." He exchanged looks with Otis and smiled.

It was the second time Abby had heard that phrase within the compound. She knew what it referenced. The book of Job said that Job was "blameless and upright." It was the Tillman cult members' way of reacting to negative thoughts about the cult. Job hadn't complained about his troubles, and neither should they.

She frowned, as if confused by his answer. "Okay . . . were you with Karl on the eighteenth of October around noon?"

"Yes." Zero hesitation.

"Don't you need to think it through?"

"No."

"I can't remember who I was with yesterday evening. I'm impressed you can remember so far back that easily."

He snorted. "I'm with Karl every day at noon. We eat lunch together, all of us."

"What, everyone on the farm?"

"Yeah, that's right," he said, his tone getting challenging.

"That's a lot of people."

"We have a large dining hall," Otis interrupted.

"And you remember Karl being there on the eighteenth," Abby said, addressing Charlie.

"We sit next to each other. So yeah, I remember."

"Who does the cooking for these enormous lunches?"

"We take shifts."

"What did you eat that day?" Abby asked pleasantly.

Charlie glanced at Otis.

"It was a Friday," Otis said.

"Oh, then it was green beans and beef," Charlie said, his face relieved.

"You didn't remember?"

"I remember. It was green beans and beef."

"Do you eat green beans and beef every Friday?"

"Yeah, that's right," Charlie said, his tone sharpening again.

"I get bored when I eat the same food every week," Abby said. "Don't you *ever* get bored?"

Another glance at Otis. "No. Routine is a privilege."

"I guess you're right. I never thought of it that way."

"You wouldn't." His smirk was victorious, as if he'd beaten her in some invisible game.

"Which is your favorite weekly meal?" Abby asked.

Otis sighed. "Detective, what does that have to do with anything?"

"Just getting to know Charlie," she said casually, keeping her eyes on O'Neal. He seemed completely stumped. That didn't surprise her. Indoctrinated cult members often couldn't handle open-ended questions that didn't relate to the cult's agenda. They were conditioned to avoid individual thinking, and that could even apply to favorite foods.

After a while he said hesitantly, "I like the fish on Monday."

She asked him about the two dates when Karl had been seen near Eden's house. Not surprisingly, Charlie answered immediately that Karl had been with him both times. Since one was in the morning and one was in the evening, he said he remembered it because they had been in their church with everyone else—morning and evening prayers.

"A witness testified to seeing Karl in Brooklyn on those dates," Abby said. "Do you think the witness is wrong?"

"Yes, because Karl was with me."

"Do you think the witness is lying?"

Charlie shrugged. "It's not my place to judge. That's the burden of God and his emissaries."

"I think it's possible that someone is trying to frame Karl for something he didn't do," Abby said. "Can you think of anyone who would wish Karl harm?"

Charlie shook his head. "Everyone loves Karl."

"Maybe someone outside the farm?"

Another glance at Otis. "He has no contacts outside the farm."

"How about people who lived here and left?"

Charlie let out a snort. "That would be impossible."

"Why?"

"Because they're dead."

Out of the corner of her eye, Abby noticed Otis tense. She frowned. "What, all of them?"

"Yeah," Charlie said. "Only five people left since Karl got here. And God—" At that point he glanced at Otis, and his mouth snapped shut.

"What happened to those five people?"

"I don't know," Charlie said. "We never heard from them again."

"You said they're dead."

"It's a figure of speech."

"A pretty dark figure of speech," Abby said. "Don't you think?"

She noticed Wong tense. The detective was probably wondering if Otis would really go that far—killing anyone who threatened to leave the cult. Abby seriously doubted it. But she was sure that he'd *told* the remaining members that the deserters had died. What better way to discourage future deserters?

But this reinforced what Wong had said earlier. Abby wouldn't get the names of any former cult members here. She would have to find her informer *within* the cult. Charlie was definitely out of the question. The man could hardly say hello without checking to verify that Otis approved.

"Lieutenant Mullen," Otis snapped. "Charlie testified to seeing Karl in every one of the instances you mentioned. Would that be enough?"

"Sorry, I got carried away." Abby let out an embarrassed laugh. "Sure, thank you, Charlie, you can go."

Charlie shot out from the chair as if from a cannon and hurried out of the room.

"Well, that's a pretty positive statement," Abby said. "Who do we talk to next?"

"Why are you harassing my people?" Otis asked, jaw clenched.

"Harassing them?" Abby asked. "I just asked a few questions."

"Asking them about the menu in the dining room and about their theories about your witness."

"I'm sorry," Abby said. "I need those statements to hold up in court. I can't just ask about the dates, and that's it. I need to get some details to make sure there are no mistakes. After all, like Charlie said, everyone loved Karl. They might convince themselves that they saw him just because they *want* it. I need to verify that's not the case. But feel free to tell me if you think I'm stepping out of line. Trust me, I don't want another angry phone call from the NYPD chief. One was enough."

Otis hesitated, then nodded.

"Who's next?" Abby asked.

"I think we'll call Aaron next," Otis said. He seemed more at ease now. "Aaron and Karl often work the apple orchard together."

Aaron was a large man, his eyelids slightly droopy as if he were on the verge of falling asleep. He was tight-lipped and angry, answering mostly in short four- or five-word sentences. He also glanced at Otis every single time before answering. And of course, Karl's alibi was affirmed by him as well.

"Can you think of anyone who would wish Karl harm, maybe someone who lived here and left?"

"Only five people left, and we never heard from any of them again." After responding, Aaron automatically glanced at Otis for assurance. Otis smiled at him. The answer had come so fast that Aaron could just as well have been reading it. Charlie had obviously briefed him before he walked inside.

Abby veered, asking, "What do you do in your free time?"

"We study the scripture."

"Don't you have Netflix? Books?"

"Don't need them."

"I gotta have my Netflix binge on the weekend." Abby sighed. "Did you ever binge?"

Aaron seemed confused. "Sure. Before I found my calling."

"What did you watch?"

"Comedies, I guess. Some action series."

"Which one was your favorite?"

Aaron froze, a panicky look in his eyes. Abby waited patiently.

"Didn't you tell me you liked *Stranger Things*?" Otis asked.

"Right." Aaron exhaled. "*Stranger Things* was good."

"Oh, I love that show! Did you watch the third season?"

"No. I joined the farm after the first season. We don't have Netflix here."

"Don't you miss it?"

Aaron rolled his eyes. "I'm blameless and upright."

"Yes," Abby said. "I suppose you are."

Aaron and Otis exchanged bemused glances.

Finally, Abby told Aaron she had enough, and he left.

"I just need a few more interviews like that, and I'm all set," Abby said.

"Okay." Otis smiled thinly. "Give me a minute to call the next one."

He left them alone in the room. Abby and Wong exchanged looks, saying nothing. Abby had almost no doubt that Otis had left them there alone hoping they'd talk. Either someone was listening in, or he was recording them.

He returned five minutes later, another community member following him. Wong stiffened as soon as she saw the girl's face.

It was Ruth, the girl who had been raped when she was fifteen. Wong's failure.

CHAPTER 47

"Ruth, right?" Abby smiled at the girl as she sat down.

"That's right." Ruth returned her smile.

Abby felt hopeful. Two years before, Ruth had approached a teacher and told her she'd had sex with a man on the farm. That showed an independent spark in the girl. She could be what Abby was looking for.

"How long have you known Karl?" Abby asked.

"Since he got to the farm seven years ago," Ruth said.

"How long have you been here?"

"Ruth joined with her parents when she was three years old," Otis said. "Almost a baby."

"Oh wow." Abby nodded in appreciation, feeling her own memories threatening to surface. She shoved them deep down. "Who are your parents?"

A glance at Otis. Wong let out a pained breath.

"Their names are Maria and Thomas."

"Do you want them to be present?" Abby asked.

Another long look at Otis. And then Ruth turned back and said casually, "No need. Otis will keep me safe."

It all went downhill from there. Ruth's answers were predictable and automatic, but she hardly uttered any of them without a glance at Otis. She'd seen Karl at the prayers and at the communal lunch. Of course she was sure; she saw him every day. She didn't think anyone would want to implicate Karl; everyone loved him.

Wong cleared her throat. "Two years ago you told your teacher that a man from the farm had sex with you. Do you remember that?"

"Sure," Ruth said. "I'm so sorry. I wanted attention, and I had an overactive imagination."

"Why did you want attention?" Abby asked.

"My mom and dad were busy, and I had too much time to invent little stories. But these stories were the tools of Satan."

"You don't make up stories anymore?" Abby asked.

"No, I'm done with that. I keep myself busy. I do a kitchen shift and a farming shift every single day." She glanced at Otis again and visibly glowed when he smiled at her proudly. Abby wished she could disembowel the man.

"That's a lot of work for a seventeen-year-old. Don't you want some time to meet friends? Dance? Read books? Are you frustrated that you don't have time to do any of it?"

Abby saw Wong leaning forward, a desperate glint in her eyes.

Ruth shrugged. "I'm blameless and upright."

Maybe, given time, Abby *could* intervene here, get Ruth out of the cult, awaken her capability to doubt. But she was skeptical. The girl's parents were still in the cult, and she seemed to have lost whatever fighting spirit she'd had two years before. And Abby had no time. Nathan was missing. If Otis or Karl had anything to do with the kidnapping, she needed to figure it out fast.

"Thanks, Ruth," she said sadly. "That's all we need. It's been very nice meeting you."

"I think you have enough statements," Otis said with finality. "Karl had nothing to do with any of this. You have your proof."

"Just one or two more," Abby said half-heartedly. "We'll be quick."

Otis shrugged. "Ruth, can you call Leonor here?"

"Absolutely."

Leonor was about fifteen and seemed ready for a fight. She sat down on the empty chair, folding her arms.

"Leonor, how long have you known Karl?" Abby asked.

"For about a year," the girl answered.

"How well do you know him?"

"Everyone knows Karl. He's great."

"Great how?"

"He's friendly." Leonor counted on her fingers. "Always happy to help with any problem. And he doesn't look down on anyone."

"Really? Do people typically look down on you?"

"Not here."

Leonor seemed tense. The answers came fast, rehearsed. Just like the rest of them.

But so far, she'd only glanced at Otis once, briefly. She didn't need his approval for every answer. She knew her lines.

Abby allowed herself to be hopeful again.

She asked about the dates. Leonor gave her the same lines as everyone else. Didn't hesitate. Another brief look at Otis, just making sure she wasn't making any big mistakes.

"You said you only knew Karl for a year," Abby said. "How come? He's been here for seven years."

"But I only joined a year ago," Leonor said.

"Really? How did that happen?"

"I met Ruth and a couple of other guys. We got to talking. I was frustrated. I was trying to make a difference in my school but getting nowhere."

"What kind of difference?"

"Like, change the way women are perceived. The ratio of male versus female students in classes like math and physics is abominable. And when you talk to people, they're like, nothing's stopping you from studying math. And they can't even see how the teachers and other students treat the female students." She clenched her fists.

"It seems like you're angry about that."

"Yeah, of course I'm angry."

As far as Leonor was concerned, anger wasn't the burden of God and his emissaries. Not yet, at least.

"Is there anything you miss? From your old life?"

"Detective—" Otis began.

"No," Leonor said resolutely. "Nothing."

Otis tensed, and Abby had to mask the sudden spark of joy in her heart. The girl had interrupted Otis. She hadn't even noticed it. She would pay for it later, no doubt.

Abby had to get her out. Not now, she needed some time to prepare. But she had to have a reason to do it later.

"We think maybe someone's trying to implicate Karl or someone else in the community," Abby said. "Any idea who would want to hurt Karl? Or Otis?"

Leonor seemed shocked. "No. We aren't bothering anyone. We're just minding our own business."

"What do you do on the farm?"

"Well, after trying my cooking, they won't let me near the kitchen again." Leonor grinned. "I do field work and patrols."

"Patrols?"

"I walk the perimeter of the fence twice every day. Make sure the fence is intact."

"Are you armed?"

A glance at Otis. "No."

"And did you see anything?" Abby made a show of leaning forward, hands on her knees. "Anything suspicious?"

Leonor shrugged. "Not really."

"You patrol the perimeter twice a day, and you never saw anyone?"

"I didn't say I didn't see anyone," Leonor said, annoyed. "I saw a few people. There's a field across from the farm. Some guys sometimes work there."

"Can you describe them?"

"Um . . . three guys. Two of them Latino. One's bald and white."

"The white guy," Abby said quickly, tensing. "The bald one. How many times have you seen him?"

"I think three times? Yeah, definitely three times."

"Anything else you can tell me about him?"

"He has a tattoo on his neck, but I couldn't see what it was."

Abby glanced at Wong, who nodded at her.

"Thanks, Leonor," Abby said. "Is there any way to get in touch with you?"

"Just talk to Otis," Leonor said. "He'll pass on the message."

"You don't have a phone?"

"We don't have phones here," Leonor said. "They're a distraction."

Abby smiled at her. "I bet it was hard giving *that* up. I have a daughter your age, and she spends every minute with her cell phone."

Leonor stood up. "I got over it."

CHAPTER 48

Will knocked on the door, checking his watch. He'd read the lab's report three times and consulted with a friend who worked in image editing. He was convinced the image of Nathan in his room was either authentic or a masterful photoshopping job that had managed to fool even the FBI's experts. He needed to know which.

Eden Fletcher let him in and asked him desperately if there was any news.

When Will's daughter was younger, she'd been hospitalized with life-threatening meningitis. Both Will and his wife had spent four days in the hospital with their daughter, taking her for different tests and to various experts, constantly terrified for her life. And whenever a doctor passed by, Will would lunge at them to ask if they'd gotten the test results or if he had a prognosis. He recalled the helplessness and frustration, begging doctors to tell him if there was any news.

"We have a few promising leads, Ms. Fletcher," he said. And heard the doctor in his mind tell him they had to run another test, consult another expert, try a different treatment. "We'll let you know as soon as we have anything definite."

Her face fell. She said nothing.

"Can I please inspect Nathan's room? Just to see if there's something we missed."

"Sure," Eden said listlessly. "It's on the second floor. Can I get you anything to drink? I was making myself a cup of tea."

"No thanks."

"I used to drink a lot of coffee, but I stopped," Eden said. "Don't need anything else to keep me awake at night. It's jasmine tea. Are you sure you don't want any?"

"Uh . . . sure, why not. I'd love a cup," Will said, more out of politeness than anything else. "Second floor?"

Eden nodded and trudged to the kitchen. Will went up the stairs and looked around. Three doors. He opened one. Gabrielle's room. The girl lay on the bed tapping on the phone, her jaw clenched.

"Sorry," Will said. "I thought this was Nathan's room."

"You're that cop," Gabrielle said, raising her eyes. "You're the one who asked me for my Instagram password."

"It's been very helpful—"

Gabrielle handed him the phone. "I need you to answer these assholes. Tell them the kidnapping is not made up."

Will blinked in surprise. "What?"

"These guys think that I made the kidnapping up. That I'm using it to get more followers on Instagram." A sob caught in Gabrielle's throat. "As if I'd use my brother like that."

Will took the phone and looked at it. It was a Reddit thread, twenty-eight upvotes to the original post. The Redditor Truth777 had suggested, like Gabrielle had said, that the entire kidnapping was made up. He'd "proved" in six bullet points that this was the case. A few Redditors had commented enthusiastically on the thread.

"Just ignore them," Will suggested. "Don't engage."

"I can't ignore them. That's how it always starts," Gabrielle said. "Someone says on Reddit that I'm a scammer, and the next thing you know the internet picks it up, and I start to see articles about it. It happened before."

"I know," Will said. Twice before to be exact.

He'd researched both scandals, found nothing interesting there. In one case Gabrielle had bungled an online order of one hundred signed photos. The other scandal was about her promoting a protein powder that later turned out to increase the risk of cancer. Gabrielle had been very publicly shamed in both instances.

"If the police comment on this thread, it'll give them validity," Will pointed out. "It won't convince them. You know that."

"If people start saying I faked this kidnapping, the ransom contributions will stop," Gabrielle said tightly. "I need to make this go away."

"Then keep posting on your regular page. *Don't* say anything about this crackpot theory—or this Reddit thread. Just keep reminding people that your brother is still missing and that the police are searching for him."

Gabrielle snatched the phone from Will's outstretched hand. "Nathan's room is over there." She pointed at the adjacent door.

Will thanked her and entered Nathan's room. He'd studied the image of Nathan holding the newspaper in that room for so long that he felt like he'd already been in it, even though it was his first time. He scrutinized the chair by the desk, where Nathan had sat in the picture. It wasn't in the exact location as in the image. He walked over, adjusted it slightly, then took a step back.

He opened the image on his phone, then compared it to the room. The photo had been aimed at the desk and the chair. A pizza box lay on the desk in the photo, as well as a few crayons and a blurry drawing. The bottom left corner of the Harry Potter poster was caught in the frame, and a bit of the bed. In the top left part of the image, the corkboard with the drawings was visible, with two of the drawings on display. One was partially hidden by Nathan's head, and the other was mostly out of the frame. The window was completely out of the frame in the photo; it was too high to be visible—

Will frowned. Was it? Something was wrong. Wouldn't part of the window be visible in the photo as well?

He took a pillow from the bed and set it on the chair to simulate Nathan's upper body. He doubted the height was an exact match, but it was close enough. Then, using his phone, he tried to aim the lens so that it more or less matched the photo they had. He took a step back, pointing the phone high to get Nathan just right, but then the corkboard was out of the frame. But if he included both the corkboard and the Harry Potter poster, he could easily see part of the window, and *that* didn't match the kidnapper's photo.

He tried to move the chair, positioning the photo farther to the left—no good, the bed was completely out of sight, and the corkboard was much more visible. And if he went to the right . . .

No matter what he did, he couldn't get it to fit.

A different phone might have a different lens, but the rules of geometry still applied. To get the corkboard, the poster, and Nathan in one picture, a significant part of the window would have to be on display. He looked at the kidnapper's photo again. Enlarged it so he could see Nathan's drawings up close.

Then he compared them to the drawings on the corkboard.

"Holy shit," he muttered.

The drawings weren't the same. There were minute differences. Unnoticeable unless you searched for them.

He dialed Abby.

"Mullen here," Abby said. It sounded as if she was on speaker, driving.

"Abby, it's me. I'm in Nathan Fletcher's room."

"Yeah?"

"The photo of Nathan? The one with the newspaper? It wasn't taken here."

"What do you mean?"

"The proportions of the room don't match. And there are small differences if you look carefully. I think the kidnapper's photo was taken in a room that was meant to appear like Nathan's room."

"What, like a studio with a setting?" Abby asked.

"Yeah, exactly."

A long silence followed, only the sound of the car's engine assuring Will that Abby was still on the line.

"Did you tell Eden? Or Gabrielle?" Abby finally asked.

"Not yet."

"Okay, then don't. It'll mess with their heads, and I don't want them mentioning it if the kidnapper calls. Send this to Carver. Oh, and Griffin. I'll get back this evening, and we'll talk this through."

"Why would the kidnappers do that?" Will asked.

After a long pause Abby finally said, "I have no idea."

CHAPTER 49

Over the years, Abby had talked to dozens of cult survivors and their families, and she already knew the scary truth. Cults could recruit anyone. Rich, poor, educated, ignorant, religious, atheist, it didn't matter. Coming from a loving, caring family didn't protect you. Being skeptical didn't protect you. Having firm beliefs didn't protect you. The misconception that people held, that "it would never happen to me," was the cults' best asset. Because there was only one vaccination against cult recruitment—being on guard. And if you assumed you were already immune, if you underestimated cults, then you were at risk.

This was why it didn't surprise her to see that Leonor's parents were a warm, sweet couple. They lived in a lovely house with a well-tended garden. Inside, the house was clean and smelled of warm bread. The living room had a large couch on which Leonor's parents huddled together. Abby sat in front of them on an armchair. A gray cat eyed her with unbridled hatred, and Abby suspected she occupied the cat's favorite seat.

"Dale makes the bread in a bread maker every other morning," Leonor's mother, Helen, told Abby. "So we eat only homemade bread."

Dale was an attorney. Helen was a librarian. They had that aura of numbness that followed a sudden, unpredictable catastrophe. When people realized the sense of control over their life was an illusion.

"Is your coffee okay?" Helen asked.

"It's great," Abby said, smiling. It was a bit weak, but it was hot, and she was mostly just grateful to be out of her car. It had taken her almost two hours and over twenty phone calls to locate Leonor's parents, and she had done it all from her driver's seat.

"I keep trying to understand what we did wrong," Helen said. "We might have been too controlling. Leonor kept asking to go with her friends to Manhattan, and I was worried, so sometimes I said no. And maybe we invaded her private space. I kept cleaning her room even though she told me not to. And—"

"Mrs. Craft," Abby said gently. "You did nothing wrong."

"Then why did she join that . . . that—"

"Cult," Dale said gruffly. "Why did she join that cult if we did nothing wrong?"

"She didn't join that cult," Abby said. "Almost no one *joins* a cult. She was recruited."

"Same thing." Dale shrugged. "They recruited her, and she made the choice to—"

"No," Abby said. "She made no choice."

"Detective Mullen, Leonor wasn't taken against her will. She started seeing those people, and after a while she packed a bag and moved to that farm. She's not gone; she still talks to us. But it's like we don't matter anymore."

Abby sighed. People who were recruited to destructive cults left behind family and friends who were hurt and angry. They felt abandoned, spurned. Parents often felt like they had failed in their upbringing. It was another tool that played into the cult's hands. When people in your old life were angry, you had good reason to stay away from them.

"It's likely there *was* something that the cult recruiters used to get to Leonor," Abby said. "But it could be anything. Maybe she had a bad breakup. Or she just fought with her best friend. Or her friends changed, as they often do at that age, and she didn't feel like she belonged anymore. Almost no one is completely whole. Not to mention she's a teenager. It doesn't mean you did anything wrong. Or that *she* made a conscious choice."

"She was frustrated," Dale said. "About something at school. About how they treated the girls and the boys differently."

Leonor had mentioned that. "Imagine she felt particularly down about that. Maybe her math teacher talked to her in a patronizing way."

"Her math teacher was a nice man," Dale said. "I'm sure that—"

"Go on," Helen told Abby. Helen knew what she meant. Dale had no idea and couldn't even begin to understand. But Helen could.

"She sat in the school cafeteria," Abby said. "Or the park. And she saw a group of friends her age. Boys and girls. And the way they talked to each other was different. Respectful. At *that* moment, it seemed just what she needed. They talked to her. And they showered her with love. Told her how smart she was, how clever. How she wasn't like everyone else in that school. She was more like them. She hung out with them a few times, nothing too serious, and then they invited her to spend a weekend on that farm."

Helen let out a gasp, and Abby knew she'd gotten it exactly right. There had been a weekend on the farm. There was almost always a weekend, or a three-day workshop, or a short, fun camp.

"They worked hard on the farm," Abby continued. "Leonor hardly got any sleep. But everyone around her was happy, and they *all* worked hard. She wanted to keep up with her new friends who thought so highly of her. And they didn't leave her alone for a single second. Kept talking to her. Feeding her the cult's agenda. At first, it sounded weird, but Leonor's polite; she didn't want to argue. Or she argued, and they told her she made good points, and they should discuss them later. But the harder she worked, the less she slept, the more sense they started to make."

"Did she tell you all that?" Helen asked.

"No," Abby said. "But I've heard it all before. That weekend on the farm, was it longer than she expected?"

"It was during the summer vacation," Helen whispered. "She meant to go for two days but ended up staying five."

"And she didn't call you during that time, right?"

"She said they frowned upon phones on the farm," Dale said. "But she made it sound like a good thing. Like she was detoxing from her phone. I was proud of her for doing it. I hated all the time she spent with that phone."

"Zero communication with the outside world," Abby said. "Hardly any sleep. And everyone around her acting so sure of themselves. So full of purpose. When she asked questions or argued, they acted like they had the answers, but she'd have to stay longer to discuss it. Can you imagine how she felt?"

"Are you saying that's when they convinced her? In those five days?"

"Mr. Craft, I'm saying when Leonor returned home after those five days, she was no longer the daughter you knew."

"They brainwashed her?"

"No. Brainwashing is something different. They influenced and twisted the way she thought. They built rigid walls in her mind and conditioned her to avoid asking questions. And with that, they gained almost complete control of Leonor's mind."

Dale and Helen sat in shocked silence.

"I think we might be able to reverse the damage they did," Abby said after a minute. "I saw very encouraging signs when I talked to her. And you mentioned she still talks to you . . . ?"

"She calls every week," Helen says. "To tell us she's fine and to check up on her cat."

"The cat is Leonor's?" Abby asked, surprised.

"Yeah, Leonor found Silver in the street when she was a kitten," Helen said. "She said they don't allow pets on the farm."

"That's good," Abby said, encouraged. "Frankly I'm surprised they let her call every week. Usually destructive cults employ a more severe regime when it comes to contact with family or friends. Does she have a cell phone?"

"No, she calls from the office," Dale said. "She mentioned it to me a month ago. They let her use the phone there."

Abby frowned. It was almost bizarre. Letting Leonor call her family was one thing, but actually allowing her to use the farm's phone? Otis could have easily told her the phone was for emergencies only. It was almost like he wanted her to keep in touch with her family.

"Have you been encouraging her?" she asked. "Telling her this community was beneficial to her in any way?"

"Of course not," Dale said, his voice rising. "I told her several times she needs to come home. I told her that place was messing with her mind."

Abby nodded, her mood dampened. Dale's visible opposition to the cult wouldn't make things easier. "Helen, what about you?"

"I told her the same," Helen said. "We even had an argument about it. She was planning on going to college, but soon after she joined, she said she didn't think she'd go. She said her time was better used there on the farm. I was furious."

Both parents were actively against the cult. Why was Otis letting Leonor talk to them? "Did you feel like she was trying to convince you to join the cult?"

Dale snorted. "Fat chance. She knows better."

Abby thought for a few seconds. "You said she was planning to go to college. Do you have a college fund for her?"

"Absolutely," Helen said. "We've been saving for years both for her and her brother."

"Does she have access to that fund?"

"No," Dale said. "Not until she's eighteen. And she'll need our approval to withdraw it."

"Did she ask you to give her the money?"

"Once," Helen said. "She wanted to give it to the community so they could rebuild the barn or something like that. I flatly told her there was no way in hell that was going to happen. We had a long fight about it, and she didn't call for several weeks after that."

That was why Otis let Leonor call her parents. He wanted that fund. He encouraged her to stay in touch just enough so her parents would agree to give her the money when she was eighteen. Abby didn't mention it out loud. Better for Leonor's parents to think she was calling to hear their voices.

But Otis had miscalculated. By letting Leonor call her parents, he gave her a weekly taste of her old life. There was a good chance this was the reason that she was still showing signs of individuality.

"I want to try and get Leonor out of that farm," Abby said. "The best chance is if she sees a familiar, friendly face she trusts when we do this."

"I'd be happy to be there," Helen said.

Abby hesitated. "I think that's a good idea, but not right away. You've both made your opinions of the cult very clear. Which means as far as Leonor's concerned, you're out. She's wired to think of you as the enemy."

Helen flinched, covering her mouth.

"I'm sure she still loves you," Abby said. "But in there, anyone who says anything negative about their community is the enemy. She won't want to talk to you about it. You mentioned Leonor has a brother?"

"Yeah." Helen wiped her eyes. "Brian. He's upstairs."

"Can you get him?"

Brian was Leonor's big brother. He seemed like a man who'd already grown but was uncomfortable with his own body. His movements were hesitant, clumsy, and he didn't walk so much as lumber into the living room.

"Hello," he said. "Mom told me you're here about Leonor?"

257

"That's right." Abby smiled at him. "How close were you with your sister before she left for the Tillman cult?"

Brian shrugged. "I don't know. Pretty close, I guess. I found her feminist shit annoying. But she was fun to be around when she was in a good mood."

"Have you talked to her since she left?"

"Twice."

"Did you tell her anything about the cult? Did you tell her to leave it?"

"Nah. She never listens to anything I say anyway. I didn't want to pick a fight with her."

Abby grinned at him, relieved. "Brian, would you be willing to come with me for a few days?"

CHAPTER 50

For a second, when he opened the supply room's door, he thought the kid was dead. His face was pale and pasty, his body completely still. But then, exhaling with relief, he heard the kid's breathing. Weak and raspy. That wasn't *his* fault. He'd wanted to keep the kid as safe and comfortable as humanly possible. Wasn't that why he'd gone to all that effort?

It was Nathan's fault for using his kindness against him.

He pulled the kid to his feet, dragged him, moaning, to his room.

He'd spent the last hour stripping this room of anything that might be used against him. So if Nathan now had to stand by his desk while drawing, because there was no chair, he could only blame himself.

The kid's back looked bad. He took off the bloody shirt, eliciting a groan of pain as the wound began bleeding again. Peering closely, he saw the skin around the scratch was inflamed. A few fibers still stayed caked under the clotted blood.

He soaked a rag and cleaned the scratch. The kid whimpered.

"It's your fault. Your fault," he kept saying through clenched teeth. "*You* did this. It was your fault I had to defend myself and get rid of that man. That's all on you."

The sensation of his knife sinking into that man's throat was still fresh in his mind. An unpleasant feeling. A nauseating feeling.

But it had been self-defense. It was the kid's fault he had even been in that position. He'd had no choice. He'd given it a lot of thought, and there was nothing he could have done. Surely not once that kid had pointed him out as his abductor.

He dressed Nathan in a fresh shirt and took off the boy's other shoe and sock. Then he left the room, his nerves rattled.

He picked up his phone and checked Gabrielle's Instagram account again. Skimmed the comments on the latest posts with the links to her own interview and Eric Layton's interview. The fake sympathy her fans threw at her made him sick. If they cared, they'd do more than post a broken heart emoji. They'd contribute to the fundraiser.

A sudden worry nagged at him as he stared at his phone. A lurking anxiety, like the feeling he got when he thought he'd left the oven on or that he'd forgotten to lock his car.

He checked it to make sure he had nothing to worry about.

But there was a reason to worry after all. It was right there on his phone's screen.

Eric Layton had something. Something too dangerous to be left alone.

He would have to be dealt with.

There was no choice. It was self-defense.

CHAPTER 51

Eric was finally putting his photoshopping skills to good use.

As a teenager, he used to edit photos for fun. He could lose himself for hours tweaking photos to create ridiculous images. Adding Nicolas Cage's face to family pictures. Or giving people cat whiskers. Or his magnum opus—manipulating the group photo of the school's football team by shifting their faces around. He'd managed to get the manipulated image in the school paper, and *no one had noticed the switch.*

When he'd first met Gabrielle, she'd asked him to help her adjust a photo of hers. That was the word she always used. *Adjust.* They weren't making her thinner; they were "adjusting" her hips. They weren't changing her eye color; they were "adjusting" it.

But Gabrielle was always so sweet and kind to him, and he enjoyed spending time with her. He didn't mind adjusting her photos. When her Instagram profile became popular and began making money from sponsored products, he was happy to keep helping her. His friends said he should charge her money, but it wasn't like it was a job. Besides, she didn't really need his "adjusting" services; she was beautiful without his editing assistance.

Still, he knew he wasn't exactly making the world better when she constantly asked him to make her hips slimmer and her lips more pronounced.

But now he was actually trying to make a difference.

He had the image of Nathan holding the newspaper enlarged on his screen. He scanned it pixel by pixel, searching for signs of editing. It was easy when you knew what to look for. He went over the objects in the image, hunting for jagged edges or mismatched lighting—the telltale signs of photo manipulation.

That was what people didn't realize. Editing a digital image was an art. And if you were an amateur, it showed.

After three hours, his neck and right hand were completely cramped, and he took a short break, groaning, moving his head left and right. Maybe his interview had been published. He checked the *New Yorker Chronicle* website and saw that it was there. For a second, a rush of excitement flooded his body at seeing his name like that online. Then a wave of guilt washed over him. The only reason his name was there was because Gabrielle's brother had been kidnapped. Was he *happy* that a child had been kidnapped? Really?

Still, she'd probably want him to post a link to the article on his Twitter, right? She'd told him she needed as many people as possible to hear about the abduction. She needed the followers for the ransom contributions. He'd just post the interview. He wouldn't say anything in the caption about himself. This was not about him. It was about her.

When he logged in to Twitter, he noticed a new tweet from Gabrielle. It instantly drew his eye because it was the same image he'd been meticulously scrutinizing since that morning.

Gabrielle had posted Nathan's picture and written, *The kidnapper sent us this image of Nathan, to prove he's still alive.* She'd cropped the background, leaving only the part of Nathan holding up the newspaper. It was a smart move. Eric had already seen people commenting online that Gabrielle had made up the kidnapping. If they saw a picture of Nathan in his own room, they'd point it out as proof.

He frowned at the image. Something was wrong.

There.

He dialed Gabrielle's number.

"Hello?" she answered immediately.

"Gabrielle, it's Eric."

"What is it?" Abrupt, impatient, but it was understandable. Her nerves were shot to hell. She probably hardly slept. His heart clenched for her.

"Listen, the photo you posted—"

"Not you too," she said, annoyed. "I already had that detective call me and rant about it. I needed to post it. To make people see."

"But is that the image the kidnapper sent you?"

"Of course it is. What, you think I took it myself?"

"No, it's just . . . is it the only one you got?"

"Eric, I don't have time right now. I need to talk to the guy organizing the donations; there's some kind of problem with the money. And the kidnapper might call at any moment."

"But this is important—"

She hung up.

He stared at the image again. There was no doubt.

Then he dialed 911.

CHAPTER 52

"What if they don't let her leave?" Brian asked.

"They'll let her leave. It's in their best interest," Abby answered distractedly.

They were leaning on the hood of her car two miles away from the Tillman farm, waiting for Wong and Leonor to show up. Wong had agreed to go into the farm alone and tell Otis that the bald man with the tattoo Leonor had seen might match a suspect in the kidnapping. They needed to talk to Leonor at the station. Abby believed if the NYPD stayed out of it, Otis might be in a more cooperative frame of mind, since it was established that the Suffolk County Police were in his pocket.

But deep in her heart, she shared Brian's misgivings. What if Otis told Leonor she couldn't leave? If she refused to come, there was nothing they could do.

Wong had seemed confident that she could present a good case, make it sound like it was in everybody's interest to finally get the NYPD off Tillman's back. She'd hint that once Leonor identified the bald guy with the tattoo, the NYPD would have no reason to keep Karl in custody.

Otis surely cared more for his nephew than he did for a girl who dared interrupt him when he talked.

Or maybe not.

"If she doesn't want to come with us, can we just . . . take her?"

"No. Back in the seventies, they used to do that. People would abduct cult members, lock them up somewhere safe, and forcefully deprogram them, sometimes for weeks. In many cases it did more harm than good. Even if the process was successful, it was traumatic for the subject. Not to mention it's illegal. No, she has to agree to come."

"Yeah, but—"

"There." Abby pointed as Wong's vehicle rounded the curve. The sun reflected off the windshield, and Abby squinted, searching.

"Leonor is with her," Brian said, relieved.

"Yeah." Abby grinned. "Are you ready?"

"I guess." Brian sounded doubtful. "I wasn't kidding before. Leonor *never* listens to me. I'm her dumb stoner brother."

"Just convince her to hear me out," Abby said. "I'll do the rest of the talking."

Wong pulled the car to the side of the road and said something to Leonor. Then she got out and took a few steps away from the road, finally pausing by a large tree. She leaned on it and lit a cigarette.

Abby joined her. Wong offered a cigarette, and Abby shook her head.

"Detective Mullen," Wong said in a monotone voice. "Fancy meeting you here. What an amazing coincidence."

Abby turned around and watched Brian approach Wong's car, leaning to wave hello at Leonor. Leonor's smile was confused, but there was no doubt in Abby's mind. She was overjoyed to see her brother.

"What did you tell her?"

"Exactly what we agreed. She's supposedly coming with me to the station to look at mug shots. She was crying when I showed up."

"Crying? Why?"

"No idea. They had just gotten out of their communal lunch. She walked out alone."

"Did she ask for permission to leave?"

"Oh yeah. Went directly to Otis and asked him in front of me. He gave her permission and told me if she wasn't back in a few hours, he'd make a few phone calls. Told her she was 'under his protection.'" Wong uttered the last words with uncharacteristic disgust.

"What will you do if she comes with me and your commander gets another angry phone call from the county executive asking where the hell Leonor is?" Abby asked, watching the brother and sister talk. Brian shook his head, pointing behind his shoulder.

"I'll say we left together, but halfway to the station she changed her mind and demanded I let her out." Wong shrugged. "Don't worry; my career will survive."

"Thanks for doing this."

Wong gave her a tight smile. "I'm not doing it for you, Mullen. I'm doing it for this kid. I'm doing it so she doesn't end up like another Ruth."

Leonor got out of Wong's car looking pissed off. Brian motioned Abby over.

"Good luck," Wong said.

Abby walked over to them, smiling. "Hi, Leonor. It's good to—"

"You have ten minutes," Leonor said coldly. "And then I'm out of here." Her eyes were still swollen.

"It seems like you've been crying," Abby said.

"We're not talking about that. Brian said you have something you want from me. Out with it."

Abby shrugged. "It's not important; I just wanted to iron out some details about what you saw. Why were you crying?"

"You almost never cry," Brian said, staring at the ground. "It had to be something really—"

"Shut up, Brian," Leonor snapped at him. "It's nothing. A misunderstanding."

"You know, I was born in a religious community," Abby said. "I was really happy there. But our preacher was under terrible stress.

Sometimes he hardly slept. And he would snap." Abby snapped her fingers. "Start yelling at someone during prayer. Just screaming at the top of his voice."

Leonor said nothing.

"This one time I went somewhere I shouldn't have."

A door left unlocked. She would have just a small peek. No one would even know. She opened it enough to peep and saw stacks of dark packets. Strange jars and pots. And guns.

"He screamed at me for what felt like an hour. In front of everyone." To Abby's surprise, tears clogged her throat. The memory, even after all this time, still brought pain. "It felt like the end of the world. No one would talk to me afterward. No one would even look at me."

Brian blinked at her in shock. But in Leonor's eyes she saw something different. Leonor knew what she was talking about. Leonor had just gone through something similar.

Abby blinked and cleared her throat. "He was under a lot of stress, that's all. He told me that later. Other than that, I was happy there. I had a purpose. Can you imagine, a seven-year-old with a purpose?"

"What was your purpose?" Brian asked.

"I was to be the mother of the Messiah's children. And they would all be winged angels. My parents were ecstatic."

"Your parents believed that?" Leonor asked, incredulous.

"Not at first. My mother was very educated. She was a pediatrician. And my father was an engineer. But they were searching for spiritual growth, and they went to this weeklong workshop. Just for fun. It was out in the woods, away from their friends and family. They didn't sleep so much because they spent a lot of the time studying. The workshop was about finding new interpretations of the Old Testament. And after a few days in which they didn't sleep and talked nonstop with other believers, they both had a moment of enlightenment. It convinced them to sign up for another, longer workshop." Abby shrugged. "One thing led to another, and I was born in a cult, thinking I would give birth to angels."

"That's crazy," Brian said. Leonor nodded but said nothing.

"Isn't it?" Abby said. "Anyway, like I said, I was happy until it ended."

"How *did* it end?" Leonor asked.

"The police showed up to arrest our preacher. It turned out that under his guidance, our community members were producing and selling heroin. The cops initiated a siege on our compound. Maybe you heard about it. The preacher's name was Moses Wilcox."

"Moses Wilcox," Leonor said, stunned. "The Wilcox massacre?"

"You've heard about it. The police wanted to break through the door, so Wilcox held a gun to my head and made me tell them that if they entered, he would blow my head off. I guess I was very convincing. The police held back, and Moses used the time to set the dining hall on fire. We had two large cooking cylinders in the hall, and they blew up. Only three of us survived." Abby pulled down the collar of her shirt, exposing a scar. "The burn scar never completely healed."

"Why are you telling me this?" Leonor asked.

Abby shrugged. "I think strong beliefs and a purpose are great. I mean, I donate monthly to Greenpeace. But some of these groups can cause harm. You have to be on your guard. Do your research. Did you do your research on Otis Tillman's Progressive Christian Community?"

"I'm not stupid; I wouldn't join a cult."

"I'm not saying you're stupid. Like I said, my parents weren't stupid either. And Brian is worried about you."

"He shouldn't be," Leonor said, a little too sharply.

"You moved out a year ago to join this religious group," Brian said. "We only spoke twice on the phone. We used to talk all the time. If our roles were reversed, wouldn't you be concerned?"

"I'd trust you if you said it's the right thing for you," Leonor snapped.

"Okay, cool," Brian said. "But you didn't say that. I'm crazy scared, Leonor. I just want to spend a day or two with you, see you're okay."

"I'm not going back to Mom and Dad's," she said quickly.

"That's fine," Abby said. "I have a place you can stay. And just talk. Tell us about this group. Convince us it's not destructive. You can leave whenever you want. And you get to spend a few days with your brother."

She saw the yearning in Leonor's eyes. She missed Brian. She wanted to spend time with him.

"I can't," Leonor said.

"Why?" Brian asked, his tone getting angry.

Abby shot him a warning stare. "What do you think will happen if you come?" she asked. "What's the worst-case scenario? You trust your brother, right?"

"I trust my brother. I don't trust you."

"It sounds like you think I'll lead you into a trap," Abby said lightly. "How can I convince you that's not the case?"

Leonor thought about it. "I ride with my brother," she finally said. "Not with you. You're not coming with us."

"I didn't intend to; I have a job."

"We stop by the place, and if I don't like the looks of it, we drive off."

"No problem." Abby saw the fear in Leonor's eyes. "Like I said, you're free to leave whenever you want."

"What about Detective Wong? She needs me to identify the person I saw."

"She can do that later. Brian, is that okay with you?"

"Sure. Just give me the address."

Abby gave him her parents' address. Brian and Leonor went to his car and drove off. Abby gave Wong the thumbs-up, and for the first time, Wong grinned at her, a wide smile. Then Abby stepped into her own car and drove after Brian.

She dialed her mother, who answered almost immediately.

"Hi, sweetie."

"Mom, they're coming. I won't be joining them; I have to check in with the task force."

"I'll prepare the spare bedroom."

"Don't do anything that will make her feel trapped. I told her she can leave whenever she wants."

"Then I'll throw the shackles away."

"Not funny, Mom." Abby grinned. "Did you drop Ben at Steve's?"

"Yes. Sweetie, you need to talk to Sam. She's *really* angry."

"It's your fault."

"She's angry because you almost didn't talk to her all weekend, not because of the dumb snake."

"I'll see her today," Abby said guiltily.

Brian's car veered abruptly to the left.

"What the—"

To her alarm, the car zigzagged out of control. An oncoming bus honked frantically as it hurtled toward it. Abby could only watch with mounting horror as the bus tried to stop before it crushed the car, but it was too close, going way too fast. Then, at the last moment, Brian veered back to the right, spinning onto the shoulder of the road.

"Shit!" Abby shouted.

Brian managed to turn away from a cluster of trees, his right side mirror hitting one, smashing into pieces. The car stopped, a spinning cloud of dust in its wake.

"Abby, is everything okay?"

"Mom, I'll call you back."

Abby stopped behind Brian's car and leaped out, then rushed to the passenger's side.

"Are you two okay?" she blurted.

Brian's cheek was bleeding from three long scratches. Leonor trembled, her face pale.

"Y . . . yeah," Leonor said. "We're . . . oh god, we nearly crashed."

"What happened?" Abby asked.

"Nothing," Brian said, rubbing his cheek. He stared at the blood on his fingers. "Nothing serious."

"I . . . I scratched him," Leonor stammered.

Abby looked carefully at the girl. She seemed frightened, but it wasn't a full-blown panic attack. Cult leaders often scared their members with threats of untold horrors that would occur if they ever left. What lies had Otis threatened Leonor with? Whatever they were, the girl wouldn't divulge them. Not right now.

Abby took a deep breath and softened her voice. "Leonor, remember. You're just taking a day off with your brother, okay? You can return to Tillman's farm whenever you want."

"O . . . okay."

"Brian, are you okay to drive?"

"Sure." He seemed shaken, but his voice was steady, resolute.

"Okay." Abby exhaled and returned to her car. She called her mother again.

"Abby, what happened?"

"Mom, when Leonor and Brian get there, just . . . be gentle, okay? That bastard did a number on her."

CHAPTER 53

Eric was working on a new project. Every now and then he'd grab the scotch bottle and take a swig.

His head spun, and he felt nauseous. He didn't normally drink so much. Sometimes one glass in the evening while watching TV. But the circumstances were appropriate.

He wasn't searching the image of Nathan for any marks of manipulation. He now knew he'd find none. He'd been played for a fool. They all had. No, instead he'd found that classic Disney photo of Snow White's stepmother, the evil queen. She stood in front of the mirror, but Eric had given her a cell phone, which she held in her hand. He was proud of his work—he hadn't been as drunk when he'd done that part.

The caption came easily. *Instagram, Instagram, on the phone, who's the fairest of them all?* He still giggled when he read it. It would go viral for sure.

Now, he worked on pasting Gabrielle's face instead of the queen's. It was going badly. What was that quote? "Write drunk, edit sober"? One of those things people *thought* Hemingway had said, even though he'd never actually said it. Eric had his own quote for posterity. "Meme drunk, photoshop sober." It was easy enough to cut Gabrielle's face, but he did it sloppily; the light was all wrong, and the size didn't fit.

He'd phoned her three more times, but she hadn't answered.

Eric had to admit to himself he'd been in love with her for years.

It had been his idea to go on that road trip that ended up making her famous. And he was the driver; Gabrielle didn't have a license back then. He took a lot of the photos. He worked on them to make them better. Didn't ask for payment—she had no money back then; her family was barely scraping by. But that set a precedent, so he never asked for money after that either.

Perhaps it really had been dumb. He was a sucker.

Someone knocked on the door. Gabrielle? Of course not. Pathetic. Still feeling that hopeful yearning even now.

Then he remembered he'd asked the woman who'd answered his 911 call to tell the detective to drop by. Because he had something to show him.

Zigzagging to the door, he peered through the peephole. Oh, it was neither.

He opened the door. "Hello. What—"

A fast movement in the dark, a vicious jab. Sudden, sharp pain tore through Eric's torso, robbing him of his breath. He gasped, taking a few steps back, trying to push the man away clumsily. The man held on, pulling Eric to him, grunting. Eric tumbled, fell forward onto his attacker, whose legs buckled under the weight. They crashed to the floor.

Eric's chest was on fire. He rolled off the man, stumbled away, but his chest still throbbed, and something was *wrong*. He looked at himself.

"Wha . . ."

A knife was lodged in his body. He grasped the hilt feebly, tried to pull it out, and let out a weak scream. The knife was stuck.

But now the man was on his feet, lunging at him. He grabbed the hilt and pulled. Eric grunted in pain, trying to push the hand away. The knife wouldn't budge, but every time the bastard yanked it, his insides were being torn to shreds.

He scratched at the man, kicked at him, managed to get away. He crawled now, toward the front door. He needed to escape.

Something struck his head, and he collapsed. The knife hit the floor first and cut into him as his weight forced the blade deeper inside. He cried, desperate for the pain to stop, desperate for help, desperate for oblivion.

CHAPTER 54

Abby sat across from Samantha in the small café. Around them, customers were chatting, eating dinner, and having a good time.

Samantha and Abby were not chatting, nor were they having a good time. In fact, Abby was having a bad time. An abysmal time.

A short temper was not one of Samantha's faults. She rarely got angry. She got irritated, but it almost never escalated from there. Instead, Samantha had a sort of constant simmering rage that, left unchecked, could boil into a roaring inferno.

Abby estimated that when Samantha had stormed out of the house because of the snake, she had been, at most, very annoyed. But instead of fixing the problem by getting rid of the snake, Abby had let their new resident remain. And instead of talking to Samantha, trying to reason with her, coddle her with platitudes and declarations of how she missed her daughter, Abby had ignored Samantha for the entire weekend.

And the annoyance had simmered—and boiled.

Previous experience dictated that when Samantha was angry, she dredged up every memory in which she had been wronged or suffered injustice. She added those memories to her soup of fury. So by now she could be mad about that one time when Abby had forgotten to pick her up from the swimming pool, or that day Abby had embarrassed her in front of her friend, or any of the other abundant mothering fails Abby had accumulated over the years.

When Abby had shown up at Steve's, Samantha had refused to speak with her or even look at her. So Abby had to grovel just to get a grunt at the suggestion that they go and talk it over in the nearby café. Samantha made it a point to be very sweet to her father, literally *kissing him goodbye*. And then she made it a point to be very nice to the waitress with multiple polite questions about the menu, finally asking what the waitress liked best. All the while completely ignoring her mother.

Abby was getting the full Samantha treatment. Which was fine—she knew she'd earned it.

She would let Samantha go first. It was important that Samantha get the feeling her mother actually listened to her. She leaned back, an apologetic expression on her face, hands to the side, her entire body signaling *come at me*.

Samantha gritted her jaw and folded her arms.

One minute. Two minutes. Five. People couldn't abide silence for long; Abby knew that. Eventually they broke. And Samantha was a social creature; she loved talking. Eventually, she'd start.

Ten minutes. The waitress came over and placed a cup of coffee and a danish in front of Abby and a fried tofu sandwich in front of Samantha.

"Enjoy," she said.

"Thank you so much." Samantha smiled at her. "It looks delicious."

The waitress smiled back and walked away. Samantha ate, ignoring her mother.

Okay, waiting her out wasn't a good strategy at all. Abby decided to change tack. She'd go first.

"It seems like you're angry at me," she said.

"I'm angry at you?" Samantha repeated Abby's words dispassionately and took a bite of her sandwich.

"How can I help you forgive me?" An open-ended question that would make Samantha think from Abby's point of view.

"I don't know, Mom. What do you think you should do?"

Okay, this wasn't working at all, and Abby lost her patience. "Can you please stop repeating my words to me?"

Sam put her sandwich carefully back on the plate, her cheeks flushing. "It depends. Can *you* stop treating me like one of your cases?"

"I'm not—"

"Yes, you are. You're talking to me like I'm holding a hostage at gunpoint or threatening to jump off a building. I'm not a psycho on drugs, okay, Mom?"

"Well, what do you want me to say?"

"I don't *want* you to say anything! You didn't call the entire weekend. It's *Monday*. You didn't even ask how my math test went! I had a fight with Julia yesterday, but you wouldn't know because you didn't pick up the phone. I had to talk to *Dad* about it."

"I'm sorry, Sam, but I'm on a very important case. A kid might die if I don't do my job right. So deal with it! I know it sucks, but your mother is also a cop, and sometimes, that takes precedence."

Both of them were breathing hard. Some people in the café were staring while others were making an effort to look the other way.

Sam picked up her sandwich and took another bite. "You should eat," she said, her mouth full.

Abby took a large bite from her danish and chewed angrily. Steve sometimes didn't call for a week, but as far as the kids were concerned, he did the best he could. Damn fathers everywhere, with their double standards. If Steve worked late, only showing up for half an hour to half-heartedly ask the kids how their day was, he was an overworked father making time for his son and daughter. But when Abby went to *literally* save lives and forgot to call, she was the mother who neglected her children.

Once, when she and Steve were still married, they went to the mall, and Samantha, only two years old at the time, threw a scene because they wouldn't buy her a stuffed animal. When Abby tried to calm her down, she got disgusted stares from everyone around her. She was the mother who couldn't get her shit together. Then, finally, Steve picked Samantha up and held her while she screamed, and *he got admiring looks* from people. Because he was a sweet father trying to calm his daughter. Abby had never forgiven him for that day even though she knew he hadn't done anything wrong.

"You know," Samantha said, "you never give Ben that shit. Talking to him like he's wearing an explosive vest."

"Ben always does what I tell him."

Samantha shrugged. "So I don't. Don't start handling me. Yell at me."

"Will that help?"

"No, I'd get angry and yell back, and we'd have a fight, but at least I won't feel like my mother treats me like a terrorist."

"Okay." A wave of guilt washed over Abby, and she nearly burst into tears. Samantha was right; she *did* treat her like a jumper or a crackhead on a violent rampage. She'd thought it was the best way to handle Samantha and her mood swings. But Samantha was too smart for that. She'd realized what Abby was doing.

"How *was* your math test?"

"It was fine, Mom."

"What did you fight with Julia about?"

"It doesn't matter." Samantha ate the last bite of her sandwich. "That kid you talked about. Is it Nathan Fletcher?"

"You heard about him?"

Samantha shrugged. "Sure. It's all over social media. Gabrielle Fletcher is sorta famous. I mean, now even more than usual. Did you meet her?"

"Yeah, a few times."

"What's she like?"

"A self-absorbed, impulsive girl."

Samantha grinned. "Yeah, that's what I figured. You know that a lot of people online are saying Nathan is hiding somewhere and that Gabrielle is doing all of this to get more followers?"

"That's not true," Abby said. "Nathan really was kidnapped. "

"There was a fitness guru in Florida who faked her own daughter's kidnapping," Samantha pointed out.

"I haven't heard of that," Abby said, surprised.

"And there's a superfamous gamer girl who maybe faked her own arrest. I mean, I'm not sure she wasn't arrested, but it sounds like that was the case. Oh, and there's Marina Joyce."

"Who?"

"She's a YouTuber that everyone really thought was kidnapped because she seemed kinda scared in one of her YouTube videos. So she did a live video to tell people she was fine, and it just freaked people more because they found clues in *that* video that she really was kidnapped and was trying to send signals to her fans." Samantha smiled, bemused. "Then a lot of people said she did it intentionally as a publicity stunt. Look it up; it's a crazy story."

"How old would I sound if I said you kids spend too much time on social media?"

"About two hundred."

"That sounds about right." Abby's phone rang, Carver's name showing up on the screen. She glanced at Sam apologetically. "I have to get this. It'll be just a moment."

"Whatever."

She sighed and answered the call. "Hey."

"Hey, Abby." He sounded tired. "Listen, that friend of Gabrielle Fletcher's, Eric, tried to reach me. Left a message with dispatch. I tried to call him back a few times, but there's no answer. I'm about to start interviewing Liam's customers from recent weeks. Can you call him, or drop by his place and see what he wants?"

"Sure. Text me the phone number and address."

"Thanks."

"Any update?" She eyed Samantha, making sure she wasn't stewing up a new rage, but her daughter was focused on her own phone, tapping.

"We got Liam Washington's recent debit card transactions. He bought a burger and fries at a place called Dallas Barbecue in the Bronx at nine forty-five p.m. on Saturday night."

"Okay."

"That matches his stomach contents. So our time of death according to the ME is between ten thirty and midnight on Saturday night. Turner went there to see if we have footage of him or if anyone happens to remember seeing him. Maybe he met someone there."

"An accomplice?"

"Maybe." Carver sounded doubtful. "Listen, did Will talk to you about Nathan's room?"

"You mean the fake Nathan room?"

"Yeah. He sent me a few images. It's crazy. They literally redrew some of Nathan's drawings. Or they made Nathan redraw them; I don't know. What do you make of it?"

"Well . . . whoever did this is highly obsessive. It could be an attempt to induce Nathan's cooperation."

"I thought along similar lines."

"It's good news in any case."

"How do you figure?"

She eyed Sam and lowered her voice. "They wouldn't have gone to all that effort if they intended to simply kill Nathan. This indicates they want to keep him alive."

"Huh. Yeah, that makes sense. Well, I'll take good news when I can get it."

"Glad to help. Listen, I gotta go, I'm with my daughter—"

"Sure, no worries. Let me know what Eric wanted."

"Okay. Bye." She hung up.

A few seconds later she got the text with Eric's details. Abby immediately tried to call him, but there was no answer. She checked the address and was relieved to see it was almost on the way from Steve's house to her own. She wanted to get this done with and go to bed.

"So," she said. "Are we cool?"

Samantha didn't raise her eyes from the phone. "No. But we're getting there. And please don't say *cool*. It makes me cringe. Oh, and I'll need a few things from my room. If you can drop them when you pick up Ben from Dad's, it'll be great."

"You're not coming home with me on Wednesday?"

Sam raised her eyes. "Is there still a snake in the house?"

"Yes."

"Then no, I'm not coming home with you."

"Sam, you can't stay at your dad's."

"Watch me."

Abby sighed. "And I figured I could get you that electric violin you've been talking about."

Sam put the phone down. "Are you trying to bribe me?"

"Will it work?"

Samantha considered it. "If you pay for another weekly violin lesson."

"Okay," Abby said brightly. "Done." Her mother would pay for the violin and the weekly lessons. Abby couldn't afford it, and it was her mother's mess to begin with.

Samantha nodded, glowing happily. "Fine. I'll come back home on Wednesday. Are you going back to work?"

"Not really. Just a quick visit to talk to someone, and then I'll drive home. I'm exhausted. It's been a long day."

CHAPTER 55

No one answered when Abby knocked on the door. She yawned and knocked again, wondering if she should just go home. She doubted Eric really had crucial information. If he did, he wouldn't just have left a message; he would have gone to the police or called Gabrielle and told her about it.

She dialed his number and waited. No answer. She'd drop by his place again tomorrow on her way to her mother's. She was about to hang up, but her finger hovered above the screen. Was that . . . a phone ringtone? She listened carefully. It was muffled, but she could definitely hear it. As she hung up, it stopped.

She put her ear to the door and dialed again. The phone was inside the house.

It meant nothing. Eric could have gone to the nearby drugstore, forgetting his phone at home. Or maybe he was home but asleep, and the phone wasn't waking him up.

But something was off. She couldn't put her finger on what, but it didn't matter. She knew from experience not to ignore the warning signs in her gut. Maybe it was that stillness in the air that made her skin prickle. Or just those vague connections—his interview that morning followed by his message. Would someone call 911 and then go to sleep or forget his phone at home?

She unholstered her gun and quietly crept through the dark yard. There was a light on inside the house. Carefully peering through the window, she scrutinized the room. It looked like a sort of office coupled with a home gym. A treadmill covered with unfolded laundry. A desk with a large monitor.

And in the doorway, on the dusty floor, a sticky reddish-brown smear.

She went back to the door, tried the handle. The door was unlocked. She pushed it quietly with her body, both hands on the gun now, holding it steady.

Signs of a struggle, a chair knocked to the floor. Taking a shallow breath, she took a step inside. There. An inert body lying facedown on the floor in a large pool of glistening blood.

Stepping softly, she made her way to the closed bathroom door. Turned the doorknob and kicked it open, gun aimed ahead. A few bloody footprints on the creamy floor. Shower curtain hiding the bath. She pulled it aside with one swift movement, made sure there was no one there, already swiveling around, pausing, listening for any sound.

Next came the bedroom. No one under the bed or in the closet. She checked the office, heart leaping at the silhouette of a man, but it was a coat and a hat hanging on the wall. The computer was still on, and her mind registered that it was Gabrielle on the screen even as she checked for anyone hiding inside the room.

The house was clear.

She hurried to the inert body, checking the pulse, finding none; the vacant eyes stared at nothing, the hair matted and sticky. So much blood everywhere.

Dashing outside, she reached her car in less than ten seconds. She grabbed the mic and hit the button.

"Central, Lieutenant Abby Mullen, I have a ten-twenty-four, man down. I need backup and medical assistance."

Static, then the choppy, interrupted voice of the dispatcher: " . . . the location, what's the location?"

Abby gave them the address and repeated the need for patrol assistance as well as an ambulance. The radio crackled as the dispatcher called all units in the area to respond, but Abby didn't stay to listen. She slammed the door and went back into the house, heart thrumming in her chest. She leaned down by Eric's body, checking again for vitals, noticing the blood-matted hair, the crimson trickle on his forehead, the ragged wounds in his back. He was well beyond anything she could do to help him.

CHAPTER 56

"No rigor mortis," Dr. Gomez told Abby. "Livor mortis just starting to show. Body temperature still almost normal. He's been dead for less than three hours."

Abby kept her eyes on Gomez, avoiding the gaping wound in Eric Layton's skull. The smell of blood was overpowering. The pool of glistening blood surrounding the victim was still fresh, and it was difficult to avoid stepping in it. Abby and Gomez had both put on shoe booties in addition to the gloves.

Abby ignored the nausea that assailed her. She'd been involved in worse crime scenes than this. She would deal. "Did the head wound kill him?"

"I don't know if it killed him, but I doubt he kept moving after getting it. There's major trauma to the skull. See the bone fragments here?"

"No, I don't." Abby glanced away.

Gomez's eyes softened. "Well, they're there. But the actual cause of death might be from the blood loss, and most of it didn't come from the head wound."

"Where then?"

"I'll show you." Gomez glanced up at the police photographer. "Are you done? Can we move him?"

The photographer nodded. Gomez motioned to her paramedics. "Try to avoid stepping in the blood."

They walked over and picked Eric's body up, flipped him, and placed him on the gurney faceup. His shirt was soaked with blood. A ragged tear in the fabric exposed another deep wound.

"Stab wound in his chest," Gomez said. "You're searching for two murder weapons. A blunt weapon bashed his skull. And a blade."

"Looks like the murderer also stomped him," Abby said, pointing at a faint outline of mud on the victim's shoulder. "See? That seems like a footprint."

"Maybe," Gomez said. "I'll tell you if there's any bruising to the shoulder."

"When's the autopsy?" Abby asked.

"I'll let you know, but if this case is linked to the Nathan Fletcher kidnapping case, I suspect it's high priority," Gomez said. "So probably tomorrow morning."

The paramedics rolled the gurney out. Abby stood up and glanced around the room, her breathing shallow. The coppery smell of the blood was slowly clogging her nostrils. A sudden image of Eric sitting next to Gabrielle Fletcher, trying to console her, flashed through Abby's mind.

There were blood smears everywhere, a red handprint on the kitchen counter. A spatter of blood on the wall. Eric had struggled. Abby inspected the fallen chair, wondering if this was what had been used to bash Eric's head. It didn't look like it; the chair was clean. Then she noticed the small black dumbbell in the corner of the room. It was the type sold in pairs. Where was its twin?

"Did you find the other dumbbell?" she asked a masked woman from the forensic crew.

The woman shook her head. "Didn't see it."

Maybe that was the blunt weapon the murderer had used. He'd stabbed Eric and then, in the struggle, somehow lost his knife. Grabbed one of Eric's dumbbells and bashed Eric's head with it.

Okay, fine, but why? What had Eric done? He'd called to say he'd found something, but how would the murderer even know what—

The interview.

The realization intensified her nausea. That journalist had published Eric's interview that morning. He must have said something that had caught the murderer's attention, made him think Eric knew something he shouldn't. And maybe later, Eric had figured out what it was. Called the police, left a message for Carver to get back to him. Except by the time Carver called him, the murderer had shown up.

She stepped into Eric's spare room. Ahmed was dusting the keyboard of the computer carefully. Abby examined the computer screen, where the image Eric had been working on was still displayed. It was a picture from Disney's *Snow White and the Seven Dwarfs*. The evil queen held a cell phone, and the caption below said, *Instagram, Instagram, on the phone, who's the fairest of them all?* Gabrielle's face was pasted crudely on top of the queen's face. A half-empty bottle of scotch stood on the desk, no glass. Eric had been drinking straight from the bottle.

"You taking the computer?" she asked.

"Yup," Ahmed said. "We'll start looking through it tomorrow. Emails, browsing history, porn preferences, everything."

"How long will that take?"

He shrugged. "It might be a while if this guy used his computer often."

"I think he did," Abby said.

She called the photographer and asked him to capture a few shots of the desk, including the image on the screen.

After he was done, she said, "Would you mind if I take a quick look?"

"Do you need the keyboard?"

"I don't think so."

"Then I don't have a problem," Ahmed said. "Keyboards are a treasure trove of dead skin cells, fingernails, and fingerprints."

"A treasure trove, huh?" Abby smiled despite herself. "You would have made a shitty pirate."

"Shiver me timbers," Ahmed said in a droll tone.

Abby gently moved the mouse with her gloved hand, checking the recent projects that Eric had been working on. The most recent was Nathan Pic. She clicked it. It was the image the kidnapper had sent Gabrielle of Nathan holding the newspaper. What had Eric thought about it?

"Do you know how to use Photoshop?"

"A bit."

"Can you see if any changes were made to the photo on this computer?"

"Sure, give me that." He took the mouse from her and checked one of the panels. "No changes. This image wasn't modified from what I can tell. In fact, this isn't even a project file; it's an image opened in Photoshop."

She took the mouse back and checked the two files before that. They were called Gabi_110219 and Gabi_102719.

She clicked one of them. It was one of Gabrielle's pictures. Abby vaguely remembered a similar picture on Gabrielle's Instagram account. "Any changes to this photo?"

Ahmed checked again. "Yup. He worked on this one. Here, see? Before—and after." He clicked between two similar thumbnails. It was almost imperceptible, but Abby knew where to look. Gabrielle was thinner in the modified picture, her breasts slightly larger, a small skin blemish on her neck gone, eyebrows sharper.

She sighed and checked the folder that contained the Gabrielle projects.

It had over seven hundred files.

"Okay," Abby said. "Let me know once you're done with it. I might need to go through it again."

"Will do." Ahmed was carefully applying translucent tape to the neck of the scotch bottle to lift the fingerprints.

"And if you find either the missing dumbbell or a misplaced knife, call me immediately."

"Right."

Abby moved toward the hallway, careful not to step in the blood. She followed the bloody footprints to the bathroom. They stopped at the sink. Pink water drops stained its scratched porcelain surface. The murderer had cleaned himself up after killing Eric. She noticed a speck of mud on the edge of the faucet. She placed an evidence marker on the sink, then called over the photographer to take a close-up photo of the mud.

He'd even washed his shoes of the blood. Taken his time. How long had he been there after killing Eric? Twenty minutes? Half an hour? An hour?

If Abby had shown up faster, would she have caught him inside?

She gritted her teeth and left the bathroom, her plastic-covered shoe kicking something tiny that clattered on the floor. Abby approached it and inspected it closely. What was it? An eggshell?

No, too thick. It was another skull fragment.

She stood up, about to call Ahmed's attention to it, when the nausea rose. She had a few seconds. She lunged to the front door, yanked it open, took two steps, and threw up on a large bush to the side of the path.

"Abby?" Carver said behind her. "Are you okay?"

"Oh shit." Abby wiped her mouth, staring at the bush.

"I just got here. Is Eric—"

"He's dead," Abby said numbly, still gawking at the spray of vomit. "I can't believe I did that."

"Don't worry about it," Carver said softly. "I won't tell."

"I think I'm going to have to," Abby said, pointing. "I just vomited on the murder weapon."

On the wet ground, under the bush, lay a black dumbbell, spotted with Abby's half-digested danish.

CHAPTER 57

Abby tossed and turned in her bed, thinking of Eric Layton lying dead on the floor. He'd called them just hours before. If she'd gone there earlier . . .

A cop's life was full of regrets. Decisions made in seconds that could mean life or death. A hair not properly labeled at a crime scene could mean a killer going free. A moment's hesitation in a conflict could mean a person getting hurt or killed. The wrong action or word in a crisis could escalate into a disaster.

Over years of police service, these moments piled up, hounding you at night. You had to learn to push them away. No matter how much regret you poured into a single moment, it never changed its outcome. Time moved only in one direction.

Still, if she'd gone there just a bit earlier.

She threw the blanket off her and plodded to the bathroom.

The skin on her palms itched. She had an urge to turn on the faucet. Let the cool water run over her hands. Some soap. Wash them clean. Really, methodically wash them, peeling away all the dirt, that satisfying feeling of the fingernails scraping the filth, and dead skin cells, and yes, the germs . . .

She forced herself to step back and shut the door.

She returned to her bed, picked up her phone, and sent a message to Isaac asking if he was awake. Usually he stayed up late. This night, however, there was no answer. Sighing, she picked up her laptop from the night table and turned it on. She intended to write some emails, maybe read an article about cult intervention.

Instead, she dragged the cursor over to the transcript icon. If icons could have wear and tear, that one would have been tattered and frayed at the corners. She double-clicked it, the familiar report filling her screen.

N: Hello?

A: Hello.

N: Hi. My name is Nick. What's—

"—your name?" His voice was kind, but Abihail knew he was one of them.

"My name's Abihail." She clutched the phone in her sweaty palm. Eden was sobbing in the background. People sat huddled all around her.

"Abihail, that's a lovely name," Nick said. "How old are you, Abihail?"

"Seven and a half." The cold, hard gun muzzle pressed against her temple, hurting her. "I have a gun pointed at my head."

Abby shivered as she read the transcript, the events of that night more vivid than they'd been for years. Things had escalated so fast. A terrible armed conflict ending up with seven dead and numerous wounded on both sides. And then a cease-fire. And the phone call.

A: He says—

"—that if you come closer, he will shoot," Abihail said. "He says you should stay back."

She glanced at Isaac. He was sitting on the floor, clutching his small backpack, frozen in fear.

"Who has a gun to your head?" Nick asked.

"Father Wilcox."

"Can you put him on the phone?"

The muzzle dug into her temple. She looked up at Father. His eyes flinty, unrelenting. "Tell them," he said.

"No," she answered Nick. "He says you should all stay away."

"Okay, Abihail. We'll stay away. Where are you right now?"

She looked around her at the benches, the upturned tables pressed against the door, blocking it. The members of the Family grouped together in the center of the room. "We're all together in the mess hall. All sixty-two of us. It's important that you stay back. Or he'll shoot me. He says if you stay back, he'll start sending people out in one hour."

"Okay. Is there an adult who can talk to me?"

There wasn't. Only Abihail could talk to the cops. Only she was allowed. "I have to hang up."

"Wait—"

She placed the phone in the cradle. She raised her eyes to Father Wilcox again. Saw the satisfaction in his eyes. Her chest swelled with pride.

"Now lock the door," he said softly.

She walked over to the door. There was no lock, just a bolt. She could just reach it if she stood on her tiptoes.

It slid easily, locking them inside. All the members of the Family were protected now.

Abby shut the laptop and set it aside. She recalled her childish belief that they were safe, that the danger was outside. She tried to recall the moment that Moses Wilcox lit the fire, but couldn't. All she remembered was the flames and the—

—smoke. People screamed. The air was hazy, and she was coughing violently. She had to get the door open.

She ran, hand over her mouth, to slide the bolt back, to open the door. Behind her, she heard Eden shout, "Abihail, get away from there!"

She had to open the door.

Isaac grabbed her, pulled her back.

An explosion, the searing pain on the back of her neck.

Her hand flew to her neck, and she let out a shuddering breath, tracing the decades-old scar.

Exhaustion settled over her like an extra blanket.

Thinking about the past wouldn't change it. Just like she couldn't go back a few hours and save Eric Layton.

And Nathan Fletcher still needed her. She had to get some sleep.

CHAPTER 58

Nathan hardly managed to get out of bed. The floor tilted this way and that, and for a second, he wondered if he was somehow on a ferry. He'd gone on the Staten Island Ferry with Mom and Gabrielle a few times, and it had felt a bit like this. But after a moment, leaning against the wall, he felt the room steady.

He shuffled to the bucket and peed in it. He had no water to wash his hands with this time, and he wouldn't have wasted it in any case. His throat was parched; his tongue felt swollen. He needed to drink.

A door slammed somewhere in the house. He heard the man muttering to himself. Nathan knew he needed to call the man, ask for water. He took a few stumbling steps to the door and leaned against it, steadying himself.

"I had to. I had to!" the man was saying to himself. His words were slurred. "You asked me to do it. I didn't want it to happen this way. I never wanted any of this."

Nathan's resolve died as he listened to the man stomping around the house, cursing and moaning.

"You bitch! You and your shit of a brother. This wasn't how I wanted it to happen. I'll show him! I'll show him right now."

The trudging footsteps thumped louder, and Nathan backed away from the door, his heart thudding. The doorknob rattled, the door juddering.

High-pitched laughter. "I forgot it was locked." Then a moment of silence. "I'm sorry. I know you didn't want any of this either. I know that. We're almost done. Just a few days more. Almost done."

The voice faded as the man probably stepped away from the door. Nathan collapsed onto his bed, swallowing. Maybe he would ask the man for some water later. Right now wasn't a good time.

He could wait.

CHAPTER 59

Carver stared at Eric's body lying on the steel table, the bruises and blemishes on his face and neck accentuated in the sterile white light of the morgue.

"If you need to throw up, use that," Gomez told him, gesturing at the bin in the corner.

"I won't need to throw up."

"I'm just saying, you people were puking on evidence yesterday. If this case goes to trial, I don't want you to mess up my autopsy report."

Carver glanced at her. "I'm fine, thanks, Doctor."

He watched as Gomez and her assistant prepared Eric's inert body, checking the paperwork as they proceeded. They stripped the body, examining each article of clothing carefully under the UV light.

"Traces of mud on the shirt's right shoulder," Gomez said, collecting a few clumps with tweezers and placing them in an evidence bag. "One rough tear on the front of the shirt. That's the stab wound."

"Right," Carver said, staring at Eric's blood-covered chest.

Gomez measured and photographed the tear in the shirt while the assistant clipped Eric's nails, placing the clippings in evidence bags. Maybe Eric had managed to scratch his attacker. Carver could sure use a break like that.

Once they finished removing Eric's clothes, Gomez began examining him as her assistant combed Eric's hair.

"Take a look at this," Gomez said, motioning Carver to come closer. She pointed at Eric's shoulder. "Slight abrasions, but there's no real bruising. This was done postmortem."

"He killed him and then stomped on him for good measure," Carver said. "Must have been angry."

Gomez shook her head. "The abrasions aren't extensive. I don't think he stomped on him. I have a different theory. But I'll do some x-rays to be sure. Step out of the room for a bit; you don't need the extra dose of radiation."

Carver nodded and walked out, grateful to leave the smell of blood and antiseptic fluids behind him. He dialed Ahmed Nader's phone.

"Hey, Carver," Ahmed answered almost immediately. "I'm still not done."

"That's fine," Carver said. "I was just checking in to hear what you've got so far. Anything at all."

"Well, I can tell you what we probably *don't* have," Ahmed said. "The murderer's fingerprints. We have a lot of smudges that indicate the murderer wore gloves. We found a lot of prints at the crime scene, of course, but I'm betting they belong to the victim and his friends. There is one surface in the entire crime scene that was wiped clean."

"Which was?"

"The victim's phone."

Carver thought about it. "The phone touch screen wouldn't work well with his gloves. So he took a glove off, did something with the phone, and then wiped the screen clean from the fingerprints."

"Exactly."

"Any idea what he looked for on the victim's phone?"

"The phone was reset completely. Factory reset."

"So there was something on it that he didn't want us to find. Why not take the phone?"

"Maybe he was worried you'd be able to locate it. Or he didn't want to call your attention to the fact that the phone was missing. Next we have footprints. We have a few good ones, as you know, because our perp stepped in the victim's blood. Size twelve."

"Like the footprint in Liam Washington's vehicle."

"Exactly like it. We can't say if it belongs to the same person because the footprints we have here are from the right foot, and the footprint from the vehicle is the left foot. But we can say that it's the same boot type, that Hawkwell boot."

"Okay. What else?"

"Nothing else. I told you, I'm not done."

"The victim has traces of dried mud on his shoulder. If you get a sample of it, can you compare it to the mud we found from Liam Washington's crime scene?"

"Sure, send it over."

"I'll tell Gomez. Thanks." He hung up.

"Carver." Gomez stood in the doorway to the autopsy room. "Come take a look."

Carver followed her back inside. Gomez sat down by the computer in the corner of the room. An x-ray of the skull was displayed on the monitor.

"There's our fracture," Gomez said. "We'll probably be able to say if that's what killed our victim in a few hours."

"Okay," Carver said, inspecting the large dark spot at the back of the skull.

"But that's not the interesting part." Gomez shifted to a different image. An x-ray of the ribs. "The second intercostal space. See these spots here? And here?"

She pointed at two spots on two adjacent ribs, one dark and one white. Carver would never have noticed them.

"What are those?"

"This is where the attacker stabbed the victim. And the blade jammed between the ribs." Gomez pointed at the light spot. "The white spot is almost certainly metal. A chip from the blade."

Carver imagined the scene of the crime. The smears of blood on the floor. Two murder weapons. The attacker had stabbed the victim, then bashed his skull with a dumbbell he'd found nearby. "He couldn't pull the knife out, so he went for a different weapon. The dumbbell."

"That would be my guess," Gomez said grimly. "And then, after the victim was incapacitated, the killer really wanted his knife back. So he flipped the victim to his back—"

"Put his foot on the victim's shoulder and yanked the knife out," Carver said.

"Exactly."

"Can you give me any details about the knife?"

"It was a long blade. I can't say how deep it penetrated, but once we remove the ribs, I'll be able to give you a good estimate. At least five inches. And to get stuck in that intercostal space, it would have to be between 0.7 and 0.8 inches wide. And sharp. Very sharp. Not just the tip—I think the entire blade would have to be sharp to cut like that. And like I said, it'll probably be missing a chip."

"A steak knife?"

"Something like that, could be, but not necessarily. I have a knife at home I use to cut tomatoes that could do this."

"Okay. Oh, listen, can you send that mud sample from the shirt to forensics?"

Gomez rolled her eyes. "What do you think I was going to do with it? Flush it down the toilet?"

Carver raised his hands in a conciliatory manner. "Sorry, just making sure."

He took one last look at Eric Layton's face. The kidnappers had killed twice. Nothing would stop them from killing again. Getting Nathan back home safely was more urgent than ever.

CHAPTER 60

Abby paused to collect her thoughts before knocking on Gabrielle's door. She was there to talk to the girl about Eric's death, hoping Gabrielle hadn't heard about it yet.

Due to the wiretap on Gabrielle's phone, which had been placed with her consent in case the kidnapper called her phone instead of Eden's, Abby knew that Eric had called Gabrielle repeatedly before his murder. Abby thought of the half-empty scotch bottle on the desk. Of the evil queen meme he had been working on. That meme couldn't be anything but Eric's accusing finger, pointed at Gabrielle. Had he just been angry because she hadn't returned his calls? Or had he found something?

Gabrielle's followers had tripled since Nathan had been kidnapped. Each post had been liked thousands of times, garnering endless comments of support.

Like many parents, Abby had done some superficial research when her daughter had first used social media. Instagram and Facebook, she'd found out, literally rewired your brain. Likes and comments on a user's post were found to release bursts of dopamine, which made the user happy. That made sense; everyone enjoyed getting likes on a Facebook post. But this essentially turned the phone into a personal dopamine stimulator. Brain scans showed that in cases of people who were addicted to social media, the brain rewired itself, making them desire more likes, or retweets, or smiling emojis.

Abby had seen drug addicts do terrible things to get their next fix. Young girls prostituting themselves, kids stealing from their parents, men stealing from their jobs. Crack-addicted parents leaving their kids hungry because they could either afford a single rock or dinner. But that was for crack or heroin. Not for a heart emoji.

She tried to imagine what Gabrielle had gone through. Two years ago, her Instagram account had gone ballistic after one viral photo. It must have been an extraordinary feeling, tens of thousands of people suddenly vying for her attention, showering her with what she perceived as love. And then, as time went by, they trickled away. She got fewer and fewer responses; the number of likes per post dropped significantly. No more dopamine for Gabrielle.

Could she really have something to do with Nathan's disappearance, just to get her fix?

Abby knocked, three sharp taps.

"Yeah?" Gabrielle's muffled voice sounded tired.

Abby opened the door. "Can I talk to you for a moment?"

Gabrielle sat on her bed, leaning against the wall, a tablet in her hand. As Abby stepped into the room, she let the tablet drop into her lap, and Abby caught a glimpse of the ransom contribution page.

"Sure," the girl said. "Is this about me posting that image?"

"No." Abby shut the door behind her. "I'm afraid I have some bad news." She stopped, letting the gap in her words do her job for her, letting Gabrielle jump to her own conclusions.

The blood drained from Gabrielle's face. "Is it Nathan?" she whispered.

In her job, Abby had seen and heard countless liars. Most were surprisingly good. But if Gabrielle was lying, she was one of the best. The terror in her voice, the quiver of her lips, they felt real.

301

Then again, this girl had been manipulating the truth in one way or another for years.

"No," Abby said. "Sorry, I should have said that first thing; this isn't about Nathan. It's about Eric."

Gabrielle blinked, relief and confusion on her face. "Eric?"

"Eric was found dead in his home yesterday evening," Abby said.

"What? No, that's impossible," Gabrielle blurted. "I talked to him yesterday."

"Really?" Abby feigned surprise. "When did you talk to him?"

"I don't know . . . sometime in the afternoon. He called me."

"What did you talk about?" Abby already knew the phone call's contents.

"Something about Nathan's photo. He kept asking if that's the image the kidnapper sent me. He sounded angry, or . . . I don't know. He talked really fast. Is he really . . . are you sure . . . ?"

"What do you think he meant? When he asked about the image?"

Gabrielle hugged herself. "Some people online are saying I made up the whole kidnapping thing. So I figured he thought the same thing. That no one sent me that picture. That I took it myself."

"What did you tell him?"

"I told him that it's the picture the kidnapper sent me," Gabrielle said, eyes brimming. "Is he really dead?"

"I'm afraid so," Abby said softly. "Did he call again?"

Gabrielle paused as if trying to remember. Abby wasn't fooled. Eric had called three more times, and Gabrielle hadn't picked up. There was no question in Abby's mind that Gabrielle remembered that. But she was probably deciding if she should say that to Abby. Did she think it would depict her in a bad light?

"Yes," she finally said, voice cracking. "He called again, but I didn't answer. I was busy writing an email to the guy in charge of the ransom donations. And I wanted to keep my line free in case the kidnappers called my number instead of my mom's. How did he die?"

"We're still looking into that," Abby said.

"Do you know . . . is there a funeral?"

"You'll have to ask his parents," Abby said. "I can get you their number."

"Thanks, I'd appreciate that." Gabrielle sniffed.

"Can you think of anyone who would want to hurt Eric?"

"I don't know. Nothing like *that*. Nothing that would get him killed. He told me he used to post some funny photos back when he was at school, and some people got mad. But that was *ages* ago. Can you . . . can I have a minute? Please?"

"Sure," Abby said. "Take your time." She walked out of the room and shut the door behind her.

She found Eden in the kitchen, flipping the pages in a photo album. Abby sat next to her and looked at the photos. Pictures of a toddler grinning at the camera, a pouting girl standing by his side. Nathan and Gabrielle, years ago.

"I made this album when Nathan was three years old," Eden said, her voice drained. "I kept telling myself I should make an album every year. When the pictures are on the phone, you never really look at them."

"I guess not," Abby said.

"But I only made this one album. Never made the time to make more."

"Any photos from the farm here?"

"No. By the time Nathan was born, almost no one had a phone or a camera on the farm anymore. It was discouraged. Otis said we should live our lives, not view them through a lens."

In general, Abby agreed with the sentiment. But like almost everything else, when taken to extremes, it did more harm than good. "You know," she said, "I met a girl from the Tillman farm yesterday. A special girl. She's called Leonor. Did you meet her?"

Eden flipped another page. Nathan in a Halloween costume, grinning, holding a Kit Kat in his hand. "No, I don't think so."

"Right, she joined after you left. She seems like she wants to leave as well . . . but she's very scared."

"It's scary," Eden said. "When all your friends are on the farm, and you hear all those things about the world outside. It's terrifying."

"But you left," Abby said. "On your own. With two kids. That's impressive. Amazing, really."

"It wasn't easy."

"No, it wasn't." Abby placed her hand on Eden's arm. "Why did you leave?"

"I told you. Otis started talking crazy stuff. And he told everyone to come nude to the private confession sessions. I just had to leave."

"Your husband was in the cult. Otis had been talking about Armageddon for years; you told me that yourself. I talked to people there, Eden. They believe every single word he says. They do everything he tells them. I think you're an incredible woman. But you wouldn't have left because he made you uncomfortable. What happened?"

Eden let out a sharp sob.

"What did they do to you?"

"It's so . . . I'm so ashamed."

"There's no reason to be ashamed. Whatever happened, you weren't in control of the situation."

Eden shook her head, covering her mouth with her hand. Abby got up and brought her a glass of water. She waited as Eden emptied it.

"Otis came to me one day," Eden said. "And said he wanted to marry Gabrielle. He said he'd found the perfect guy for her."

Abby kept her face blank, shutting away the disgust. "How old was Gabrielle at the time?"

"Twelve."

"So you got up and left?"

"No," Eden whispered. "That's why I didn't tell you. I was happy. Otis told me this guy would take care of Gabrielle when the end of the world came. David was thrilled to hear it too; his daughter would be safe. Can you imagine? A mother happy to marry off her twelve-year-old girl?"

"I can imagine," Abby said. She could. She'd seen worse.

"This guy was about to join the community in a week or two. And when he joined, Otis would marry them. A date was set. People were preparing things for the wedding. I made a white dress for Gabrielle. A wedding dress. A size eleven wedding dress."

"Did Gabrielle know?"

"No!" Eden's eyes widened. "She still doesn't. Please don't—"

"I won't tell her. What happened then?"

"Otis told me Gabrielle should arrive pure to her wedding. She should do her first private confession session with him."

Abby shut her eyes.

"I knew what happened in those confession sessions," Eden said. "I already did several of them. Otis didn't schedule them often for me. Some younger women had weekly confession sessions. And when he told me Gabrielle had to do one . . . I just couldn't let her do it. I couldn't. I wanted Nathan and Gabrielle to be far away from there. At the time, I was in charge of the everyday administration of the community. I bought clothing, hygiene products, anything basic we needed and couldn't make on the farm. So I had some access to the community's cash. I stole three thousand dollars and left with the kids. I planned on giving them up for adoption."

"Adoption?" Abby asked, surprised. "Why?"

"Because I thought I would die," Eden said. "It was something we all knew; people who left the farm died. The FBI killed them, or they got sick or had a terrible accident. No one survived for long."

"That's what Otis told all of you."

"Yeah. I believed it. So I figured I'd give the kids up for adoption and then wait for death. But I couldn't even figure out how to start the adoption process. And a week went by. And then another week. And I didn't die."

"So you went back for a divorce."

"Yes. I went back to the farm and told David I wanted a divorce. I said if he didn't give me a divorce, I would tell the police about everything that went on in that community. I think Otis nearly had me shot."

"You're lucky he didn't."

Eden nodded. "Instead, he ordered David to sign the papers. That I was possessed by Satan and that my soul was already gone."

"Do you know the name of the guy Gabrielle was supposed to marry?"

"No. I never met him. But I think he was related to Otis in some way. That's part of the reason we were excited about it at first."

Abby's heart sank. "Otis's nephew?"

"I think so."

Karl Adkins. He was the one who had been supposed to marry Gabrielle when she was twelve. Abby had had it all wrong. She'd thought Otis had recruited Karl because Eden had left, but it was the other way around. Eden had left because Karl was about to join—and marry her daughter. Later, Karl had found Gabrielle online and stalked her.

"I need you to repeat that story to someone else," Abby said. "It might help Nathan."

CHAPTER 61

"Thanks for coming," Carver said, his tone dry.

He sat in one of the precinct interview rooms with Tom McCormick, the journalist. Carver, and the rest of the cops in the station, had little love for the *New Yorker Chronicle*, which had published an article about police ineptitude in the 115th Precinct a year before. McCormick hadn't written that article, but it still rankled.

News about the Layton murder had broken that morning. The journalist seemed dazed. He must have heard about it recently. "Of course. I'm horrified by what happened. Whatever I can do to help."

"When did you interview Eric?"

"Two days ago, on Sunday evening."

"And how did he seem when you talked to him?"

"Well, he was obviously upset because of the kidnapping."

"Did it seem like there was anything else on his mind?"

McCormick frowned. "I . . . don't think so. The kidnapping was all he talked about. The kidnapping and Gabrielle Fletcher."

"Did you record the interview?" Carver asked hopefully.

"No, I transcribed it while we talked."

"Can I have the transcriptions?"

"Of course, I'll send them to you . . . are you investigating a possible connection between the murder and the kidnapping case?"

"We're looking into all possibilities," Carver said carefully. He hated interviewing reporters. Every question he asked would be analyzed later by McCormick and his editor, and would provide background material for the *Chronicle*'s articles about the case. "Did Layton tell you anything beyond what appears in the interview?"

"He gave me some background material about his friendship with Gabrielle. And about her life before the kidnapping."

"What did he tell you about her life?"

"Well, I'd have to check my transcriptions for all the details, but it was mostly about her parents. Her parents got divorced when Gabrielle was young. Her mother struggled to support them, so she was out of the house a lot. And her dad never talked to her since, even though she tried to reach out to him—"

"Gabrielle tried to talk to him?"

McCormick nodded. "He still lived in some sort of Christian community that Gabrielle grew up in. So she called the community three years ago and asked to talk to him. But the people she talked to said her dad wouldn't talk to her on the phone."

Carver leaned back in his chair, his mind kicking into high gear. This was probably how Otis had found out where Eden and her kids lived. "You said the people she talked to said her dad didn't want to come to the phone. Did she talk to *several* people?"

"I'm not sure; maybe it was an expression. Could be she only talked to one guy. But you can ask her."

"And they said he wouldn't come to the phone?"

"According to Eric they suggested she come in person, but she wouldn't. She said they creeped her out. And she was furious at her dad for refusing to talk to her."

Carver doubted whomever Gabrielle had talked to had even mentioned it to David. Whom had she talked to? Otis? Karl?

"Did he tell you anything else about her life there?"

"No. He kept dropping hints about it. Like he knew some stuff I wouldn't believe. But I think it was just talk."

"During the interview, was there a point he seemed thoughtful? Or distraught?"

"When I showed him Nathan's picture with the newspaper, he was very upset. He began crying." McCormick's eyes suddenly widened. "Do you . . . do you think he was murdered because of the interview?"

Carver twisted his mouth. He had to raise the subject eventually. McCormick could be in danger as well. "This is strictly off the record."

"Of course."

"It's a possibility we're investigating. Did you see anything strange in the past day? People you don't recognize near your home? Maybe someone following you?"

"I live in Manhattan. I see people I don't recognize all the time. Do you think I might be in danger?" McCormick blinked.

"I don't believe it's likely. But if you notice anything out of the ordinary, call me immediately."

"Well, that's reassuring." McCormick's mouth twisted.

Maybe another police ineptitude piece was about to be published soon. He gave McCormick his card. "If you think of anything else, don't hesitate to call. And send me those transcripts as soon as you can."

Whatever Eric had said during that interview had probably gotten him killed. But Carver wasn't closer to figuring out what it was.

CHAPTER 62

Abby was thirty-nine years old with two kids of her own. And yet whenever she walked through her parents' front door, she felt that sweet safety that rose when someone else took control. It was almost as if she could stomp into the living room, shout angrily that she was hungry, and slump on the couch.

In fact, she probably could do that. And her mother would walk in, give her a sandwich and a warm cup of cocoa, and ask her how her day had been.

Her mother was in the kitchen cutting vegetables, and as soon as Abby stepped inside, she put down the knife and swept Abby into a warm, slightly suffocating hug.

"Hey, sweetie," she said. "Who's your friend?"

Abby drew back. "Mom, this is Eden Fletcher. Eden, this is my mom."

"You can call me Penny," her mother said. Her face betrayed nothing, but Abby felt the slight tension in her mother's body when she realized who Eden was.

"Nice to meet you, Mrs., uh . . . Penny," Eden said meekly.

"Can I get you both something to drink?"

"A cup of coffee would be amazing," Abby said.

"Just water," Eden said.

Penny turned to make the coffee. Everything she did in the kitchen was a statement. She moved fast, her movements sharp and assertive. She slammed the cutlery drawer as if it were an enemy that needed vanquishing before it would give up a spoon. Abby's dad had to fix a broken drawer or cupboard door every few months due to her mother's aggressive stance toward kitchen furniture. Eden visibly flinched when her mother shut the cupboard door. Abby was used to it—loved it, in fact; it was part of her childhood's music.

"Is Dad at work?" Abby asked. Her dad worked at an advertising company.

"Yes. He's been working really hard. They got the pizzushi project, so you can imagine what that's like."

Abby snorted. "Good luck advertising *that*. No one wants a pizza rolled like sushi."

"We'll see. Hank has done miracles before."

"Where's Leonor?"

"Upstairs with her brother."

"How has she been?"

Penny put a spoonful of sugar in Abby's coffee, stirring it vigorously until the entire brew swirled in a vortex that threatened to spill out of the mug. "Scared," she said, handing Abby the mug. "Wouldn't come inside until her brother looked through the house. And I could hear her pacing in her room until two in the morning."

"But then she slept?"

"I think she slept almost until ten." She gave a glass of water to Eden. "Are you sure you don't want tea or coffee? It's cold outside. Tea will warm you up."

"No thanks." Eden seemed aghast at the prospect of Penny starting to bang cupboards and drawers again.

"I talked to Leonor when she woke up," Penny said. "I told her I was your mother. She seemed surprised."

Abby nodded. "I didn't mention that yesterday."

"I also told her I adopted you after the Wilcox cult disaster." A brief glance toward Eden. "She was interested to hear it."

"Good." Abby had agreed with her mother that if the opportunity presented itself, she should talk to Leonor about Wilcox. "But you didn't mention Otis Tillman?"

Her mother folded her arms. "I'm not a rookie to this, you know."

"I know, Mom." When she'd been a child, her parents had gone through a lot to help Abby move on, leaving her past behind her. And Penny had done most of the heavy lifting. "I'll go have a word with her, okay?"

"Sure, sweetie. I'll keep your friend here company."

Abby gave Penny a grateful look and went up to the second floor. Penny had put Leonor and Brian in her old room. The door was closed. Abby stepped quietly to the door.

Brian was speaking, his voice sharp, angry. "Leonor, for god's sake, cut that out. I can't . . . would you stop that? For just one moment?"

Abby knocked at the door. After a moment Brian opened it. His face was flushed, teeth clenched.

"Oh, it's you," he muttered. "Leonor can't talk right now." He gestured behind him.

Leonor sat on the bed, her eyes shut tight. She muttered softly to herself, her hands clasped together.

"I actually wanted to talk to you," Abby said lightly. She grabbed Brian's elbow and pulled him out of the room, then shut the door. Not letting go of his arm, she led him to her dad's office, and shut that door as well. The office was a mess—a good indication Dad was working hard. The large whiteboard he used for brainstorming was scrawled with possible pizzushi slogan ideas.

"She won't listen to anything I say," Brian exploded as soon as the door was shut.

"Keep your voice down," Abby said softly.

"How can I get her to see things clearly if she won't listen? Whenever I say something about that damn cult, she starts praying again."

"Chill, Brian." Abby said. "It's not your job to convince her, okay? You said so yourself: your sister never listens to anything you have to say."

"Then why am I even here?"

"Because she needs someone who loves her to be by her side. Your role here is to hug her, and tell her how good it is to see her again, and talk about your happy childhood memories. Make her feel good."

"Then how will we convince her to leave that place?" Brian looked helpless.

"We don't," Abby said. "She needs to decide for herself."

"She had a whole year to decide for herself, and she didn't."

"She was sleep deprived with no access to information, surrounded by people who were taught to be afraid of anyone and anything outside the cult. Now she's sleeping well. She's away from the cult's agenda and twisted thinking. She has time to think for herself. She can research things online. She can talk to people outside the cult's circle of influence. And we can give her information if she asks for it."

"So that's it? We wait?"

"*You* wait, and have fun with your sister. Worst-case scenario, you got a three-day vacation with her. Is that so bad?"

"Yes," Brian said. "I want her back. Not for three days. For good."

Abby sighed. "I know. But whenever you start arguing with her, you're making it worse. Leonor has been conditioned to resist anyone who criticizes the cult. You're becoming *the enemy*. Why do you think I brought you along and not your mom?"

"Beats me. I thought it was because my mom nags."

"It's because your mom has made her opinions about the cult very clear. She's the enemy now. Leonor won't listen to *anything* she has to say."

"Oh. But now I said some bad things about the cult."

"Then we're lucky you're her dumb brother, and she doesn't really listen to you, right?" Abby grinned at him.

"I guess."

"One of the practices used in cults is teaching the members to handle negative thoughts. For example, in Leonor's case, whenever she voiced questions or thoughts that were perceived as negative, she was ordered to pray on it. After a few months, she learned to pray when those thoughts occurred, even if she didn't voice them out loud. They had short-circuited her brain, teaching her how to shut away negative thoughts about the cult."

"Is that what they did in the cult you were in?"

"Among other things," Abby answered. "That's why she prays whenever you confront her about the cult. She's shutting you and your negativity out. Don't get angry at her when it happens. She can't help it."

Brian seemed as if he was about to cry. Abby wasn't sure she could handle a blubbering six-footer.

"Make her feel happy, okay?" she said. "We'll take care of the rest."

"Okay."

"Now I need to talk to your sister."

"What if she doesn't listen?"

Abby shrugged. "Then I'll try again later."

She returned to her old room, knocked on the door, and opened it. Leonor still sat on the bed, but she wasn't praying anymore.

"Hey," Abby said. "Is my mom treating you all right?"

"She's very nice," Leonor said.

"Glad to hear it."

"I want to make a phone call. People in the community are probably worried sick about me."

"You can do that." Abby shrugged. "There's a phone line downstairs; feel free to use it. But if you call, they'll tell you to come back. You know that, right?"

"So? I *should* go back."

"Maybe you should. But I don't think it's such a bad idea to stay with your brother for just a day or two. He misses you."

"He can come visit me at the farm. It's not prison. People visit all the time."

Abby sighed. "What are you worried about, Leonor?"

"Why am I here?"

"Why do you think you're here?"

Leonor stared at her deadpan. "I think you're trying to convince me to leave the community."

"Did I say anything to try and convince you so far?"

"No. And it won't work anyway. You're wasting your time. And mine."

"Maybe that's true," Abby conceded. "But if you believe so strongly that Tillman's community is the place for you, then you shouldn't be worried that I'll convince you to leave, right?"

Leonor said nothing.

"We let Karl Adkins go yesterday evening," Abby said.

Leonor's eyes narrowed in suspicion. "Really?"

They had. Not because of Leonor's actions, like Abby let her believe, but because they couldn't charge him with anything. Abby wished she could charge him for his intention to marry Gabrielle when she'd been twelve. But that was impossible.

"Once you go back, you can tell them everything," she said. "That you went with me, compelling us to let Karl go, and stayed here while we wasted everyone's time. Would that be so bad? Do you think anyone will be angry you did that? For Karl?"

"I don't care what anyone thinks. I'm doing what I think is right."

"Okay. Good." Abby opened her bag, took out a folder, and laid it on the dresser. "This is for you."

"What is it?"

"This is the police file on Otis Tillman," Abby said. "You can look through it or not. It's your call."

"How do I even know it's real?"

"I guess you'll have to take my word for it." Abby smiled. Leonor didn't smile back.

"One more thing," Abby said as she turned to leave. "There's someone here I want you to meet."

"Who?"

"She's named Eden. You probably heard of her. She used to be David's wife."

The blood drained from Leonor's face. "She's here?"

"She's downstairs with my mother," Abby said. "You can ask her anything you want. I'm sure you have a lot of questions."

CHAPTER 63

The kid was shivering in the bed, the bedsheets smudged with sweat and dirt.

He placed the soup on the desk and went over to shake the kid. Gently at first, then more insistent. "Hey. Wake up. I made you soup. It'll warm you up."

Did the kid even need warming up? His body was burning hot.

"Hey. Nathan, wake up."

The boy's eyelids fluttered, but his eyes rolled up. He convulsed, his body suddenly rigid, jaw clenched shut. A drop of drool ran down his chin.

"Stop that! Wake up!"

Something was wrong with him. It was that ugly scratch. It kept getting worse all the time, swollen and inflamed, seeping pus. That idiot, why had he done that to himself? It was all his fault. His fault— and his sister's fault for taking her time with the ransom. She should be interviewing twenty times a day, doing road tours, enlisting celebrities for her cause. What was she waiting for? He'd given her the perfect platform for this, like she'd always wanted, and she couldn't even take the initiative. What the hell was wrong with her?

It was *her* fault that her brother was sick now. Her damn fault.

He left the room, slammed the door behind him, and grabbed his phone. Was almost about to dial her, but his finger wavered above the screen.

Stupid. So damn stupid. If he dialed now, they'd have his location. The police would be here within half an hour, surrounding the place, game over. All because he'd lost his shit, forgotten the basic rules. The rules they'd all planned together. Only burner phones. Always call from Manhattan, far from the hideaway. Always disguise your voice.

But this had to be dealt with. Gabrielle needed to understand time was running out. If Nathan died, it wouldn't be on *him*. Not after everything he'd done for the kid. Everything he'd done for her.

There were other ways to send a message.

He returned to the boy's room and took a picture. He then went to the kitchen and turned on the laptop, opening Tor Browser. They'd planned this part as well, of course, and he'd learned the basics of the dark web long ago. He logged into ProtonMail using the temporary email address he'd created. A burner email account, easily discarded, untraceable.

His jaw was clenched as he typed the short email, each keystroke an angry punch. Attaching the image was a hassle, since it was on the phone, but he managed. A single click and the email was sent. He exhaled, his body trembling from the effort. He imagined his words, bits of information, zipping through the cloud of computers in the dark web, finally emerging from a random computer somewhere in the world. Japan, Switzerland, Iran, anywhere at all. And then ending up in Gabrielle's inbox. Waiting to be read.

She needed to know. He was doing it for her.

CHAPTER 64

Abby had pajamas she kept for special occasions. Not the sexy kind of special occasions. No, these pajamas were for nights in which she needed something soft and fluffy to hug her body. She wore them sparingly so that their softness would not dissipate due to frequent laundering. They were light blue with a drawing of a sheep chewing a flower on the shirt. The pants were loose fitting so that her legs felt free but warm.

She decided that tonight was one of those special nights with a need for fluffiness. So when she got out of the shower, she slipped into her sheep pajamas.

There should be a word to define the pleasure of wearing really comfortable pajamas. Just the act of putting them on made some of the day's weight lift off her shoulders.

Her phone rang, and she cringed. She was about to lie down, draw the blanket over her body, and sleep well for once.

It was Carver. She answered the call. "Hey."

"Hey, Abby. I was about to grab some dinner and wondered if you want to meet up and discuss the case."

"No, not tonight. I'm already at home."

"Oh." There was a slight pause. "Did you eat dinner?"

"I . . . had yogurt."

"That's not dinner. Tell you what. I'll grab us both some Chinese food and come over to your place. There are some developments I want to talk about."

Abby wanted to explain she couldn't. That she was in her light-blue sheep pajamas already, and that meant she was *done*. But she wasn't sure Carver would understand their significance. He seemed like a man who didn't have a special pair of pajamas at home.

"Sure," she found herself saying. "Come over."

"Brilliant." She heard the smile in his voice. "Text me the address. What do you want to eat?"

"I don't know. Not rice, get me something with noodles."

"On it." He hung up.

She debated with herself if she should stay in the pajamas. But no. She couldn't eat with these pajamas on. A sauce stain would be catastrophic. And she wasn't thrilled with the idea of Carver seeing her in this attire either.

Sighing, she opened the wardrobe and grudgingly stared at the shelves, trying to decide what to wear. She could wear one of her office suits, but the idea was appalling. She ended up dressing in her blue yoga pants and a tight black shirt she hadn't worn in a couple of months. She debated with herself if she should bother with makeup and contact lenses, got annoyed with Carver for putting her in this situation, and decided he would get her with glasses and no makeup. He would deal with it.

She ended up putting in contact lenses after all. And adding some eye shadow.

By the time Carver showed up on her doorstep, she was starving.

"So, I got you some beef noodles—"

"Perfect." She snatched the bag from his hand and led him to the kitchen.

"But I guess if you're full from your yogurt, you don't have to eat it." Carver grinned.

"Don't mess with me. Do you want a beer?"

"Sure."

She got one for him and one for herself.

"You look good," Carver said, sounding slightly astonished.

"That surprised tone is uncalled for." She pried her box open, the smell making her mouth water.

"It's just that you sounded kind of tired when I called, and you've been working really hard on this case—"

"You're not helping the situation." She fished out a piece of beef with her chopsticks and put it in her mouth. It tasted amazing. "Where did you buy this?"

"Local place in our precinct," he said, pleased with her expression. "I'll take you there one of these days."

Abby eyed him, surprised. Carver, intent on his own food, didn't seem to notice her watching him.

"Where are your kids?" Carver asked.

"At their dad's. It's his day."

"His day, huh?"

"When you're divorced with kids, everything is either *his* day or *your* day. Or *his* weekend or *your* weekend. Life becomes binary."

"And which do you prefer? Your days or his days?"

She considered that. "I prefer to have the kids here. But it's nice to have the weekend off occasionally. Or to wake up in the morning without having to frantically get everyone ready for school. Or to be judge and jury when they're arguing."

"Do they argue a lot?"

She shrugged. "Didn't you fight with your siblings when you were little?"

"Oh yeah. But there were eight of us, so it was more like gang turf wars. Usually all the little ones against the big ones. Battles for the TV remote control could get bloody." He smiled dreamily, as if recalling a beautiful day. "My little sister was a biter. Now she's a lawyer."

"Do you think it's related?"

"I can't see any other option. So you're enjoying the quiet?"

"Sort of. When the kids are gone, I miss them all the time. I want to cuddle with Ben or listen to Samantha playing her violin. Listen to how their day was. Help them with their homework . . . though frankly I don't do a lot of that anymore."

"They don't need your help?"

"Not really. They're both pretty independent—and really smart."

"They'd have to be, with their parents," Carver said.

Abby felt a tingle of delight at those words. She'd heard a slight variation on that sentence multiple times from teachers, or friends. It was usually along the lines of "They're so smart; they really take after their dad." Because everyone knew the kids' dad was a math professor, one of the leading academics in his field. He'd even published books that almost no one could understand. And people sometimes said, "Samantha is so pretty, Abby; she has your looks."

But no one had ever said the kids were smart because they took after their *parents*. Plural.

Oh god, she was blushing.

"Did you ever want any kids?" she asked, her voice slightly high pitched. "I mean, with your family, I'd think it was a must."

"In theory," Carver answered. "But in practice, I always felt like it was the wrong time. Money was short, so maybe we should wait. I was really busy at work, so maybe we should wait. Our apartment was too small; maybe we should wait. And finally my wife found a guy who didn't want to wait. So we got divorced."

"Oh. I didn't know you were married."

"Four years." Carver emptied his beer. "Now Monika's with this finance lawyer. And they have a cute boy."

"You stayed in touch?"

"In the modern sense. I stalk her on Facebook. Look through all her perfect life photos and occasionally click the 'Like' button without commenting—to let her know that I'm happy for her but don't really care that much one way or the other."

Abby laughed. "That's sorta creepy."

"Don't you look at your ex's photos?"

"Sure, every one of them. But I don't click 'Like' on *any* of them—to let him know I don't give a shit."

"Who knew the Facebook 'Like' button could have so many subtle meanings."

Abby laughed again. "You said you wanted to discuss the case."

"Right." Carver's face became serious. "I talked to McCormick, the journalist who interviewed Eric Layton. Apparently Gabrielle had told him that she called the Tillman farm three years ago. She was searching for her dad."

Abby blinked. "She said they weren't in touch."

"They weren't. I called her and followed up. She told me a guy she didn't know answered the phone and went to get Otis as soon as he realized who he was talking to. Otis told her David didn't want to talk to them. He tried to convince her to come over and talk to her dad in person. But she didn't. She said she wasn't even convinced her dad was still there. Otis seemed creepy to her."

"Good instincts."

"So that was probably how they found out where Eden and her kids lived."

"Did she say who she talked to? Before Otis?"

"She didn't know him. I figured maybe it was Karl."

"That's definitely possible. And it's worse than you think." She filled him in about the arranged wedding between Karl and Gabrielle. "I bet he got very excited when he found out she was alive—and not that far away."

"And that's when he began stalking her Instagram account."

Abby leaned back in her chair, thinking this through.

Carver got up. "Where's the bathroom?"

"Down the hall to the left."

Carver left the kitchen. Abby picked up her takeout box and fished around for any beef pieces she'd missed.

"Shit!" A sudden scream shot through the house.

Abby dropped the box and bolted down the hall. Carver stood in the doorway to Ben's room, body tense.

"Are you okay?" Abby asked, heart pounding.

"There's a snake in there! It lunged at me when I opened the door."

Abby glanced through the doorway. The snake was in its vivarium, staring at both of them, probably trying to decide who was tastier.

"It lunged at you? It's inside its vivarium," Abby said, bemused. Carver's hand was at his side—where his gun would've been if he hadn't taken it off when they sat to eat.

"Well . . . I didn't see the glass. It's very clean. And that thing just hissed." Carver glanced around the room, taking in the other vivaria with the tarantula, the chameleon, and the crickets. "It's a zoo. You have a zoo in your home."

"It's not a zoo. This is my son's room. The bathroom's the *second* door to the left. Did you want to shoot the snake?"

"That thing hissed at me," Carver said again. "I don't like snakes. And that aquarium is really clean. I didn't see the glass."

"It's a vivarium. My son does like it clean."

"Okay. So . . . *second* door to the left, yeah?"

"That's right."

"Are there bats there or something?"

"No, but take a look before you use the toilet, because sometimes we keep piranhas in it."

Carver blinked, as if for a second he thought she was serious. "You're hilarious," he said dryly.

Abby returned to the kitchen, decided to get two more beers, one for herself and one for Carver. He came back from the bathroom, his cool demeanor still shaken.

"So . . . all those things are your son's pets?"

"Well, the snake's new; I told you about it. And the crickets are food for the tarantula; they're not actual pets." She held out the beer for him.

"Aren't these creatures poisonous?" He took the beer, their fingers brushing. He opened the can and took a long swig.

"They're definitely not poisonous. If anything, they're *venomous*," Abby said. "And in any case they're not dangerous to people. A bite from the tarantula or the snake would just sting."

"I used to have nightmares about snakes as a kid after watching that *Indiana Jones* movie."

"Oh, the Well of Souls scene," Abby said. "Do you know some of the snakes there are actually legless lizards?"

"What's the difference?"

"Snakes don't have earholes. Ben used to watch the scene repeatedly and point out different things in it. The different types of pythons, the fake snakes. He loves the cobra."

"Are you into snakes too?"

"Not so much," Abby admitted. "To be honest, I hate them. And spiders. And even the crickets. I guess the chameleon is okay."

"You're an amazing mom for letting him keep those things."

"Tell that to my daughter."

"If you told me back at the academy that one day you would have two kids, and that you'd be the kind of mom that lets her son have a pet snake, I'd have said you were delirious."

Abby frowned. "Is that a compliment?"

"I think so." Carver smiled at her and took a long sip from his beer.

"What *did* you think I'd be, back in the academy?"

"I don't know." Carver stared at the table. "I guess I thought . . . I mean, I hoped . . ." The sentence evaporated into silence.

"What did you hope?"

"I was disappointed to meet Steve at that barbecue when we graduated." Carver shrugged. "I was thinking of asking you out for a drink."

Silence settled between them. Abby drank her beer, telling herself that her head was spinning because of the alcohol.

Her phone rang, Gabrielle Fletcher's name appearing on-screen. "Hello?"

"Lieutenant Mullen?" Gabrielle's voice was strained, close to tears. "I . . . I just got an email. From the kidnappers."

"An email? What does it say?" She caught Carver's eye.

"It says Nathan is sick," Gabrielle sobbed. "That his time is running out. They also sent a picture. He looks bad."

"Okay, first of all, I'm sending someone to check your computer," Abby said. "The image could contain a virus."

"Why would they send me a virus?" Gabrielle sniffled.

To take over her computer and web camera. To listen in on whatever was going on in their home. "It's just a precaution," Abby said. "Can you forward the email to me?"

"O . . . okay. But what should I do? Should I answer the email?"

"Let me see the email first. Send it over now." Abby gave Gabrielle her email address.

While Gabrielle did this, Abby retrieved her laptop. It was routinely maintained by the IT department at the police academy, and she was confident the antivirus installed would alert her if a virus was attached to the email.

"Okay, sent," Gabrielle said.

Abby waited for a few seconds, then refreshed her inbox. There. An email from a temporary email address—a random sequence of letters and numbers. She opened it and read the short text, Carver looking over her shoulder.

> This is taking too long, and your brother doesn't
> have a lot of time. He's sick, and we're losing our
> patience. If he dies IT'S ON YOU!!!!

Nathan's image definitely looked bad. The kid was pale, one of his eyelids half open, his face scratched and dirty.

Gabrielle cleared her throat. "Do you think he's already . . . already . . . ?"

"He's alive," Abby said, hoping she was right. "They wouldn't send us this image if he wasn't."

"Should I answer the email?"

"Yes. But I want to write the reply myself. I'll send you the text later." Abby doubted the kidnappers would even check it. The temporary address indicated this wasn't an email account they intended to use again. "Give me an hour."

"But what if we don't get the money in time? Do you think they'll let Nathan die?"

"We'll do everything we can to get to him on time, okay?"

"Okay."

"I'll call you once I have the reply to the email ready."

"Please hurry," Gabrielle whispered and hung up.

"Send me the email," Carver said. "I'll talk to the tech guys, see if we can track it back to its source."

Abby nodded distractedly, already opening a blank document, thinking about the reply to the email.

Carver got up. "I'll let you know what they say."

"Okay. Carver?"

"Yeah?"

"The kidnapper doesn't sound stable in this email. We need to find Nathan fast."

CHAPTER 65

Abby parked the car in front of her mother's house at just after nine in the morning. She checked her email again to see if there was any update. Nothing so far. The night before, Carver had called her to tell her they couldn't trace the email back to the sender. Whoever had sent it knew what they were doing.

Gabrielle had replied to the email using Abby's text. A calming message with a few open-ended questions that were meant to give the kidnappers a feeling of control over the situation. Hopefully they'd answer the email, supplying the task force with some much-needed information. But Abby suspected the kidnappers wouldn't even open it. When they wanted a dialogue, they talked on the phone. This was their way of sending a message without engaging.

The image of Nathan lying unconscious left her with a desire to act. But there was nothing to act on. She could only continue doing what she'd done so far. Lean on Leonor, and get answers.

She got out of the car and walked over to the door. She'd barely knocked before Penny flung the door open and pressed a finger to her smiling lips. Abby followed her, doing her best to avoid making any sound as they climbed the wooden steps to the second floor.

The door to Abby's old room was shut, but beyond it, she heard the sound of a loud conversation. For a second her gut twisted as she heard Brian shouting at his sister, but then Leonor answered, her voice cheerful and giddy.

"It was on your thirteenth birthday, assbutt." Leonor's voice was slightly muffled, but Abby managed to piece the words together. "And I didn't fall on the cake; I was pushed."

"I'm telling you it was my twelfth birthday; I distinctly remember because Mom made me that cake that was shaped like Dumbledore. It was a beautiful cake—before you managed to smear it all over your shirt."

"Oh, come on, it didn't even look like Dumbledore. She got his face all wrong; it looked like a pervy Santa."

"You think all Santas are pervy."

And then, a sound that made Abby's eyes tear up. Leonor *laughed*. "Well, they are!" she said, still giggling. "I mean, the whole sit-on-my-knees thing?"

Abby and her mom tiptoed down the stairs and went to the kitchen.

"They've been like that for the past thirty minutes," Penny said in a soft voice. "They didn't even get out of the room yet."

"That's great," Abby said, pacing the kitchen.

"Last night I talked to Brian before going to sleep. He told me that every year after Halloween, he and Leonor would combine their loot and hide in their room, stuffing their faces with chocolate and candy. So this morning I got your old trick or treat bag—you remember it?"

"The pumpkin-shaped one? You still have it? It's probably full of mold."

"I cleaned it up. Then I went to the nearby drugstore and filled it up with candy. And I put it in front of their room. I think Leonor woke up first. She got out, found it . . . and they've been inside the room ever since."

Abby hugged her mother, a tear running down her cheek. She'd spent years studying crisis management and cult intervention. But her mother could intuitively figure out what people needed the most.

She resumed pacing the kitchen, thinking about the girl in the room above them. The information she had. She could probably refute Karl's alibi. Maybe she could testify about the systematic sexual abuse of minors within the cult. She had to have something that could help the police get a foot in the door.

Leonor was on the brink. And they needed that information right now. But if Abby barged in and questioned Leonor, she'd shove the girl right back into the cult's hands.

Cult intervention never worked under a tight schedule. The subject had to have time to process, to reach the conclusions on their own. Abby *knew* that, but still she had the urge to push Leonor, to try and convince her. Nathan's life depended on the information Leonor had.

"How are the kids?" Penny eyed her.

"They're fine. I talked to Steve this morning. They're staying at his place until Thursday."

"Oh, that's nice of him."

"Whatever." It was. He hadn't even sounded too superior when he'd agreed. Well, maybe a little. But that didn't prevent Abby from feeling she was the worst mother *in the world*. And she'd met some pretty atrocious mothers, including the mother of that friend of Ben's who let him watch four hours of TV every single day. But did that mother abandon her kids for a whole week? No, she did not. Because only Abby was that awful.

She pushed the thought away.

"I've been remembering some things from my childhood," she said. "From the cult."

"Bad memories?"

"Some. It wasn't all bad. There was a wildflower field . . . well, you know that. Where they grew the poppies. But it was beautiful."

"I remember," Penny said.

"You were there?" Abby asked, surprised.

"We all were. Hank and I took you there a year after we adopted you. We thought it might help. You were so unhappy."

"Did it help?"

"Maybe, a little. It was a long process."

Abby nodded, pacing the kitchen, tracing the chair with her—

—*fingers. She glanced at Penny, who stood by the counter, humming to herself as she made dinner. She wasn't paying attention. A perfect opportunity.*

Abihail sneaked away, stepping softly. She paused by the stairs for just a second, listening. Hank was talking on the phone in his study upstairs. He talked a lot on the phone. Penny had explained to Abihail that it was part of Hank's job.

She slid into the bathroom, leaving the light off, the door half-closed. When she closed the door, they always noticed.

Then she took out the green scouring pad from her pocket. She'd pinched it from the sink in the kitchen when Penny wasn't looking.

It was perfect.

Penny and Hank didn't like it when she washed her hands. She'd explained about the germs, and Penny had said that she was right but that twenty seconds with a bit of soap was enough. They didn't understand. You couldn't get rid of the really nasty germs like that. Some germs had to be scraped away.

Hank had told her that if they caught her scraping her skin with her fingernails again, she would be punished. But he'd never said anything about scouring pads.

She turned on the faucet and began scrubbing, the rough material peeling away the germs. She poured a large dollop of soap on it and scraped harder, soap running down her wrists, turning pink with blood. It hurt, but it was good pain, cleansing pain. She had to get rid of all the germs.

"Oh no! Abihail, what are you doing!" Penny's horrified scream made her drop the scouring pad into the—

—sink.

Abby stared down at the sink. At some point she'd stepped out of the kitchen, walked over to the bathroom. It wasn't the same sink; Penny and Hank had installed a new one since then. But there were still remnants of her childhood in that bathroom. Same mirror on the wall, even after all these years. Same tiles.

How horrified they'd been. She still recalled hearing them as she—
—*lay in bed.*

"We need to be tough about this," Hank said, his voice angry. "We can't let her harm herself. What if she cuts herself next? I'm going to tell her that there's no TV for a whole week, and if we catch her doing that again—"

"Oh, stop that, Hank," Penny said sharply. "Punishing Abihail won't help. You need to be patient. You remember what the psychologist said."

"That shrink is too soft. My parents were strict with me when I was a child, and I turned out just fine."

"For heaven's sake. Are you comparing what that poor child went through to your childhood?"

There was a long moment of silence.

"That damn cult," Hank finally said. "I don't know if we'll be able to fix what they did to her."

"It's not about fixing her. It's about giving her love. You just need to be patient."

Their voices became softer after that, and Abihail had a hard time following the discussion. She was tired and was slowly drifting away, wondering what that word was that Hank had mentioned, the cult, *and if the fire and the explosion from that night was the cult's fault.*

Abby massaged her forehead, walking back to the living room. She glanced up the stairs hopefully, but Leonor and Brian were still shut in her old bedroom.

"Abihail?" Hank's voice came from the doorway.

She didn't take the blanket off her face. She didn't want to see him. Or Penny. She wanted to go back to her Family.

"I have something for you," Hank said. She felt the weight of him moving the mattress as he sat on the bed. "To wash your hands with."

That did the trick. She peeked from under the blanket. "What is it?"

He held a large bottle that contained gooey pink liquid. "It's special medical soap. Antimicrobial. You know what that means?"

She shook her head.

"It kills germs extra fast. Much better than regular soap. And you need to use it with these." He took out a large packet of what looked like white circles. "They're made of cotton. See? You dab a bit on them, and then you start scrubbing. You don't need to scrub hard, but . . ." He exhaled. "You can scrub as long as you want. Until your hands are clean."

"Even a whole hour?"

He sighed. "I don't think you need a whole hour. But you can wash them as long as you want. But no fingernails, okay? And only use these special pads." He placed the bottle and the pads on her bed. "Okay?"

"Okay," she said meekly, and then, after a slight hesitation, she hugged him, her eyes squeezed shut.

The sound of a door opening upstairs shook Abby from her reverie. She quickly wiped her eyes with the back of her hand as Brian and Leonor descended the stairs.

CHAPTER 66

"Hey," Abby said in a light, cheerful voice. "How are you this morning?"

"Fine," Leonor said, her happy smile dissipating.

"You seem better," Abby said. She didn't let a fragment of her tension show, her muscles loose, her expression distracted, as if she were just passing by.

"I guess. It's nice to be with Brian." Leonor glanced at Penny, letting a little smile show. "Thanks for the chocolates."

"You're welcome, sweetie," she said. "Can I make you both some tea?"

"I can make it," Brian suggested.

"Don't be silly." Penny began her ceremony of banging all the cupboards and drawers in the kitchen.

Abby rolled her eyes at the noise. "Let's go to the living room," she half shouted over the din. "I can't hear myself think here."

They stepped into the living room. Abby sat on the armchair, and Leonor and Brian sat on the couch, huddled together.

"Brian, did you get your side mirror fixed?" Abby asked. "You shouldn't drive like that."

"Not yet," Brian admitted.

"I think I can make a statement for the insurance," Abby suggested. "Telling them that it wasn't your fault. Maybe it'll be easier to get them to pay for it that way."

"That would be great," Brian said, sounding relieved. "I don't have a lot of cash at the moment, and my dad will have a fit when he sees the car."

"I just need to understand what happened," Abby said lightly. "There seemed to be some sort of problem; you lost control."

For a moment no one spoke, but then Brian said, "It's nothing. Forget it. It was my fault."

"No," Leonor said in a strangled voice. "I scratched him. I panicked."

Abby frowned. "Why did you panic?"

"I just figured . . . I was scared."

"What were you scared of?"

"I thought . . . look, it's dumb. I was frightened. But I'm over it."

"Did your brother *do* anything to—"

"No!" Leonor blurted, edgy. "I thought it was a trap, okay? I figured maybe there was a blockade waiting for us. And they would stop us and kill us. So I shouted at Brian to turn around. And when he didn't, I scratched him."

"Why did you think that?" Abby probed, searching for a crack. An indicator that Leonor had doubts. That she was ready to think and act on her own.

"I don't know."

"You don't know?" Abby repeated.

"Look, all the other people who left the community were killed, okay? There are people who hate us. Who want to stop us. People in the bureau and fundamentalist Christians who think we're an abomination because we're progressive. I guess you're okay; you're not one of them, but I didn't know that back then."

"You say the other people who left the community were killed. But you met Eden. She wasn't killed, right?"

"I guess not. Maybe not everyone was killed. We might have gotten some bad info."

Bad info. There it was. For Leonor to admit *they had it wrong* was a big step. Time to lean on that crack. Widen it.

"How do you think you got the impression that everyone died when they left? Who gave you that bad info?"

Leonor shut her eyes and prayed. Brian stared into his lap, despair etched on his face. Abby gave him a reassuring look and leaned back, waiting. She'd pushed too hard. She'd have to be gentler. After a few minutes, Penny walked in and handed each of them a cup of tea. Leonor stopped praying as if embarrassed by her own behavior. Penny left, caressing Leonor's head on her way out of the room.

"Did you talk to Brian about the community in the past few days?" Abby asked as soon as her mother was gone.

"Yeah." Leonor was staring at the floor.

"What do you think he feels about it?" Abby sipped from her tea.

"You'd have to ask him."

"I want to know what *you* think he feels," Abby suggested casually. She wanted Leonor to see herself through Brian's eyes. To examine the cult from a different perspective.

"I guess he's not happy about it. Because of that woman yesterday."

"Eden?"

"She was pretty negative. But, I mean, she left. And Otis told us she stole money from us. So I don't know how far we can trust her bullshit."

"Was it all bullshit? Didn't it seem similar to things you witnessed yourself?"

"Maybe, if you have a really twisted outlook. Like, anything can sound really horrible if you say it wrong."

"Like Santa," Brian said, smiling at his sister.

"Shut up, Brian."

"So you think she was twisting reality?"

"Yeah."

A slight hesitation there. An infinitesimal pause. Abby heard it. Somewhere, deep down, Leonor knew Eden had been telling the truth.

Not a twisted version of it. Abby wanted that buried part in Leonor's consciousness to come out.

"What would fourteen-year-old Leonor think about what Eden told you?"

"What?" Leonor raised her eyes, looking confused.

"Suppose you heard Eden's stories before you ever met the people from your community. What would you have thought about it? Would you say it's bullshit?"

Leonor remained quiet. Abby waited, letting her think this through.

"I didn't know better when I was fourteen."

"But now you know better. Because you know the people, and you've studied their way. They explained everything to you."

"Yeah."

"If you met fourteen-year-old Leonor right now, how would you explain it to her so that she would understand?"

"I . . . I'd tell her that . . . I mean, there are things she didn't grasp. She'd have to talk to the people. See for herself."

"Eden told you they were about to marry her twelve-year-old daughter to Karl. How would you explain that to your past self?"

Leonor bit her fingernail, her eyes frantically searching for a way out. "Some things aren't easy to explain. She'd have to talk to Otis."

"Why? Couldn't you explain it yourself? You said you now understand it."

"He explains it better."

"What would fourteen-year-old Leonor think if she met you right now? What would she say about what happened in the car with Brian? Do you think she'd understand your fear? That you were afraid Brian was driving you into a trap?"

Leonor shut her eyes again. But to Abby's surprise, she didn't pray. It was time to lean harder. Time to shatter the walls that Otis had planted in Leonor's mind.

"What would she say about Otis's criminal record? Illegal arms trading. Two sexual assault charges."

Leonor shook her head violently.

"What would she think about what *you* went through lately?"

Leonor's eyes opened wide, full of pain and fear. There she was. The girl underneath. Hurt and broken, but she was still there. She shot to her feet. "I need to take a walk."

Brian stood up. "I'll come with—"

"No!" she shrieked at him. "Leave me alone! I'm going for a walk—alone."

She lunged for the door as if they were about to grab her. Brian stood up to follow her, but Abby put her hand on his arm. Leonor got out of the house, shutting the door behind her.

"Why did you let her leave?" Brian asked, furious. "We were getting somewhere."

"It doesn't help if she feels like we're keeping her here against her will," Abby pointed out. "We told her she can leave whenever she wants."

"What's going to stop her from calling her cult leader, asking that they pick her up? Or just hitchhiking back there?"

"Nothing," Abby said. "But she said she wanted to take a walk alone. Respecting her wishes is critical right now."

Despite her apparent nonchalance, she was worried. Leonor's sudden lunge for the door seemed like an attempt to escape. And if she was desperate for a safe haven, she would automatically turn to the place that felt like home—Otis Tillman's farm. Abby wished she could deploy barricades or have someone tail Leonor. She couldn't. All they could do was trust in the judgment and self-reflection of a frightened fifteen-year-old girl.

As minutes ticked by, Abby checked her phone, trying to read her emails, but she kept reading the same few sentences over and over. Brian turned on the TV, then turned it off. He walked out and returned ten minutes later, his expression dark, but said nothing. Abby guessed he had gone looking for Leonor and come back empty handed.

An hour went by. It was nerve racking. Penny swept the floor, did some tidying up, but she was clearly unsettled as well. Abby got ready to move on. Leonor had fled. Probably on her way to the farm by now. This had been a heartbreaking bust.

The door opened, Leonor standing there. Her eyes red and puffy.

"I don't want to go back to the farm," she sobbed.

"You don't need to." Brian gathered her into his arms.

"But I don't want to go back to Mom and Dad's either. Not yet."

"Do you want to stay here for a few more days?" Penny asked. "That's fine."

"Okay," Leonor said into Brian's chest, her voice muffled.

Abby cleared her throat. "Leonor, I need your help. Can you answer a few questions?"

Brian gave Abby a furious glare, but she ignored him. They'd broken through. Now there was no time to lose. Leonor pulled back and wiped her eyes. "I think I know what you want."

"We think that Otis or Karl may have decided to kidnap Nathan last week," Abby said. "Maybe they're even keeping him on the farm. But to search it we need a good reason. So if you can break Karl's alibi or if you have any information—"

"You're wrong." Leonor sniffed.

"I know you still think that way, but—"

"You don't understand." Leonor raised her voice. "They didn't decide to kidnap Nathan last week. They've been planning it for years."

CHAPTER 67

"Detective Carver and I have interviewed my informant, Leonor Craft, for more than two hours," Abby said. "We estimate that we have more than enough for an extensive warrant on the Tillman compound."

They sat in the task force room around the table, all eyes on her. Her body thrummed, flooded with adrenaline, as she knew the next few hours were pivotal, not just to the case but for numerous lives that would be affected by the outcome. She had to get this right.

"Leonor has been a member of the Tillman cult for over a year," she said. "During that time she has gotten closer to the inner circle of the cult's leadership, which consists of four people. Otis Tillman, who is the cult leader. Karl Adkins, his nephew and assumed successor. David Huff, who is Otis's right-hand man and also Nathan Fletcher's father. And Richard Styles, who is Otis's attorney."

As she spoke, she spread the pictures of the four men on the desk. They had recent pictures of Karl and Richard from Karl's interrogation. David and Otis's picture was the same one from Gabrielle's Instagram feed, very outdated.

"First of all, Leonor clarified that Karl doesn't have an alibi for the day of the kidnapping," Abby continued. "She says that in the past few months, he's been leaving the compound frequently. Otis had commanded the entire group to verify Karl's alibi if asked. Which, of course, is what they did. The so-called official version is that Karl almost never leaves the compound. But like I said, this claim has been refuted by Leonor."

"Can we trust her?" Barnes asked. "She lied in your first interview."

"Yes," Abby said adamantly. "The first interview was in the presence of Otis Tillman. What she said there has little relevance. Leonor added that since we showed up at the compound, she's talked to multiple members of the cult and slowly found out there had been discussions of abducting David's children for years. These discussions were mostly secret, but it's a small community. People talk. Leonor named three different people who knew of this plan. We believe their primary target was Gabrielle Fletcher, who, according to Eden Fletcher, was supposed to marry Karl Adkins when she turned twelve. This was the reason Eden left the cult."

"Why didn't Leonor come forward earlier?" Griffin asked. "If she knew they had kidnapped Nathan Fletcher?"

"Like I said, she'd only found out about it fairly recently. And Otis Tillman made sure to tell everyone the rumors were unfounded. That they did actually plan to welcome back David's children to the group but had decided to wait until the children came on their own. Leonor believed him. This morning I managed to convince her otherwise."

"Where are they keeping him?" Marshall asked.

"We don't know," Abby said. "Leonor pointed out two cabins that are off limits to most members. In addition, the basement in the main house is off limits and always locked as well. He could be in either of those locations, or they might be keeping him somewhere off-site."

"Leonor's testimony, along with the forensic evidence we have so far, gives us enough grounds for a search warrant," Carver said. "We have Eden Fletcher's testimony about Karl as well as her pointing him out in a lineup. We have Karl's digital footprints all over Gabrielle Fletcher's Instagram page. We know several members of the cult wear boots that match the prints we found in both Liam Washington's and Eric Layton's crime scenes. I sent a sworn affidavit to the Suffolk County

Police detailing everything, and they're acquiring a search warrant right now."

"Okay." Griffin massaged the bridge of his nose. "And once we get the search warrant, we'll need to approach this carefully."

No one needed to say *Waco* or *Ruby Ridge* or *Wilcox*. The collective trauma from those armed standoffs—and their horrific conclusions—was still fresh in every law enforcement officer's mind, even dozens of years later.

"Leonor was very clear about the firearms in the compound," Abby said. "There are at least a dozen automatic rifles stashed in the main house. The patrol guards and the lookout have two automatic rifles and two shotguns between them. If we show up brandishing a search warrant for the entire premises, it will almost certainly devolve into a full-blown crisis with multiple innocents and potential hostages. There are twelve minors in the compound, six of them under the age of ten. In addition, Nathan Fletcher himself might be on the premises."

"Can we negotiate their surrender?" Griffin asked, eyeing both Abby and Will.

"It's not likely," Abby admitted. "From everything Leonor told us, and from what we've seen, the entirety of the cult believes that higher-ups in the police and the bureau are intent on killing them all. I'm also concerned that if Nathan is on the premises, Otis might decide his best bet is to kill him and get rid of the body before we storm inside. And the kidnappers' recent email indicates we have very limited time. Negotiation needs time."

"So what's the alternative?"

"We need to coordinate a raid with the Suffolk Police," Carver said. "Leonor gave us the location of the stashed guns. And even more important, she gave us vital information on the cult's schedule. We know when to strike."

CHAPTER 68

"We have good satellite images of the compound, but we're not sure if the blueprints of the main house are updated," Baker, the commanding officer of the Emergency Services Unit, said.

It was a cloudy night, the moon mostly hidden. But even in the darkness, Baker was easily visible, looming over everyone, his shadow almost like a fairy-tale giant. But in this tale, the giant was on their side.

Abby and the rest of the task force stood alongside the group of ESU officers and a few select officers from the Suffolk County Police, including Detective Wong. Otis Tillman's farm, or the Tillman compound, as Baker called it, was less than two hundred yards away.

Baker continued with his briefing. "Since we don't have intel about the main house interior—"

"Lieutenant Mullen and I were inside the house," Wong said.

Everyone turned to look at them.

Baker had decided to strike during dinnertime, which Leonor promised was a two-, sometimes three-hour affair. It always started with a long sermon by Otis. And depending on how hungry *he* was, the sermon could take ages. During that time, the majority of the community was in the dining hall, listening. The sermon was mandatory. Only two armed guards remained outside, one in the lookout tower by the gate and one patrolling the perimeter. Otis himself had two armed bodyguards, but they were in the dining hall with him. The rest were unarmed.

The raid was a joint operation of the NYPD and the Suffolk County Police—with an understanding that the ESU commanding officer called the shots.

"Do you think you can find your way in it?" Baker asked.

"I believe we can," Abby said.

They were in a thicket of trees. The house stood between them and the lookout tower. Abby had been supposed to stay back while the ESU officers and the Suffolk cops raided the compound. But the plans were quickly changing.

"Put on a vest, you two, and someone get them goggles," Baker ordered.

She'd forgotten how heavy the vest was. It was like medieval armor. She dreaded the moment she'd have to run with the thing. Wong wore hers casually, as if it were a shirt. A man gave Abby night vision goggles and helped her adjust them on her head. When she turned them on, the trees were flooded in a gray-green light.

Abby scrutinized her surroundings in the new light, getting used to it. It was hard to get a sense of depth of her environment, and she dreaded walking with the thing, not to mention running. All around her, men were adjusting their gear, tightening straps, checking their guns and magazines. Wong did the same, moving with confidence and ease. Abby felt out of place, but it was hardly the first time. She could fake confidence. She just wished she could *feel* it.

Leonor had been a treasure trove of information, handing them detailed schedules, living arrangements, even recalling the blind spots of the lookout tower. She'd recited it all in a detached tone that worried Abby. Behind that tone were layers of turbulence and pain. Leonor's world had been torn to shreds, and although it was for the best, Abby knew the next few months would be fraught with hardship.

"Hey," Carver whispered by her side. "Be careful in there. Okay?"

She glanced at him and could see the concern on his face, even with the flat gray-green vision. "Don't worry; I'll leave the action-hero stuff to the ESU guys."

A voice buzzed in her earphone. "They're entering the dining hall now." It was the officer on lookout, stationed on the roof of a nearby barn and equipped with a scope.

"Can you see the patrol?" Baker asked.

"Negative. He should be on the eastern part of the compound."

They all waited, tense. Abby hardly breathed, listening intently. Somewhere in the distance, a vehicle drove by. Crickets and katydids chirped around them. Ben had once explained the difference, but she couldn't remember which were the noisier ones.

"I see him now," the lookout said. "Northeastern corner."

"Okay," Baker said. "Team one, go."

Four men moved, melting into the night. Even with her night vision goggles, Abby could hardly see them as they proceeded in the direction of the fence. She waited, shivering, not knowing if it was from the cold, or fear, or excitement. She counted in her mind, matching the beat of the insect chirping. When she reached 378, a gruff voice said on the channel, "We're in. The patrol is in custody."

"Move to the lookout tower," Baker said. "Team two, Mullen, Wong. Go."

Three men moved, crouched, following the first team's path. Wong followed, and Abby jostled behind them, keeping as low as she could. The vest made it hard to bend over, and she was breathing hard within seconds, the night's chilly air hurting her lungs. Then she saw the fence, bathed in the night vision goggles' green hue. A section of the fence had been cut—the work of the first team.

And they were inside, running through an apple orchard, branches snagging at Abby's sleeves. She tripped over a tree root, stumbling, nearly crashing to the ground, the NVGs shifting askew, and for a moment she got a glimpse of the orchard without them, a pitch-black darkness, the trees like menacing shadows. She couldn't see or hear the rest of her teammates, her breathing becoming fast, panicky. She put the goggles back on, and the world shifted back to green. There was Wong, coming back for her. Abby gave her a thumbs-up. They kept going.

At the edge of the orchard, they paused. A field lay between them and the house, and the lookout would see them if they ran out in the open. Abby squatted, catching her breath.

"Lookout in custody," the man from team one said. "We're opening the front gate."

Both armed guards were down. The rest of the cult members were in the dining hall.

Abby followed the men as they ran in the open field toward the house. She felt exposed but reminded herself that any of the cult members who happened to look out the dining hall window would see nothing. Abby and her team were shrouded by the night. And without her goggles, she'd see nothing either.

The men reached the back door and flattened themselves against the walls to either side. Abby took the left side, drawing her gun.

The man by the door turned the knob. "Locked," he murmured. He motioned to the one behind him, raising his hand, counting down with his fingers.

Three . . . two . . . one . . .

He took a step back, and the guy behind took his place. Then he kicked the door, smashing it open, the loud sound making Abby flinch. The second guy moved inside swiftly, and the "clear" signal came a second later. The other two men moved in, and Abby and Wong followed in the rear, weapons raised, pointing in alternate directions.

"The stairs are through that door over there," Wong said in a low voice. "There are two more doors to the left, the front door to the right."

How did the detective manage to recall it so clearly? Even though she'd walked through these rooms with Wong, the house seemed completely different in the green dark, the lack of color disconcerting.

They moved from room to room, making sure each was clear before continuing to the next one. When they went up the stairs, Abby climbed second. The man in front of her stopped at the edge of the stairs and signaled for her to cover the left. She nodded, tensing. When he shifted forward, turning to the right, she followed, whirling left, gun aimed in front of her. The second floor was as empty as the first.

"Tillman's office is that way." She pointed. "The guns should be in the room over there."

They split, Wong and one of the men to the office while Abby and the others went for the room with the guns. Leonor had warned them that occasionally Otis stationed a guard there. The man in the lead opened the door and cleared the room.

She followed him inside. It was a sort of storage room with boxes, mattresses, a spare bunk bed. Abby crossed the room to three mattresses that lay against the wall, and shifted them aside. Nothing. Had Otis moved the guns? For a second she was gripped by fear. What if the guns were in the dining hall? This could escalate into a horrific shoot-out with innocent children trapped in the line of fire.

A fractured memory materialized. An explosion, a searing pain on the back of her neck. Her fingers went to the decades-old burn scar.

What was that? A small latch almost perfectly hidden. She unbarred it and pulled. A part of the wooden wall shifted. Behind it, two ammunition boxes and a dozen assault rifles.

"This is team two; the guns are secured," the man behind her said.

"Team two, copy, take positions by the dining hall. Stay out of sight," Baker responded.

The men grabbed the boxes of ammunition and some of the rifles, leaving eight behind for Abby and Wong. Abby took four, slinging two over each shoulder. A mistake, the guns clattering against each other and against her legs, making each step a stumble. Wong toted all four on the same shoulder. They all went down the stairs slowly, vulnerable with their cumbersome cargo. The first team met them outside the door, and four of the men took the guns and ammunition to the front gate, where an ESU armored vehicle now waited. Abby beelined to a knoll nearby the dining hall and positioned herself behind it. Wong joined her a moment later.

"Now we wait," Abby whispered. "It might be a while."

"At least unlike the people in there, we don't have to listen to Tillman's ramblings," Wong pointed out.

Abby turned off her night vision goggles and removed them, making sure to look down to avoid being blinded by the light from the dining hall windows. The world turned black, but it was a relief to take the damn things off. She flattened herself on the ground, leaning on her elbows, letting her eyes adjust to the darkness. She lay there, shivering, deriving little comfort from Wong's presence. Her entire body ached from the tension and effort of the past twenty minutes. She was thankful for the opportunity to lie still.

Minutes ticked by, the compound silent.

"There," Wong hissed.

The dining hall door opened. People trickled outside in groups. They were talking; someone laughed. Two women came out, one holding a baby in her arms, the other walking a toddler hand in hand.

And then three men stepped out together.

"I have eyes on the target," the lookout said in the earphone. "Two armed bodyguards. I can't see if the target is armed."

"Copy," Baker said. "Okay, team three, go!"

Lights. Engines roaring. Three large armored vans drove through the open gates and circled the crowd, blocking the people in. Screams. The deafening sound of a chopper's rotors as it lowered above the crowd, a sudden blinding spotlight hitting the ground. Men disembarked from the vehicles, rifles aimed forward.

Abby ran, leaping over the knoll, gun in hand, straight at Otis and his bodyguards.

"Don't move!" she screamed, knowing no one could hear her over the chaos. "Put your hands up!"

Tillman seemed shocked as he looked around, squinting his eyes at the dozens of armed men surrounding him. Now, in the midst of the turmoil he had no control over, he was no longer imposing or confident. He looked like a trapped animal desperate for a way out.

One of his bodyguards, Abby now saw, was Karl Adkins. He took a step forward, protecting Otis with his body, still holding his rifle despite the warning shouts from the agents around him.

His eyes met Abby's, and she saw a flash of anger burning in them.

He moved fast, the barrel of his rifle training on her. Her own gun was too low, aimed sideways. She raised it, but she was sluggish, her finger trembling on the Glock's trigger.

A deafening explosion at her side, her ears ringing. Karl lurched backward, eyes widening. Several more shots echoed in the darkness around them, accompanied by screams, and Karl tumbled to the ground. Abby glanced sideways at Wong, who had been the one to shoot Karl and was already training her gun on the second guard.

"Drop it!" Wong shouted. And despite the impossible uproar around them, he seemed to hear her and dropped his rifle to the ground.

People were running, ESU forces intercepting them, the chopper hovering above. Someone shouted, his voice intensified with a bullhorn, but Abby couldn't parse the words with the ringing in her ears. She stared at Karl, who lay on his back, eyes wide and vacant, a medic by his side. More and more vehicles poured into the compound. Somewhere, a woman was crying.

An agent grabbed Otis, forced him to his knees, and patted him down, pulling a long farming knife from Otis's belt. He tossed the knife aside. Abby glanced away from Karl and spotted the blade discarded in the dirt. It was long, maybe six inches, and quite narrow.

Just like the knife that had killed Eric and Liam.

CHAPTER 69

The evening stretched into the night, fragmented in Abby's consciousness, a disjointed sequence of events.

Bright spotlights and flashlights casting blinding beams in the darkness, illuminating the terrified residents of the compound as they were herded back into the dining hall by armed men. Crying children, furtive glances at Karl's inert body on the ground. Horror and fear etched on people's faces.

A busted door, then another, then another. A room that looked like a lab. Another that was filled with papers and computers. A basement full of chemicals. No sign of Nathan anywhere.

Two K-9 handlers with dogs. One of them a search and rescue dog, the other a cadaver dog. Noses to the ground, sniffing and searching. Abby hoped one would find Nathan. Dreaded that the other would. But she wasn't even sure which dog was which.

An ambulance driving into the compound, red lights flashing. Karl's body raised on a gurney. Wong standing to one side, staring at the medical crew, her expression inscrutable.

More boots, all matching the same type. All collected and taken away to be examined for one pair with a specific tread-wear pattern. The boots of a murderer.

And more farming knives with a long, narrow blade. Found in trunks in a storage room, discarded under beds, two in the possession of congregation members.

Then, already exhausted, she stepped into Otis's office, where Carver and Marshall stood by Otis's desk, staring at a laptop's screen. Carver's face was twisted with disgust.

"What is it?" Abby asked.

"Found a flash drive hidden in a drawer," Marshall said. "It's full of videos."

Abby stepped over, the laptop's screen shifting into view. Was that . . . a porn video clip? No, it was much worse. The man in the recording was Otis Tillman. The video had been taken in this very room. Abby's eyes flickered to the corner of the room where the camera would have been. The shelf of books.

"We found the camera," Carver said, following her gaze. "It was impossible to see if you didn't know where to look."

Abby gazed back at the laptop. The sex on the screen was rough, Otis's mouth locked in a visceral sneer, the woman's face turned away from the camera. The volume was muted, and Abby was thankful for that fact.

"Some of these videos are just conversations," Carver said. "Between Otis and one of the community members."

"Confessions," Abby interjected. "He filmed their private confessions."

On-screen, the woman turned her head, facing the camera. Abby shut her eyes. Ruth. It was Ruth.

"Can you turn it off?"

"Done." Carver's voice sounded brittle.

Abby looked down at Otis's desk. The desk on which Ruth had been lying. She took a step away, distancing herself from it. How many confessions like that one had taken place there? The air was suffocating, rancid. She crossed the room to the window, flung it open, letting in the chilly night wind.

"Why did he film those confession sessions?" Marshall asked.

"Blackmail, probably," Abby answered after a moment. "Jim Jones did something similar. When people were about to leave—or to report him to the authorities—Jones would threaten to expose their secret confessions. I guess Otis went a step further. He wanted actual videos."

"Those videos go back years," Carver said.

"How many?" Abby whispered.

Marshall checked. "Over two thousand videos. Going all the way back to 2011."

That probably meant there was a video of Eden here. Had Otis threatened her with it? Shown her video to the rest of the community when she left? Abby didn't want to know.

"Any luck out there?" Carver asked, glancing through the window at the shadowy trees.

"A lot of paperwork, which might give us some good leads," Abby said. "No sign of Nathan. And the people here aren't talking so far."

"Where's Tillman? And David Huff?"

"They were taken into Suffolk County Police custody along with Richard Styles."

Carver let out a long breath. "Okay. Let's go talk to them."

CHAPTER 70

"He didn't ask for an attorney?" Abby asked, inspecting the screens in the monitor room. Otis Tillman sat in one of the interrogation rooms, leaning back in his chair, his face expressionless.

"He did," Wong said. "As soon as we got here. He asked for Richard Styles, but when we told him his lawyer was under arrest as well, he waived his right to an attorney."

Abby glanced at the time. Half past midnight.

"Let's talk to him," Carver said.

"Wait." Abby hesitated. "Maybe I should go there on my own."

Carver frowned. "Why? We can probably make it work better if we do it together."

"I'm just thinking . . . he knows me and—"

"Abby, is this about that time in the academy?"

"That's part of it," she admitted. "We didn't do so well back then."

A tiny smile twisted Carver's lips. "We were practically teenagers back then. It'll be okay. Don't worry about it. I'll let you lead, do your light, casual questioning. And when I feel like we need to lean on him, I'll intervene."

"Okay," Abby said. "Don't mention the murders until we get a few questions in. I want to start out with him assuming he can weasel himself out of this, so the less charges he knows we're throwing at him, the better."

"No problem," Carver agreed. "But you leave the confession videos and all the forensic stuff to me for when he needs to be bullied."

Carver led the way to the interrogation room. The smell in the claustrophobic chamber hit Abby as she stepped in—a noxious mix of sweat, farts, and disinfectant. Otis hardly even moved as they entered, as if they didn't matter. Abby sat across the table from him. Carver dragged his own chair to the side of the table, effectively blocking Otis in. He sat too close to the man, invading his personal space. Otis reflexively moved his chair away to distance himself from the detective, breaking his nonchalant demeanor.

"I have some good news for you, Otis," Abby said. "The Suffolk County executive is eager to keep a lid on this entire story. He really doesn't want his grandson's face plastered on the news tomorrow, labeled as a cult member. So we're willing to cut you some slack. If you tell us where Nathan Fletcher is, we'll do our best to minimize the charges brought against you."

Otis folded his arms. "We're not a cult, Lieutenant Mullen; I already told you that. We're a Christian community. Why the NYPD is conducting this witch hunt is beyond me. And when dawn breaks tomorrow, and the media starts reporting about my nephew's murder by your homicidal cops, you'll be singing a different tune."

"We're only interested in Nathan's safety. We don't care about the way you manage your community."

"I also care about Nathan's safety. He's my dearest friend's son, and I would never do anything to harm him."

Otis probably believed that come morning, the news would be filled with reports about the Christian community that had been ravaged by the police. And he was intent on wasting their time until that happened. If Abby wanted to get anywhere with him, she had to make him feel like time was his enemy. And she knew how to do it. Otis, like most cult leaders, brimmed with paranoia and distrust. The loyalty of his members was always cast in doubt. And now that they were out of his reach, it would only get worse.

"A few members of your community are already talking," Abby said. "We learned you were planning on kidnapping both of David's kids. And Karl was supposed to marry Gabrielle, right?"

A flicker of doubt, almost instantly gone. "When David lost his kids to that woman, he was bereft with grief. He approached me and asked if we could get them back. And yes, he also got Karl worked up about it. I humored them for a bit, but ultimately they came to see it was a bad idea."

"It didn't look that way. Karl kept following Gabrielle online. And he stalked her in real life as well."

"That was unfortunate. I allowed him a cell phone because of some outside work he was doing for our farm. But I didn't know he would use it to follow that girl. If I only knew, I wouldn't have encouraged that."

Abby smiled at him, sliding her hair behind her ear. "He used one of the farm's trucks to go there, didn't he? I thought you ran a tight ship. Surely you noticed he was missing for long periods of time. And using a lot of gas."

"I did. Of course. And when I asked him about it, he said he was doing some rounds, making sure our suppliers didn't cheat us." He glanced to the side, his voice breaking as he said, "He was a good kid. I believed him."

"If *my* best friend was suffering, missing his kids, I would try to help him," Abby said. "Maybe you didn't kidnap Nathan. But you sent Karl to hang around the Fletcher house. Just to see if the kids were unhappy. If maybe they wanted to come voluntarily. Right?"

"We'll be asking the rest of your people the same question," Carver said darkly.

Otis hesitated. "Like I said, Karl did this on his own. But he finally admitted the truth to me. And he *did* suggest that maybe one of the kids would come voluntarily, so I allowed him to keep a lookout. But never more than that. We only wanted to help David and the kids. Life with their mother couldn't have been easy."

"I believe everything your community did was well intentioned," Abby said. "Tell me about Friday. Did Karl go there that day?"

"No. Like some of us testified, Karl was with us."

"Really?" Abby frowned. "Because half an hour ago, I talked to one of your members, and he clearly told me that he saw Karl leave."

"Then whoever you talked to was wrong." His face remained blank, but his eyes glazed. He was trying to figure out who had talked to her. She'd purposefully let slip the gender pronoun to make it sound specific. Was he running the names through his mind now, trying to figure out who was already breaking?

She leaned back and waited, hoping Carver would take the cue. And he did.

"I've had enough of this," he growled. He placed the laptop he'd brought on the table and opened it, dragging his chair even closer to Otis as he did so. "You know, our forensic team took your flash drive. Guess what we found there?"

He turned the laptop so Otis could see the screen. "You're a very tidy person, Tillman; I'll give you that. There's a bunch of videos named after many of your community members. And you know what those videos contain? I couldn't believe it when I saw it. All their private confessions."

Tillman stared at Carver in contempt. "Just like the police to look through the private confessions of Christians."

"They're not just confessions," Carver said. "You know that, right? There's quite a few of them that end with you getting a blow job or having sex with your community members."

"It was all consensual. I don't expect you to understand; it's part of the cleansing process."

"Well, I'd argue that if you're their preacher, landlord, and boss, then none of this is consensual. But we don't even need to go there, because three of your community members in those videos are minors. So you're going to prison for multiple cases of statutory rape, asshole. And you know what I'm going to do? I'll make sure everyone in that prison knows you like to rape little girls. It'll make you *really* popular."

"Your threats don't intimidate me, Detective. What did you think? That your petty bullying would make me burst into tears? You're not the first person to try and bring us down, and you won't be the last. What next? Will you turn off the cameras and hit me? Put a bullet in my head? Go ahead. Kill me. Kill all of us. For having our own opinions on what's right. For trying to change the world."

Abby frowned. "It seems like you feel we're unjustly persecuting you."

He snorted. "I'm blameless and upright."

"I don't care about upright, but you're not blameless," Carver said. "With the rape, you're already going to prison. And we have possession of illegal firearms. I wonder what we'll find once we go through all your papers and computers."

"We needed the assault rifles to protect ourselves," Otis shot back. "You proved that when you raided us and murdered Karl. I am a preacher, Detectives. I have a large community. I try to lead them well, but sometimes, in pursuit of change, they stray."

"Maybe," Abby said. "But how do you think it would look in court?"

"My community will all testify on my behalf. It will look like what it is. A brutal witch hunt."

"Will they?" Abby asked. "All of them?" She exchanged glances with Carver, who smirked.

Otis's eyes shifted between them. "Of course. I wouldn't expect you to understand the love between a preacher and his—"

"Oh, we got an eyeful of that love, thanks," Carver said, leaning in toward Otis. "What I'm wondering is, Will that love hold? With all the charges your community are facing. Every person whose fingerprints are on those assault rifles will be charged. We will use every shred of evidence we find in your office. We have several incarcerated already. Do you think they'll still feel that love when we give them a deal? And *then* imagine their testimonies in court."

Otis was backed against the wall. His face was etched with contempt, but underneath Abby glimpsed what she was looking for. Fear.

"Like I said, we're only interested in Nathan Fletcher. If you tell us where he is—"

"I don't know where he is. We never laid a hand on him."

"We have solid forensic evidence that says different," Carver said. "Shoe prints that match those boots everyone in your community wears. And we have evidence that suggests someone used one of those knives you people have to murder two people. Murders connected to the Fletcher kidnapping. Once we match our evidence to the right boots—and the right knife—it'll be a solid case. You will never see daylight again."

"The boots we use are common—"

Carver slammed his hand on the table. "We are conducting these interrogations with each and every one of your community. How long before someone cracks? How long before someone tells us *exactly* about your plan to kidnap the Fletcher kids? I'm giving it two hours tops."

"Well, it's too bad you killed Karl," Otis snapped back. "Because even if there was such a plan, David would never tell you anything, and—"

His eyes widened, and his mouth snapped shut. Then, to Abby's surprise, his body relaxed, and he turned to her.

"I'd like to see a lawyer now," he said. "I'm not saying another word until that happens."

CHAPTER 71

"It looked like he figured something out," Abby said.

They sat in the monitor room, drinking tepid cups of coffee.

"I think he got scared and figured he needed a lawyer to make a deal," Carver said.

Abby shook her head. "The way his whole body reacted . . . there's no way he faked that. He realized something. Something important."

"He talked about Karl dying. Maybe he thought he could use that to his advantage in some way?"

"Maybe . . . he was talking about the plan to kidnap Nathan. That David would never flip on him, so it was too bad that we killed Karl. Maybe he figured out David would actually flip on him?"

"He was about to mention someone else," Wong said.

Both of them turned to face her.

"Check the footage." She pointed at the console. "He was about to mention a third person, but then he didn't."

Carver ran the footage back, and they watched the final minute of the interview. Otis lost his cool and shouted, "Well, it's too bad you killed Karl! Because even if there was such a plan, David would never tell you anything, and—"

"I think you're right," Abby said.

"I don't see it," Carver said.

"It's like he was about to say, 'David would never tell you anything, and Johnny won't either,'" Abby clarified. "Or 'Johnny wasn't there.' Or something about Johnny."

"Johnny?"

"It's an example. Much more likely that it's someone like Richard Styles. Suppose there were four of them. Otis, Karl, David, and someone else. They were the ones who planned the whole thing. And Otis listed them to us, telling us why we wouldn't be getting anywhere."

"He could have been about to say anything," Carver argued. "He could have been about to say, 'And I'm done talking to you.' Or 'And I want coffee and a pretzel.'"

"Let's check," Abby said brightly, standing up.

"Where are you going?"

"He said David would never flip on him. Let's see if that's true." She pointed at the monitor displaying David in the other room.

The interrogation room where David waited had a flickering light that kept clicking. David squinted when they walked in. Unlike Otis, he didn't look calm. He looked scared and exhausted.

"Hey, David," Abby said. "We have a few questions. To tie up loose ends."

David stared at her, saying nothing.

"Otis told us you once had a plan to kidnap Nathan and Gabrielle, but you ended up deciding not to go through with it," Abby said.

"That's right," David said. "We all agreed it was a bad idea."

"So you talked it over," she said. "You, Otis, Karl, and, uh . . . who was the other one?" She frowned at Carver, snapping her fingers.

"Luther," David said.

"Luther, right." Abby couldn't believe her luck. "You all talked it over and just decided not to go through with it?"

"Yeah."

"Don't you find it strange that Nathan was kidnapped after all?"

"Sometimes the Lord punishes us for our impure intentions," David said. "It's not my place to question his judgment. I can only strive to be better."

"Nathan's kidnapping was God's punishment for your own abduction plan?"

"I'm sure of it. Nathan was kidnapped, the police are murdering us one by one, the raid on the rest of the community . . ." He shut his eyes. "'For the wrath of God is revealed from heaven against all ungodliness and unrighteousness of men, who by their unrighteousness suppress the truth.'"

Abby exchanged glances with Carver.

"That plan," Carver said. "You were supposed to take Nathan back to the farm?"

"No, of course not," David said. "We were supposed to take him to the other . . ." He paused.

Abby leaned back, feigning disinterest. "Where did you plan to take him?"

"If Otis told you about it, why didn't he tell you *that*?" David asked.

"We didn't ask him about it." Abby shrugged.

"Then ask *him* about it."

"Why does it matter?" Carver asked. "You said you didn't go through with it."

"We didn't."

"Then why not tell us where you planned to take him?"

David didn't answer.

"Are you worried that Otis *did* go through with the kidnapping?" Abby asked. "And that Nathan really is there?"

"He didn't." His voice was completely certain.

"How do you know?"

"Because I know Otis better than anyone else. He would never do that."

"But you planned to do it."

"To get my kids back! Not to ask for ransom."

"Karl Adkins was spotted near Eden's house twice in the past month," Abby pointed out. "He was away from the farm on the day Nathan was kidnapped. What if *he* decided to go through with it? He was supposed to marry Gabrielle, right?"

"Karl would never do something without Otis's approval." David looked away. "I'm done talking about this."

He shut his eyes and prayed silently. Abby sighed.

"If Nathan is held somewhere, you should tell us," Carver said. "Do you want him to starve to death?"

David kept praying.

Carver leaned forward. "You know, this precious friend of yours, the guy you know better than anyone else? He screwed your wife. While you two were still married. He even videoed it—for posterity. Do you want to see?"

David's eyes snapped open, the prayer dying on his lips.

"That got your attention, huh?" Carver said.

David smiled thinly, contempt etched on his face. "You think I don't know about that? I gave them both my blessing."

Abby blinked, surprised.

"You talk as if I *owned* her. This is the type of patriarchal constructs we were fighting against. Sex is not *wrong*. It's not a sin. If both Eden and Otis wanted to have sex for Eden's spiritual growth, who am I to stop them?"

Otis had managed to harness gender equality as a reason for having sex with any woman he chose. How did he explain the discrepancy with the Ten Commandments? Probably by preaching about the meaning of the words *adultery* and *covet*. It didn't matter. His community members would believe anything Otis told them. It didn't have to make perfect sense.

David began praying again. After trying to ask more questions and getting no response, Abby and Carver stepped out.

"Who's Luther?" Carver asked.

"Let's find out," Abby said. "He probably has a confession video here somewhere."

She opened the laptop and reviewed the files. "There's no Luther here."

"How about Lou?"

"Nope." She saw seven files for Leonor and wished she could just delete them.

"Do you think David made that up to throw us off?"

"It didn't seem that way. And it's a pretty dumb way to throw us off." She sipped from her coffee. "Ugh, it's completely cold."

"Here, let me see." Carver looked at the screen over her shoulder. He was so close to her that their cheeks nearly touched.

"It's not there," she murmured.

"Yeah." He pulled away. "Let's call Barnes; I think he's still there, interrogating the members."

He made the call while Abby went to the bathroom. She nearly nodded off on the toilet seat.

When she returned, Carver was frowning at his phone. "No Luther among the people at the compound either."

"We'll keep asking tomorrow," Abby said tiredly. "Maybe Leonor knows who this guy is."

Carver perched on the desk next to the laptop. "What do you think David was about to say when I asked him where they intended to put Nathan?"

"He started saying the other . . . something." Abby thought about it. "The other farm? The other compound?"

"Is there another farm?"

"Not that I know of. But it's worth checking. There might be paper-work in the compound's office."

"Yeah."

Carver's eyes were bloodshot, and she was sure hers looked even worse. An evening that had seemed so promising at first was ending with only more questions. Nathan was still missing. Abby just hoped he was alive.

CHAPTER 72

Nathan was in the swimming pool, learning to swim again. He didn't like it, but his mom kept insisting that he should learn how to swim. And as long as he stayed in the shallow end of the pool, it wasn't too bad. He could go through the motions. And his mom would buy him ice cream later.

He even began to get it; he was *floating*. And Gabrielle cheered him on. He smiled at her, and she made a funny face at him, so he laughed, but that was when he swallowed some water. He coughed and sputtered, and he was glad he was in the shallow end of the pool because he could just step out—except his feet wouldn't touch the bottom.

Gabrielle was still cheering, but her voice was farther and farther away, and he thrashed in the water now, swallowing more, every breath a gurgle, and the man who'd stopped the car for him also coughed and sputtered by his side, his blood seeping into the pool, turning the water red.

He tried to get away from the bleeding man, and hands were grabbing him from below; they wanted to take him with them down down down, so he kept paddling at the water, crying, but Gabrielle didn't notice—she didn't see any of it; she just kept cheering. And the water was *cold* now, so cold; he was trembling, his body convulsing, and his throat was so dry, which was terrible, because even though he'd swallowed all that water, he was thirsty. But he didn't want the water in the pool, water that was now crimson with blood. He wanted water. Just a cup of water.

He whispered for water, but no one was there to hear him in the bed in his room. No, not in his room, in the other room, the strange mirror room. He'd been swallowed by a room that looked like his room but wasn't, and he kept whispering for water, but no one came. Not even Gabrielle, who kept clapping and cheering because she thought he was swimming so well.

And maybe he was, because he was floating again, floating away from his body, leaving it behind, which was probably better because his body hurt all over and was so cold.

Floating away would make everything better. Maybe he'd even see his mom again.

CHAPTER 73

Abby had once owned a very old Chevy Cavalier. The Chevy had accumulated mechanical problems like some people accumulate coupons. The engine would overheat in the summer. The driver's window didn't close properly, and rain would trickle in. Due to the constant puddle of rain inside the car, it smelled of mildew. The passenger mirror was fractured. The air conditioner rattled constantly.

And yet, miraculously, it kept on driving. Abby couldn't really afford to fix the car, so she kept ignoring all the problems, daring the car to live on another day. And it did. On and on, a strangely reliable piece of junk that had no business being on the road.

Until one day it wouldn't start.

She towed it to the shop, and when she asked the mechanic how much it would cost to fix, he raised an eyebrow and said, "Seriously?"

When she trudged into the station that morning after three hours of sleep and a quick shower, she felt like her old Chevy Cavalier. And she knew that soon, if she didn't get a good night's sleep, she wouldn't be able to start. She'd stopped at Starbucks and bought six coffees and some doughnuts for the team. But only Carver was there, standing in front of the map that marked the locations pertaining to the case.

"Where is everyone?" she asked.

"Marshall and Barnes are back in Suffolk County, trying to milk information," Carver said. "I have no idea where Will and Kelly are. Are those for me? I only need three cups; you didn't have to buy six."

She handed him one of the cups, sipped from another. "Will's at the academy. He said he'll be here in a few hours. Anything new?"

"Otis talked to a lawyer, and he has a great deal for us. We drop all charges, and in return he'll give us info regarding Nathan's location."

"Info *regarding* Nathan's location?"

"Yes. The lawyer was very clear. He said Otis has crucial information that might lead us to Nathan. But not the actual location."

For a second, Abby considered shrugging it off. It was probably nothing.

But Nathan's life was on the line. Could they really afford to ignore the possibility? "We could stipulate in the deal that if it doesn't lead us to Nathan, the charges stay."

"Yeah. Griffin is already looking into that. But it's more complex because the charges are not in our jurisdiction. Some are federal, and some are in Suffolk County's jurisdiction . . . it'll be tricky to coordinate this deal. It'll take time."

"Time Nathan doesn't have," Abby said heavily.

"If it hasn't already run out."

She refused to consider that possibility. "What about our idea yesterday? About the other compound?"

"Well, the Suffolk County Police actually found a deed to another farm twenty miles east of the compound in Otis's papers. He bought it four years ago."

"And?" Abby's heart skipped a beat.

"It's abandoned. We have K-9 handlers there right now, searching."

"Oh."

"Wong told me they also found some email correspondence with the real estate agent on Otis's computer. It sounds like they looked at a bunch of places but finally decided on that one. David and Otis were cc'd on all the emails. But guess who negotiated the actual purchase?"

"Who?"

"You don't want to guess?"

"For God's sake, Carver—"

"We have his private name in the email address. Luther."

Her heartbeat quickened. "If he bought the farm, he must have been in the cult at some point."

Carver turned back to the map. "Sounds right. I hope Marshall and Barnes manage to get something about this guy from their interrogations, though they say they're mostly getting chants and prayers."

"I'm not surprised. It'll take time." Abby glanced at the map. "What are you doing?"

"Trying to think it through again. Seven years ago, Eden left the Tillman cult with her kids, leaving some very pissed-off men." He pointed at the pin that marked the compound. "Then, a few years later, Gabrielle calls them, trying to get in touch with her dad. They try to get her to go there, but she refuses. Then, Otis figures they can kidnap the kids. He makes a plan, involves David, the ex; Karl, who is supposed to marry Gabrielle; and this guy Luther."

"He sends Karl to scope out the targets," Abby said. "Karl follows Gabrielle's Instagram and every once in a while goes by their house. But Otis later decides to keep David out of it. He realizes he can kidnap Nathan and use Gabrielle's popular Instagram account to get a nice ransom for the kid."

"And at the same time punish Eden for leaving them in the first place."

"Then, somehow, Liam Washington finds himself in the wrong place," Abby said. This was the weak link in their theory. "One of them takes him out."

"And later they see something in Eric's online interview that makes them think he figured something out. So they kill him too."

"Liam Washington's murder still bugs me," Abby admitted. "It doesn't fit with the rest."

"What if they kept Nathan somewhere along the road between Albany and Manhattan?" Carver said, trailing the road on the map with his finger. "Suppose Liam saw something while he drove home, something he shouldn't have."

"Yeah, that could work."

"Still a long road. We have no way to know where it happened."

Abby nodded. "What about forensics? Shouldn't we have a match to the footprint by now?"

"Maybe, I got here ten minutes ago; I didn't get around to checking." She took out her phone and dialed Ahmed.

"I was just about to call you," Ahmed said as soon as he picked up. "Do you want the good news or the bad news?"

"Let's start with the good news."

"Those boots you retrieved over there are all the right brand, matching the footprint from both crime scenes. Four pairs are even the right size. And I talked to Gomez. The knife model is a very good match for the murder weapon."

"Fantastic."

"Now for the bad news. You don't have it."

"What don't I have?" Abby asked.

"The murder weapon. Or the boots. The tread-wear patterns of the boots from the farm don't match the footprint from the Layton crime scene. And you remember the small chip that broke from the blade? We checked all the knives you brought us, and it doesn't match any of them."

Abby chewed her lip. "Okay, thanks, Ahmed."

"I'll let you know if I find anything else." He hung up.

Abby filled Carver in. "Maybe they got rid of the boots and the weapon," she suggested.

"Maybe," Carver said doubtfully.

"What's bothering you?"

"We have a missing pair of boots, a missing knife, and a missing Luther," Carver pointed out. "Doesn't it sound like they're all missing together?"

Abby thought about it. "It's possible."

"You know what else has been bothering me? Remember when we interrogated David, and he talked about how they made a plan to kidnap Nathan? And then he said God is punishing them for it, that the police are murdering them one by one."

"Right."

"The only one the police shot was Karl. Why 'one by one'? It sounds like we're killing them methodically. Otis and David are obviously not dead."

"So you think Luther was also killed by the police?"

"No. I think David *thinks* Luther was killed by the police."

Abby caught on. "Otis kept telling the community that everyone who leaves his protection dies. That the police are killing them off."

"Exactly. What if Luther is one of the people who left the cult? And Otis told the community the police killed him?"

"That's what Otis wants to offer," Abby said, feeling excited. "This is what he figured out last night! When you told him we have a match to the boots and knife, he was confused at first, because maybe they really didn't kidnap Nathan. But then he realized he knew who did. Luther, who worked out the initial plan with Otis, David, and Karl."

"Luther might still have the boots and the knife from the time he spent in the Tillman cult. And he enacted the plan that they'd originally thought of. But he did it alone."

"If Otis knows how to contact Luther, he might be able to lead us to him. And to Nathan."

"That's true. A phone number would be enough to nail him."

"We have to make that deal," Abby blurted.

Carver gave her a long stare. "Yeah."

"You don't think so?"

"I think Nathan could be dead. And that Otis is incredibly dangerous. You want him to keep on raping his community members? And what about Leonor? How would she feel about this?"

She saw his point. If they made this deal, what would she tell Leonor? And what about Ruth and the rest of the women who appeared on those thousands of videos?

"Okay," Carver finally said. "Suppose we're right. Luther is the one who kidnapped Nathan. How does that tie into Liam Washington's murder?"

"Maybe we were right the first time," Abby said. "They worked together."

Carver frowned. "It's possible, but when I investigated Liam's background, I didn't find anything that pointed to him. And we went through his schedule; all his recent engagements check out. Phone calls all correspond to his wife, friends, and clients. I don't think he's related to the kidnapping either way."

"Then, like you said, he saw something that he shouldn't have. On the way back home from Manhattan."

"Okay." Carver inspected the map closely. "So the road he would have used is the I-87."

"It's a highway," Abby said. "What would he have seen on it?"

"Maybe he saw the kidnapper with Nathan in the car," Carver suggested.

"That makes sense. But then how did he end up dead?" That car, the blood on the window. "According to forensics, Liam sat in the driver's seat, and the murderer stood outside, stabbing him through the window. I can't see that happening on a highway unless they both stopped somewhere to eat or—"

"Hang on. It's not just a highway; it's a toll road. Liam's wife told us that he avoided toll roads."

"Then maybe he drove on this one," Abby said, pointing at the alternative road. "The Taconic State Parkway. I drove on it once to take Samantha to camp. It's a regular road. Probably not a lot of traffic, particularly at night."

"And then he might have seen the kidnapper with Nathan. Suppose their car broke down or something. Liam stopped to help . . ."

"And the kidnapper murdered him, taking his car." Abby said. "That's possible. If that's the case, the kidnapper could be keeping Nathan somewhere along that road."

"It's a hundred-mile-long road," Carver said. "So that doesn't narrow it down too much."

"It's a start." Abby scrutinized the map. "A lot of small towns down this road. Maybe he bought a place in one of them."

"He was the one who was in charge of buying the second farm in Long Island. If he bought another place, there's a good chance he would have used the same real estate agent." Carver paused for a second. "We might need a search warrant for her records."

"Maybe. But we can try to convince her to give us information voluntarily. We just have to ask nicely. Do we have a phone number?"

"I think it's in her email signature. Hang on." Carver checked his phone. "There we go. Rachel Edwards."

He read out the phone number for Abby as she dialed.

After a few seconds a woman picked up. "Hello?"

"Is this Rachel Edwards?"

"Yes."

"Hi. My name is Abby Mullen. I got your number from a client of yours, Luther? He said you really helped him buy that lovely place on Long Island."

"Oh yes! I remember Luther." Rachel's voice warmed up. "Such a sweet man."

"He is! And he had only good things to say about you. Ms. Edwards—"

"Rachel, please."

"Rachel, I'm currently looking for a farm in New York State. Do you think you might have something for me?"

"Absolutely. We have some amazing deals. Did you have anything specific in mind?"

"Well, I've recently been at a barbecue at Luther's place. Not the one on Long Island. The one he bought after that. Did he buy it through you?"

"Of course, he bought both estates through me."

Bingo. "I was hoping to buy a place near Luther's. I really loved the area. Do you have anything there?"

"Let's see. What's the address?"

"Oh, I don't remember. My husband does the driving; you know how it is. But, um . . . we got there by driving down that nice road with all the trees. Uh . . . I think it's the Taconic State Parkway? It's the one between Albany and Manhattan."

"Oh, now I remember," Rachel said. "It's that place on Bowman Road, right? Let me see . . . yes, there it is, Bowman Road. Luther Gaines."

"I think that's the one!" Abby scribbled *Bowman Road—Luther Gaines* on a piece of paper and handed it to Carver.

"I'm not surprised you liked it there. Very peaceful. Those beautiful woods. I'm afraid I don't have anything else there. But if you're looking for somewhere similar, I have a place in the western part of the state that you might like."

"I'd love to hear about it . . . oh, I'm late for my aerobics class. Can I call you back tomorrow?"

"Of course."

"Thanks, Rachel, now I see why Luther spoke so warmly of you." Abby hung up.

"You know, you could have said you're a cop investigating a kidnapping," Carver said dryly.

"Real estate agents prefer clients to cops."

"Doesn't everyone? Hang on, I can't even find Bowman Road on this map. Let me check Google Maps." He fiddled with his phone. "There we go. It's really tiny. Not a lot of places there."

Abby checked the time. Just after nine. "How long to get there?"

"About two hours, maybe a bit more."

"Let's check it out. We can narrow the addresses down on the way."

CHAPTER 74

It was time.

He stared at his phone, the ransom donation fund website on-screen. The donations had gone past the $5 million threshold.

It had never been about the money, of course. It was about *her*. What she needed him to do. What she'd *asked* him to do. The money was a way to buy time. Time for her to shine. Time for her to be as famous as she deserved.

Time for him to befriend the boy.

The befriending hadn't gone as well as he'd hoped. But still, he'd done it all for her. She would eventually see that. He would, in time, find a way to explain it. And even the boy would acknowledge that he'd gone through a tremendous effort just to make him feel at home.

Until that happened, he would have a lot of money to build her the house of her dreams. Nathan's room would be just the start. After all, he knew what she wanted more than anyone else. She wanted a swimming pool like the one Ellen DeGeneres had (according to the post of July 2018). A huge dining room in which to throw dinner parties (Instagram story, November 2018). A bedroom like Sheryl Crow's (one of her first posts, August 2016). He'd taken meticulous notes. He had sketches to show the architect he'd hire.

He'd have $5 million to make her dreams come true.

And eventually, she'd understand he'd done it all for her. One day, it would be an amusing anecdote to tell their children.

He made sure the voice modulation app was working, then dialed her number.

"Hello," she said, breathless. Scared.

There was no reason to be scared. They were in this together.

"Congratulations," he said. "It looks like you managed to get the ransom. You'll see your brother very soon."

"Is he okay?"

"He's fine." Perhaps not in the best of shape, but it was the boy's own fault. "This has been a great week for you. You got all that you asked for."

"What? I never asked for this." She sounded angry and confused. But it was a lie. She was lying. She had *asked* for this. She *wanted* this.

He gritted his teeth, trying to ignore it. "Here's what we're going to do. You'll send me the money by Bitcoin. Write this down; I'm not going to repeat myself."

"Wait," she said. "You need to know. The ransom donation platform has a fee. Six percent. I managed to get them down to five. But that means they're keeping two hundred fifty thousand dollars. But I have the rest. Almost five million. Just tell me where to send it."

The surge of rage surprised even him. He'd gone through all of this for her. He wanted to use the money for her. And now she was lying to him? Trying to cheat *him*?

"Listen, you ungrateful bitch. I said five million, and I *meant* five million. I told you not to fuck with me—"

"It's not me, I swear." Her voice dripped with lies, with deceit. "It's the donations guy. And I'll add my own savings. I have a few thousand—"

"Five. Million. Dollars. You lying whore! You know what? You have only ninety-five percent? No problem. You'll get only ninety-five percent of your brother back. Which five percent should I cut off?"

"No, wait!"

He hung up, removed the battery, tossed the phone on the floor of the car. Then he thumped the steering wheel, screaming with fury.

He started the car and floored the gas pedal.

He would send her 5 percent of her brother. In the mail.

CHAPTER 75

The road to the house was rough, paved with loose gravel, dotted with muddy potholes. Distinct tire marks crisscrossed the mud. At one point, Abby asked Carver to stop the car, got out, took a photo of the marks, and sent them to Ahmed.

Finally they got to a decayed gate, locked with a chain, blocking the way forward. A rusty barbed wire fence cordoned off the area within. Beyond, barely visible through the distant trees, stood what looked like a small cabin.

"Maybe we should get some backup from local police," Carver said.

"We don't have anything yet," Abby answered. "This is just a long shot. We could park farther down the road, stake this place out."

"Wait," Carver said. "Look at the gate. It isn't electrical. Whoever lives here would need to get out of the car to unlock it, then push it open."

Abby examined first the gate, then the muddy road. She saw what Carver was saying. "You're right. We might get lucky. Hang on."

She got out of the car, studying the ground as she approached the gate. Her hand was on her holster, a reflexive reaction to a sense of danger.

She found what she was looking for to the right of the gate by the chain. A clear shoe print in the mud. She didn't have Ahmed's knowledge and expertise, but it was easy to see that it looked like the sole of the type of boots they had at the Tillman farm. The hair on the back of her neck stood as she took out her phone and snapped a photo of it. Then she returned to the car.

"Look." She showed it to Carver.

"Send it to forensics. If there's a match, we'll have enough for a search warrant."

Abby sent it, messaging Ahmed, telling him it was urgent. She stared beyond the gate at the cabin. Was Luther Gaines there?

Was Nathan?

"I'll park the car down the road," Carver said. "Buckle up."

She put her seat belt on as Carver switched on the engine and shifted to reverse.

Abby's phone rang. She glanced at it expecting to see Ahmed's name, but it was Gabrielle.

"Hello?"

"Lieutenant Mullen?" Gabrielle's voice was shaky, terrified. "He called and said he would cut Nathan. I told him it wasn't my fault, that it was the donation platform, but he wasn't listening. He's going to hurt my brother. I tried to call him back, but the phone was offline. What should I do? You have to do something."

"Wait, slow down," Abby said, heart thumping. "Who called? The kidnapper?"

"Yes," Gabrielle said. "For the ransom."

The ransom. Of course. She'd almost forgotten that the crowd-funded ransom was almost complete. "Okay. Don't do anything. Don't *post* anything, you got that? He might get angry if you post something right now. Do you understand?"

"Yes, but—"

"I will listen to the recording," Abby said. "And then we'll see, okay?"

"Okay."

"Wait for my call. Don't do anything stupid."

Abby hung up and turned on the wiretapping app. The last phone call to Gabrielle's phone had been at 12:37 p.m. Five minutes ago. Abby tapped it, letting it play on the phone's speaker. She listened to the call with Carver, both of them tensing as the kidnapper shouted at Gabrielle, threatening to cut Nathan. The call ended abruptly.

Abby raised her eyes from the phone screen and met Carver's gaze. Her mind shrieked at her that they needed to move, needed to open the gate and check the cabin. They couldn't afford to wait for forensics to tell them what they already knew in their gut. That they were in the right place and that there was no time to lose.

But would she be able to convince Carver? She was too attached to this case. She would have to be careful about what she said, the way she presented it. With enough time she could convince him. But there wasn't enough time. Every second mattered.

She cleared her throat, trying to calm her voice, to play the part of the detached, rational cop. "I think—"

"Hang on tight." Carver shifted gears and floored the gas.

The car lurched, engine screeching, as it hurtled down the few yards between them and the gate. A deafening sound of screaming metal reverberated in the car as Abby clung to her seat, her breath robbed from her lungs. The rusty gate tore open, their car hitting a knoll beyond it with a terrible jolt that caused Abby's jaw to snap shut.

Carver skidded up the drive to the front of the cabin.

"Are you okay?" he asked, breathing hard as he switched off the engine.

"Jesus," Abby whispered. She glanced back at the ruined gate, the now-sagging wire fence at both sides.

Carver had already stepped out of the car, his gun in hand, and was running to the front door. Abby half stumbled out of the passenger door. She ran after Carver, crouched, drawing her gun. She flattened herself to one side of the door, Carver to the other side.

Carver glanced at Abby, and she nodded at him. With one swift move he stepped in front of the door and kicked it. It flung open with the crunch of splintering wood. Carver pointed his gun ahead of him, stepping inside, turning to his right, Abby a step behind him, covering him on the left.

A kitchen, a shabby-looking living room.

An enormous picture of Gabrielle on the wall.

Just a few steps into the hallway, her gun leading the way, finger tense on the trigger. A door opened into a bathroom with a dingy bathtub. Two steps inside, checking each nook, each shadow for a possible attacker. No one there.

Stepping out, she glimpsed Carver as he barged through another door down the hall. She went to the third door.

A key in the lock. From the outside.

She tried the door, moving the doorknob slowly. The door was locked. She turned the lock, flung the door open.

A moment of confusion as she stepped into a room that belonged to another house more than a hundred miles away. Nathan's room.

Except it wasn't. It was a twisted replica, a cage decorated to feel like a boy's bedroom. And on the bed, lying under sheets stained with blood, was the inert shape of a child.

Two quick steps and she was by his side, pulling back the covers, heart skipping a beat as she saw how deathly pale he was.

But his chest rose and fell. Shallow breathing.

Phone in her hand, she dialed 911. The voice of a dispatcher answered, asking her what her emergency was.

"This is Detective Abby Mullen from the NYPD. I need an ambulance. I'm with an eight-year-old boy, and he's badly hurt."

CHAPTER 76

He clutched the steering wheel tightly, as if it were a throat he was squeezing. The lying whore's throat. All of the sacrifices he'd made for her, and she couldn't even own up to what she'd told him. Even worse, tried to steal money that he wanted to use for *her*.

He'd given up his life for her.

Before he'd laid eyes on her, he'd been one of Otis Tillman's closest advisers. If Otis needed *anything* done, Luther was the guy to do it. Not David, that limp rag of a man. Luther. Otis knew that. Luther stopped at nothing to get the job done. In fact, Otis didn't even need to tell him what to do. All Otis had to say was what he needed, and Luther would figure out *how*.

Which was why, when lovesick Karl found out that Gabrielle and her family were living nearby, they all went straight to Luther. Karl and David were useless; they had no idea what to do. David had wanted to *apologize* to Eden. Apologize to the woman who had stolen money from the group and taken his kids.

It had been Luther's suggestion that they pick up Nathan. Take him to the farm, teach the kid about where he came from. Then, use Nathan as bait to lure Gabrielle and Eden back as well. Or at least lure Gabrielle back. No one gave a rat's ass about Eden.

And when Otis had told Luther to go and spy on the family, figure out their schedule, find the right moment to pounce, Luther had been happy to do it. Left the farm, found a shitty apartment, used his old contacts to get some freelance gigs. Did some gun trafficking for Otis on the side. All under a false name to be safe.

He slowed down, a car driving at a snail's pace ahead of him. He leaned on the horn, blasting the air with the sharp honking. The car in front moved aside, but he didn't let go, kept pressing the horn as he shot past, hurling curses, venting his fury at Gabrielle, at David, at Karl, at Otis.

Because when he'd gotten to know Gabrielle, when he'd gotten to really *see* her every day, he had realized Karl didn't deserve her. He told Otis over and over in countless conversations. Gabrielle should be *his*. But Otis kept insisting she should be Karl's wife because he'd given his nephew his word. Never mind that Otis owed the world to Luther. Never mind that Karl was a worthless piece of shit.

Besides, Otis wasn't so keen on the plan anymore. He was excited about the steady income from the gun trafficking. Didn't want to draw the attention of the police by picking up Nathan.

Luther was almost content to let it drop. But then *she* asked for it. That was what made him act. *She* was the one who pushed him over the edge.

She hadn't even told him what to do. She'd just said what she *needed*.

And Luther had figured out how.

And now she had lied and said—

Something was beeping. An electronic, shrill sound. It had been beeping for a while, but he'd ignored it, too caught up with memories and anger. Where was that sound coming from?

His phone. He took it out of his pocket and glanced at it. It was a notification from the alarm app he'd installed. The app that notified him when any of the doors in his cabin had been opened.

Had the boy escaped *again*?

He pulled to the side of the road and opened the app, checked the security footage of the boy's room. His heart nearly stopped. There were strangers in the room. A man and a woman. Their backs were to the cameras, but the guns were easy to spot.

Cops.

They'd somehow found his cabin. He was finished.

No, not yet. He still had some time.

He would get what he *deserved*.

CHAPTER 77

Abby stood in the doorway of the cabin watching the ambulance drive off, apprehension gnawing at her. Nathan's fever had been high, and he hadn't woken up, not even when they'd put him on the stretcher and carried him to the ambulance.

Were they too late?

She stepped back inside the cabin, trying to push the anxiety away. She'd already called Eden and told her they'd found Nathan and that he was being transported to St. Peter's Hospital in Albany. There was nothing more she could do for Nathan now.

Carver was in the room Nathan had been kept in. He'd slipped on a pair of gloves and was going through one of the drawers. He turned to face her when she walked in.

"How is he?"

"He was still unconscious when they drove off."

Carver nodded and turned back to the desk. "Why do you think Luther went to all that effort? Re-creating Nathan's room from scratch like that. What's the point of it all?"

"I'm not sure yet." She looked around the room, flinching as her eyes skimmed over the bloody bed. Then she noticed the tiny magnetic panel above the door. "There's some sort of alarm mechanism over the door."

"Yup. The front door too."

"In that case, Luther might know we found Nathan."

Carver shut the drawer and opened the next one. "Nothing we can do about that."

Abby went to the bedroom. It was small, most of the space taken by the double bed. The room smelled . . . sticky. Above the bed, a page was taped to the wall, the words *Just because you're paranoid doesn't mean they aren't after you* printed in a large font.

She went over to the nightstand. A framed picture stood on it, a selfie of Gabrielle smiling seductively. A sentence adorned the bottom of the photo, typed in one of those obnoxious generic cursive fonts—*You'll have my undying gratitude.* Abby inspected the picture closely. Luther had woken up every morning to this photo. What did it mean to him?

She searched through the drawers in the room, finding nothing much. Clothing, a handful of coins, sunglasses, a box of tissues, a flashlight.

She returned to the living room and inspected the enlarged photo of Gabrielle on the wall. Not a photo at all but a collage, hundreds of tiny images of Gabrielle creating a mosaic of Gabrielle's face. This picture, the room Nathan had been caged in, the photo on the nightstand—it all spoke of an obsessive mind. An obsessive mind focused on Gabrielle.

She imagined Luther, a man who'd spent years in the Tillman cult. Years following Otis, treating him like a king, a messiah. And then, for some reason, Luther had left the cult. Or perhaps he had been kicked out. She knew from experience that the mind didn't let go that easily. Eden *still* had a photo of Moses in her bathroom. And Abby herself had taken years to get over the sudden vacuum in her life, and that was thanks to her loving, patient parents.

Luther had filled the emptiness with a different obsession. A different person to follow. To idolize.

She inspected the photos closely. They mostly looked like images from Gabrielle's Instagram account. She even recognized a few. There were several nudes that caught Abby by surprise until she realized what they were—manipulated images. Luther had used freely available photos from Gabrielle's Instagram account, editing them to create his own private porn stash of the one girl he was interested in.

She spotted the image that had made Gabrielle famous. The photo in the mist. Then she saw the same image in a different section of the mosaic. And there was a third. Apparently Luther had used some duplicates.

Strange, that someone so obsessive wouldn't go the extra mile to make sure each photo was used only once.

No, it wasn't the same image. They were from slightly different angles. In one of them Gabrielle's eyes were shut. Luther had somehow laid his hands on the other photos from that occasion.

She scrutinized one of the images closely. It was from the time just before Gabrielle's popularity blew up. At the start of it all.

I've been following you from the start. Wasn't that what he'd told her?

Three different images from the same occasion. It went without saying there would be a few. That was how everyone took pictures these days, right? You aimed the phone, snapped half a dozen photos, and chose the best one. But you didn't share the rest.

So how had Luther gotten his hands on those photos?

He had to have been there—at that photo shoot. Maybe he'd taken them himself. She'd gone on the road trip with a few of her friends. Could Luther be one of Gabrielle's friends? No, that didn't make any—

The world tilted, something snapping in her mind. A connection she should have seen earlier.

She took out her phone and searched for the email from Ahmed, the one where he'd sent her a link to all the photos on Eric Layton's computer. She tapped on the second-most-recent photo—the image of Nathan holding the newspaper. She examined it carefully.

"Oh shit," she muttered. "Carver!"

He stepped into the living room. "What is it?"

"Do you have the photo that the kidnapper sent Gabrielle?"

"Sure, hang on." He took off his latex gloves, then fiddled with his phone while Abby tapped her foot impatiently. "There."

Abby held out her phone. "Put yours next to mine."

He did, and they looked at both photos.

"They're not the same," Carver said.

The changes were minuscule. A tiny shift in perspective. And on Abby's phone, one of Nathan's eyelids was shut a fraction more than in the other.

"Eric asked Gabrielle," Abby said, her voice hollow. "He asked her if this was the only photo she received. This is what he noticed. The photos aren't the same. The kidnapper snapped a few photos of Nathan. These are two of them. But why would Gabrielle have them both? That's what Eric thought. He figured the only reason Gabrielle would have both is if *she* took the photos. Especially since she told him repeatedly that the kidnapper only sent her one."

"Are you saying Gabrielle is in on this?" Carver frowned.

"No, but that's what Eric thought. Gabrielle didn't send him *this* photo." Abby shook her phone.

"Then who sent it?"

"The journalist. Tom McCormick."

Carver squinted. "The journalist?"

"Remember the interview? Eric had seen Nathan's photo for the first time when McCormick interviewed him. And he must have asked McCormick to send him that photo. But McCormick sent him the *wrong* photo."

"And not the one he'd originally sent Gabrielle," Carver said, catching on.

"McCormick later realized his mistake, so he killed Eric and wiped his phone. He didn't know there was a copy of the photo on Eric's computer." Abby gritted her teeth. "Gabrielle told me McCormick interviewed her before. Of course he has. He's probably the journalist who originally got her famous. The one who wrote that article about her photo that went viral. There are other photos from the same photo shoot in that collage on the wall. Remember what Will told us? A reporter tagged along on the road trip. *He was there.* He might have even been the one who took the pictures."

She imagined Gabrielle asking McCormick to take her photo in that misty swamp. Him, taking a dozen photos, then sending her the best one. And keeping the rest.

I've been following you from the start.

"Tom McCormick is Luther Gaines," Carver said slowly.

"And he's been stalking Gabrielle for years under the guise of a journalist who's interested in influencers." She recalled how in his interview, McCormick hadn't followed up on Eric mentioning the strange stories about the community Gabrielle had lived in. Any reporter worth his salt would have asked about that. But McCormick preferred to avoid the topic. Now it was clear why.

"Do you have McCormick's number?" Carver asked, tapping on his phone, then putting it to his ear.

"Yes."

Carver gave her the thumbs-up, then said, "Hello, Natalie? How are you doing . . . yes, I've been busy. Listen, I need you to ping a number for me." He paused. "I know, but these are exigent circumstances. I'm taking full responsibility for—you're a peach, thanks. Okay, you writing this down?"

Abby found McCormick's number on her phone, and Carver read it aloud to Natalie. They waited.

"You have it?" Carver finally said. "Where—" The color drained from his face, and he bolted toward the door.

Abby hurried after him as he thanked Natalie and hung up the phone. He yanked the driver's door of his car and slid in. Abby quickly entered, dropping into the passenger seat.

"What is it?"

"He's within a hundred-yard radius from the LaGuardia Plaza Hotel," Carver said.

Abby's heart plunged. "That's near Eden's house."

"Radio it in. Eden and Gabrielle might be in danger."

CHAPTER 78

They've found Nathan.

The thought, almost too good to be true, kept floating in Gabrielle's mind, a cloud of relief, of joy. *They've found Nathan.*

He was at the hospital, but Mom had already talked to the doctor, and he'd said Nathan was going to be fine; he just had some kind of infection. But they were treating him, and he was going to be fine.

She was in his room, packing a bag for him, hearing her mom's voice downstairs talking on the phone. She sounded so different now. In the past week, it had been as if there were a spring coiled within them, and it kept getting tighter and tighter and tighter. Their bodies so strained, a couple of rubber bands stretched to the limit. Now her mom sounded more like a puddle, wet and relaxed. She could finally let go. Because Nathan was safe.

She took his Yoda plushy too; that was important. And crayons so he could draw.

"Gabi! Let's go," her mom called.

"Coming!"

She went by her room, grabbed her phone. She would take a picture of the three of them to upload to her feed. Thank all of her amazing followers, old and new. What about the money? Not now, later. She bounced down the stairs as if gravity had lost its hold on her. She felt much lighter than she had this morning. A revolutionary diet.

Mom was already at the door, waiting for her. "Did you pack his plushy?"

"Yeah, I got him everything."

"Okay." A happy, loving grin.

Her mom's phone rang. That was an amazing feeling, to hear the phone ring and not wonder if it was *him* calling with his strange metallic voice, threatening to kill her brother.

Mom took out her phone, glanced at it. "Oh, it's Abihail. I need to thank her. Just a minute." She stepped away from the door, answering the call.

Who was Abihail? Did her mom mean Abby Mullen? But a knock on the door distracted her.

"What?" her mom said behind her, talking on the phone. "I don't understand."

Gabrielle peered through the peephole, then opened the door.

"Tom." She smiled happily at him. "You won't believe what happened."

Why was he staring at her like that? What was he . . . was that a knife? Her smile died.

And he shoved her—hard. He stepped inside and slammed the door behind him.

CHAPTER 79

The usually quiet block where Eden and her family lived had lost its customary sleepy atmosphere. Abby took it all in—the patrol cars, the ESU vehicle, the negotiation truck, the men in vests, the sound of a helicopter overhead. A large area around Eden's house was cordoned off, cops in vests turning the media and the curious onlookers back. A young patrol officer waved them past as they flashed their badges. Carver parked the car on the sidewalk, Abby already leaping out of the car and walking straight toward Griffin, who was talking sharply into his radio.

"I want *all* the houses on the block vacated," Griffin barked. "And push the media back. I want those damn cameras out of here." He turned to face Abby.

"Sir." Abby breathed hard. "Are you the incident commander?"

"Yes. You're the one who called it in, right?"

"Yes sir."

"Okay. The tactical commander is Baker. Sergeant Vereen was the negotiations commander, but I want you to take charge."

"Yes sir. How many hostages—"

"Get Vereen to fill you in, I don't have time." Griffin checked his watch. "It's three fifteen. I want an update on how the negotiation is going by three thirty."

Abby turned to the negotiation truck, slid the door open, and hopped inside. After the NYPD had bought the negotiation truck, it was Abby who'd redesigned it to make use of the cramped space in the rear part efficiently. One side had an enormous whiteboard, which Abby preferred over the multiple computer screens that some police forces used. Officer Tammi Summers—a capable young negotiator—was scribbling on the board. At the far end of the work space stood a desk with two phones and a radio. It was the primary negotiator's workstation.

Will sat by the desk, a phone to his ear. He turned toward her, his face awash with relief. "I'm glad you finally got here."

"Griffin wants me to take charge."

"Okay."

There was no time for bruised egos, and they knew each other too well for that.

"Trying to get him to answer?" Abby asked, pointing at the phone.

Will hung up. "I call every five minutes. He picked up twice so far."

"Brief me."

"After you called dispatch, I tried to get both Eden and Gabrielle on the phone with no success."

Abby nodded. She'd been talking to Eden, warning her about McCormick, when suddenly she'd heard a scream, and the call had disconnected. When she'd called again, there had been no answer. After that, both Eden's and Gabrielle's phones had gone offline.

"At ten minutes past one, a patrol car got here. They knocked on the door, and a male voice screamed at them to get away from the door, or she gets it."

"Who's 'she'?"

"We don't know. One of the cops tried to talk to the man, but he kept screaming at them to get back. Finally they did, calling it in. Meanwhile, the person inside closed all the blinds on the windows. One of the officers saw him dragging a woman with him, but the interior was too dark to see who it was. Griffin got here and took charge. We arrived at two oh five. I called McCormick's phone several times, and we could hear it ring inside the house. Finally he picked up, shouting at me to get everyone back, or he'd kill them both."

"So both Gabrielle and Eden are there."

"That's the assumption, but we have no verification of that. After half a minute, he hung up. Didn't answer for twenty-five minutes. Then he answered the phone again, calmer, still demanding to get everyone back. He also wanted us to clear the street completely. I tried to engage him, and he hung up again."

"Okay. You were the primary negotiator the entire time?"

"Yeah. And Summers acted as secondary negotiator and intelligence officer."

Not ideal—Abby wished Will had asked for a third team member. If Tammi acted as secondary negotiator, she couldn't focus entirely on intel. "Okay. I'm secondary negotiator now. Summers, what do you have on McCormick so far?"

Summers cleared her throat. "Tom McCormick started writing articles for the *New Yorker Chronicle* in July 2017. At first his articles were mostly political, but after a few months he began focusing on influencers. He covered several up-and-coming local influencers, including Gabrielle Fletcher. He has a social media page for his work but no personal page. Same for Twitter and Instagram. He owns a white Nissan Sentra, which we already located. It's parked nearby, so it looks like he drove here. As far as we can tell, he has no legal firearms. No medical records. No police records. I didn't find anything before July 2017 so far."

Abby massaged the bridge of her nose. "Okay. I'll give you some leads to start with. Tom McCormick is a fake name. His real name is Luther Gaines, and he was a member in the Tillman cult. At some point in the past three years, he left the cult; I'm not sure if it was before or after he started writing for the *Chronicle*. I want you to talk to his editor.

Tom probably gave them references. See if you can find those." She paused as she recalled the photograph on Luther's night table. "Also, I want you to check Gabrielle Fletcher's Instagram account. Will had it indexed, so hopefully you can find things easily. I want you to look for any sentence that has the phrase *undying gratitude*."

Summers scribbled furiously in her notebook. "Okay."

Abby turned to the board. "Divide the board into topics; this is a mess. Here's what I want from left to right. Info about Tom. Info about Luther. Anything we find on Eden and Gabrielle—I want their medical records here." Her finger moved, pointing at various parts of the board as she kept numbering topics. "Demands. Deadlines. I want a list of all the good stuff we did for him, okay? If we delivered him an espresso, I want to see it on the board. We need a diagram of the house—don't draw it yourself; get some blueprints. Leave the right side for a surrender plan. And every single important phone number we can get. For starters, I want Tom, Eden, Gabrielle, Tom's editor, and the number of the doctor currently taking care of Nathan Fletcher at St. Peter's Hospital in Albany. You got all that?"

"On it."

Abby checked the time. Nearly three thirty. "I'll go brief Griffin. Will, show Summers the indexed data of Gabrielle's feed. When I return, we'll call him again."

CHAPTER 80

It was like Gabrielle wasn't even hearing him.

She was supposed to understand by now. He'd always assumed she was a brilliant girl. But when he outlined how he'd only tried to help her, explaining about all the effort and time he'd invested, doing what she'd *asked* him to do, she just stared at him, her eyes vacant. He slapped her. She tumbled off the chair, gasping, her mother screaming at him to stop.

"Are you even listening?" he roared, then whirled toward Eden and pointed at her face. "Shut up, or I'll cut your throat."

"Sorry, I'm listening," Gabrielle sobbed on the floor.

The guilt had already begun sinking in. He shouldn't have hit her. She was confused. And the damn phone rang again. They called all the time—like they had something important to say. He rubbed his eyes with his fists, trying to concentrate. If he only said the right words, Gabrielle would understand. She would see all he had done for her.

He would have her undying gratitude.

Her love.

That was all he'd ever asked for, wasn't it?

He knelt by her side. "You asked me to do it. I would never have done it all if you didn't ask . . . if you didn't practically beg for it."

She blinked at him. "I don't understand. Tom . . . when did I—"

"Don't act like you don't remember!"

She flinched, and he realized his hand was already raised. Ready to slap her again. It was that damn phone. It was driving him insane. It wouldn't stop ringing.

He snatched it from the table, ready to lob it through the window. But no, he needed it for later. Instead he accepted the call.

"Tom?" that guy, Will, said from the other side.

"Listen, asshole!" he shouted. "Don't call again unless it's to tell me the street is clear. You got that?"

"But how can—"

"You're not listening!" None of them listened. No one listened to him. No one. "I'll hurt them, I swear I'll hurt them. Don't call again!" He hung up.

For a few seconds, there was blessed silence from the phone, just the sound of the women sobbing. He didn't want to make Gabrielle cry.

If only she'd listen.

"Don't call again!" The line went dead.

Abby and Will exchanged glances. She'd been listening in on the conversation as the secondary negotiator. Her heart thrummed in her chest, the angry words still echoing in her ears. McCormick was furious. And rage mixed with fear was deadly.

"What do you think?" Will asked.

"I think the initial communication might have tainted you," Abby said.

The first contact with the subject was always tricky. Adrenaline flooded the subject's body, making them erratic and unpredictable. The negotiator's only role during that first contact was to calm the subject down, mostly by using active listening. Except sometimes, like in this case, it wasn't enough. McCormick had been too angry, or too scared, or both. He'd lashed out at Will and marked him as an enemy. For

McCormick, Will wasn't someone you could talk to, negotiate with. He was someone you threatened—or raged at.

"I don't know," Will said. "There was a moment during the second conversation when I felt we were building a rapport. I can make this work."

"Let's hear it." Abby put on a pair of earphones.

Will turned to the control panel and played the recording of the call.

It was similar to the one she'd just heard. McCormick talked in angry outbursts with Will doing his best to be receptive, to draw McCormick into a conversation. At one point McCormick calmed down enough to stop screaming. He said he wanted them to clear out. Will asked him how he expected them to do that. McCormick said it wasn't his problem, and hung up.

Abby looked at Will. He was one of the best negotiators she knew. But her gut told her she was right. McCormick wouldn't talk to him. They needed a fresh start.

"We're going to switch," she said. "I'll be primary."

Will nodded, and she saw the hurt and concern on his face. *His* instinct told him he was the right man for the job, and she had just effectively told him he wasn't. Even if she was right, it was no fault of his, but that didn't lessen the sting. Even worse, a transfer between negotiators was always risky. The subject in a crisis never responded well to surprises. If she was wrong, it might mean that Eden and Gabrielle would get hurt. It might mean they'd die.

The point of the knife dug into Gabrielle's cheek. She was frozen, a statue sculpted by sheer terror.

"When you lie to me, it feels like someone is cutting me with a blade," Tom hissed at her. "Do you know how much that hurts? Do you want to find out?"

She didn't. She didn't dare shake her head. She tried to speak, but her voice was gone, robbed. *Please don't,* she mouthed. She could vaguely hear her mother's sobs. Tom had handcuffed her mom and shoved her onto the couch. He'd told her mom that if she moved, he'd kill them both.

The blade withdrew from the cheek, wavering an inch from her face. She tried to look away from the knife's tip as it hovered in front of her eye. *Oh god, what if he cuts my eye? No, please no, please please please.*

"You'll stop lying to me, right?"

"Yes," she managed to whisper.

"You remember asking me to help you now?"

"Yes." Anything. She'd say anything.

"When?"

She blinked. "What?"

"When did you ask me to help you? You said you remember." His voice had an edge almost sharper than the knife. "I think about it every. Single. Day. I hope you do too."

Her mind whirled, thinking about the few conversations they'd had, the interviews. What could he possibly be talking about? What could it be?

"We need to call again," Abby said.

"He said he'd hurt them if we do," Will warned her. "Perhaps we should wait until he calls us."

She shook her head. "It's an abstract threat. He won't act on it."

When people made threats they intended to act upon, they were usually specific. If McCormick had said, "If you call again, I will slit Eden Fletcher's throat," Abby would have been warier. But a generic "I will hurt them" wasn't as strong.

There were exceptions. She hoped this wasn't one of them.

She turned to Summers, who sat in front of a laptop, scrutinizing the screen. "What do you have so far?"

Summers turned to face her. "I found the phrase *undying gratitude* twice in Gabrielle's feed," she said. "One is in a post where she said that another Instagrammer had her undying gratitude for introducing her to a brand of protein bars."

"And the second?"

"There was a contest post. She offered a signed picture to the fan who got her the most followers in a week. A fan joked, asking what if he quadrupled her followers, and she said he would have her undying gratitude."

Abby blinked. That was it. "Find me that post. And get me everything you can on the fan who made the comment. He's our guy."

She picked up the phone and called McCormick. It rang.

There was a certain feeling Abby always got as she started every negotiation. A terror in the pit of her stomach, the weight of responsibility crushing down on her.

Second ring.

A bitter taste in her mouth. Sweaty palms. She breathed in through her nose.

Third ring—and he picked up.

"Do you want me to kill them, you asshole?" McCormick screeched at her.

And the fear faded. She was in control.

"Luther Gaines," she said.

A stunned silence on the other end. She'd caught him by surprise, invoking his real name. His name gave her power, like in a fairy tale.

"Who the hell are you?" he finally snarled. "Put the other guy on the phone. I was talking to him."

"Will had to leave. My name is Abby. I'm the one talking to you now." A low voice, calm and controlled.

He let out a tortured laugh. "The famous Abby Mullen, huh? Well, the other guy should have told you I said not to call again. I said that—"

"It seems like you were caught in a bad situation." She kept her voice low. "You did what Gabrielle asked you to do, right? For her undying gratitude."

"Yes," he breathed. "That's right. I did it for her. She *asked* me."

"She asked you," the woman on the phone agreed. "She said she wanted more followers."

"And I got them for her!" he said, eyeing Gabrielle with fury. *"Twice."*

"You got them twice," Abby said. "Once with your article that went viral, making her famous, and then with her brother."

Finally, someone who understood. Who *listened* to what he had to say. "I sacrificed everything for her."

"Sacrificed everything?" Abby asked, sounding curious.

"*Everything.* I left the community for her. I endangered myself for her. Even the money . . . I never wanted the money for myself."

"No," Abby agreed.

"I wanted to use it for her. It was all for her. I wanted to build her dream home. I know just what she loves—she told me; I have sketches. I would have been able to get her *everything*. I own a large plot of land. She told me last year she wanted to live outside the city." The truth poured out of him, a torrent of words. Was he saying it to Abby? Or to Gabrielle, who listened mutely? He didn't know, but it didn't matter. He couldn't stop talking. "No one was supposed to get hurt. I even did my best to make that boy feel at home. I didn't want him to be scared. She told me once that he loved his room. His man cave, she called it. So I made it for him so that he would be happy."

"You wanted to make him more comfortable."

"Yes! I wanted it to be the same. Literally identical. If she only knew how much time and money I put into it . . . would I do that if I wanted to hurt him?"

"You wouldn't."

He kept talking, explaining how he'd searched for the right plushy, how he'd even copied Nathan's drawings. Abby listened, clearly impressed, and asked questions about the furniture. He told her how hard he'd worked copying Nathan's signature, and Abby chuckled, and suddenly he laughed as well, realizing there really was something funny in it. All the while, as he and Abby talked, he had one eye on Gabrielle. Did she get it now? Did she finally understand?

He was vomiting information.

Abby kept egging him on, mirroring his sentences, pulling him further with simple open-ended questions, trying to judge his tone. Will listened in on the conversation, occasionally turning to Summers, instructing her, as she frantically scribbled on the board.

Information and time were a negotiator's oxygen, and Abby was getting both. At first, when Luther had said that Gabrielle had told him something, she'd assumed Gabrielle had told him in an interview. But then she realized he meant that Gabrielle had posted it on her page.

For Luther, those posts were an ongoing conversation. He was clearly contemptuous of Gabrielle's fans; he didn't see himself as one of them. For him, the fans were like parasites, listening in on his chats with Gabrielle. As far as he was concerned, he and Gabrielle were already in a relationship.

She glanced at the board, where Summers had written *delusional* and *obsessed*. Could she use his obsession with Gabrielle in her favor?

"It seems like you and Gabrielle had a good connection," she said when there was a lull in his monologue.

"We still do!" His tone sharpened. Will shot Abby a warning look.

"You still do," she agreed, repeating his words, keeping her voice cheerful and light. She needed to get him to talk about the past. To remember better days. "When did you realize you had a special connection?"

"Two years ago." There was a smile in his voice. "She bought a yellow T-shirt and took a photo with it. She said it was for a special someone, and I realized it was me."

Will snapped his fingers at Summers, and she nodded, sitting by her laptop, searching for the post.

"How did it make you feel?" Abby asked.

"It was . . . it's hard to explain. It made me feel special. It gave me a purpose." His tone shifted, becoming angrier. "But now, *this* girl won't even look at me. After all I've done for her. I've made her famous! *Do you hear that?* I've made you famous!"

A frightened sob in the background. Abby clenched the phone tightly, trying to control her own voice. "It sounds like you were expecting a different reaction."

"You're damn right. The whore won't even look at me."

Make him pause. Force him to think it through. "How did you imagine this meeting?"

A long silence. "I don't know," he finally said, sounding defeated. "I did everything right."

He was exhausted. Exhausted from the noise outside, exhausted from the looks that the girl and her mother gave him, exhausted from talking.

"Luther?" Abby said. "Are you still with me?"

"I'm here." He should finish it. He and the girl would die together. And that way, they'd stay together. He leaned forward, the knife at her throat. She whimpered. A tiny drop of blood trickled down her perfect skin.

"I was thinking about that day she first talked to you," Abby said. "That day with the yellow shirt. I bet it wasn't the only time she made you feel special."

"No." He smiled sadly. "There was her nineteenth birthday. We were both so happy. And that trip to California. She kept posting updates—like breadcrumbs—so I could follow her." The memories flooded him. Tears welled in his eyes. They had been so happy. Did it really have to end now?

"That sounds lovely," Abby said. "And you said you still have a special connection, right? You said you are confused and surprised. Do you think she could be too?"

"Maybe." He pulled the knife away. "Maybe it's just a misunderstanding."

"Then how can I help?" Abby asked.

"What?"

"How can I help to make this better?"

He blinked, surprised. She wasn't screwing with him. He heard the concern in her voice, the sadness. She understood him.

"I don't want to go to prison."

"Go to prison?"

"For the kidnapping. And for . . . for this."

"Well, I think we can get you a good attorney. I know someone who might be perfect. We can show in court how you did everything you could to make the boy feel at home, right? Because it was never really a kidnapping. And you were just doing what his sister told you to."

That was true. They didn't know about the murders. They couldn't connect those to him. And the rest was a misunderstanding. With the right legal protection, even if he went to prison, it might be for a short time. And when he got out, Gabrielle would be there, waiting. "The money," he blurted. "Gabrielle collected the ransom. She was about to transfer it. Can I use it for legal fees? Can you check it for me?"

"How can I convince them to do it?" Abby asked doubtfully. "I can't even promise that Gabrielle is alive."

"She's alive. She's here."

"But they won't believe you're telling the truth."

He frowned. "I can let you talk to her. Would that work?"

"Well . . ." Abby paused for a few seconds. "I think that would work."

He put the phone on speaker but then hesitated. He didn't trust the girl. "Tell her you're fine," he said, placing the knife at her throat.

"H . . . hello?" the girl sobbed.

"Gabrielle? This is Abby. Are you okay?"

"I'm . . . I'm fine. I'm scared."

"We'll fix this," Abby said, her voice calm. "Don't be scared. Is your mother okay? Is anyone hurt?"

"N . . . no."

He muted the speaker and put the phone to his ear. "Is that enough?"

"I think so," Abby said. "Let me check regarding the money. I really appreciate your cooperation, Luther. We'll get through this, okay?"

"I only did what she asked for. I got her followers. I made her famous."

"You definitely made her famous. I think she'll see that in time."

"Right," he said slowly. He had an idea. In time? Maybe he could make the girl realize it right now. The remote for the TV was within reach. He leaned forward, keeping the knife on the girl's throat, and switched on the TV.

"Luther? Are you still there?"

"Yeah, are you checking about the money?"

"I sent someone to check. It might take some time. You know how these things are."

"Yeah." He switched between the channels, searching. Then, suddenly, he paused. A local news channel. Gabrielle's face was on-screen.

"See that?" he said, smiling at the girl. "You're famous. Just like you always wanted."

She didn't answer, her eyes glued to the TV. He watched with her, the reporter saying there was a police siege at the house of Gabrielle Fletcher. That sources claimed she'd been taken hostage. Abby was saying something in the background; he wasn't listening to her. His smile faded as the reporter said the man holding Gabrielle hostage was believed to have murdered Eric Layton.

They'd found out about Layton's murder. He wasn't going to get a short sentence. He would spend his life in prison.

Screaming, he threw the phone at the TV, and the screen fractured, the picture fading away into nothing.

CHAPTER 81

A stunned Abby stared at Will. "What just happened?"

"There was a noise in the background," Will said. "I think he turned on the TV."

Abby hadn't noticed; she had been so focused on the conversation. It had been going so well. And then a shout of rage, and the call had disconnected.

Will was already playing the last minute of the call again. Now she heard it, the faint sound of someone else talking. Not Eden or Gabrielle. The calm, detached voice of a news anchorwoman. Will paused the recording and ran it through filters, his fingers moving fast. When he played it again, Luther's voice—and her own—were turned down. The background was enhanced, and they could make out the words.

" . . . Sources within the police claim the man who barricaded himself in the house is also wanted for questioning regarding the murder of Eric Layton, a twenty-one-year-old resident of—"

And then the scream. The recording ended abruptly immediately after.

"Shit." Abby exhaled.

The media had snatched away the hope she'd managed to cultivate in Luther's mind. Maybe she could convince him the people at the news knew nothing, that they had no evidence connecting him to the murder. But she doubted it. Luther was delusional, but he was not a fool.

The phone rang again. Luther clenched his jaw, his fists trembling. He'd been gripping his knife so tightly for hours that his fingers were tired; his wrist ached.

Not much longer now. He'd say what he needed, and then he'd finish it. Kill her, kill himself. He wasn't afraid of the pain. Life had hurt him much more than the blade ever would.

"You weren't right for Karl," he told the girl. "Once I got to know you, I saw that. It wasn't right, making you marry him."

He saw the bewilderment in her eyes, the confusion, and he laughed hysterically. "You don't even know, do you?" he asked. "Your precious mother never told you about the man she intended to give you away to when you were twelve."

The girl glanced at her mother, then back at him. Her lips moved, pleading, the same words they had before. "Please. Don't hurt me. Don't kill me. Let us go."

And the phone rang on. His head pounded. He was tired. He was ready to let it *all* go.

"He's currently not answering our calls," Abby summarized for Griffin. "We'll keep on trying. And we need to get the media to stop talking."

They were standing outside by the negotiation truck, looking at the house.

"I'll deal with the media," Griffin growled. "Baker, what are our options?"

"If we enter by force, we can storm in through the window on the second floor and the front door in tandem," Baker said. "We'll use stun grenades before entering. If he's on the ground floor, we have a reasonable chance of taking him. But if he's on the second or third floor, it's more of a crapshoot."

"You said you heard a TV in the background," Griffin said. "Is there only one TV in the house?"

"Yes," Abby said. "In the living room."

"Then it's probable that's where he still is. On the ground floor."

"Maybe it's our best choice," Baker said. "He's not answering your calls. You said yourself that he's desperate. If he thinks he's on his way to life in prison, he might decide to die here, take the hostages with him."

"Give us ten more minutes."

"Are you willing to bet Eden and Gabrielle Fletcher's life on it?" Griffin asked.

Abby hesitated. Either way, it was a gamble. "Yes," she finally said.

Griffin stared at the house, jaw tight.

"Sir?" Baker said. "What's it going to be?"

Gabrielle knew the end was near. Every time he came at her with the knife, she thought *this* time, he was going to cut.

He spoke, but she couldn't make out the words anymore. The man was deranged. Insane. Talking about a man called Karl. About her father. Cursing them, then cursing her, then trying again to explain that he'd done it all for her. Didn't she see?

No, she didn't. All she knew was that he was about to kill her. And the police did nothing.

Her mom knew it too. And as he talked on and on, the blade at her throat, her mom slowly got off the couch, her hands still handcuffed behind her back. She inched toward him. Gabrielle forced herself to keep her eyes on *his* face as she saw her mom creeping ever closer.

And then a lunge. Her mom crashed into him, and his legs buckled. He staggered sideways, the knife clattering to the floor.

Gabrielle shot up from the chair, ran to the stairs. He tried to grab her, fingers brushing her ankle, just a bit too slow, and she was leaping up the stairs, three at a time, up to her room, slamming the door shut. Locking it. Breathless.

Two steps to the window—she opened the shutter, stared out at the cops.

"Help!" she screeched as she heard him rattle the door behind her.

"Help!"

Abby stared at the window. Gabrielle waved at them frantically.

"Help us!"

"Get over there!" Griffin shouted, but there was no need. Men were rushing toward the house.

Gabrielle must have realized she could jump, and was hesitantly climbing onto the window ledge.

And then, the silhouette of a man behind her. Grabbing her, pulling her back. The glint of a knife. A scream.

Gabrielle struggled with Luther, the window still open, and Griffin was shouting over the radio. Abby watched, horrified, hearing the radio chatter, everything slowing down, seconds stretching.

"Do you have a shot?" Griffin shouted.

"Negative. I don't have a clear shot," the sniper on the radio answered.

"If you have a shot, take it," Griffin snarled.

And then Luther pulled Gabrielle back. For a fraction of a second, only his silhouette remained framed in the window. He was already moving away.

A sudden blast echoed in the street. Luther stumbled back. Disappeared from view. The shutter closed.

"Damn it!" Griffin shouted. "Did you get him?"

"I hit his shoulder," the sniper said. "He's not dead."

"Sir, we should break inside now while he's down," Baker said urgently.

"Break in," Griffin said.

Abby could only stare as the ESU crew moved in.

He dragged Gabrielle to the stairs, shoulder pounding with pain, sleeve wet from blood. *His* blood. The bitch. The goddamn whore. She'd done this to him. She'd gotten him shot.

They would break in now, kill him. But he would take her down with him.

"Up," he grunted at her, knife at her back. "Up the stairs."

She hesitated, and he let the knife cut, just once. She screamed and stumbled up the stairs. He climbed after her. The world spun. One stair. And another. And another.

They reached the third floor; he was breathing hard.

Explosions rattled the house, making his ears ring, everything confusing and slow. He shoved Gabrielle into a room on the third floor. Only one window there. Too small to break through. Downstairs, he heard men running, shouting.

He forced her to the side, flattened himself against the wall. "I'm upstairs with the girl!" he screamed as loud as he could. "If anyone comes near, I'll kill her! You got that? I'll kill her!"

Listening, striving to hear them above the constant ringing in his ears, he prepared himself to do it. Slit the girl's throat.

But they stayed back.

Abby watched as someone ran outside, shouted for a medic. She prayed fervently for Gabrielle and Eden to be all right.

"Sir, the suspect is barricaded on the third floor with the girl," Baker said on the radio. "He says he'll kill her if we get near."

"What about Eden Fletcher?" Griffin asked.

"We have her. She's hurt."

The medical crew ran inside with a stretcher.

"Mullen," Griffin said. "I'm going to order them up to the third floor."

"No," Abby blurted. "He'll kill her. If cornered, he'll kill her."

"He's already cornered—and desperate; you said so yourself. And he won't answer the phone. We're out of options."

"If he wanted to kill her, he would have done it already instead of barricading himself upstairs," Abby argued. "He wants a way out."

"If he won't talk to us—"

"He won't talk to us on the *phone*," Abby said—and ran toward the house.

He was losing too much blood.

His vision was blurry, spots dancing in front of his eyes. Soon, he would faint. And the girl would be free to run downstairs. They would come up and arrest him. He would spend the rest of his life away from Gabrielle, unable to make contact.

No.

He grabbed her hair, pulled it hard. She let out a scream, forced to raise her head, expose her neck. One cut was all it would take.

"Luther." Abby's voice from downstairs.

His hand hesitated. He would not answer. It was too late to talk. Much too late. It was time to finish it all.

He didn't answer. Abby tried again. "Luther?"

Could he have killed himself and Gabrielle already? Abby was about to climb the stairs when she heard a frightened whimper. Gabrielle. Still alive. Listening carefully, she also heard the labored breath of Luther Gaines.

He didn't want to talk. But he hadn't finished it either. It was up to Abby to say the right words. To label his thoughts and fears.

"It looks like you're afraid that if you surrender, you'll go to prison," Abby said.

No response.

"I'm not going to lie to you; it might happen. But we can get you that attorney. Remember what we talked about? Whatever you're charged with will have to be proved in court. Anything could happen."

No movement. No answer. He didn't believe her.

What did he want? What was he trying to do? During their conversation he'd been furious at Gabrielle. He felt betrayed by her. He felt—

No. Not by Gabrielle. By *this girl*. That was how he kept talking about her. When he mentioned his interactions with her online, he called her Gabrielle. But whenever he talked about her in the flesh, he called her *this girl*.

Almost as if they were separate people.

It was that well-known problem of social media—with a perverse twist. When you followed a person online, they always seemed perfect. Their family was the happiest family; their trips were the best trips; every picture was wonderful, enviable, something to be desired. But it hardly ever reflected the truth.

Luther had been obsessed with Gabrielle. Even when he'd met her as a reporter, she'd presented her fake persona, her public face. Now, meeting the real girl for the first time, a girl who pleaded for her life and refused to love him, he was disappointed. And enraged.

He still loved Gabrielle. And on an emotional, subconscious level, he couldn't believe the Gabrielle he loved and *this girl* could possibly be the same person.

With such a volatile, delusional mindset, an emotion left unspoken was dangerous. He could act on it, not even knowing why. Abby would have to bring those thoughts to the surface.

"It seems as if you can't understand how Gabrielle and this girl could even be the same person."

He stayed frozen, listening to Abby's voice, low and calm.

"You love Gabrielle Fletcher, a beautiful, smart, caring girl," Abby said. "She talks to you every day, makes you feel special. Maybe you're wondering, How could *this* girl even be the same person? This girl, who acts as if she doesn't understand you—and doesn't care for you."

He ground his teeth together. Of course he knew they were the same person. He knew it. She was being ridiculous. It was time to end this. He glanced at the girl's throat. At Gabrielle's throat. One cut was all it would take.

"It sounds like you have such a wonderful connection with her. A connection that could return back to the way it was one day. In time. If you let Gabrielle go. This girl you're holding up there. She's the same person you talked to. It doesn't feel like it. But she is."

His eyes welled up. This was going nowhere. Why was he hesitating? He should have done it already.

He placed the blade on the girl's skin. On Gabrielle's skin.

Abby kept talking. "She's the same person who bought the yellow shirt just for you. Who shared her trip with you. Who promised you her undying gratitude. In time, you might have it."

Still nothing. Abby couldn't even hear him breathing—or Gabrielle's whimpering.

"I saw what you did for Nathan. I saw that room. All the thought you put into it. Gabrielle will see it as well. You can tell her; she's with you right now. She's confused and scared, but it's the same Gabrielle. She just needs time."

"Remember that day on the road trip? That day you made her famous? How did it make you feel?"

He remembered. Of course he remembered. He shut his eyes, feeling the tears in his throat. How had it gone so wrong?

"You've made Gabrielle famous again. She'll see that. What do you think she'll tell you about it tomorrow? And the day after that? And the day after that?"

He opened his eyes, looked at the pale, shivering girl. At Gabrielle. What would she tell him tomorrow? He could already imagine tapping the Instagram icon. Watching her thanking everyone for being there every step of the way. Blowing a kiss to the camera. To *him*.

He let his hand drop, and the knife clattered to the floor. His body slumped.

Abby's throat was raw from talking loudly, but she kept on going. "It seems—"

A floorboard creaked. Abby squinted up the stairs.

Gabrielle appeared in the doorway, trembling, pale as snow. She walked down the stairs one by one, stumbled, fell.

Abby was there to catch her before she hit the floor.

CHAPTER 82

Abby lay curled in her bed, her thoughts as light as a cloud, Ben's small body snuggled against her. It was Saturday morning, sunlight filtering through the window, and life was perfect. She planned on taking the kids out, but for now she couldn't find the willpower to get out of bed. Heavy, warm blanket; cute little boy; and a day full of nothing.

Sam knocked on the door, then opened it, still dressed in her pj's. "My violin is on its way," she announced. "It'll be here next week!"

"Oh good," Abby said sleepily. Her parents had paid for it, which made it even better. "Get in here. We're snuggling."

Sam looked at the bed, her mouth twisting. "Yeah, I don't think so."

"Come on. We want to hear about your violin."

"Ugh. *Fine.*" She got in the bed and pulled the blanket over.

Ben squawked as his foot emerged from under the covers. "Hey! Stop hogging the blanket!"

"I'm not hogging it! Let go!"

Abby shut her eyes, grinning. In a few minutes the shouting and arguing would drive her insane. But right now it was the sound of heaven.

"Moooom, tell her to stop pulling!"

"So? What's the violin like?" Abby said.

"It's wonderful! It's made of acrylic, and it's really light. Do you remember that clip I showed you of Lindsey Stirling two weeks ago?"

"Of course." Abby had no idea what she was talking about. "So is that the violin she used?"

"No, but it's really similar. And I heard it play; the sound is just amazing. And once I get it, I'll solve that feedback problem I've been having with the microphone because I'll plug it in directly, so everything will be so much easier. And I'll be able to play it super loud . . ."

"The neighbors will be thrilled."

"Once I save up a bit, I'll buy a distortion pedal for it, which everyone says is *amazing*. Distortions in electric violin sound so cool; I'll play an example for you in a bit . . ."

Abby let her mind float away as her daughter talked. She usually did her best to listen to her children, accumulating a ridiculously detailed knowledge of the mating habits of spiders or the various solos of the modern violinists. But right now, her mind was in a porridgy state, as was good and proper for a Saturday morning.

As Sam spoke, her body became more and more relaxed, melding into Abby's. A snuggle sandwich. Abby etched it in her mind, making sure to remember this moment forever.

"I want to take Pretzel for a walk today," Ben said happily when Sam paused for air.

"I don't think we can take Pretzel for a walk," Abby said, caressing his hair.

"Why not? We take Sam's stupid pet for a walk."

"Because my pet isn't disgusting," Sam said.

"Mom! She said my pets are disgusting."

"Sam, don't say that. Ben's pets are very nice."

Sam snorted and then suddenly tensed. "What the . . . Ben, did you bring your spider here?"

Abby had turned to look at Ben when she felt the gentle tickle of a spidery leg. She shrieked, leaping out of the bed, the drowsiness in her body evaporating.

"What's the matter, Mom?" Sam grinned at her. "I thought Ben's pets are nice."

"I didn't bring Jeepers here," Ben said defensively. "Sam was tickling you with her finger."

"Oh god," Abby groaned, trying to soothe her hammering heart. "You are a terrible daughter."

"Did you hear how loud she shrieked?" Sam whispered, smiling at Ben.

Ben giggled. Sam tickled him. His giggling turned to laughter.

It was a perfect Saturday morning.

CHAPTER 83

"I'm joining a table for two," Abby told the hostess. "Reserved for Jonathan Carver?"

"Absolutely, this way please," the young hostess said, leading her into the dimly lit restaurant.

Abby took off her coat and slung it on her arm as she followed. She wore her khaki off-the-shoulder dress and her over-the-knees gray boots. Dressed to kill. Even Sam had conceded that Abby's outfit was "not bad." As far as Abby was concerned, that was high praise from her teenage daughter.

Carver sat in the corner of the restaurant in a private booth. The padded seat was a circular bench around the table. Abby smiled at him as she slid in to join him. Carver had called that morning and asked if she wanted to meet for dinner. She'd suggested meeting for lunch, assuming he wanted to go over the case summary. Flustered, he'd clarified that he was asking her out.

And now, there she was.

"I already ordered a bottle of red wine," he said, gesturing at the bottle on the table.

"Is it a good wine?" Abby asked, picking up her glass.

"Absolutely. Because I told our waiter I want a good red wine bottle. That's how I literally phrased it."

She sipped from her glass, looking at him over the rim. She'd never seen him dressed up before. A dark sweater over a blue shirt, looking casual with a hint of fashionable taste. Was the taste his? Or did it belong to one of his numerous sisters? Or maybe an ex-girlfriend?

The waitress came over, and Carver ordered the spaghetti alle vongole. Abby asked for the butternut squash tortellini, which she'd glimpsed on a neighboring table and instantly craved. The waitress tapped on her small tablet, whisked the menus away, and left.

"How are things at home?" Carver asked. "Back to normal? I mean, with your daughter and everything."

"If by 'back to normal' you mean she mostly ignores me and rolls her eyes when I talk to her, then yes, they're back to normal. I'm getting things ready for Ben's birthday party."

"Oh." Carver sipped from his own glass. "So . . . what does that mean? Making a cake and buying M&M'S?"

Abby grinned at his naivete. "Well, M&M'S can be contaminated with peanuts, so that could kill at least two of the children in attendance unless I'm ready to stab them with an EpiPen. We have a very health-conscious group of mothers in the school, so I had to give up Smarties and Skittles as refreshments even though Ben loves them, or I would be burned at the stake. I *am* making a chocolate cake, which got a grudging approval after I refused to make a carrot cake. And the birthday party intersects with the marriage of one of Ben's friend's aunts, so I had to go through a fifteen-minute conversation with the mother in which she made it clear that her son really wanted to attend, but they just can't, and I had to explain we'd have scheduled it on a different day if we only knew. There was a last-minute cancellation by Professor Boggle—"

"I'm sorry, what?"

"Professor Boggle is a sort of scientist for hire for birthday parties. But he canceled because his father died. So I had to find a last-minute substitution, and it was either Dowey the Clown or Torrinimo the Magnificent Magician. I went with the magician because the clown sounded sleazy on the phone. My son hates magicians, so I needed to find a way to tailor the act to his taste. Ever try to convince a magician to pull a snake out of the hat instead of a rabbit? Let's just say it's a good thing I'm a professional negotiator." Abby paused to sip from her wine. "So yeah. Making a cake and buying some M&M'S."

"Oh." Carver mulled it over. "Would they really burn you at the stake for Smarties? That sounds harsh. Do we even have stakes?"

"Every neighborhood has stakes now. We only use them to burn mothers who failed as a parent."

"Dads get a free pass?"

"Of course. We're very lenient with dads. But they're not allowed to participate in the actual burning. Only the mothers are allowed to burn each other."

"That's a relief."

Abby leaned back, grinning. She was enjoying this, sitting in this lovely place with a man, her mind reasonably free of worries.

"Oh, you know who I met the other day?" Carver asked. "You remember Hughie? From the academy?"

She frowned. "Was he the one who accidentally swallowed a fly at the shooting range and almost shot the instructor when he tried to cough it out?"

"What? No, that's Tyler. Hughie is the one we called Hughie the Gooey? Because he was always sweaty."

"Oh yeah! He made a pass at me the very first day at the academy."

"He's in the Animal Cruelty Investigation Squad now. He was actually pretty passionate when we talked about it. I think he really changed."

"So he's not sweaty anymore?"

"I don't know if his sweat glands work differently. I just got the impression that he got much nicer. Like . . . really relaxed."

"Maybe it's because people aren't calling him Hughie the Gooey anymore."

The waitress came over and placed a basket of breadsticks on their table. Then she left. Abby tried to decide if she should eat the bread before her dish came. A momentous decision.

"You look beautiful," Carver said.

"Oh." Blood rushed to Abby's cheeks. "Thanks." She took another large sip from her wine to gather her bearings.

Carver took a breadstick from the basket. "How's the snake?"

"Who? What?" Her head was starting to spin. She'd drunk too much on an empty stomach.

"Your son's snake. How is it?"

"Crawling and slithering as ever. Yesterday he ate a large frozen mouse, so today he's resting."

Carver let out a shudder. "I don't even know how you can sleep in the same house."

"Not easily," Abby admitted. "It helps I'm on the second floor. But I guess he can climb up steps if he ever escapes the vivarium. And he's plotting his escape. I can see it in his eyes."

"You could lay a snare for it."

"Uh-huh."

"No, I'm serious! I'm really good at this. My sister Holly is really good at drawing. So we used to spend hours drawing plans for elaborate traps for our big sister. Here, let me show you. Give me your napkin."

"Why can't you use your napkin?"

"Yours is way better." Carver took out a pen from his bag, snatched Abby's napkin, and began to draw. "These are the stairs. You have a laundry basket at home, right? So you position it like this . . . you have to hold it up, like that. You place the bait—"

"Bait?"

"Yeah, something the snake likes eating."

"He likes eating mice. Are you saying I should leave a dead mouse on my stairs every night?"

"Don't bother me with details. If you put the bait like that, it slithers over to it . . . it moves the broomstick—"

"What broomstick?" Abby was smiling widely. She took another sip of her wine.

"How else do you think it would work? You need a breadstick. I mean a broomstick." Carver took another breadstick as he scribbled. "The snake moves the broomstick, and the trap springs! Bam, it's in the laundry basket."

"Did your sister ever fall into one of your elaborate traps?"

"No, but it doesn't mean they weren't any good. Here." He gave her the napkin back. "Free of charge. A trap planner would charge thousands for this."

"A trap planner? Is that a thing?"

"When I was a kid, I wanted to be one."

"That doesn't mean it's an actual profession."

Their food arrived, and Abby barely waited for the waitress to leave before digging in. Her pasta was delicious.

"Did you talk to Eden?" Carver asked after they'd eaten in relative silence for a few minutes.

"Yeah. She and Gabrielle both needed stitches. Eden also had a blood transfusion. But they're much better now. Nathan too. They transferred him to the same hospital."

"That's good."

"What about Luther?" she asked.

"He'll live." Carver didn't sound particularly happy about it. "We have a solid case on the murder charges too."

Abby nodded. For Eden's and Gabrielle's peace of mind, it was best if Luther stayed in prison until the day he died.

"It's all thanks to you," Carver said after a second. "You didn't let your past with Eden impair your judgment at all. If you hadn't figured out who Luther was in time . . . or if you weren't there to talk to him . . ." He shook his head.

"We don't know what would have happened," Abby said, staring at her dish. Dark thoughts that had invaded her mind the past few nights began creeping in.

"I know," Carver said.

She cleared her throat. "When I talked to Gabrielle on the phone that day, she sounded so . . . out of it. So scared. She could hardly piece a sentence together."

"He had a knife to her throat. It's very understandable."

"Yeah . . . of course it is. I . . ." A storm brewed in her mind, threatening to break. She didn't think she could stop it. "Do you know, when I was seven, during the Wilcox massacre, I talked to the police negotiator on the phone. I remember talking to him. There's also a transcript; I've read it a million times."

She put her fork down, realizing her fingers were trembling. "Moses Wilcox had a gun to my head. I remember it. The way it felt."

"Tell them what will happen if they come near us. Tell them about the gun."

The cold muzzle, pressing against her temple.

"What did you say to the negotiator?"

"I . . . in the transcript I tell them Moses is holding a gun to my head. I told them that if they broke inside, Moses would shoot me. They asked if I was okay. I said I was okay, that all sixty-two of us were okay, that no one was hurt."

She held a paper in her hand. On it was the number sixty-two, underlined. She couldn't read yet, but she knew how to read numbers up to ninety-nine.

"He probably told you what to say."

"He did. I remember it."

"Tell them."

"And then, after the phone call ended, I remember he told me to bolt the door. I did. I walked to the door and bolted it, locking us all inside the hall. Which he later set fire to."

"You were seven; you can't blame yourself for—"

"Why did he tell me to bolt it? Why didn't he do it himself?"

Carver said nothing, looking at her intently.

"And when the fire started, why didn't anyone open it? Sixty-two people in a burning hall. Are you telling me no one ran to the door to open it?"

"There probably wasn't time. I read the report about the incident. The cooking cylinders in the hall exploded."

Abby shook her head. "There was time. There was . . ."

The smell of smoke. Screaming for help.

The bolt. She ran to the door to slide the bolt open. Behind her, she heard Eden shout, "Abihail, get away from there!"

She had to open the door.

Isaac grabbed her, pulled her back.

An explosion, the searing pain on the back of her neck.

"Eden doesn't remember it the same way," she said hollowly. "Memories get warped during traumatic experiences. And cult members' memories often change to match what they believe."

"That makes sense."

"Gabrielle sounded so scared. And back then I had a *gun* to my head. I was completely cool. I read the transcript a million times. I didn't cry. Didn't stutter."

The number sixty-two on a piece of paper.

"I don't think there was a gun to my head," Abby said.

"Tell them about the gun." His finger pressing against her temple—just like a gun. "Tell them all sixty-two of us are together. Will you remember that, Abihail? Sixty-two." He scribbled the number on a piece of paper. In the background, she heard Eden crying. But Abihail didn't cry. She was brave. Moses always said she was a brave girl. That was why he wanted her to do this and not Eden or Isaac. He only trusted her.

"I don't think I was in that hall with the rest of them. Everyone in that hall died. He told me what to say, and then he went to that hall to join them, and I . . ." She shut her eyes.

"After I leave, call them. Tell them what will happen if they come near us. Tell them about the gun. And then, go to the dining hall door and bolt it."

"The bolt was on the outside," Abby whispered. "I locked them in—like he told me to. Eden, Isaac, and I were *outside* the hall."

"You can't be sure—"

"I'm sure."

They screamed for help. Mommy and Daddy—and everyone else. There was smoke.

She ran to slide the bolt open. She had to let them out.

Eden's scream. "Abihail, get away from there!"

Isaac grabbed her, pulled her back.

An explosion, the searing pain on the back of her neck.

She raised her fingers to touch the scar on her neck. "I made the call to the negotiator to buy Moses some time. I locked them inside the dining hall. And he set it on fire. They were locked in. They couldn't get out. By the time I went to open it . . ." Tears ran down her cheeks.

Carver swept her into a hug. She buried her face in his chest, weeping.

"You were only seven," he kept saying. "You were only seven."

CHAPTER 84

Abby slowed the car down as she got to the crossroad, fields of green in every direction. She turned left, listening to the music from her Spotify, trying to tune out Eden. The woman was speaking to the babysitter. Again. Fourth time in a three-hour drive. And as they got farther and farther from home, the anxiety in Eden's voice was more and more apparent—until it was almost unbearable.

Abby didn't judge her. It'd been only two months. And it was the first time Eden had left Nathan and Gabrielle for a whole day since . . . well, since they had been born.

"Can I talk to Nathan?" Eden asked. Then, a second later, "Hey sweetie! Yes, we're nearly there. We'll be home late afternoon. Yes, before bedtime. Did you eat?"

Ben and Samantha were at Steve's this weekend, so Abby didn't need to worry about anything. Besides her eternal concerns that the kids ate junk food at Steve's, watched things they shouldn't watch at Steve's, played violent video games at Steve's, and went to sleep too late at Steve's. But she was getting good at pushing away those nagging concerns, never voicing them, and healthily letting them fester. Because letting dark thoughts and anxieties fester in your brain was a big part of being a parent.

Finally, Eden hung up the phone. "Are we here?"

"Yup," Abby said. "Welcome to Georgetown, Delaware."

"It's very . . . spacious," Eden said, sounding a bit jealous.

"Tell me about it." Abby didn't share Eden's newly found desire to leave the city. She loved the city. Here, every house was dozens of yards from the next one—and nothing but grass in between. It seemed so dull.

"Do you think he'll be home?" Eden asked for the tenth time since they'd left.

"I hope so."

They had no way of being sure. Isaac hadn't answered their texts in which they'd announced they were coming together to visit him.

Ever since that night with Carver, Abby's trust in her own memories had been disintegrating. Discussing things she remembered with Eden and Isaac raised endless contradictions and gaps. Isaac recalled the day they'd hidden in the poppy field but claimed that they'd found a weird-looking rock and not a bullet. Eden insisted that the sinks they'd washed their hands in hadn't been outside at all; they had been indoors. Each of them remembered Moses Wilcox differently. And the three of them had varying memories of that last, terrible day.

Eden and Isaac were content to let it drop, but Abby couldn't. The guilt from that day, intertwined with the uncertainty of her own recollections, kept gnawing at her at all times. She slept badly and during the day was tense and irritable. She needed to put those days behind her once and for all.

It was Eden who suggested that they all meet together. Abby instantly said yes. Isaac was less than thrilled. He couldn't get time off from work, and the workload spilled into the weekends as well. He suggested that they meet in a few months when things calmed down. The idea was unbearable to Abby, and finally she suggested that she and Eden come over to his place during the weekend. He explained that wouldn't work, though couldn't really give them a straight answer why.

He was hiding something. And Abby had a hunch what it was. Unlike Eden and her, Isaac had had a few things packed when they'd left the Wilcox cult. He'd mentioned it a few times during chats, and had even sent Eden the picture of Moses Wilcox. Perhaps he had something else there. Something that would shed light on past events.

Was he hiding it to protect her? Or was there something there that cast him in a different light? She needed to know.

She'd managed to track him down. He lived in Georgetown. Less than four hours away. They could drive to see him and get back home in the same day.

"How's Nathan?" she asked, trying to distract herself.

"During the day he's fine, but at night . . ." Eden sighed. "He ends up in my bed every night."

"What is the therapist saying?"

"To give him time."

Gabrielle paid for the therapist with her increasing income. Abby had no doubt that she was outearning her mother now. In fact, she was probably outearning Abby and Eden put together. Abby still occasionally checked Gabrielle's Instagram account and found it confounding that a person could make so much money doing . . . well, practically nothing. Though Eden explained that Gabrielle worked from the moment she woke up until the late hours of the evening. Answering fans, reading comments, connecting with other influencers . . . apparently it was constant work.

"This is the place," Abby muttered, parking the car. A tiny white-tiled house. The yard was covered in grass, only one bush breaking the monotony. The windows were shuttered, uninviting. During the long drive Abby had avoided thinking about the actual encounter, meeting Isaac, the three of them together for the first time since the Wilcox massacre. She knew how he looked, of course; they'd sent each other countless photos over the years. But she couldn't imagine his expression when he opened the door.

She got out of the car before she had time to let her anxiety settle in. She imagined him glancing at them through the shutters, watching his past as it marched toward his house.

A man opened the door before she had the time to knock.

"Can I help you?" he asked guardedly.

She had no idea who this was.

"Um . . . we're looking for Isaac. Is he home?" Abby asked.

"I'm Isaac."

"Oh." Disappointment filled her. This had all been for nothing. She'd tracked down the wrong man. "I'm sorry; I thought this was Isaac Reed's home."

"I'm Isaac Reed." He frowned, squinting at her. "Who are you?"

"So sorry, we've definitely got the wrong—"

"Isaac?" Eden whispered behind her.

The man glanced over Abby's shoulder, his eyes widening. He grasped the doorway as if to steady himself. "Eden?"

Abby stared at him, then at Eden, confounded. What the hell? This wasn't Isaac. He didn't look *anything* like the photos.

"Yes," Eden said. "It's me. And this is Abihail. She looks different. I know."

He gazed at them, frozen. Abby now saw it. Not his similarity to the photos he'd sent her. But his similarity to that black-haired boy with the bucktoothed smile from her childhood. Something was deeply wrong.

Finally he said, "What are you doing here?"

Abby blinked. "We . . . we told you we were coming."

"What? When?"

"We both sent you messages."

"Abihail, I haven't talked to either of you for more than . . . thirty years."

Her world was spinning. No. That couldn't be. She had stacks of letters from him. They'd chatted just a few days ago. She wrote him messages *almost every single day*.

"Then who have we been talking to all this time?"

ACKNOWLEDGMENTS

Writing a book is tough. Starting a new series is even tougher. After I'd spent so long with Zoe, Tatum, Marvin, and the rest of that lot, creating a whole new series with a new protagonist with family and friends—and possibly a pet or two—felt like an impossible task. And it really would have been impossible without a lot of people helping me throughout.

My wife, Liora, first and foremost. She was the one who announced I needed to write about a hostage negotiator. I wasn't sure—I wanted to write about an undercover agent, to which she said, "Meh." And then when I told my editor, Jessica Tribble, that I was thinking of writing about an undercover agent but that Liora insisted I should write about a hostage negotiator, *she* said, "Listen to your wife."

So I did, and Abby was born. Liora then helped me every step of the way, from building the character and her terrifying background to the plot. And then she read the thing when it was done and told me what I needed to change. Which turned out to be a lot.

And thanks to Jessica, who, after telling me to listen to my wife, helped me work on my original draft and add much-needed background on Abby, giving her more texture and depth. As always, she did a phenomenal job while editing the book.

Christine Mancuso read one of my original drafts (there were quite a few) and helped me restructure the book to improve the pacing. Did you grip the book extra hard when Nathan fled from his kidnapper? A lot of that was Christine's doing.

My dad read an early draft, too, and helped me polish Abby's professionalism. He's a psychologist and was offended by the irresponsible way I scattered technical terms and cheap psychological observations throughout the book.

Kevin Smith, my developmental editor, did a fantastic job, helping me polish the book until it shone. He was super patient and helpful throughout our back-and-forth. Working with him was, as it has been before, pure pleasure.

Emily Havener and Stephanie Chou received the final draft and caught my endless grammar and spelling mistakes, as well as some ghastly continuity errors.

Thanks to Laura Barrett, the production editor, who did a lot of the coordination and administration involved in producing this book.

Wayne Stinnet read my raid chapter and helped me through it so that it felt more like a raid and less like a group of people bumbling in the dark haphazardly.

Richard Stockford answered my layman's questions about how the police work, helping me through some issues regarding coordination among different law enforcement agencies.

Thanks to Sarah Hershman, my agent, for always doing everything she can to make my books soar.

And thanks to all of my readers for making my dreams come true.

ABOUT THE AUTHOR

Mike Omer has been a journalist, a game developer, and the CEO of Loadingames, but he can currently be found penning his next thriller. Omer loves to write about two things: real people who could be the perpetrators or victims of crimes—and funny stuff. He mixes these two loves quite passionately into his suspenseful and often-macabre mysteries. Omer is married to a woman who diligently forces him to live his dream, and he is father to an angel, a pixie, and a gremlin. He has two voracious hounds that wag their tails quite menacingly at anyone who dares approach his home. Learn more by emailing him at mike@strangerealm.com.